AQUA TERRA IGNIS AER

ZODIAC
ACADEMY
THE RECKONING

CAROLINE
PECKHAM

SUSANNE
VALENTI

Zodiac Academy

Earth Cavern

Pitball Stadium

Saturn Auditorium

Uranus Infirmary

Aqua House

Neptune Tower

Lunar Leisure

Water Lagoon

Pluto Offices

The Shimmering

Place
Terra House
er Hall
Mars Laboratory
King's Hollow
The Howling Meadow
The Wailing Wood
The Orb
Earth Observatory
Venus Library
Aercury
hambers
Aer House
Fire Arena

The Reckoning
Zodiac Academy #3
Copyright © 2019 Caroline Peckham & Susanne Valenti

Interior Illustration by Sarah Goodman & Sloane Murphy
Formatting by Sloane Murphy

The Reckoning/Caroline Peckham & Susanne Valenti – 1st ed.
ISBN-13 - 978-1-914425-05-9

WELCOME TO ZODIAC ACADEMY

Note to all students: Vampire bites, loss of limbs or getting lost in The Wailing Wood will not count as a valid excuse for being late to class.

ORION

CHAPTER ONE

Twelve deaths. Eight from Starlight Academy, four from Zodiac. All students.

I was still caked in mud and blood long into the evening, the scent of smoke hanging over me.

Countless were injured but I'd healed as many as I could, then carried even more to Uranus Infirmary. I sent Darius off with the Vega Twins back to Ignis House to ensure they were safe. And when the last of the students were either back in their rooms or being tended to, I headed to my own place with a heaviness descending on me.

How the fuck did this happen? How did they get in? Why weren't we more prepared?

I headed into Earth Territory, curving through The Wailing Wood which was eerily quiet, the leaves not even rustling in the still air. I soon arrived at the faculty quarters and unlocked the tall gate to Asteroid Place.

The yard was aglow with lights, breaking up the thick darkness on its verges. The long row of brick chalets stretched out ahead of me before the pool and I spotted Washer sitting on a deck chair, his hair damp and his clothes freshly changed. He held a bottle of something in his hand and as I drew closer the acrid scent of vodka hit my nose. I wasn't in the mood to be picky as he wordlessly offered it to me and I took a long drink, grimacing as I swallowed and passed it back to him.

He looked me up and down, eyeing the state of me with horror in his eyes. "I read the cards. Nova didn't believe me."

I nodded stiffly, moving to walk away but he caught my wrist. His Siren power pushed gently against me in a silent offer.

"Let me," he said before I could shut him down. "It's the least I can do to take away some of your anxiety. I should have done more to make Nova listen to me, but even *I* started to doubt the reading. I have made mistakes before..."

The promise of relief tingled against my skin, but I pulled away from him, my lips tight.

"It was only by chance I did the reading at all," he went on. "I was practising for teaching Tarot – you know how I dislike Pitball," Washer said, clearly desperate for me to say something.

I sighed. "Nymphs act spontaneously to get around our predictions. It is what it is, Brian."

He nodded, his throat rising and falling. "What was the final count?"

I released a long breath, not needing to ask what he meant. "Twelve. Four from Zodiac. Two juniors who stayed to fight and two freshmen."

"It's a damn miracle it wasn't more," Washer muttered, sipping on the vodka again.

"Thanks to the Vega Twins."

He nodded slowly, his eyes darting to me then back to the pool. "I suppose you have a theory on what their Order is?"

I didn't answer that. Mostly because I didn't have one. And partly because I could still smell death on me and I seriously needed some time to myself instead of discussing this.

"Elaine's calling an assembly at midnight," I growled then headed down the alley between mine and Washer's chalets.

I hadn't fed from Darcy and I was nearly tapped out magic wise. It might have been tempting to let Washer syphon off some of this stress but I was down to the last of my power reserves. And I didn't want to be completely empty right now. Just in case this hellish night wasn't over. Maybe I should have fed from her. But it had felt like a dick move all things considered.

Since I'd left Blue with Darius, the lasting imprint of her ashen cheeks and wide eyes were burned into my retinas. She'd fought at my side tonight with the fierceness of a warrior. And she'd saved my fucking life.

Now, I was adrift without her, my heart trying to tear its way out of my chest in a bid to go to her.

Does this change things?

No. It couldn't. I couldn't let it. I'd sworn to keep away from her, but after tonight, after how close we'd both come to death, a small voice had awoken in my head that whispered, *fuck it, we could be dead tomorrow.*

I unlocked my door halfway down the alley, stepping into the large chalet I called home. I locked up behind me, sealing the door with a shield like usual before switching on the light. The open plan kitchen-diner swept out ahead of me in tones of grey and white. I'd lived here for nearly four years now and it was the one place on campus I felt I could really remove the professor mask.

I peeled off my filthy Pitball kit, tossing it in the trash and heading into the bathroom. I practically scalded myself in the shower in an attempt to burn away the blood of students and Nymphs alike. And when I was done, I pulled on a shirt and smart pants, snatched a bottle of bourbon from the cupboard and flung myself onto the couch.

Tiredness wracked every inch of my body and as I drank way more than I should have before a formal assembly.

I found my eyes drifting closed and let myself be swallowed by the sweet nothingness of sleep.

My Atlas was pinging and someone was pounding on my door. I groaned, shifting to sit up on the couch and finding my bottle of bourbon spilled all over the floor. Alright, a *third* of a bottle of bourbon.

I snatched up my Atlas, finding it was only a quarter to midnight – *so why is everyone hounding me right now?*

"Lance! Open up!" Francesca's frantic voice called from the other side of the door.

I grunted, checking the message on my Atlas and finding it was just a reminder from Elaine.

I really need the backup at the assembly, Lance.

The FIB are breathing down my neck and we need to show them we're handling this like the professionals we are.

Don't be late.

Elaine Nova.

"Lance!" Francesca banged harder. "I'll break the door down if you don't answer in five seconds."

I tried to conjure enough healing energy into my body to force myself to sober up. But shit, I was running on fumes.

I headed toward the door, trying to compose my face into an expression that didn't give away how much I'd had to drink. I disabled the shield around the door and unlocked it, pulling it wide, unable to fight a wince as the glaring lamp above Washer's porch pinched my eye sockets.

"You look like shit." Francesca pushed past me with an eye roll and I groaned, pulling the door closed and pressing my back to it.

She was dressed in her black FIB jumpsuit, her hazel hair pulled up into a high ponytail and her features set in a disapproving frown. She gave the room a sweeping glance, taking in the spilled bourbon on the floor then turned to me with an even harder expression. "You can't do this. Not right now."

"Skip the lecture." I moved into the kitchen, pouring myself a glass of water and draining it in two long gulps. Now I was half-cut, my emotions were muffled like I had a pillow pressed over them. Being numb made everything so much easier.

"I need to see what happened. The students are too traumatised right now and Principal Nova is too busy. Show me." She strode forward with her hand outstretched.

I caught her wrist, a low snarl rolling out of my throat. "I've got a pounding headache, Francesca, I don't wanna throw-up from Cyclops invasion as well."

She twisted her hand free, her brows drawing together as she finally dropped the FIB act.

"Are you alright?" she breathed, her eyes dancing with sympathy.

An uncomfortable feeling stirred in my chest as she looked at me like that. "I'm Fae." I barged past her, heading to the mirror on the wall to see precisely how much of a train wreck I was right now.

"That's not an answer," she pushed just as I looked at myself. My eyes were bloodshot and darkly shadowed; I looked like death warmed up. *Oh shit, I can't go to The Orb like this, Elaine will have my balls for earrings.*

I pushed a hand into my hair, flattening it down while Francesca stepped up beside me with a heavy frown. "You don't have to act like this isn't affecting you."

"That's what I teach the students though, isn't it? Fae are tough, they don't break." *Now we're all going to gather in The Orb and keep up that lie.*

She stood there for so long in silence that I had to shatter it again.

"Don't you have an investigation to be conducting?" I headed to my room to get a more suitable shirt because this one looked like it had been stuffed under a rock for a week.

Francesca followed me and I ignored her as I stripped off my shirt and took a black one out of my closet, shrugging it on. I turned and found her up in my personal space, her head tilted to one side. "I worry about you sometimes. And I mean that as a friend." She gave me an anxious frown and I sighed heavily.

Francesca was one of my Nebula Allies. She'd been in Aer House with me at Zodiac and since she'd joined the FIB she'd helped me out more than a few times when she was off-duty.

The Nymph situation had been growing out of control for months and Darius and I had taken it into our own hands to help keep their numbers under control. She tipped me off any time there was a sighting within a ten mile radius of Zodiac. Which was strictly illegal, but she knew the FIB could use all the help they could get even if they wouldn't admit it. She kept my secrets and I kept hers. Our trust was implicit. But she never looked at me like *that*. Like I wasn't handling shit.

"Well don't," I said simply, glancing at the clock on the wall. It was just before midnight. "I've got to go."

She nodded, tugging at a loose lock of hair by her ear. "I'll wait here. Top up while you're out so I can look at your memories." She flopped down onto my bed, looking exhausted and I was hit with a knee-jerk reaction.

"No," I blurted and she stared up at me like I'd grown an extra head.

"What?" Her brow creased with confusion. Even *I* was confused about where that reaction had come from. All I knew was that I needed my bed to myself tonight - with the exception of Lady Bourbon.

"You can't stay here tonight." I strode out of the room, snatching my Atlas on the way as I headed for the door. I heard her walking after me and knew she deserved more of an explanation than a flat refusal. "I need some space, alright? Vampire needs." I glanced at her and she gave me a pointed look before shrugging.

"Fine, but you owe me those memories." She gave me a teasing grin as we headed out of my house and I locked the door.

"I'm sure Washer will offer them to you more than willingly," I mocked as we walked out of Asteroid Place and along the path through The Wailing Wood.

"Ew," she breathed. "God, does he still make the students wear those skimpy bathing suits?"

"Yep."

"I remember mine used to give me the worst wedgie and he just *loved* watching me try to sort it out."

"Oh yeah, I remember that. That's why everyone called you Wedge-cesca."

"They did not!" She smacked my arm and I chuckled, a weight easing from my chest.

I was still lightheaded and I wasn't sure if it was from the alcohol or my lack of magic. Francesca eyed me with a frown then held out her wrist. "Here. Just don't tell anyone you bit an FIB agent."

My fangs prickled and I couldn't resist as I caught her arm and slid my teeth into her veins. We paused in the woods and Francesca rested her other hand against my shoulder as I fed. Her fingers trailed up to my neck and wound into my hair, causing a tight squeeze in my chest. The well inside me started to fill and relief spilled into my gut alongside it.

I pulled away, swallowing the last of the metallic taste and finally healing the haze in my brain. "I'd better be on time tonight," I said and she nodded, understanding what I meant. She checked her watch then rolled her eyes to the sky.

"Well I guess five minutes late is on time for you."

I gave her a slanted grin then shot away into the trees, using my Vampire speed to eat up the distance between me and The Orb.

I arrived outside and an icy wind gusted across my neck. I glanced behind me with the gut feeling of being watched. I bared my fangs, hunting the buildings circling The Orb for any sign of an enemy. But all was quiet apart from Nova's voice carrying from inside. A few FIB agents appeared, patrolling the paths and I nodded to them before turning away.

I silently stepped into The Orb, moving to the right of the door and pressing my back to the wall. The place was packed with students, everyone listening attentively to Nova at the far end of the room while the rest of the faculty sat behind her.

On instinct, I hunted for Darius, but I found Blue first. She was with her sister, the two of them surrounded by an army of A.S.S. I had to figure out what that fire was they'd cast. It was driving me mad. I'd fought alongside Darcy and seen the full extent of her power. And I was worried as all hell about what it meant. With magic like that, she and her sister were an official threat to the Heirs. To Darius. And no matter what strange connection I had with Blue, it could not stand in the way of me ensuring Darius sat on the Celestial Council and unseated his father in the process.

I can control this.

Diego Polaris shifted beside her, dropping his arm around her shoulders. My jaw locked and white hot energy built in my chest. I had the completely irrational urge to go over there and drag him out of The Orb by the throat.

Be sensible, Lance. It was a one time thing. She's not yours to be jealous over. Leave it alone.

I spotted Darius sitting on his usual couch with the rest of the Heirs. Seth's jaw was tight and emotion flickered in his eyes. Some of his pack were quietly sobbing in their chairs and my mouth twitched. Ashanti Larue had fallen today. She'd been on the Pitball team since the start of the year after the former Airsentry had graduated. From the red eyes around the room, I could figure out who had been friends with the other three who'd died too.

A fierce anger rose in me, knowing that the Nymphs had taken Ashanti and several others of our kind. Their magic stolen along with their lives. The Nymphs would pay for this. No doubt the Celestial Councillors were already preparing a retaliation which would see them brought to their knees.

"We are all deeply saddened by the losses our academy has suffered today," Nova said gravely. She looked preened to perfection, her dark locks coiled into a shining bun and her clothes immaculate. There wasn't a single sign she'd fought in the battle earlier on as a powerful Manticore, but she had. Just like plenty of others in this room. But that was the way of Fae. We kept going even through the hardest of times. "The FIB have sent the bodies home to their families. We will all greatly miss Darren Torkin, Lily Jessops, Harriet Kent and Ashanti Larue-"

The wolf pack howled as one, the sound piercing my gut. Caleb wrapped an arm around Seth and Max reached out to hold his hand, taking his pain away with his Siren gifts.

"Although this tragedy has rocked us to our core, we must remember that we are Fae. We do not falter in the face of adversary. We lift our heads high and walk on. Tomorrow, classes will continue as normal and freshmen will begin preparation for The Reckoning which will be held this coming week. We will show those cowardly Nymphs who skulk in the shadows that we cannot be broken. Not even for a moment."

A few people clapped, but most of the students seemed subdued.

Nova pressed out an invisible crease from her button-down jacket then clasped her hands together. "Now," she said sharply and everyone lifted their heads. "Zodiac Academy is officially on lock down. We will not lose a single other student to the hands of the vile creatures who have declared war on us this very day. Curfew will start at nine pm sharp every night without fail, including weekends. Any student found out of their Houses after this time will face severe punishment. Two hundred and fifty points will be docked from your House and you will face detention with Professor Orion." She gestured to me and a sea of eyes turned my way.

I gave them a dark look to stoke a little fear in the hearts of any rebels considering breaking those orders. Darcy's eyes locked with mine and my lungs compressed. Why was it so fucking difficult to cut her out of me? One look was enough to make me consider risking everything I'd ever worked for.

So stop looking, asshole.

Nova continued on, "Werewolves will have to run under the moon early in the evening-" They groaned as she went on and I searched for Darius again as I realised the major issue this curfew posed for us.

His gaze butted against mine as if he was thinking the same thing and I jerked my head to beckon him. He slid out of his seat and no one paid him much attention as he moved to the far wall and started a subtle trail toward me.

I slipped back out of the door and a moment later, he joined me outside. He said nothing as we headed away toward the shadowy path between Pluto Offices and Mercury Chambers. The FIB were crawling all over this place so I kept walking without a single word, turning into the entrance to the offices and shutting the door behind us with a loud clunk. It was deathly silent in the atrium and the darkness was penetrated by the dim blue glow of lights on the sorting machines. I opened my palm, casting a silencing bubble around us as a precaution.

"Curfew presents a real issue for your training," I said, folding my arms.

Darius nodded. "Yeah and I still don't even have my own draining dagger to practice with."

"Have you got back everything else that your pal Milton stole?" I asked in a dark tone. I'd gut that kid for burning down Darius's room if I wouldn't lose my damn job for it.

"I got back a few coins that were in his room," he growled. "It's hard to say if he took any more than that and I can't ask him outright about the dagger. It'd draw too much attention to it. But he's too thick to realise what it is."

"Stupidity is dangerous around something like that. What if he starts cutting himself?" I hissed, running a hand down the back of my neck.

"Well he'll fuck up his whole life if he gets caught doing that."

A tense moment passed between us as the weight of his words settled in the air. We'd both lose everything if we got caught, but we were too far down this road to stop now.

"The last thing we need is the FIB getting their hands on it," I said anxiously. "It's not traceable but if they know an artifact like that is floating around campus, they'll start a witch hunt."

"Your fuck buddy will keep them off our backs," Darius taunted but I wasn't in the mood for games.

"Francesca covers for me when we go after Nymphs. She's not aware of my other *hobbies*," I said dryly, even though Darius knew that. He just wanted a rise out of me, which meant he was in a seriously bad mood and playing with fire.

"I think she'd still take a bullet for you even if she did figure out that you-" I stole the air from his lungs with a twist of my fingers and he spluttered heavily.

A crunch had sounded outside. A footstep for sure.

Darius glared at me as he caught his breath but the look I gave him told him exactly why and his eyes whipped to the door. I'd cast a silencing bubble around us but an FIB agent could have breached it if they'd sensed it.

I leaned in close, speaking into Darius's ear. "I have a feeling the FIB aren't being transparent with their investigation this time. They're watching all of us. I'll message you privately. Delete everything I send the second you've read it."

He nodded and I dropped the silencing bubble just before he shoved me hard in the chest. "My friend died out there! I can't keep calm and just sit in that assembly, Professor!"

"You need to take a breath," I boomed. "If you lose control of your Order form I'll dock you twenty House Points."

"Fuck you!" Darius stormed out of Pluto Offices and I marched after him into the night.

"Twenty House points and you can meet me in detention Thursday evening!" I bellowed after him. *That ought to give us a chance to practice.*

The air was eerily still but a shadow moving in my periphery alerted me to the slinking FIB agent, strolling along as if he hadn't been there the entire time.

"I wouldn't want your job," he joked but his eyes trailed over me in a way that made me uncomfortable.

"It'd be fine if the kids actually behaved," I said, slapping on a smile and he nodded slowly.

"I hear that. I've got a ten year old who starts a rebellion every other week. You got kids?"

"Nah. Not really my calling in life."

"Says the teacher." He cocked a brow.

"Well if there's one way to put you off having kids, it's being around a bunch of teenagers twenty four seven."

"You'll change your mind on that one day. Besides, you're only young. You can't have been graduated long, you look about the same age as my eldest..."

I kept my smile in place but it was beginning to hurt my face. *Don't presume you know shit about me, asshole.* "Four years out."

He looked me over. "And you're a professor? At *this* academy? How'd you pull that off?"

Nosy shit. "Straight As in my finals." *And Uncle Acrux pulling strings so I'd have to be within a mile radius of his son at all times.* I didn't even wanna be a goddamn teacher. Though I doubted anyone else could tell that...

He released a low whistle. "Well I bet you make friends with the students easier than you do the faculty, eh?"

My eyes sharpened and my smile fell away dramatically. This guy wasn't casually interested in me, he was fucking interrogating me. And that riled up a fierce storm in my blood.

You wanna dance, shitbag? I've been to hell and back tonight, so you're a walk in the park.

"I don't make friends with *anyone* very easily, least of all students, Mr..?"

"Malone. Gordon Malone. It just struck me as odd that you brought Lionel Acrux's son all the way out here to have a private chat. I hear on the grapevine that your family have a special kind of relationship with theirs." Triumph flared in his eyes like he'd won this game. That he'd caught me out at something. But hell if he had.

My eyes slid over him as I hunted for his badge and rank. Jackpot. This loser was beneath Francesca. Because just like me, she aced every job she took on in life. She'd climbed the ranks at the FIB faster than anyone else in her training class. And she hadn't stopped climbing since.

"Well Mr Malone, I suppose your superior Agent Sky will be wondering where you've run off to."

His brows jumped up. "You...know her?"

"Yeah I'd like to think I know my girlfriend pretty well." I watched the blood run from his face all the way down to his shiny little boots with a twisted satisfaction. It wasn't *entirely* accurate but she wouldn't deny it if he brought it up. Not that I expected he would now he knew he was interrogating the man that kept company with his boss at night.

He cleared his throat. "Yes well, you're probably right. You won't um, tell her that I..."

"That you what?" I smirked.

"Nothing." He dipped his head. "Have a good night." He hurried away and my shoulders dropped.

That was one crisis averted but I had much bigger problems facing me this week. It looked like the Vega Twins were about to emerge in their Order forms and they'd proved that they were now a genuine threat to the throne.

On top of that, the Lunar Eclipse coincided with The Reckoning. Which meant I was about to be worked off my ass preparing freshmen for both events while trying to figure out a way to stop Darius's father from bringing a plague down on Solaria.

At Zodiac, they called this Hell Week. And this year, it was more literal than ever.

TORY

CHAPTER TWO

"**T**or?" Darcy's whispered voice reached out to me where I was hiding in slumber and I recoiled from it with a groan. "Tory?" she said a little louder.

"No," I mumbled, pulling a pillow over my head.

I was dog tired. We were in my room in Ignis House, neither of us wanting to part company since the horror of the Nymph attack. After everything that had happened after the Pitball match yesterday and attending that assembly where Nova had basically told us to suck it up and get on with our education, we'd stayed up into the small hours talking.

I guessed at some point we'd both passed out but I had no idea why the hell Darcy thought it was a good idea to wake me up again. From the aching in my limbs and foggy brain I could only imagine it was the armpit of dawn and I had no reason to want to see that time of day.

"Can you hear that?" Darcy asked, the note of concern in her voice making me lower the pillow an inch.

I groaned again as I rolled onto my back and lay still until a strange sound reached my ears. It was like the distant clang of a metal gong.

"What is that?" I asked, forcing myself up a little onto my elbows and blinking the sleep from my eyes.

Darcy was sitting up in my bed, her arms folded as she cocked her head to listen.

"It could be anything in this crazy school. Maybe Manticores play the gong to replenish their magic or Harpies like to dance to gong music under the light of the moon just for the hell of it," I suggested.

Darcy laughed half-heartedly and we both fell silent as the dull chime of the gong rang out again, sounding a little nearer this time. It wasn't really a dancing under the moon kind of sound though; it was more ominous than that, like the promise of something to come.

A shiver ran down my spine at that thought and I pushed myself upright.

"I can't believe I'm going to say this, but shall we get an early start, maybe head for breakfast at The Orb?" I asked. Now that I was awake and that damn gong was ringing out I didn't imagine I'd be getting much more sleep anyway.

"I was thinking the same thing," Darcy replied, relief lacing her tone.

I moved to get out of bed but my Atlas suddenly released a loud ring which I'd never heard from it before. Darcy's did the same on the desk across the room and we exchanged a look before I hooked mine off of the nightstand to see what this was about.

As my gaze fell on the message, my eyes widened in surprise and I held it out so that Darcy could read it too.

WELCOME TO HELL WEEK!

You and the rest of the freshman class are now formally beginning the week leading up to The Reckoning.

During this week you must pass the trials of your Elements before taking part

in the final assessment which will determine whether you are worthy of your
place at our prestigious academy.
To make sure you are thoroughly challenged, the rest of the student body will
be throwing further tests your way at every turn and making your lives hell!
Will you make the cut for this year's official enrolment?
It's time to prove how Fae you are.

Yours - Principal Nova

"What the crap?" Darcy breathed in disbelief. "A bunch of people died yesterday. I get that Nova said we have to carry on with our education if we want to be strong enough to stand against the Nymphs in the future, but this seems like a bit much."

"Everything in this fucking place is a bit much," I growled.

"What do they mean the rest of the student body will be making our lives hell?" Darcy questioned.

"Well that bit at least won't be any different," I joked. "In fact, if they've got to spread their attention between all the freshmen instead of just focusing on us then maybe we're in for an easier time than usual."

"That'd be nice. Though I get the feeling it will just make the target on our backs even bigger," Darcy sighed.

"Maybe you're right. At least we're used to it." I pushed myself upright and ran my fingers through my hair as I fought against the urge to crawl back into bed.

The clash of the gong was getting louder and I got the sense that it was to do with this Hell Week shit.

"Freshmen!" a girl's voice carried loudly from out in the corridor and I hesitated as I looked towards my closed door. "Hell Week is upon you! You have fifteen minutes to get yourselves ready for class and get out of your rooms. Anyone who doesn't appear voluntarily will be dragged out. You have been warned!"

I looked back at Darcy and groaned. "Why does it have to start so early in the morning?" I asked. "It really is going to be hell if they wake me up at this time every day."

"Let's hope that's the worst of it," Darcy replied as she got up too.

We exchanged a look which said we both knew that was unlikely before I headed into the en-suite. I clipped my hair up before jumping into the shower, letting the hot water wake me up despite the longing I felt for pillows and soft sheets.

I emerged quickly, leaving Darcy to take her turn as I dressed in my Academy uniform and tamed my hair into something respectable. As I started applying my makeup, my Atlas pinged with a private message.

I reached for it automatically, my lips parting in surprise as I saw who it was from.

Caleb:

So I'm thinking we need to draw a few lines in the sand...

I frowned in confusion, wondering what he meant by that before replying.

Tory:

Talking in riddles only makes you seem like more of a douchebag.

Caleb:

And there was me thinking that was impossible. I'm talking about keeping the two sides of our relationship separate.

Tory:

We don't have a relationship.

I tossed my Atlas onto my bed dismissively and returned to the task of completing my makeup. Darcy appeared from her own shower and claimed another uniform from my closet without bothering to ask. As we were the same size in everything, we'd long since taken to stealing each other's clothes as standard. And even though we weren't as short on options as we used to be in the mortal world, it was a habit that we weren't likely to break any time soon. It was familiar and natural, and one of the few things that hadn't changed when we'd come to this insane academy.

My Atlas pinged behind me. And again. And again.

"You're popular this morning," Darcy commented, eyeing it with interest.

I grunted in response. "Caleb's just trying to get into my pants again."

She snorted a laugh. "How hard are you going to make him work for it?"

"He took part in the whole throwing us in a pit business. So I'm thinking I'm done with him," I said dismissively.

"Yeah, you totally should be," she agreed. "But that look in your eye says you're not."

"That's just the part of my brain which is blinded by his hotness. I refuse to listen to her because she's a slut. The sensible part of my brain says hell no and I'll be keeping company with her and her chastity belt from now on."

"Okay," Darcy said in a way which told me she wasn't totally convinced but there wasn't much I could do about that. My track record spoke for itself.

The Atlas pinged again. And again.

"At least let's see how hard he's grovelling," she said with a wicked smile.

I laughed and moved to grab my Atlas from the bed.

Caleb:

That's so cold, Tory. I know you felt things too... the noises you were making in response to them are kinda hard to deny ;)

Caleb:

Do you want me to beg? Do you like the idea of getting me on my knees for you?

Caleb:

Are you ignoring me now? Can't we just agree to disagree about the whole throne issue and take out our frustrations over the situation on each other? I promise, I'm super frustrated over it and it will take a lot of work to make me feel any better about it...

Caleb:

You wanna see how frustrated I am...? I really need help working through this...

The last message contained a photograph which Caleb had taken of himself in a mirror after getting out of the shower. His blonde curls were damp and looked darker than usual and every inch of his exposed, muscular body glistened with fat drops of moisture. The picture cut off at his waist and his navy eyes blazed with an intensity which made me swallow a lump in my throat.

Caleb:

Want to come over and see the rest?

Darcy released a breath of laughter. "Well he certainly knows what he wants."

My gaze raked over the picture of his tight abs glistening with water and I groaned. "Why does he have to be such an asshole?" I complained.

"Well if he wasn't, you probably wouldn't like him at all," she reasoned and I couldn't help but laugh at that.

"That is a tragically accurate assessment," I agreed.

I decided to leave Caleb hanging and closed down the private messages with a smile tugging at the corner of my mouth.

"Time's up freshmen!" the girl's voice came from beyond my door again and we looked around at it with concern. "Come on out to face hell - it'll only be worse if we have to come get you!"

"This school is insane," Darcy groaned as she placed her satchel over her shoulder and we prepared to head out there.

I stuffed my Atlas into my own satchel and threw it on as we moved towards the door.

"Shield?" I suggested at the last second, imagining someone waiting outside the door to throw a bucket of water over our heads or something.

"Good idea," Darcy agreed.

We both threw up a strong shield of air magic and I opened my door with my heart in my throat.

The door swung wide and I held my breath as we stepped out to find... nothing. The corridor was abandoned.

I exchanged a look with Darcy and quickly locked up behind us as we headed for the stairs which led down to the common room.

The only sound was the persistent clang of that far off gong which my heart was quickly falling into rhythm with.

We descended in silence but the second my feet landed at the foot of the stairs in the common room, I fell still. The whole room was full of students clad in long black robes with plain white masks concealing their faces.

For a moment nothing happened, they all stared at us through the eye holes in their masks and I felt like I'd just stumbled into a creepy ass cult nightmare.

Opposite me, I recognised Marguerite's flaming red hair falling behind her white mask as she raised a hand to point at the two of us. "Fresh meat!" She cried and as one, every student in the room lunged at us.

I screamed, throwing more energy into the shield I'd created and accidentally creating a blast of air magic which crashed out from us and slammed into them, knocking students from their feet and tumbling across the red carpet.

"Oh shit," I breathed, glancing around at what I'd done but Darcy had already caught my hand and she yanked to get me moving as the Ignis students recovered from their shock and came for us again.

We ran through the centre of the room as flames crashed into the outside of the shield Darcy was maintaining and I scrambled to throw up another of my own to help her.

"*Stop running and drop your shields!*" Marguerite demanded, her voice thick with Coercion. With our focus fully on maintaining our magic, we hadn't even been attempting to keep our minds guarded from that kind of attack. The two of us stumbled to a halt, the shields blinking out of existence instantly.

We were swamped by a group of guys big enough to make me think they were seniors and they wrenched us away from each other.

I swore at them, thrashing as I fought to break free of their hold but they only laughed as they carried me back through the common room and shoved me to my knees before Marguerite. Darcy was pushed down beside me and she swore at the guys restraining her with enough vigour to make a few of them laugh.

"*Don't fight back,*" Marguerite commanded and my traitorous body fell still as I cursed myself for not expecting that.

Her eyes sparkled with excitement beneath the creepy, expressionless white mask and she leaned towards me with a black marker in her hand.

Her Coercion glued me in place as she scrawled something across my forehead before turning and offering the same treatment to Darcy.

"*Now run along to class,*" Marguerite ordered.

I sprang to my feet and hurried from the room with Darcy at my side, the Coercion forcing us to run. The crowd of robed Ignis students parted to make way for us, laughing their asses off as we went.

As we made it outside, I felt the grip of her power loosening and I gritted my teeth as I finally managed to throw it off and stop running.

Darcy halted beside me and I looked at her with a frown. The words *just talk to my raven* were scrawled across her forehead in thick black marker.

"What does mine say?" I asked after telling her what they'd written on her.

"Whore," Darcy replied with a sigh. "She's not very original is she?"

"I don't think she's ever had an original idea in her life," I agreed. I channelled some water magic and tried to use it to clean the marker from Darcy's skin but it wouldn't budge.

"I'm guessing this is stuck on magically," Darcy sighed after the third attempt failed.

"So we're stuck like this?" I asked.

"Yep," Darcy replied.

"Great."

We trudged towards The Orb while I offered up many creative insults about Marguerite and Darcy smirked appreciatively. As I finished venting, I noticed a crowd of students in black robes hanging out near The Orb ahead and paused.

"I'm suddenly not feeling so hungry," Darcy muttered.

My stomach growled its disagreement but I turned away too. It didn't look like there was anything but trouble waiting in The Orb today anyway.

A hiss drew my attention to the shadows beside Venus Library and I turned to find the cause of it with a frown.

"Hey guys!" Sofia whispered, waving us closer as she spotted us. She was deep within the shadows, her back pressed to the brick wall of the library as she glanced about nervously.

"What are you doing?" I asked with a smirk as we drew closer to her.

"Trying to avoid the attention of the Terra House juniors," she explained.

"They're tying freshmen to the spire of Neptune Tower with vines."

I turned to look in that direction and my eyes widened as I spotted a ring of students bound to the roof ten floors up exactly as she'd said.

"Oh my god," Darcy breathed.

"Did you know about this Hell Week stuff before today?" I asked Sofia, dragging my gaze from the terrified freshmen.

"No. But I just called my mom and she was laughing her head off. Told me good luck and said that's how it's done here - it's kept secret from the freshmen on purpose."

As Sofia leaned forward a little to get a look around, I noticed the words *Vega ass-licker* written on her forehead and I pursed my lips angrily.

"So did your mom give you any other advice on how to survive this week?" Darcy asked her.

"She just said that we can't take it lying down. We have to try and fight back. Which is why I came to the library actually." Sofia produced a book and opened it to a page where she'd wedged her thumb. "I think I've found the spell we need to unstick this pen from our faces."

"Really?" I asked excitedly. I hadn't exactly been thrilled about walking around with the word *whore* branded to my forehead for the foreseeable future.

"Yeah... if I get it wrong it might take off a chunk of skin though," she added with a nervous laugh.

I exchanged a glance with Darcy then released a deep breath.

"Just try it out on me," I offered. "I can always go to Uranus Infirmary if it goes horribly wrong."

"Are you sure?" Sofia asked though she was already raising her hand towards me, sparks of magic twisting between her fingers.

"I trust you," I confirmed, closing my eyes.

Sofia's fingers brushed my skin followed quickly by a wave of cold energy. There was no pain and I slowly opened my eyes as she drew back, finding the two of them grinning at me.

"It worked?" I confirmed.

"It did!" Sofia said with a squeal of excitement. She quickly performed the magic on her and Darcy and I glanced out towards the path once more to keep watch as she did.

A bolt of fear ran through me as a group of ten juniors rounded the corner, vines curling around their arms as they wielded their magic. Before I could duck out of sight again, one of them spotted me.

"Fresh meat!" he bellowed and the three of us screamed as we darted away down the darkened path between Venus Library and Mercury Chambers.

I threw a handful of flames over my shoulder to slow them down and we scrambled around the building, turning left as we ran on.

The juniors were bellowing a battle cry as they chased us and my heart thundered with panic.

"Any ideas?" I gasped as Darcy directed a crash of wind behind us, knocking the juniors from their feet for a moment.

They were already scrambling upright again before I turned my attention back to the path before me.

"I've got one!" Sofia cried. She tossed Darcy her satchel then yanked off her blazer, quickly followed by her shirt then skirt.

I grabbed the clothes from her as she threw them my way and she ripped her shoes from her feet, leaving her in her socks and underwear. She didn't waste time on removing those before bursting into her Order form and shredding through them.

Her beautiful pink Pegasus form towered over us and she dipped her wing so that Darcy could jump onto her back.

The juniors were yelling curses at us as they saw their prey preparing to escape and huge vines sped our way like a thousand slithering snakes.

Darcy yelled out as she threw a fireball at the vines, destroying them and giving me time to leap up onto Sofia's back behind her.

With an excited whinny, Sofia took off at a gallop and the wind swept through my hair at the immense speed.

The juniors yelled behind us as we escaped and with a few powerful beats of Sofia's wings, we launched into the sky.

I let out a whoop of triumph, my heart soaring as the ground sped away beneath us.

Darcy was laughing excitedly in front of me and the smile on my face was so wide it made my cheeks ache.

Hell Week at Zodiac Academy had just begun, but we'd survived a whole lot of crap already since coming here so we could handle this. The wind whipped through my hair and the beautiful sight of the Academy grounds sprawled out beneath us, filling me with a joy so intense it made me ache.

The Heirs didn't think we could make it through The Reckoning but as I looked down upon the Academy I'd begun to think of as home, I was determined to prove them wrong. We were Fae. And we belonged here. And we'd be staying no matter what.

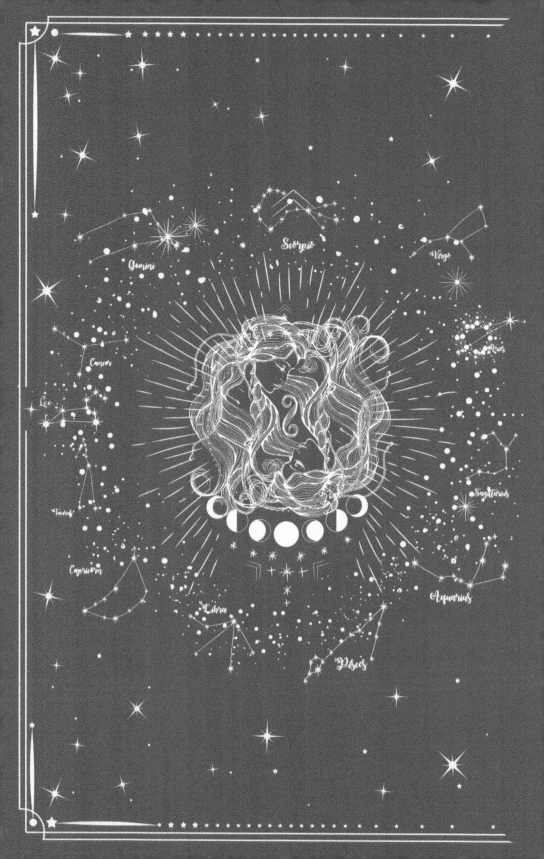

DARCY

CHAPTER THREE

I sat in Cardinal Magic class between Tory and Diego, coming down from the high of riding across the grounds on Sofia's back. The longer I sat there, the more the thrill in my veins gave way to anxiety. The thought of seeing Orion again in the cold light of day was making me feel all kinds of messed up emotions. None of which I wanted to concentrate on. Because if I boarded the over-analytical train to insanity town, I'd be stuck on it all day.

Tyler Corbin hurried in five minutes late, but it didn't matter considering Orion still wasn't here. The class was loud with chatter as they spoke about Lily Jessops who had sat in the back row of our class all term. I felt bad that I'd never spoken to her. She'd been quiet and I hadn't known whether her allegiance had laid with us or the Heirs. It saddened me to know she'd been lost to the hands of the Nymphs.

Someone had cast a tribute of moss and glittering flowers all over her desk which continually closed up then bloomed all over again.

"It's just so hard to lose such a dear friend," Kylie was sobbing, her friends grouped around her as she dabbed her eyes. "Lily was such a sweet girl."

I'd never once seen Kylie hanging out with her and I shot a glare over my shoulder at the attention-seeking act she was performing. Why did she think it was alright to use someone's death to get herself a few pats on the back? It was disgusting.

My Atlas pinged along with everyone else's in the classroom and I frowned as I took it out.

Zodiac Academy has been mentioned in The Celestial Times.

I clicked on the article with a feeling of dread in my stomach and my gut lurched even more when I found what I'd suspected: it was written by Gus Vulpecula.

ATTACK ON ZODIAC!

Zodiac Academy remains on high alert while the Fae Investigation Bureau continue to shed light on the mass Nymph attack which occurred yesterday afternoon on the school's grounds.

At the end of the Pitball match between Zodiac and Starlight Academy, which kicked off the inter-school tournament, the stadium was over-run by nearly fifty Nymphs, many of which possessed Elemental magic stolen from Fae they'd killed in previous incidents.

Twelve students (eight from Starlight and four from Zodiac) have been named amongst the dead and a vigil is expected to take place in a week's time to commemorate their loss.

In true Fae fashion, Principal Elaine Nova has informed all parents that there will be no hiccoughs in the education of their children and school hours will continue as usual. With the freshmen facing their official enrolment exams this week, it is predicted that a higher number of drop-outs will occur than usual. That being said, the potential of the Fae who do make it under such pressure will be celebrated for their strength in times of adversary.

Amongst those taking part in their exams and who were also present for the attack, were Tory (Roxanya) and Darcy (Gwendalina) Vega. Reports from eyewitnesses state they saw both Vegas casting a mysterious red and blue fire during the battle. One witness and student at Zodiac Academy, Miss Marguerite Helebor, gave this statement, "They seemed to think they were helping, but their magic was rogue and dangerous. I wouldn't be surprised if some of the deaths were caused by their attacks."

Other witnesses have spoken of the Vegas' ineptitude during the fight and many are calling for them to have a mental examination before being allowed to proceed with The Reckoning. Though it once seemed that the Vega Twins were nothing but a slightly unbalanced yet relatively harmless duo, it now seems we have more to fear from them than first understood.

Bets are being made kingdom-wide over which Order the two of them will emerge as. But the rumours are rife about the possibility of two more Dragons rising to power. High Lord Lionel Acrux was unavailable for comment, but his son, Darius, had this to say.

"We are all greatly saddened about the event which occurred at our beloved Zodiac Academy. Alongside my fellow Heirs, I intend to take measures against the Nymphs for bringing such tragedy on our people. In regard to the Vega Twins, I have little to say except that in this time of great need it would be most appropriate if they publicly renounced their claim to ensure the future of Solaria falls into capable hands."

The other Heirs have expressed similar wishes, but with rumours circling that the Vegas do indeed intend to make a bid to claim their throne, one must wonder why they haven't yet come forward to state their own views on the coming war and how they would hope to handle it. Upon reaching out to them late last night for a statement, I was refused by both parties.

Pressing for more information, I discovered from a reliable witness who wished to remain anonymous that Tory Vega was engaged with multiple sexual partners throughout the night, whilst her sister circled the halls, anxiously looking for a raven she had apparently lost sight of during the battle.

The only possible conclusion I am able to draw from their behaviour is that the two Vegas Twins share the mad streak of their father, and will certainly bring another reign of savagery down upon Solaria if they were to lay their claim and win.

"Bullshit," I hissed, tossing my Atlas onto my desk with a clatter. "This is complete lies."

"That Gus guy has a date with my fists," Tory snarled.

Sniggers sounded from plenty of our classmates but not as many as

I'd expected.

"It's okay, chicas. No one believes anything written in The Celestial Times," Diego said and Sofia nodded, her eyes glimmering.

"I'd like to be there on that date though, Tory," Sofia said proudly. "I'd bring the fury of my hooves."

"You sure did in the battle," I said to her with a grin and a glow filled her eyes.

"Hey, er, Darcy... Tory?"

I whirled around, finding Tyler standing before us, looking slightly awkward as he raked a hand through his blonde-tipped hair.

"Yeah?" Tory asked with a look that said she was preparing to blast him into oblivion if he said something about that article.

"I just wanted to say um.... well what you both did when the Nymphs showed up... it was really brave. And I'm not sure I would still be here if it wasn't for you two. That Gus Vulpecula guy is a filthy liar. My mum works for The Daily Solaria though, so I'll make sure she gets the truth. The real truth." He placed something down on my desk then on Tory's before hurrying back to his seat.

I picked up the green leaf he'd given me which turned to a deep rust colour then gold before words spread across it. Shock took hold of me as I read them.

Thank you.

I found Tory holding a matching one and she looked to me in complete surprise.

Orion strode into the room and slammed the door so hard, I nearly dropped the leaf as my gut knotted and I was suddenly too hot everywhere. He half glanced my way then looked firmly forward, marching up to the head of the room.

I frowned as I noticed he had a watermelon under his arm and as he arrived at his desk, he planted it down and took something out of his suit jacket pocket. I recognised Diego's beanie hat as he slid it over the watermelon, picked up a pen and started drawing a face on it that looked like an angry little gremlin.

He angled it toward Diego then pointed at him. "You want this back?"

"Yes, sir," Diego said, rage making his temple pulse.

"Then I encourage you to try and get it back before the lesson ends."

Diego gawped at him, making no move to get up as Orion swiped his electronic pen from the desk and turned to the board. It was Seth who'd taken that hat from Diego and it was hardly fair he had to work to get it back from Orion now. I sensed it wouldn't be as simple as him walking up there and grabbing it either.

Orion stepped aside, revealing what he'd written on the board.

YOU ARE ALL BOTTOM-FEEDING LOSERS.

My mouth fell open as he glared at the class, looking like he was about to unleash the apocalypse on us.

"This is Hell Week," he snapped and everyone flinched from his ferocious tone. "And you're all fucking useless."

"Oh my god, sir!" Kylie piped up. "Lily *just* died, how can you even-"

Orion lifted a hand and snapped his fingers together. She spluttered and choked, holding her throat and rising from her seat in a panic. Orion strode casually down the aisle and my heart thrashed against my chest as he paid her absolutely no attention.

"She's suffocating!" Jillian wailed, patting Kylie on the back as she turned blue.

"Professor!" I gasped as he drew near me and he shot me a dark glare.

"Yes, Miss Vega?" he questioned, totally calm, that twisted smile pulling

42

at his mouth.

"She's choking," I hissed and he shifted his gaze to Kylie as if he'd just noticed her.

"Five points from Aer for stating the obvious." He strode past me and I swivelled in my seat, glaring at his back as he went.

"Miss Minor." he pointed at Jillian. "Name three constellations in their Latin names that aren't star signs."

Jillian opened and closed her mouth, shaking her head.

"Do so or your friend here is going to pass out. I'll give you a clue: both your and her surnames are part of several constellation names." He folded his arms, waiting and Jillian's eyes widened to saucers.

"U-ursa Minor, Ursa M-major and, and-"

"And?" he inquired.

"Monoceros!" she blurted and Orion waved his hand.

Kylie collapsed down into her seat, coughing heavily as she drew in deep lungfuls of air.

"It seems your friend is not a complete waste of oxygen, Miss Major. So be sure to prove to me that you're also not wasting precious air in my classroom."

Kylie nodded, panting as she held her throat, staring back at him angrily. I was kind of impressed at how unaffected she seemed after nearly choking to death.

"So perhaps we aren't all entirely useless. Maybe you just need the right motivation to work harder." He turned back up the aisle, his hand landing on Sofia's shoulder. His other palm shot out toward Tory and he stole the air from her lungs.

Tory sat bolt upright, her hand flying to her chest.

"Miss Cygnus, name the seven Cardinal Magics that all Fae are capable of before Miss Vega turns blue," Orion commanded and Sofia squeaked in alarm.

My heart thumped madly but Sofia was the smartest Fae in the class and she gave his answer immediately. "Healing, Coercion, Levitation, Summoning, Illusion, Divination and Atmospheric Manipulation."

Orion released Tory from his power and she gasped for air, managing to choke out, "Ass-hole," as he marched back to the front of the room.

I gave her a sympathetic look and she pursed her lips.

Orion leaned back against his desk, folding his arms. "We have a serious fucking problem. Corbin, tell me what it is." He pointed at Tyler who remained dead silent, shrugging his shoulders.

"Polaris?" Orion asked Diego who shook his head.

His eyes skipped onto me. "Miss Vega?"

"That our Cardinal Magic teacher is a psycho?" I offered, rage still simmering in me from him attacking my sister.

His jaw ticked in a deadly way and my heart thumped out of rhythm. "I prefer the term unbalanced and frankly it's the least of your problems." His mouth twitched with amusement as he looked away.

Unbalanced was right. Plus totally unpredictable. And I didn't think it was the least of my problems at all, it was right up there with Nymphs declaring war on Solaria and some crazy ass fire living in my veins.

"If I don't get an answer in the next ten seconds, someone's head is going to be introduced to the ceiling," Orion said coolly.

Everyone started calling out answers as he held up two hands, counting down fingers one at a time.

"The Nymphs?!" someone cried.

"The Reckoning?" someone else tried.

"Hell Week is going to kill us?" Jillian wailed.

"We suck?" Diego blurted and Orion paused one second from finishing his countdown and used that finger to point at him.

"What specifically do you suck at?" he demanded.

"Um, everything?" Diego tried and I couldn't help the snort of laughter that escaped me.

"No," Orion sighed, lifting his finger again, ready to count it down.

"Practical magic!" Sofia supplied just before he curled his finger.

"Yes," he cheered with a bright smile. "Ten points to Ignis." He stared around at all of us with gleaming eyes.

"Tell me, Corbin, how many Vampires drank from you last week?" Orion shifted closer to him as Tyler frowned.

"Um… four maybe?" he said with a shrug.

"And did you try to fight them off?" Orion asked.

"Well… it's easier to just, ya know, let them get on with it," Tyler said awkwardly.

"Precisely. And some of you..." He swept through the class with his Vampire speed and everyone stiffened. His hand landed on Tory's shoulder as he leaned in close to her ear. "Actually enjoy it, don't you?"

Tory blushed which was saying a lot for my sister. "That's not really your business, is it Professor?"

"Isn't it? I beg to differ." he stood upright then shot back to the front of the class. "What is the point of you all being here if you're content with sitting at the bottom of the food chain? I'm not going to waste my time training Fae who don't want to climb the ranks." His sharp eyes scored over us all, cutting us down to the quick. "Raise your hand if you've been drained by a Siren recently."

Everyone raised their hands, even the Sirens in the class.

"And keep your hand up if you fought back."

Nearly everyone's hands dropped except Tory's and I threw her a grin.

"Oh yeah! Tory Vega totally throat punched Max Rigel," Tyler said excitedly.

"Did she now?" Orion asked with a hint of a smile.

"Well yeah." Tory shrugged innocently, but her eyes lit up with the memory.

45

"And I suppose you've attempted that with Caleb Altair too, have you?" Orion deadpanned and the smile fell from her face. "I thought not."

"Sir – we're not trained to fight off other Fae yet," Kylie called out. "Most of us aren't from the gutter with street fighting skills."

"Maybe you'd better go spend some time in the gutter then, Miss Major, because you won't be trained to fight off other Fae magically until after The Reckoning," Orion said and Tory and I started grinning. "The fact is, I don't care if you get knocked on your ass every time a Fae takes advantage of you. If you don't even try to fight back, you don't deserve your place in this school. Do I make myself clear?"

A murmur of *yes sir* filled the room.

"Good. Your first assignment this week is to embrace your inner Fae. Don't take any shit lying down. No one's judging you if you lose, but if you don't even try to win, you're not one of us. And if you can't hack it, get out of my class." He gestured to the door and one boy actually gathered up his things and hurried out. The door slowly swung closed behind him and my lips parted in surprise.

"This is called Hell Week for a reason," Orion growled. "We're going to try and break you. You might even *get* broken. But so long as you persevere and make it through The Reckoning you will be accepted as true Fae. Your place at Zodiac Academy will become official. Even if you don't make it through the rest of the year, no one will be able to take that away from you. So suck it up. And face the heat with everything you've got. Remember to look out for yourself, because not everyone in this classroom is going to be here next week."

Ho-ly shit. Am I ready for this?

Orion tapped the board and the screen changed to the lesson title.

The Reckoning: How to Prepare for the Worst Week of Your Life.

"The Elemental Trials will be held this week leading up to The Reckoning." He tapped the screen and the schedule flashed up.

Thursday: Air Trial
Friday: Water Trial
Saturday: Fire Trial
Sunday: Earth Trial
Monday: The Reckoning

"You will attend the trials of whatever Elements you hold." He looked to Tory and I with a terse expression. "That means you will attend every trial of *every* Element you hold."

"Great," Tory muttered and my gut clenched.

"That's crazy, chicas." Diego shook his head, pushing a hand through his curly black locks.

"The trials are top secret so I won't be giving you any pointers. However, what I can say is that it will test the abilities you have learned in your Elemental classes, but most importantly it will test your mettle. The older students have been instructed to make your lives as difficult as possible during this week, so when you face your trials, you will be exhausted, you will be angry and you will be ready to go home. So you'll have to call on the strongest part of your nature if you're going to survive it."

"I changed my mind." The guy who'd left the room poked his white-blonde head back through the door and everyone turned to look at him.

"I've already forgotten your name," Orion snarled at him but the boy opened the door, edging back in with his Atlas clutched to his chest.

"It's Elijah Indus," he said firmly, lifting his chin.

"Talk to me in the hall," Orion ordered, a malicious look on his face as he hounded forward and Elijah backed out of the door. Orion stepped after him and as the door closed, several people darted out of their seats, clustering against it to listen.

It was totally unnecessary as Orion's booming voice made the whole classroom shake.

"DO YOU THINK IT'S APPROPRIATE TO INTERRUPT MY LESSON WITH YOUR INDECISIVENESS!?"

Diego shot out of his seat, running up to the desk and swiping the beanie hat from the watermelon. A noise somewhere between an amused laugh and a gasp of terror escaped me as he pocketed it and returned to his seat.

"He'll search you for it," I said, my heart thumping harder.

"You're so dead," Tory laughed.

"You're right." Diego frowned deeply.

"Here, give it to me." I held out my hand and Diego's eyes rounded.

He shook his head firmly "No, it'll get you in trouble."

"He won't know I have it," I said as Orion's voice split the air apart again.

"I DON'T CARE IF YOUR PARENTS SOLD ORGANS TO GET YOU INTO THIS ACADEMY, THAT'S ENTIRELY IRRELEVANT TO WHETHER YOU MAKE THE CUT!"

I wiggled my fingers at Diego and he hesitantly took the hat out and placed it in my hand. "Are you sure?"

"I'm sure."

"Good luck with that," Tory jibed while Sofia stared at the hat like it was about to explode.

I stuffed it into the back of my skirt where Orion wouldn't dare go, arranging my blazer so it concealed the lump. I sat up straighter as the door flew open and the students scattered, fleeing back to their seats.

Orion shoved Elijah into the room, pressing his hands to his shoulders as he guided him to the head of the class. Elijah was pale faced, but had a determined expression in place as Orion prepared to dole out his punishment. He prodded Elijah so he was front and centre then stepped back so we were all staring at him.

"Mr Indus has something to say," Orion announced.

Elijah cleared his throat. The class waited attentively and some people sniggered. "I'm pathetic."

"And?" Orion prompted.

"And a coward."

Orion cocked his head, still waiting.

Elijah sighed. "And I'd like to apologise to you all for being an embarrassment to the school. And to Solaria. And to the entire race of Fae."

"If you walk out again you're done," Orion snarled and I sensed he really meant that. He stalked down the aisle to Elijah's chair and carried it to one side of the room. "Twenty points from House Aqua. And you can stand up in every one of my classes until you earn your seat back."

Elijah nodded quickly, hurrying back to his desk and standing awkwardly where his chair had been.

"Right." Orion returned to the board then his eyes floated down to the hatless watermelon. A dark chuckle rolled from his throat and he turned smoothly toward Diego with a challenging grin. "Stand up, Mr Polaris."

Diego did as he was told, shaking a little as Orion moved to stand in front of him. The hat seemed to burn against my flesh as he studied Diego like he was deciding specifically how he was going to destroy him.

"Hand it back." Orion held out his hand and Diego shook his head in response. He leaned in closer, his eyes calculating as he looked Diego up and down. "Hmm... you don't have it, do you?" His eyes whipped to me and my heart nearly combusted.

I quickly schooled my expression and felt Tory leaning closer like she was gonna grab it if he got too close to his prize.

Orion cast his gaze across me, Tory and Sofia, then back to me, curling a finger to make me stand up. A little thrill danced through me as I stood. He couldn't shove his hand down my skirt. He was a teacher. A fact he had reminded me about quite clearly at Lionel Acrux's house.

He held out his hand and I shrugged.

"I don't have anything, sir," I said innocently.

"Are we really going to play this game?" He leaned into my face and my throat closed up as the all-too-familiar cinnamon scent of him washed over me, reminding me viscerally of the kiss we'd shared. Danger tingled my senses as I read the double meaning to his words. A smile caught the corner of my mouth and I nodded.

He gave me a devil's grin that made my confidence plummet. He thought he'd won. But had he?

He stepped back, still smiling. "Everyone will lose five House Points for every minute Miss Vega keeps hold of that hat."

I gasped, immediately feeling hands on me from the students behind. I lurched away, snatching the hat out from my waistband and throwing it at Orion, releasing a noise of frustration. He caught it out of the air, strolled back to the watermelon and redressed it.

"How the hell am I supposed to get it back if you threaten everyone in class?" Diego huffed.

Orion leaned back in his chair, resting his feet up on the corner of the desk. "That, Mr Polaris, is exactly what you have to figure out."

TORY

CHAPTER FOUR

I left Cardinal Magic feeling even more anxious about this Hell Week stuff than I'd been before it. Professor Orion's teaching method left a lot to be desired. In our last high school back in Chicago I'd had this over-interested guidance counsellor called Mrs McGravy who had tried to smother me with warm and fuzzy feels. I remembered wishing for her to be an asshole instead. Now I was beginning to think I'd been wrong to want that. Mrs McGravy would have given me constructive advice about how to make it through Hell Week and bolstered my confidence in my own ability for good measure.

Orion publicly humiliated me, made me feel worthless and called me names before telling me straight to my face he fully expected me to fail. And I got the impression he actually *wanted* me to fail too. Not like the other students who he wanted to push into succeeding. With me and Darcy it came down to his allegiance to Darius and the other Heirs and at the end of the day he didn't want us on the throne.

The freshmen all stuck together as we headed towards The Orb for lunch and it was kind of amusing to find that all of the cliques, House divides and social circles melted away into nothing as we were faced with a greater threat.

Every older student I saw was wearing one of those long, black robes and I guessed it was to make sure the freshmen stood out as easy targets in our uniforms.

I kept a shield of air magic raised around me as well as making sure I was protecting myself from Coercion too. It took a fair bit of concentration and we stayed silent as we walked. It was probably the least excited I'd ever been about food in my entire life.

"Your Majesties!" Geraldine called loudly the moment we entered The Orb and I turned to find her waving both of her arms above her head as she stood on a chair. In all honesty, she was one of the tallest girls I knew and it was completely unnecessary for her to raise herself up any higher to be seen over the crowd, but she seemed to like doing it.

I sagged in relief as we moved to join the A.S.S. to the left of the room with Diego and Sofia keeping close as we went.

"I saved your table for you," Geraldine gushed as we approached. "It's the darndest thing, but after all of your help with the Nymph attack, we've had over a hundred new members join the Almighty Sovereign Society!"

"Oh wow," Darcy said, summoning some enthusiasm from somewhere even though I knew this fan group still made her as uncomfortable as it made me.

They wanted us to rise up and take back our throne and despite the fact that I was becoming more and more tempted to challenge the asshole Heirs, I still didn't have any intention to place a crown upon my head. So their faith in us was more than a little unwarranted. Still, in this particular situation, I'd gladly accept any help going and if the Ass Club could protect us while we ate our lunch then so be it.

Geraldine was wearing a black robe just like all of the older students and her friend Angelica smiled warmly as we came to sit at the table beside them.

Geraldine had already brought over a selection of sandwiches and bowls of french fries for us and I dropped into my seat with a groan of longing after missing breakfast.

I fell upon my food while listening with one ear to Geraldine rattling off the names of the newest members and occasionally offering out my hand to shake when one of them moved forward excitedly to meet us. I doubted I was really what any of them expected from a princess on my best day and I internally apologised to them for the fact that I wasn't going to be distracted from filling my face while these introductions continued.

When I finally finished my fourth sandwich, I leaned back in my chair and started picking at an overflowing bowl of french fries. Diego was stewing over his missing hat, coming up with more and more pathetic ways to get it back while looking like he might start crying over it.

"Why don't you just buy a new hat, dude?" I asked eventually.

Darcy kicked me beneath the table and I raised my eyebrow questioningly but apparently her warning had come too late. Diego dropped his head into his hands and started murmuring about his abuela knitting it before descending entirely into Spanish. Sofia tried to comfort him, offering me a look that said it was my fault and I rolled my eyes dramatically as I took a sip of my drink.

I quickly placed the coke back down on the table and glanced at the others. "Did someone want diet coke?" I asked, wondering whose drink I'd ended up with by accident. As much as I argued against Geraldine getting our food and drinks all the time, she insisted on doing it and never forgot our preferences so I doubted she would have made that mistake.

Before anyone could respond, Geraldine and Angelica burst into a fit of hysterical laughter, drawing our attention away from Diego's display of self pity.

"I g-g-got you diet!" she cried, barely able to force the words out between her laughter.

"What?" I asked in confusion.

"The mayo in your sandwich was half fat too!" Angelica added, clinging to Geraldine as she wiped tears from beneath her eyes.

"Why?" I asked in confusion.

"H- h -hell week!" Geraldine spluttered through her laughter, her eyes sparkling with amusement.

My lips parted and I threw an extra dose of false outrage into my expression in response to the ridiculous prank, placing a hand over my heart. "How could you, Geraldine?" I gasped. "I thought we were friends!"

Her laughter turned to howling and it was actually kinda addictive, forcing a laugh from me as I exchanged an amused look with Darcy.

I almost didn't notice a figure winding their way between the A.S.S. tables and I looked up at the guy from Terra House as he smiled down at me like we were best friends.

"Can I help you?" I asked with a frown, wondering why he was interrupting our conversation.

"I have a message for you," he said brightly. I eyed his black robe suspiciously, reinforcing my shield as best I could.

"Okay..."

"Caleb says two minutes."

"What?" I asked, glancing beyond him to the red couch where Caleb was perched on the arm of it beside the other Heirs who must have all appeared in The Orb while we ate.

The boy walked away having delivered his message and I was left locking eyes with Caleb across the room.

He smirked at me knowingly and a little wave of heat built in my core. He lifted his Atlas from his pocket and typed something on it. A moment later my own Atlas buzzed and I pulled it from my satchel.

Caleb:

Tick tock.

I glanced down at my half eaten french fries before catching Darcy's eye.

"What?" she asked, reading my expression.

I offered her my Atlas to see the message and she frowned. I'd told her all about the lead up to Caleb and I hooking up in Acrux Manor and she clearly understood what he meant by his message.

"He's not seriously expecting you to play that crazy game *now* is he?" she asked.

"What game?" Sofia asked curiously and even Diego peered between his fingers.

Darcy raised an eyebrow at me, asking my permission before she told them and I only hesitated a moment before nodding. There wasn't much point in hiding it from them if it was something that might become a regular occurrence.

"She got Caleb to hunt her while we were at that party at the Acrux Manor. If he didn't catch her within fifteen minutes then he couldn't bite her," Darcy explained.

"And you thought it was a good idea to do that with a *Vampire*?" Diego asked in disgust.

"Hey, less judgment dude," I snapped. "I'm not the one sobbing over knitted goods."

"Sorry, I didn't mean it like that," he muttered. It had seemed like he meant it like that to me though.

Caleb was still looking at me across the room and as I caught his eye, he tapped the watch on his wrist, reminding me that I was running out of time for my headstart.

I pushed my chair back and got to my feet suddenly.

"You're going to play?" Darcy asked in surprise.

"Orion said I shouldn't just accept getting bitten any more. If Caleb can't catch me, he can't bite me," I reasoned as my heart rate picked up a notch.

"I don't think this was what he had in mind..." Sofia frowned.

"Whatever. Caleb is the most powerful Vampire in Solaria. This is the best chance I've got to avoid a bite. And my headstart is going to run out if I don't go now."

"Class starts in ten minutes," Darcy said half heartedly.

"Cover for me. I'll be there!" I promised before turning and running for the exit.

I glanced back at the red couch in the centre of the room just before I ducked outside and found all four Heirs looking my way.

Caleb was saying something to the others with a smile playing around his lips. Max and Seth seemed mildly interested but Darius looked pretty damn pissed. As his heated gaze met with mine, my heart leapt a little at the anger I found there. I hadn't spoken to him properly since we'd fought together against the Nymphs and I really wasn't sure what I'd have to say anyway. In the moment, we'd been weirdly united. I'd saved his life and he'd saved mine. I'd even cried while he lay dying in my arms. But then Orion had appeared and healed him and the momentary insanity which had come over me, making me think I cared about him had gone in an instant. I only had to remember the way he'd tossed me into that pit to know all I needed to about him and who he was. And he was my enemy. The look he was giving me right then said he felt exactly the same.

I ducked out of The Orb and looked around quickly, wondering where the best place to hide would be. I didn't have many options and I didn't really have a good headstart either so I crossed the path and headed straight into Venus Library.

The librarian wasn't at her desk as I entered and I hurriedly shot down the closest aisle, racing between texts on Fae biology before swinging left at the end.

I leapt onto one of the spiralling metal staircases which led to the upper levels, running up and up until I reached the fourth floor.

I darted along a narrow balcony which looked down over the rest of the library and glanced over the railing just as the doors opened and Caleb stepped inside.

My footsteps were ringing along the wrought iron walkway and he looked up instantly, his eyes locking with mine.

A devastating smile pulled at his lips as he spotted his prey and I couldn't help but laugh as I kept running. I doubted I'd escape now but he still had to make it up to me without the aid of his Vampire gifts.

As he disappeared between the stacks, I found a ladder leading down a level and quickly descended.

Caleb's footsteps rang out as he started running up the staircase I'd used to get to the top floor and I looked around, trying to find another way down. I tiptoed along the walkway, keeping my movements as quick as I could while trying to remain quiet and I found another staircase hidden between two shelves in the far corner.

I scrambled down to the bottom floor and sprinted between the shelves, aiming for the door again.

Before I made it half way, Caleb dropped down from above and landed in front of me, releasing his hold on the vines he'd magicked into existence to assist him in dropping four floors to catch me.

I skidded to a halt and he smiled widely as he stepped closer to me.

"Got ya."

Before I could respond, Caleb shot forward, lifting me into his arms and propelling me through the library with his Vampire speed until we ended up inside one of the private study rooms at the back of the building.

I gasped in surprise as he kicked the door shut behind us and pushed me back against the wall before sinking his teeth into my neck.

His grip on my waist tightened to the point of discomfort and I tried to push him back a step but he held on tight, releasing a growl.

"Ow," I protested irritably and he finally released me with a sheepish grin.

"Sorry, I've been running on empty since the fight with the Nymphs and I don't wanna bite anyone else."

"Orion thinks I should be putting more effort into fighting you off," I said, touching the tender skin where his teeth had pierced my skin. "I'm thinking he has a point."

Caleb stepped forward slowly, reaching out for me and I let him. His fingers brushed against my neck and his magic slid through the wound as he healed it.

He stayed there, his hand on my skin as he held my eye.

"Don't look at me like that," I muttered, trying to shake him off but he didn't budge.

"Like what?"

"Like you didn't take part in that whole shoving me in a pit bullshit right before the Nymph attack. Like we aren't on two different sides of some fight I never asked to be in," I spat, surprising myself with how angry I felt at him.

"We *are* on two different sides of it though," he said and there was no apology in his voice, just acceptance. "But shit, Tory you don't understand how freaking much I like playing this game with you. Ever since we got back from that party I've hardly been able to think about anything else. The feeling of you in my arms, the taste of your blood on my lips, the rush I get when you run from me..."

My pulse spiked in response to his words despite myself and as he drew a little closer to me, I didn't push him back.

"You're not even sorry, are you?" I breathed.

"Can't be sorry for it. I've got responsibilities. To the other Heirs, my family, Solaria... I have to think of what's best for all of them and if you take the throne then the Nymphs might just get the leg up they need to win this war. You have to know I can't let that happen." He hadn't released me and I found I didn't really want him to.

"I have a bit of a weakness for assholes," I admitted slowly. "But I'm used to them lying about what they are. At least you own it."

"I do," Caleb said with a smirk, his hand travelling up my neck ever so slowly. "I'm an honest to god asshole. Do you want to keep playing with me, Tory?"

"Maybe," I breathed because in that moment I didn't even know anymore.

I should have been trying to keep away from him and his psycho friends but one way or another our lives all seemed to be destined to tangle up with each other's. And at least Caleb wasn't lying to me. He wasn't offering me the world, but he was offering me freedom, at least in this. So maybe I could try keeping the two things separate, when we were alone we could forget about being an Heir and a lost princess. And outside of that, we could stay on opposite sides of this stupid feud. It seemed kinda like a recipe for disaster but maybe I wanted a little rebellion.

"I'll take maybe." Caleb leaned forward to kiss me and I didn't make any move to stop him.

His mouth was hot and demanding against mine and the passion that burned between us sprang to life instantly, urging me on.

My heart thumped harder and his fingers twisted into my hair, tugging just enough to elicit a moan from my lips.

Before he could push me any further, I pressed him back. "I have to get to class," I protested. "I can't afford to miss lessons before my Elemental Trials."

"No, we wouldn't want you to fail The Reckoning, would we?" Caleb teased, moving his mouth across my jaw and working really damn hard to

61

keep me here.

"I mean it," I said on a laugh, pushing him back more firmly.

Caleb pouted at me, refusing to step back while he kept me caged in with his body.

"Come to Terra House tonight then," he asked, his navy eyes sparkling with promises.

"I won't be going anywhere tonight, there's a curfew, remember?"

"Those rules don't apply to me. Besides, I'll keep you safe if you're with me. You'll just have to stay the whole night."

I rolled my eyes at him. "I can keep myself safe, thanks. But now I'm going to be late-"

"If I run you to class will you come tonight?" he asked, his mouth slipping to my neck and sending shivers right through my spine.

"If you get me there on time, I'll consider it," I replied.

Caleb glanced at his watch then cursed, sweeping me into his arms before speeding back out of the tiny room.

I managed not to shriek like a nine year old on a roller coaster, but I did cling onto his blazer like my life depended on it as the world shot past us in a blur so intense I couldn't concentrate on a single thing.

Caleb skidded to a halt right outside the Fire Arena locker rooms and placed me back on my feet before leaning close to speak in my ear.

"One minute to spare. I'll expect you tonight, sweetheart." He pressed his mouth to mine and my heart leapt a little at the fact that he'd done so in plain sight. I had no intention of being marked as his in front of the whole school and I pulled back quickly, looking around to make sure no one had seen us. Luckily, we were already so close to being late that everyone else had already headed inside so I was spared the drama.

"Don't go getting ahead of yourself," I warned as I headed into the girls' locker room. "I only said I'd consider it."

The door swung closed between us and I bit down on a smile as I headed in to get changed. I almost considered refusing to wear the flame resistant outfit required for the class, but I decided that today wasn't the day for me to have that argument with Professor Pyro. I'd just have to accept the fact that I wouldn't have the same level of control over my fire magic as I would without it. But I'd keep practicing without the outfit until I was confident enough to prove her wrong.

In the meantime I had to get through this class and hope she would just be pleased that I'd finally managed to get in a training session with Darius.

The thought of the Dragon Shifter set me on edge. But I'd known I'd have to face him some time. Hopefully there would be enough going on in class to ensure that that time wouldn't have to be now.

I jogged into the locker room and found Darcy and Sofia waiting for me, already dressed for the lesson.

"Did he catch you?" Sofia asked with wide eyes.

"Yeah," I sighed, though the memory of him kissing me took the sting out of the bite. Maybe Orion had a point about me starting to like it. I'd have to consider going for the throat punch next time.

"Well maybe it's not worth playing his games if he's just going to catch you anyway?" Darcy suggested as I started stripping out of my uniform.

"It gives me a shot at escaping," I replied. "Besides... it's pretty hot."

"There it is," Darcy said, rolling her eyes as Sofia laughed.

I smirked as I quickly changed into the fire proof outfit required for the class and we hurried outside. I plucked at the material irritably as we went. I was sure it was affecting my ability to shape my fire magic but Pyro just wouldn't listen to me.

I tied my hair into a high ponytail and headed out into the Fire Arena keeping my focus on my sister and Sofia, not sparing a glance for the two Heirs who were lurking at the back of the assembled students.

We moved to join the other freshmen and Pyro tasked us with creating a ring of fire then shooting fireballs through it.

Sofia moved away to work with the lower powered members of the class while Darcy and I made sure we had a good amount of space around us before we started so that we didn't end up accidentally hurting anyone.

We began to practice and my magic instantly started to go haywire, not listening to what I wanted from it and alternating between blazing out of control and sputtering away into wisps of smoke.

Darcy was in a similar position beside me and I sighed irritably as I tried to decide how best to overcome these issues without removing the fireproof outfit.

Professor Pyro approached us with a frown on her face and I prepared myself for another lecture on how we were failing to grasp the essence of the flames.

"Roxy managed a lot better than that in our session together, Professor," Darius called before Pyro reached us and I glanced over at him in surprise.

After the quote he'd given for that article in The Celestial Times I'd presumed we were back to hating each other. But then everything else Gus Vulpecula had written was a load of shit so maybe I shouldn't have paid much attention to the quote either.

My gaze skimmed over Darius as I tried to gauge his mood. He was in the process of coating his fists and arms in gloves made of fire and I couldn't help but stare at the impressive display of magic.

"Well perhaps you'd like to assist her again for this class?" Pyro suggested.

I opened my mouth to protest but what could I really say?

"Of course, Professor," he said, offering her a wide smile like he couldn't think of anything better.

"And perhaps Mr Altair would help Darcy?" Pyro added, waving Caleb closer too.

He was looking my way but I ignored him, walking to meet Darius instead. There was no point in me trying to argue my way out of it and I wasn't going to let him see that his company made me uncomfortable.

"Let's see if your theory about that outfit has any merit to it then," Darius said as I closed in on him. His gaze swept over my skin tight shirt and trousers and I resisted the urge to fold my arms over my chest. Something about the clingy material made me feel more exposed than I would have in something more revealing.

"At least if you agree with me, Pyro will have to listen," I muttered.

"That's where you're going wrong, Roxy. You keep asking her to let you wear something else but Fae don't ask permission to do what we want. Especially when we're more powerful than the person saying no."

"So you think I should just tell the teacher I don't agree with her and do whatever the hell I want?" I asked, raising an eyebrow at him. No doubt he was hoping I would so that I'd get into trouble for it.

"I'm just telling you what I'd do," he said with a shrug.

Before I could reply, he snatched my hand and his power slammed into my body like a tidal wave. I gasped as my own magic fought back instinctively, shoving him out so that his power could only dance around the edges of mine.

Darius grunted irritably. "You let me in last time," he reminded me in a low voice. "Why did you trust me then and not now?"

I cleared my throat uncomfortably. "I didn't trust you then either. I just had to push past my natural inclination to protect myself from sociopaths. You'll have to give me a moment before I can easily do so again."

The pressure of Darius's power increased against mine and he tugged me a step closer to him. "Let me in, Roxy," he breathed and for a moment it seemed like he was talking about more than our magic.

Why did we have to hold hands for this? My palm was tingling and it had nothing to do with magic and everything to do with the insanely attractive asshole in front of me. He shifted his thumb over the back of my hand, making heat dance beneath my skin and I was sure it was intentional. But I wasn't going to let him throw me off my game.

I looked up into his dark eyes and released a long breath as I removed the shields around my power.

His magic tumbled into mine with a shudder of ecstatic energy which filled me from the soles of my feet right through to my core. My back arched involuntarily and I shifted a little closer to him despite myself. Darius caught my other hand too, his gaze holding me captive as I adjusted to the feeling of his magic in me.

"Push back," he commanded, his voice rough.

I was about to ask what he meant but his magic was so entangled with mine that I could feel what he wanted. Our power slid out of me like the pull of the tide and passed back into him through the point where our hands connected.

There wasn't a moment of resistance as my magic tumbled into him but as I held his eye, I watched his pupils dilate with the rush of taking in my power.

I bit my lip as his grip on my hands tightened and he tugged me closer again, our chests almost brushing as I looked up at him.

"Stop power fucking her and start working on what Pyro wants," Caleb called and I flinched, yanking my magic back again as I looked around at him and Darcy.

"Are you afraid I'm going to steal her attention from you, Cal?" Darius asked Caleb with the hint of a smile playing around his lips.

"Not likely," Caleb replied dismissively but his eyes narrowed.

"I'm still here," I reminded them irritably. "And neither of you are interesting enough to keep my attention for long so there's no point in you getting your panties in a twist over it. Maybe we should just get on with this class?"

Darius smirked at Caleb tauntingly and I rolled my eyes at him.

"Well I'm happy enough to practice without help if you wanna leave me to it?" Darcy suggested, not-so-subtly trying to tug her hand out of Caleb's grip.

"Don't worry, sweetheart, I promise to be gentle with you," he said, ignoring her attempts to break free.

My sister obviously had reservations about this activity and I couldn't really blame her. She shot me a look which basically said she'd rather be pretty much anywhere else than holding Caleb's hand and I glanced at Darius before raising an eyebrow at her as if to say 'who's got it worse?'. Darcy snorted a laugh and the two Heirs looked between us like they were trying to figure out what we'd just communicated to each other.

"Come on, Roxy, let's see what you've got," Darius said, releasing one of my hands so that I could cast with it.

He drew me away from Darcy and Caleb and I threw an apologetic look back at my sister as we walked across the sandy arena.

Darius was slowly pushing more and more of his magic into me as we walked and heat was building in my chest with the force of it.

I pulled on my hand, forcing him to stop walking when it seemed like he was going to drag me all the way across the arena to the shadows on the far side of it. I had no intention of being alone with him and this spot right in the centre of the arena had plenty of space for us to work in.

Darius smirked at me as he gave in and came to a stop. It was either that or release my hand which he didn't seem to have any intention of doing.

"Okay, Roxy. Why don't you make a motorbike for me again?" he asked.

"Well I don't think you really know anything about them so how could you correct me if I shape something wrong?" I asked dismissively.

I didn't really like that he'd discovered my love of bikes. It felt like I'd given him ammo to use against me and I had no intention of letting him find out anything else or even letting him see how much that passion meant to me.

"I know plenty about them," he assured me. "Like how to ride them faster than anyone else I know."

"Those are very big words for someone who doesn't know a gasket from a gas tank." I shrugged.

"Well how about, if you manage to make one with your fire magic, I'll let you back up your talk with a race?" he suggested.

I hesitated. This was not a good idea. But... I really wanted to get back out on the road. I'd been missing the purr of an engine something chronic in the last few weeks and Darius's collection of top of the range speed machines were oh so tempting.

"If I win, I get to keep the bike," I said.

"You won't win," he replied dismissively.

"Then you won't be afraid to agree to my terms."

"Fine. What do I get when I win?" he asked.

I looked up at him, my mind whirling with anything at all I might be able to offer him. But what does an asshole who lives in a palace filled with gold even need?

"I'll work on one of your bikes. Give it the mods you don't think it needs and prove you wrong for a second time," I offered.

"But if I'm right and it doesn't need your so called modifications then I'm not ending up with much of a prize, am I?" he mused.

I rolled my eyes. "You're not right but getting you to admit that is probably an impossible task so what do you want instead?"

Darius pushed his tongue into his cheek as he considered it, his gaze trailing over me in a way that made me shift my weight onto the other foot.

"I'll think of something," he assured me.

"Sure. Whatever you want. I'll be winning anyway, so it doesn't really matter," I said with a shrug.

I turned away from him and pulled on his magic as I worked to create a bike out of fire.

As expected, my magic was going haywire with the stupid suit on and even with Darius's help I really struggled to wrangle it under control. He even had to admit that the damn thing was causing me issues after fifteen minutes of struggling against it.

"You could just take it off," he suggested as I managed to turn my latest attempt at a bike into a fireball which almost took out Marguerite's eyebrows as she scowled our way.

"Not going to happen," I replied dismissively.

Pyro was looking rather unimpressed with my efforts and I had to bite my tongue against my irritation so I rolled my sleeves back and folded the hem of the shirt up to reveal my waist.

"I'm going to use both hands," I said to Darius without looking him in the eye.

He didn't need any further encouragement and stepped forward to grip my waist like he had before. This time I didn't press my body to his though and instead focused on harnessing my magic in the way I wanted.

My frustration meant I threw more power at the task than I'd intended and I yanked on Darius's magic too.

A full sized motorbike materialised in the flames before me and with a surge of triumph, I sent it tearing across the arena.

Pyro stopped what she was doing and actually applauded me and I grinned to myself as more than a few of my classmates joined in.

I started making the bike weave between the students as it did a circuit of the arena and Darius leaned close to my ear as he maintained his grip on me.

"Congratulations, Roxy. Looks like we've got a date Wednesday night then."

I ignored the flutter in my chest as he called it a date because it absolutely didn't take place. "Maybe I've already got plans Wednesday," I said.

"Yeah, you do. With me."

He released his grip on my waist and my control over the magic faltered as the bike burst apart into a thousand flaming tendrils which burnt out quickly without anything to maintain them.

I turned to give Darius a response to that comment but he was already half way across the arena on his way to the locker rooms. The rest of the class were disbanding too and I rolled my shirt down again as I turned to look for Darcy.

She was walking towards me and I had to fight to school my expression before she arrived. From the few glances I'd cast her and Caleb's way during the lesson, it didn't look like they'd managed to power share at all.

My plans for Wednesday night had definitely not included spending any more time with Darius Acrux. But if I backed out now I'd be letting him win. And I really couldn't live with doing that.

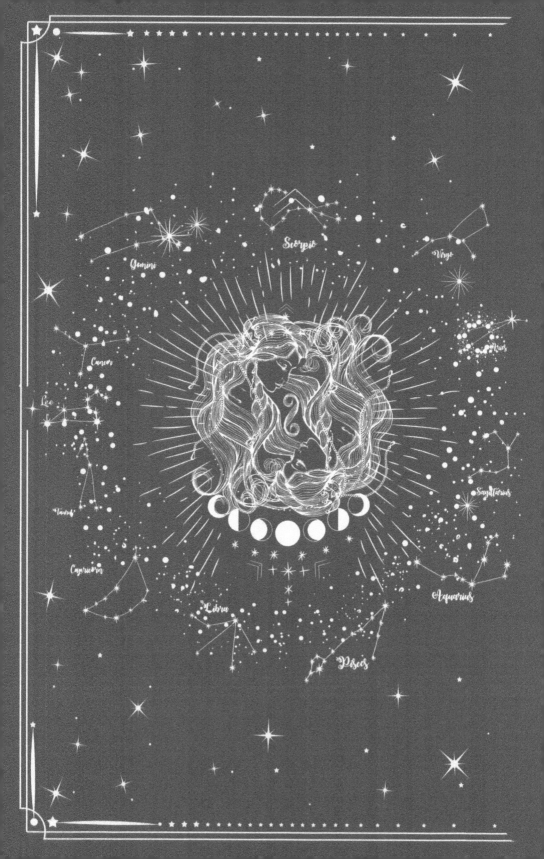

DARCY

CHAPTER FIVE

My stomach writhed with vomiting butterflies as I stood outside Orion's office ready for my Liaison session. I wasn't sure I could handle how awkward this was going to be.

Maybe he could just assign me a new Liaison? Yeah, I should definitely suggest that. That would make this whole off-limits thing a whole lot easier to deal with.

I was annoyingly early because I'd heard a bunch of Aer students plotting a massive attack for the freshmen in my House. To avoid being caught up in that, I'd arrived here at a quarter to seven. *And the prize for worst idea ever goes to...*

Orion appeared at the end of the corridor dressed in an immaculate suit unlike the grubby Pitball kit or shirt and slacks he usually showed up in. *I guess the Pitball pitch is still off limits.*

My mind reeled as I suddenly realised he was on time. And not just on time. Goddamn *early*. I half expected him to do a U-turn and come back later, but he kept walking toward me. His Atlas was in his hand and his eyes were fixed on the screen. I didn't know if it was better or worse that he wasn't looking at me. All I knew, was the closer he got, the less air made it into my lungs on each breath.

He finally stopped before me, dropped the Atlas to his side and looked up.

Echoing silence seemed to fill the void between us.

He scratched his beard then moved toward the door to unlock it, his arm bumping mine as he did so. I quickly scooted back, hovering behind him and decided now might be a good time to just call quits on this whole agonising lesson. Which was actually gonna be a full damn session for once. *Why today? Why would you be early today?*

"La- *sir?*" I corrected half way. *Where did that come from? I almost said his first name!*

"I don't speak French, Miss Vega."

Hilarious.

He stepped into the room, leaving the door wide but I remained in the corridor. I moved half way through the entrance and found his back to me as he walked across the room.

"Um actually, I was thinking maybe it might be a better idea if I just get a new Liaison," I suggested, but my voice was followed by another bout of excruciating silence.

Orion settled into his chair and didn't reach for his bourbon for once. "No, that won't be necessary. Come in. Close the door."

There was a large tan leather book on his desk and as I moved into the room, I spotted the name on it. *Orders of Fae.*

I shut the door and the click resounded in my ears. I wet my achingly dry mouth, heading across the carpet and lowering into the chair opposite him.

The clock on the wall ticked so loudly I swear it was making my left eye twitch.

He pulled the book toward him, flipping it open to a page marked with a long blue feather and started reading something in silence. While he did that, I studied his expression, trying to work out what he was thinking. My eyes shifted to his mouth and heat surged up my spine as the memory of that kiss made me want to just-

"Dragons." Orion looked up. "I think you and your sister might be Dragons. Though a kind thought to be extinct."

"Oh," I said, leaning forward to try and get a look at the book. My mind whirled with that idea. Darius always looked so incredibly fierce in his Order form and he was also so damn *big*. I couldn't imagine what it might feel like to have my body transform like that. Would it hurt? And would I know how to use my wings and shoot fire instinctively?

It was absolutely insane and so much to process that I finally forgot about the tension in the room. I tried to pull the book toward me and Orion pointed out the passage at the same time, causing our skin to graze. White hot energy raced under my flesh and I immediately yanked my hand away.

I sat back in my seat, combing my fingers through my hair just so I had something else to focus on. "Right, er- so Dragons?"

"Dragons," he echoed, clearing his throat. "Potentially this one." He pushed the book toward me, tapping on the passage before withdrawing entirely.

I leaned forward, reading the paragraph with intrigue.

The long extinct Ismenian Dragon was once a powerful Order. As the largest of the Dragon Orders, its fire was three times the strength of its smaller cousins. Often darkest blue in colour, it had a forked tongue and poisonous breath which could kill a Fae up to ten metres away.

I lifted my head, my mind spinning. "How big does this Dragon get?" I asked, thinking of Darius and his already huge form. If we *were* one of these Ismenian Dragons we'd be even larger. And despite the kind of frightening possibility of actually shifting into something that size, I didn't mind the sound of being bigger and badder than Darius Acrux. Him and the other Heirs would never be able to push us around again.

"I think they could be as much as double the size of a regular Dragon. So..." He didn't finish that line of thought, instead drawing the book away from me and closing it. He got to his feet, turning to place it back on the book shelf which arched over the doorway in the centre of the wall.

"What's in there?" I asked just to break the penetrating silence.

"A storage room," Orion said, taking another book from the shelf and putting it down on the desk.

"Oh," I breathed. "Do you store anything interesting in there?"

Orion gave me a taut frown. "Miss Vega-"

I rolled my eyes and he stopped short, a low noise leaving his throat.

"What?" I huffed. "It's really stupid that you keep talking to me like we didn't-"

"Don't," he growled and I sighed, my eyes falling to the book on the desk.

The Wonders of Being a Dragon.

I exhaled a laugh at the name and Orion fought so hard against a grin that he almost busted a tooth.

"Read it. And I'll sign you up to attend the Dragon Order Enhancement class tomorrow." He managed to get the moody mask back on his face and I nodded, taking the book and putting it in my bag.

"Don't we have enough to worry about with our Elemental Trials starting on Thursday?"

"Finding out your Order is essential," Orion said firmly. "I imagine you'll emerge any day now. Don't you want to be prepared?"

I considered that and nodded. If I was going to burst into a forty foot Dragon maybe a heads up *would* be nice.

I checked the clock on the wall and found it was only a quarter past seven and my stomach dropped. I still had forty five minutes left of this session.

Orion followed my line of sight and a deep v formed between his eyes.

He sighed heavily. "Fuck this. Come on, let's go for a walk." He got up and I looked up at him in surprise.

"A walk?" I asked in confusion, getting to my feet.

"Yeah, maybe you'd like to try out that fire again, huh?"

"That *almost* sounds like fun," I teased.

"Yes, well I can be fun sometimes. Especially when I'm not wearing this suit."

I stared at him and his eyes widened as he realised what he'd said.

"I meant when I'm not working," he said quickly.

"Right yeah." *And when you're diving into swimming pools. And pressed against me with your tongue in my mouth.*

I moved toward the door, bumping into him as he moved too. *Oh god why are we even trying to pretend this isn't the most awkward evening ever?*

I was relieved when we exited the painfully quiet corridors of Jupiter Hall and the evening call of birds, chatter of students and music from The Orb finally broke the pressure in the air between us.

He took off at a purposeful stride down the path and I headed after him, falling a step behind so we didn't have to look at each other.

The air was icily cool and the sky crystal clear, brushed with deepest orange and pastel peach as the sun began to set. My breath fogged before me and I sensed the keen clutch of winter in the air.

Orion headed through The Wailing Wood and I practically had to jog to keep up with his long stride.

We finally emerged in The Howling Meadow and a gust of wind sailed through the long grass, causing a sweeping ripple all across the huge field.

A smile pulled at my mouth as Orion stepped into the grass and I headed after him toward the very centre of the meadow. I reached into the well of magic inside me, wondering if I'd be able to cast that intense fire again. I could almost feel that power there, but it was like a sleeping beast. And I wasn't sure how to wake it.

The breeze grew stronger as I stopped in front of Orion, dragging my dark hair out in a wild tangle of tendrils. His tense jaw relaxed a little and his eyes skimmed over me in a way that unravelled me from the inside out.

I took a breath, angling my face away so I didn't drown in memories of his mouth and hands on me.

Okay now we're in the middle of a field alone. How is this better exactly?

"Raise your hands to the sky, let's not burn the entire meadow down," Orion instructed and I did as he said. "Order powers are different to your Elemental powers. You should feel those channels in two different parts of your body."

I kept my eyes on the sky, my hands raised as I nodded.

I'm feeling a hell of a lot of fire in my body right now but none of it is Dragon Fire.

"I can sense my magic and it feels like there's another part of me, but it's not awake," I explained.

"What were you feeling when you used it before?" he asked and I couldn't blink, couldn't even breathe as I recalled the exact moment when Orion was about to die as two Nymphs stood above him.

"I was afraid."

"Good. Afraid we can do," he said, then a scream ripped from my lungs as I was launched a hundred feet into the air.

The wind rushed over me and my stomach lurched wildly as I flew up on the magical gust Orion cast at my back. With a yell, I hit the peak of my momentum, the sky staring down at me as my arms cartwheeled like mad.

Cast air!

I forced out my palms, stifling my screams and trying to gain a handle on my terror. But I started tumbling, falling at a furious pace, hurtling toward certain death.

Air exploded from my hands and blanketed my fall just a foot from the ground. My hair was a mess over my face and as I released my magic and my knees hit the ground, I pushed it out of my eyes with a groan of relief.

"Did that wake it up?" Orion asked casually.

I looked up at him with a scowl and he started laughing his head off.

A feral noise escaped me and I launched myself at him. I shoved him in the chest before I could even think about the consequences and his eyes lit up with the challenge as he stumbled back a step.

"Oh you wanna fight? Come on then, no more physical contact though, Miss Vega." He brushed his shirt down like where I'd touched him had left a mark.

"So you keep reminding me," I said tauntingly.

He gave me a taut frown in answer to that.

I raised my hands, knowing this was a crazy, stupid idea but I was sick of him having the upper hand on me all the time.

A flick of his wrist just sent you a hundred feet into the air!

I squashed that thought away. I was powerful; at the very least I could blast him across the valley through sheer force.

Orion backed up through the grass, raising his palms with a demonic glint in his eyes, the grass rustling around him in a building storm.

Oh shit.

"Ready?" he asked, flexing his fingers.

I brought magic to my palms, planting my feet then nodded firmly.

"Maybe *this* will wake up the beast." He threw out an arm and water shot toward me in a swirling blast. I staggered to my right, throwing up a shield of air so the wave scored across the side of it and splashed over the ground.

I used the power of earth to my advantage and willed the grass to grow longer behind him, wrapping around his arms. It worked to an extent, but he yanked his arms out of it easily enough and I gritted my teeth in determination.

He flicked a hand and the power of air slammed into my shield. The force of a hurricane battered against it and I dug in my heels as the sheer pressure pushed me back, tearing up dirt beneath my boots. I held out for as long as I could but my shield finally crumbled and I gasped as I was left exposed. With the feeling of being punched in the chest, I was thrown backwards across the meadow and slammed onto my back in the grass, wheezing heavily.

Get up. Fight back.

I couldn't see him from where I'd landed, the long stalks reaching high up around me.

I kept entirely quiet and my tactic paid off as he called out, "Hey, are you alright?"

I rolled onto my knees, crawling deeper into the grass with a mischievous grin on my face.

I'll be alright when I beat you.

"Darcy?" Orion demanded anxiously, the sound of his footsteps pounding this way. My heart jolted at the sound of my name and I wondered if he was genuinely worried he'd killed one of the Vega Twins. *That would certainly make headlines.*

"Shit," he cursed the second he found the empty patch of grass. "Very clever, Miss Vega."

I stilled, making sure I didn't shift the long stalks brushing my arms as he hunted for me.

"Shame about the rain though." He cast a torrential downpour into existence and I winced as the ice-cold water soaked me through.

I heard him moving to my right, shivering as I waited for my moment to strike, peering between the long stems. Through the sheet of rain I spotted the back of his jacket and launched myself upright with my hands raised. In a heartbeat, I realised it was *only* his jacket, a gust of wind making it drift across the top of the grass in the shape of his body.

I lurched around in fear but I was already too late as he propelled me up into the air again on a ferocious breeze. I screamed as I was thrown around in a vortex, the world a tangled blur of sky and earth as I tried to figure out which way was up.

My head pounded, my gut lurched and frustration burrowed through to my core. I desperately tried to wrangle the wind around me, casting a gust of air and forcing it to spin in the opposite direction to Orion's tornado. The wind eased just enough for me to get my whereabouts and I spotted Orion ten feet below. I shot a propulsion of water at him, catching him in the arm and making him lose concentration.

The vortex abruptly died and I plummeted toward the ground with a gasp, colliding with him before I could get a handle on my power again. We slammed to the floor and my arm got trapped beneath him, snapping my wrist beneath his weight and making me cry out in pure agony.

He lurched upright and I fell onto my butt, cradling my arm to my chest and hissing through my teeth. Pain sliced across the bone and I bit into my lip to stop myself from screaming.

"Here, give it to me," Orion commanded as he knelt before me in the dirt, reaching for my wrist and gently curling his fingers around it.

I winced as pain daggered down my arm but a warmth built beneath his fingers which sank into my skin, soothing it away. It felt like heated wax pouring all over the wound. I drew in a breath, gazing down at the green light which shone beneath his palm. The pain ebbed away and I felt the bone resetting, shifting into place and fusing back together.

"Thank you," I whispered, swivelling my wrist to test it and marvelling at the magic he possessed.

"Well it was the least I could do seeing as I broke it," he said, sitting back on his heels.

"That was sort of my fault," I teased and he grinned, making my heart squeeze hopefully.

We were in a little cocoon, the grass beneath us flattened and the stalks around us tall enough that no one would see unless they were flying overhead – which was an actual possibility in this place.

"So I won right?" I beamed and he lifted a brow.

"No chance. It's got to be a five second hold down or the game is still on."

Oh really?

I threw out my hands, not giving him any warning as I cast a forceful gust of air to try and knock him onto his back. He was so fast to react that he blocked it before it even got close to holding him down. I cursed as he launched himself at me, trying to scramble away but I wasn't fast enough. I didn't even really try to fight him off as he threw his weight down, pinning me to the ground with his entire body.

"You're supposed to use magic," I said breathlessly, his throat bobbing as his mouth hovered an inch from mine. The scent of cinnamon rolled over me and fire reached deep into my belly, making me consider leaning in for a kiss. We'd made a solid decision to stay away from each other and look where we'd ended up already? *Great effort.*

"Maybe brute force is just as efficient sometimes," he said in a rumbling tone which delved into my chest and sent a hungry shudder through me.

"You said no physical contact," I whispered as his muscles hardened, keeping me caged beneath him. I was losing my mind. I should have tried to fight him off, but I didn't want him to go anywhere. And from the intense look he was giving me, I could tell how close he was to crossing this line again himself.

"What if I'm having second thoughts?" he growled.

"You're fickle," I pointed out. "And confusing."

"I don't mean to be." He dipped his head so his mouth was by my ear and goosebumps rose to meet the heat of his breath. "I can't think straight around you," he said heavily, his hand clawing into the earth beside my head. "I could have lost you in that battle, or I could have died without ever knowing how this might have played out…"

My throat thickened and I almost gave in to the craving rising in me. But there was too much at stake for the sake of lust. It was stupid. He could lose his job and be 'power-shamed' and I could lose my place at the Academy.

"I owe you my life," he breathed and my heart nearly detonated as he pressed his lips to my cheek. "Thank you."

"The rest of Solaria aren't feeling so grateful," I said as he drew away, leaving a burning mark on my skin. "Not after that Vulpecula guy printed that article."

"Fuck what he said," Orion growled then he frowned as he realised he shouldn't have said it.

"You should be glad he's spreading lies about us. You're firmly Team Heirs." I jerked my chin up as I held his gaze.

"You're right," he muttered. "I am."

My heart sank at hearing him confirm it. On top of him being my teacher, we were on opposing sides of a feud which was never going to be bridged. With a sigh, I pressed my hands to his shoulders, pushing him back. He moved as easily as if I'd shoved him, standing up and pulling me after him. Our hands parted and the wall grew thicker.

"I need a new Liaison," I said through the gnawing lump in my throat.

He nodded stiffly, looking boyish and broken for a moment as he hung his head.

A magnetic energy hung in the air, trying to force me toward him. It was so powerful I had to consciously take another step back to try and shake it away.

"This has to stop," I said firmly then turned away and marched off through the meadow, not daring to look back even though my heart pounded painfully in my chest.

As I made it into the woods I started running, racing in the direction of Aer House, needing to hide away until I smothered this desperate longing in my heart.

I was panting by the time I reached my room, hurrying inside and twisting the lock. I sank down against the door, knocking my head back against the wood as my pounding heart started to slow.

My Atlas pinged and I took it out of my bag, my gut fraying as I found a private message waiting for me from Orion.

Lance:

What if I don't want it to stop?

SETH

CHAPTER SIX

I stripped off my clothes in the male locker room in Lunar Leisure, stuffing them into my sports bag. A splinter drove into my heart as I thought of Ashanti. Losing a pack member was like cutting out a piece of our hearts simultaneously. We all shared this pain and it was my responsibility to make sure we all pulled through it.

"Capella, Castro, Cray – you're up!" Professor Prestos called beyond the door.

I scratched a raging itch behind my ear as I headed out of the room followed closely by the other two wolves. They weren't part of my pack. I was the highest ranking Alpha in the school, but I wasn't the only one. We tended to build packs in our Houses out of convenience. Though occasionally a Beta would catch my eye from another group and I'd have to challenge an Alpha for them. I always won.

I headed along the corridor of white walls, the scent of something minty rising under my nose. As the smell thickened around me, I was slammed back into my childhood in an instant. Werewolves emerged in their Order forms younger than any other Order and I hadn't been flea dipped since I was eight. It was damn humiliating to have to do it now. For a moment I was just a white cub looking at my siblings as we splashed in a bath full of that minty potion which tingled my nose and made my eyes water. A child with no responsibilities and no reputation to uphold.

I stuffed the memory away as I pushed through the doors into the huge pool room, the shining glass roof towering overhead. Heated air wafted around me and that peppermint scent became even more powerful. The pool water was gone, replaced with the cool, creamy potion instead.

The Physical Enhancement teacher, Professor Prestos, strode over to me with her Atlas in hand. I couldn't help but check out her tanned legs beneath her tight shorts. Her dark hair was tied in a fishtail down one side of her neck. Prestos didn't take any shit, but I didn't plan on giving her any today.

"Shift and get in the pool for fifteen minutes, Capella," she instructed, ticking me off on her Atlas.

A group of wolves were climbing out of the dip in their Order forms and my heart lurched as I spotted Frank amongst them. His huge black form seemed smaller with his hair coated to his sides by the flea treatment.

My pack hadn't slept in my room since I'd somehow picked up these damn fleas. The night Darcy had come to see me. Now that I was down a member of my pack, my instincts were burning even more fiercely, telling me to initiate her. She wasn't even a Werewolf. It was ridiculous. But I didn't know any other way to stop these wild emotions apart from ensuring she was made an official member of my pack.

Maybe I'll ask Professor Canis. My Order Enhancement teacher was pretty knowledgeable when it came to our kind. If there was a way to break this bond I had to Darcy Vega, I had to know what it was. Since I'd made her my Omega, the thought of hurting her was unbearable. I hadn't even thought I meant it. I'd just gone to her room that day to remind of her place. But I was hardwired to protect my own. And now I'd claimed her for my pack, the longer I put off initiating her, the more I'd be driven to insanity.

I cut off her hair. I broke her fucking heart. I can't bear it.

I shifted into my Werewolf form, my paws meeting the pale blue tiles beneath me. I stepped up to the edge of the pool and waded into the shallow end, followed closely by the two other male wolves. A handful of girls appeared too and I spotted Alice amongst them. She'd been close with Ashanti and I'd been desperate to comfort her and the rest of the pack, but they still wouldn't spend any time with me. It was understandable; Werewolf fleas were a plague. Their bites set off a searing itch that dug deep under the skin. So after this treatment, I hoped things could go back to normal. Because being alone at night was starting to break me.

I sank up to my neck in the pool and had to stand there in the thick substance as it tingled against my skin.

Alice shifted into her mottled grey form and waded into the dip. I lifted my nose to beckon her over but she turned away, grouping together with the other girls as they entered the pool.

My heart thumped out of tune. Why were they still ignoring me? It was only fleas, and they'd be gone after this. Were they angry that I was putting them through this? It wasn't *that* bad; just a mild inconvenience. Not worth shunning me over. Especially as I was their fucking Alpha.

I barked sharply and the sound echoed back to me off of the glass roof. Alice turned my way, baring her teeth in a clear warning for me to stay back. The other two males swam away and I was left in a corner of the pool with fear threatening to swallow me up.

Why are they doing this?!

I was jerked into the past again, this time reliving the worst week of my life. I could almost feel the snowflakes melting against my tiny wet nose, the cold inching into every part of me as it delved under my fur.

A whimper escaped me as I blinked away that memory, forcing it down deep where it couldn't resurface any time soon.

"Time's up!" Prestos finally called and I waded back out of the pool, following the rest of group through to the huge shower room. My instincts burned through me. I didn't *follow*, I led.

I snapped at Alice's heels, trying to get her in line as I bounded to the front of the pack. She fell back but didn't look at me as I passed.

What the shitting hell is going on?

The hot water flooded over me from the showers above, washing away the milky liquid into drains around my paws. When my coat was clean, I shifted back into my Fae form and snatched a towel at the far end of the chamber.

The others shifted too and the second Alice drew close to get a towel, I caught her arm and bared my teeth at her. "What's up with you?" I growled and she snarled back at me.

She yanked her arm free, grabbing one of the fluffy white towels and wrapping it around her body. She tucked a long ebony lock behind her ear, giving me a firm look. "The pack and I have been talking."

"And?" I demanded, practically barking at her as the other wolves scurried out of the room.

"And Frank says you've made Darcy Vega an Omega," she hissed, her dark blue eyes narrowing on me with rage. "She's not even a wolf."

"You don't know that, she hasn't emerged," I snapped, but I'd seen that hellfire she'd cast at the Pitball pitch. She wasn't a wolf and everyone knew it. Hell, it was all the school could talk about. And initiating some other Order into the pack was an insult to our way of life.

Alice yanked her hand free from my grip. "We love you, Alpha. But you need to get rid of her. We won't follow you again until you do." She stalked out of the changing room and I was left alone, my shoulders trembling as the space seemed to grow too wide. Too empty.

"Alice!" I called after her, my voice pitchy.

It wasn't that simple to get rid of Darcy. I'd already claimed her as one of my own. That meant I *had* to protect her. And banishment only happened when an Alpha was challenged. If she fought me and I won, I could dismiss her from the pack. But the challenge had to come from her; I couldn't control that part. And a quiet, resilient piece of my heart didn't want her to either. I liked the idea of being her Alpha a little too much.

Shit, I am so screwed.

I hurried back to the changing room, drying off and pulling on my jeans and a shirt, throwing my sports bag over my shoulder. I tied my damp hair up into a bun then checked my Atlas, revelling in the way my skin had finally stopped itching.

The message waiting for me soothed my rampant heart.

Max:

We're staying at King's Hollow tonight. Get there before curfew – Orion's gunning for House Points this evening.

Thank the stars for my brothers. If it wasn't for them, I really would be alone.

I hurried out of Lunar Leisure, heading for The Wailing Wood as the icy wind brushed against me. At least I was myself again; no more fleas. No more scratching like a stray mutt. But my wolf needs were not being met at all and I was growing desperate for affection.

I ran the last mile to King's Hollow, pushing through the wards surrounding the huge oak tree and heading up to the door. I was admitted into the hollow tree trunk and hurried up the winding stairway into the wide lounge filled with wooden furniture and fur throws.

A fire was burning to one side of the room and Darius was stretched out on the sheepskin rug beside it, shirtless as he toyed with the fire in his palms. My eyes lingered on his abs for a moment and I blinked sharply, turning away.

Max was on his Atlas, splayed across the large couch and Caleb was nowhere in sight.

"You smell like mint." Max looked up from his Atlas with a grin.

"Flea dip," I said, mirroring his smile. "No more scratching. How's your rash?" I couldn't see any sign of it now but as Max lifted up his shirt, a faint raised line of flesh was revealed across his stomach.

"Nurse says this should go in a couple more days, but the rest of it's gone. She said it was the worst case of Griffin rash she'd ever seen."

"Well you do have sensitive skin," Darius said with a frown, sitting upright so the firelight danced over the broad muscles of his shoulders. He looked like a demi-god, his skin so inked and-

I bit down on my tongue. *Man* I needed to get laid.

"Where's Caleb?" I asked.

"Where do you think?" Darius said, dropping back down on the rug again as he pointed to the door across the room.

"I'll go see him." I walked away, taking the short stairway up to the door and stepping outside. The wooden rope bridge stretched out ahead of me to the opposite tree where Faeflies hovered and sparkled, weaving through the branches. I headed across it, the wind picking up and making the bridge rock beneath my feet. An owl hooted somewhere close by followed by the distant call of wolves.

My heart clenched as I froze, listening to the familiar call of my own pack running without me. It was as painful as if the moon itself had turned its back on me.

I forced myself to keep moving, finding Caleb in his favourite spot. The treehouse on this side had a veranda built around it and a swing bench hung from the roof. Fairy lights glittered along the railing and all the way up around the edge of the roof. Caleb was sitting on the bench, his Atlas in his hand and his face sketched with irritation.

"Hey man, what's up?" I sat beside him, pushing away all thoughts of my pack running without me – *who was heading it right now? Fucking*

Maurice? Better not have been.

"Tory Vega just shut me down. I asked her to come to my room tonight but she just messaged me saying she's not coming and that I should use this time to 'work on my personality'." He sighed, furiously thumbing through FaeBook posts absentmindedly, kicking out against the railing and making us swing backwards.

"The Vegas are hard work." I leaned my head back with a grunt.

Caleb threw me a curious look. "You're not judging me then? Because every time I mention her name in front of Darius he looks like he's about to burst into flames."

"Well I've got a little Vega issue of my own. Can't exactly judge you right now."

"You do?"

I hadn't told them about Darcy being in my pack. I always told them everything, but this seemed like a betrayal somehow, even though I hadn't intended to do it.

"I accidentally made Darcy an Omega."

"You *what?*" Caleb blurted and I nodded, frowning at him. My eyes lingered on his mouth a moment too long and I cleared my throat. *Grr. Damn wolf needs.*

"I know, it's so fucked up. And now I can't stop thinking about her. She has to officially challenge me or please me so I can initiate her. So how well do you reckon that's going? Oh and not to mention my entire pack have shunned me because I now have to initiate someone who isn't even of our Order."

"Shiiit," Caleb breathed.

"Yeah."

My gaze snagged on a FaeBook post on his Atlas and I snatched it out of his grip, my gut wrenching as I spotted a topless selfie of Maurice accompanying it.

Maurice Galaxi:

Heading out for a run with my new pack. Are Alpha fights really necessary when you have abs like these?

#topdog #sethwho? #newalphaintown

Comments:

Alice Telesto:

Watch out sugar I might fight for the position myself ;)

Maurice Galaxi:

Well maybe we should challenge him soon but I want a proper taste of the pack first to make sure it's worth it...

Lisa Canis:

What's happened to Mr Capella?

Maurice Galaxi:

He betrayed us, Professor :(#traitor #somewolvesarebetteroffalone

Lisa Canis:

Oh no! #frownyface

I snarled furiously, tapping out a reply to Maurice's comment about challenging me in shout caps.

Seth Capella:

I AM YOUR ALPHA. IF YOU CHALLENGE ME I WILL DESTROY YOU!!!!!!!!

Caleb wrestled the Atlas from me before I could hit post, my finger still jamming down on exclamation marks as he finally got it from me.

"Don't rise to it," he demanded. "You can't be seen losing your cool. The press could get access to this."

"*Cal.*" I pawed at him. "He has to know I'm his Alpha. I've been giving

94

them time to deal with Ashanti's death but-"

"He's trying to anger you," Caleb pressed, holding the Atlas out of reach. I glanced at the screen and realised the newsfeed had scrolled down to a professional photograph of Caleb which had been printed in The Rising Moon Magazine last year. His chest was bare and his body gleaming with seawater as he smirked at the camera. In his hand was an ice cream he was leaning in to lick but someone had cropped it out, replacing it with a glittering Pegasus dick.

Caleb followed my gaze as I tried to reach for it before he could see.

"Assholes!" He crushed the Atlas so hard in his hand I could have sworn he was going to break it.

"Chill," I sighed. "Take your own advice."

"Fine. Fuck them." He tossed the Atlas into a chair with a scowl.

A howl sounded off in the woods again and a whine escaped me as rejection dug into my heart.

Caleb patted my arm and the contact made me ache. I needed more. I needed someone to just...

I moved into his touch, invading his personal space and nuzzling against his chin. He knew I couldn't help myself and though his Order was almost the exact opposite of mine in terms of our tactile behaviour, he let me do it because he knew I had to or I'd go mad. But tonight, it felt like more than that. My senses came alive with the musk of his flesh and the heat of his body.

"*Seth*," Caleb warned as I moved my mouth to his ear.

"Remember that time in The Shimmering Springs last year?" I burrowed my hands into his hair and he released a deep growl in his throat.

"That was one time. And there was a girl there too," he pointed out.

"Not the whole time," I said with a smirk, brushing my mouth across the line of his jaw. He still didn't push me away so I planted a hand on his chest and ran it down the hardened lines of his abs. "Are you tempted?"

He growled, catching my hand at the edge of his waistband and pushing me back. A whine left my throat but I didn't force the issue. If he didn't wanna go there then that was up to him. I just needed to get some attention right now. *Any* attention.

"You have a girlfriend, remember?" Caleb said. "If you need a blowjob, go find her."

Oh yeah, I do have a girlfriend. In the last couple of days I'd been all alone and so messed up over Ashanti's death, but I'd not once thought about going to Kylie for comfort. I seriously had to break that off.

She'd grown up next door to me and had gotten crazy hot the summer before she was due to start Zodiac. I'd been home from the Academy and a series of sweaty nights with her had kept me thoroughly satisfied while I wasn't with my pack. We'd both had fun and I'd maybe once or twice told her she was my girlfriend because well, it had felt that way at the time. But now...the only girl I craved was Darcy Vega. Which was an impossible dream. She'd never touch me after what I did to her. *Unless I made things up to her somehow...*

I looked to Caleb, readying to voice something deeply traitorous. But he was screwing Tory, so I knew he'd understand. "Do you think Darcy would ever forgi-"

"Hey are you talking about the Vegas?" Max called and we both turned to find him doing a pull up on a low hanging branch above the bridge. My eyes lingered on his muscles and I let my gaze wander appreciatively. I didn't normally perv on my friends. But tonight felt anything but normal.

"Sort of." I shrugged one shoulder.

"We all need to talk about them. Come inside." Max dropped onto the bridge and it shuddered from the impact of his weight before he headed away.

I stood up, sensing Caleb following but before I made it two paces he caught my arm, wheeling me around and dragging me into a tight embrace.

"Your pack will come back to you." He clapped me firmly on the shoulder.

I wrapped myself around him, needing that hug more than anything in the world right then.

"*Ashanti*," I choked out and he held me tighter.

"I know," he sighed. "Fuck the Nymphs. We'll destroy them all one day."

I nodded against his shoulder and he released me. We headed across the bridge and I felt miles better by the time I reached the other side. With my brothers around me, I'd get through this. We could pull through anything so long as we stuck together.

"And to think I almost got desperate enough to try and kiss you," I muttered as we walked up to the door.

"Only in your dreams," Caleb whispered.

"And memories." I cocked a brow and he pursed his lips.

"I have no recollection of that," he lied.

"Keep telling yourself that." I punched him on the shoulder as we headed into the den.

Darius was standing up, his hands resting against the mantelpiece as he stared at the fire. I'd been so caught up in my own worries I'd totally missed how fucking stressed he clearly was.

I walked straight up to him, wrapping my arms around him from behind and nuzzling his shoulder.

"Dude," he growled, his body tensing beneath me.

"You're upset," I insisted and he sighed, letting me remain there.

"Yeah he is, but he won't let me syphon off his anger," Max said, dropping down onto the couch as Caleb joined him.

"I don't *want* to let go of it," Darius snarled and I released him so he could turn around. He clapped my arm and I gave him a nod, moving to sit between Max and Caleb, pushing them aside to make room.

Max leaned his shoulder against mine and I felt him drawing some of my grief over Ashanti away. I gave him a look of thanks and he nodded, a silent understanding passing between us.

Darius folded his arms, looking across us all. "My father just called. He believes our claim is officially under threat. Before Sunday, the Vega Twins were easy prey. It was a joke to think they'd ever be considered for the Solarian throne, but now..."

"That fire they cast was fucking powerful," Max said in agreement, sitting forward and resting his elbows on his knees.

"They still don't actually want the throne though," Caleb pointed out.

"That's not what they said after the Pitball match," I reminded him, a rumbling growl leaving my throat and Caleb nodded seriously.

"Even so, that article in The Celestial Times did a good job of downplaying what they did. They won't ever get the backing we have," Caleb said.

"That's one newspaper, Cal," Darius said, shaking his head. "It will get out elsewhere. There's footage online already."

"Let's address the elephant in the room here," Max said in a dark tone as he gazed at Darius unblinkingly. "It looks like they're gonna emerge as Dragons."

A line of smoke left Darius's nostrils as he exhaled. His shoulders trembled and I had the feeling he was holding back the urge to explode into his Order form and take his fiery rage out on the sky.

"Deep breath," Caleb encouraged and Darius nodded slowly.

"Well look at the bright side," I said. "You could marry one of them and avoid marrying your buck-toothed cousin?"

Darius's eyes whipped to me, his anger seeming to dissolve for a second. "That's not a terrible idea. Tory Vega has dry humped me on more than one occasion so I could probably win her round."

"I do hope you're fucking joking right now," Caleb said in a deadly low voice and I turned to him with a smirk.

"Someone's jealous," I taunted, shoving his thigh with mine and he pressed his lips together into a tight line.

A smirk pulled at Darius's features as he played up to Caleb's reaction. "That would be one way to keep her in line, huh Caleb? Surely you don't mind if I claim your play-thing. You're only passing time with her anyway, right?"

"Right," Caleb ground out, his shoulders becoming rigid and I glanced at him, knowing that wasn't true. Caleb didn't do exclusive very often, but it seemed like he was trying to do it with Tory. Which meant he actually gave a shit about her. And with my emotions all knotted up over Darcy, I sensed we were both about to cause a real issue when it came to keeping them both under heel.

"That was the least convincing act I've ever seen," Max jibed. "And I can feel your jealousy from here, mate, so you're not fooling anyone."

"She's my Source, it's natural for me to be possessive. That doesn't mean I care about her," Caleb insisted, glaring at Max to try and make him back down.

Their fighting made me uncomfortable and I snarled at Max to try and make him back off too. He raised his hands in innocence and I relaxed, getting to my feet and moving to stand next to Darius instead.

Darius's playful expression fell away. "If the Vegas are revealing their strength, we're all gonna have to remind everyone that we're stronger."

"But we're not stronger. Not once they're trained," Caleb said.

Max leaned back in his seat with a dark smile. "But we *are* trained. We've got four years on them. No strength beats that and you all know it." Even though we were only sophomores at Zodiac, we'd had private tutors since our early Awakening at fifteen years old. There was no way they could catch up on us.

"So what are you suggesting?" I asked.

"We remind this school who the real monarchs are," Max said keenly. "It's time we put the Vegas back in their box."

I shared a brief look with Caleb, our secrets radiating between us.

How am I going to put Darcy in her place when my body is telling me to protect her? And how is Caleb going to beat down Tory when he's clearly catching feelings for her?

I sighed, knowing I had to say it as I looked to Max. "Sorry bro, I can't do shit right now. Darcy's my Omega."

"What?" Max snapped and a low growl sounded from Darius.

I raised my hands in innocence. "It was an accident."

"Well fix it," Darius demanded.

"I'm working on it," I sighed, but was I really?

"I'm enjoying my fun with Tory," Caleb said with a casual shrug and Darius shot him a death glare. "I say we just hope for them to fail The Reckoning."

"And if they don't?" Max snarled.

"We'll deal with it then," I said and Caleb nodded in agreement. "It's only a week."

"Fine," Max huffed, sitting back in his seat. "But if they pass, we've gotta come up with a better plan than the last one."

"Sure," I said offhandedly. I didn't like to admit it even to myself but I knew I was holding off on forcing Darcy from my pack on purpose.

Heat radiated from Darius and I could tell something was still bothering him.

"What is it?" I nudged him and his scowl grew.

"If they *are* Dragons, Father is going to have his own thoughts on the best way to deal with them."

"Do you think you might really end up married to one of them?" Caleb asked with a worried look.

"No...that's the thing." Darius shook his head, his brow heavily furrowed. "If he believes they're about to emerge as Dragons, I don't think he'll take that lying down. In fact, I think he'd rather kill them before that ever happens."

TORY

CHAPTER SEVEN

Dragon Order Enhancement was held to the southwest of Fire Territory on an open plain close to the thermal pools which divided it from Water Territory.

The scent of sulphur hung thickly in the air and steam rose from geysers and shallow pools which swept across the plain in coiling tendrils. I eyed The Shimmering Springs with interest, remembering Sofia suggesting we head to them for a swim some time. But I still felt a little trickle of fear at the idea of getting into deep water and I wasn't convinced the experience would be very relaxing all the time I felt that way.

Although as I thought about it, I imagined that the hot, thermal water could be a good place for me to work on facing my fear. At least it wouldn't be cold, reminding me so viscerally of that river I'd crashed into or the pool the Heirs had frozen over. And if I wanted to make sure they couldn't use that fear against me again in the future then I really needed to work on facing it. Not to mention the fact that if I went into my water Elemental Trial with a deep fear of cold water hanging over my head, I might be setting myself up to fail before I'd even begun.

With that thought in mind, I decided to come back to the pools and see if I could do something to at least stifle the terror I felt when looking at deep water. Perhaps I could desensitise myself enough to make it through the assessment. Although I had to wonder if a few days would be anywhere near enough for that.

Darcy and I walked side by side as we approached the marker on my Atlas to show us where the lesson was going to be held and I wasn't sure which of us was dragging our feet more. Spending an hour with Darius Acrux wasn't either of our ideas of fun and I hadn't even spoken to him about the Nymph attack where we'd fought alongside each other so ferociously. I'd gotten pretty damn up close and personal with his Dragon form then and I wasn't really sure why Orion thought it was necessary to make us spend even more time with him in lizard form.

There were only six students gathered together when we arrived and five of them were guys. I smiled widely as I spotted Geraldine's friend, Angelica, who was surrounded by the other four guys while Darius stood separate to them. She extracted herself from the group, much to their disappointment, and moved over to greet us with a wide smile.

"Hey! I didn't know you were joining us today," she said, throwing a look at Darius who shrugged dismissively.

"I didn't realise it mattered," he said.

"You could have just posted in the group chat," she complained. "It's not exactly hard."

"I keep leaving that group chat for a reason," he replied irritably.

"And I keep adding you again for a reason too," Angelica protested. "It's meant to be a way for the Dragons who attend this academy to bond and as you're the biggest-"

"It's just a forum for these assholes to try and land you as a bride,"

Darius said, pointing at the four guys who said nothing to correct him. "And I don't need to read constant updates about the way your scales shimmer with the beauty of all the stars or how your fire is so fucking impressive that they all have wet dreams over it."

"You just have wet dreams about your own fire power then do you, Darius?" I asked casually.

His gaze slid to me and he didn't miss a beat in replying. "Well it is a lot more potent so it would be more likely," he agreed.

I snorted a laugh despite myself and Darcy raised an eyebrow at me. The other Dragons were eyeing the two of us with interest like the idea of two new female Dragon shifters appealed to them. With my knowledge of the Dragons' preference for breeding with their own kind, I imagined the idea of two new girls emerging in their Order was great freaking news. But even if I did turn out to be a Dragon, I had zero intentions of marrying one. Especially if Darius Acrux was an example of the kind of men their Order produced. Distractingly good looks aside.

"So is the Professor late or something?" Darcy asked, looking around.

"There are no Dragon Professors at the Academy," Darius said. "So I run these sessions as I'm the biggest and most powerful Dragon here."

"Could you try to take your head out of your ass the next time you say that?" I asked and Angelica bit down on her lip to stop herself from laughing. The other Dragons didn't seem inclined to say anything but their eyes swivelled between Darius and us like they were watching a tennis match.

"Can't do much about the truth, Roxy," Darius said, sounding every bit the cocky asshole he was. "And I think you know full well how big I am after straddling me during the Nymph fight."

"When I saved your life you mean? I was wondering when you were going to thank me for that."

"Well I saved your life in that fight too so we can call it even I think," he replied. If he was at all grateful to me for what I'd done in that fight he wasn't showing it now. But I didn't know what I expected, it was hardly like Mr Full-of-Himself was going to admit that he'd needed me in that moment.

"Orion said that he thinks we'll be even bigger Dragons than you if his theory about us is correct," Darcy cut in before I could escalate this little chat into a full on row.

"Well Orion likes to think a lot of things are bigger than they really are," Darius joked but I didn't miss the flicker of irritation that had passed through his eyes at Darcy's comment. "And there's a lot more to being a Dragon than just size."

"Such as?" I asked.

"We're the most powerful Order there is. There might be less of us than there are of other Orders but it would take a whole pack of Werewolves to take on a single Dragon in shifted form. And even then the Dragon would likely win."

The other Dragons all perked up proudly in response to that and I had to admit that I wouldn't really mind if I found out that I was one of them.

"So how does this go?" Darcy asked. "Are we going to ride you or-"

"No," Darius said firmly. "Dragons aren't pack horses, we don't offer out rides to people. Ever."

"But I'm sure I saw Orion jump from your back in the fight," Darcy countered.

"I grabbed him and helped him cross the pitch so that the Nymphs didn't kill either of you. If they got their hands on a power like yours it would be disastrous. He did *not* ride me."

The other Dragons were all nodding firmly and it was clear that this wasn't actually Darius being a dick but really was a rule they followed.

I tried not to let the disappointment show on my face. Riding a Dragon through the clouds had been the one thing about this lesson that I'd been looking forward to.

"Do you want to try and create that Nymph killing fire with us? See if it can match up to ours?" Darius challenged.

"We can give it a go." I shrugged. Neither of us had managed to summon the red and blue fire since the Nymph attack but I was willing to try it.

Angelica smiled widely as the six Dragons all moved to stand in a row. Darius beckoned us over to join the end of the line beside him and I positioned myself just out of his reach.

Angelica went first, throwing her hands up towards the sky and releasing a wave of fire which burned so hot that the grass beneath her withered away even though it was in the opposite direction to the flames. The other guys followed suit, each of them managing to throw Dragon Fire up several meters above their heads into the sky.

Darius planted his feet firmly before taking his turn and the strength of his fire almost forced me back a step as it shot into the sky, further than I could measure by eye. I felt the heat of it warming me right down to the pool of magic in my core which seemed to swell in response to the flames. I wondered if that could be a Dragon thing or if his power was just so intense that I couldn't help but have a physical reaction to it.

My lips parted and I couldn't deny I was impressed by the display of his power.

Darius turned to me and Darcy with a smirk on his lips, gesturing for us to take our turns.

I exchanged a glance with my sister and she shrugged, raising her hands at the same time as me.

I tried to call on that otherness inside me which had awoken during the battle with the Nymphs. It was like it was hiding behind a glass wall; I knew it was there but I just couldn't get through to it.

I scrambled with the attempt for several minutes but eventually gave up. Darcy sighed loudly as she stopped trying too.

"Maybe it only works when there's Nymphs around?" she suggested halfheartedly.

"Or maybe you're not Dragons at all," Darius said and I wasn't really sure if he sounded happy about that or not.

"So what now?" I asked.

"Now, you two might as well go back to your Houses," Darius suggested as he pulled his shirt off, exposing those muscles to the sun and forcing me to check him out. Which he totally noticed. He smirked at me as he started to unbuckle his belt and the other Dragons began to undress too. "We're going for a fly."

"Urgh, then I'm leaving before you flash me your junk again," I said, turning away from him before he could drop his pants.

"Your loss, Roxy."

Darcy turned away too and we started walking as the sounds of clothes hitting the ground followed us.

"Catch you later, guys," Angelica called. "Hopefully you'll be flying with us soon!"

"See you later," Darcy called back without turning around and I threw a wave over my shoulder at her.

We kept walking but before we could get any distance, a huge roar tore through the air behind us and a massive fireball blossomed to life above our heads.

We both screamed, dropping to the ground in fright just as an enormous golden dragon swept over our heads, his wings almost clipping us where we cowered on the ground.

I leapt upright as Darius twisted away, throwing my hands out and casting a spray of ice cold water at his scaly ass. He deflected it with a flick of his powerful tail, releasing another roar before turning sharply and soaring towards the clouds.

We watched as he and the other Dragons flew higher and higher. Angelica's red scales glinted in the sun and the other four Dragons chased around her playfully as they tumbled through the clouds.

Darius turned away from them, beating his powerful wings hard and disappearing in the direction of Earth Territory to the north, clearly having no intention of staying with the other Dragons for the rest of the session.

"Well at least if we do turn out to be Dragons we won't have to worry about spending these lessons hanging out with that jackass," I said as I watched him fly away. "He clearly prefers his own company over hanging out with his kind."

"The idea of transforming into that is insane," Darcy commented, her eyes on the group of Dragons who still chased each other above us. "But it does look like fun too."

A smile tugged at my lips as I watched them. "Yeah," I agreed. "Being a Dragon would be pretty badass."

"Shall we head to The Orb and grab an early lunch before the Hell Week pranksters show up?" Darcy suggested.

"Yeah, I'll just grab my satchel." I moved away from her to retrieve my bag from where I'd left it on the far side of the plain but stopped as Darcy gasped behind me.

"Ohmagawd, I've got to pee!" she exclaimed.

"Okay hang on we can go as soon as I've-"

"No, like right now! I'll meet you at The Orb!" She turned and sprinted away from me before I could even get another word in and I frowned after her in complete surprise.

"When you gotta go, you gotta go, right?" Max called, stepping out from behind a craggy rock face and spinning an orb of water between his fingers casually.

"Did you do that to her?" I demanded, drawing magic to my own palms as I waited to see what he was going to do.

"Manipulating the water in someone's body is fairly easy for someone as powerful as me," he said with a shrug. "She'll feel better once she gets far enough from my influence."

"Why the hell would you do that?" I demanded.

"I just need a word with you. I could have actually made her wet herself but I was being nice. I come in peace." He crossed his finger over his heart, leaving a shining cross made of water hanging in the air before it while he gave me an earnest expression.

"Not interested," I said coldly, turning my back on him as I made a move to follow my sister.

I bumped into a wall of hard air and turned to glare at Max as he smiled at me. "Just hear me out," he pressed.

"Why?"

"Because, you and me are in a pickle. You know my secret and you're keeping it for me. I don't like being indebted to you."

"Just make sure you keep your freaky powers away from me and my sister and you can forget about it," I assured him. I had no intention of blurting out the secrets of his heritage and weakening the Celestial Council while the Nymphs were circling anyway.

"For a debt this big that won't really cut it. I owe you. And I don't want to. It makes plotting against you awkward. So I have an offer for you." He smiled like he thought this offer was irresistible and I pursed my lips.

"Spit it out then."

"I'm willing to teach you any piece of magic that you want to learn."

"We're in a magic school, dude, there are teachers here paid to do that job and I'm guessing they're better at it than you." I made a move to walk away from him but he caught my arm.

"Isn't there something your need help with? Something you wish you didn't have to be afraid of anymore?" Max asked and he used his Siren gifts to tug an answer from my lips before I could stop him.

"I don't want to be afraid of deep water," I breathed.

I jerked my arm out of his grip and swung my other fist to punch him. He wasn't going to be caught out by me fighting dirty a second time though and he caught my fist before I could land the blow, grinning at me like we were playing a game.

"I can work with that. How about I take away your fear of drowning?" he suggested.

"I don't want you in my head," I growled, yanking my fist out of his grip as I stepped back.

"Not like that. Sirens can't just pluck fear out of you and leave you free of it. That's moronic. We can't manipulate you once you're out of range of our power."

"Good to know," I said darkly. "So how are you supposed to take my fear then?"

"You have air and water magic, I can teach you to breathe underwater. You'll never have to worry about drowning again." Max smiled widely, waiting for me to accept and I hesitated. It was a damn good offer but I didn't trust him one bit.

"How do I know this isn't some trick?" I asked carefully.

"You'll have to trust me."

"No deal." I went to turn away from him again and he closed in on me. Fire sprang to life in my palms and I glared at him.

"You're so distrusting, little Vega. You should really work on that. But if you want, I'll let you take another peek into my head so that you can see I have good intentions." He offered me his hand and I frowned at him.

"Do you expect me to kiss you again?"

"Not necessary this time. But we can if you want to." He waggled his eyebrows suggestively and I rolled my eyes.

His outstretched palm hung between us and I eyed it warily. On the one hand I wanted to tell him to fuck off, leave him squirming over the fact that he felt like he was in my debt. But on the other, his offer sounded so damn good I wanted to bite his hand off.

With a sigh that let him know I still wasn't sure about this, I reached out and took his hand.

It wasn't anywhere near as intense as kissing him when I was Song-Spelled but for a moment I felt his mind opening up to me. He let me feel the honesty in this offer and I was quickly convinced that it wasn't some plot before he pushed me back out again.

I moved to release his hand but he held on for a second, a wicked glint in his eye. "Do you wanna screw Darius?" he asked quickly, catching me off guard.

"What?" I snapped, snatching my hand back. "Of course I don't."

"There was a lot of hate there, little Vega," Max said. "But there was lust too. Maybe you should just do it to work through your frustration with him."

"I've warned you about messing with my head," I snarled at him.

"I didn't mess with anything," Max replied innocently. "I just felt what you felt."

"Are you going to teach me this water shit or not? There are a thousand places I'd rather be than hanging out with you. Like falling from a cliff into a pit full of shit," I snapped.

"Nice. Maybe we should work through this frustration too?" he suggested with a smirk. I narrowed my eyes at him and he held his hands up in surrender. "No more Siren gifts," he promised. "Come on, I'll show you what you need to know."

Max took off down a path towards The Shimmering Springs and I only hesitated for a moment before following him.

The smell of sulphur grew stronger as we approached the springs and steam rose up all around us as little pools of bright blue water appeared between the rocks. It was beautiful, the sound of burbling water drowning out all else the further we went.

Max finally stopped by a wide pool big enough for around ten people to sit in it and dropped down to his knees before the water. He gestured for me to do the same and I did, intrigued despite my reservations.

"You don't get taught this until Junior year but as I'm ahead of my class, I already have it mastered and I'm sure with your power, you'll be able for it too. The easiest way is using your magic to create a pocket of air around your mouth and nose and hold it in place. It's a little harder to do than creating a shield around you on land because the water is pushing back against you all the time. But you can use your water magic to help with that too. And because you're strong you should be able to maintain it for a good hour or more once you've got the hang of it."

"Really?" I asked. Now that he explained it, it seemed kinda obvious but I'd never even considered the idea of creating my own air supply when I'd been trapped beneath the ice in that pool.

"Simple as that. Watch me then try it yourself." Max swiped a hand across his mouth and nose for a moment, creating a bubble of air around his face before leaning forward and pushing his head beneath the surface of the hot spring.

The clear water made it easy for me to see the pocket of air that remained in place around his face and I grinned to myself at the thought of being able to do that.

Max sat up again and gestured for me to give it a try.

I took a deep breath then ran a hand down my face the same way he had, working to create a bubble of air not unlike the shields that Professor Perseus had taught us in our Air Elemental class, just a lot smaller. Once I was pretty confident that it was in place, I leaned down and pushed my head beneath the water.

I half expected Max to shove me in but he didn't lay a hand on me and I was able to concentrate on maintaining the pocket of air.

The first breath I took was beyond strange. Water pressed against my eyes and neck but I managed to breathe just fine in the pocket I'd created for myself.

I could feel the water in the pool weighing in on my bubble of air and I worked on guiding it away with my water magic until the pressure eased off. It took a fair bit of concentration to wield the two powers at once but after a few minutes I felt confident that I had the hang of it.

When I finally drew back, I found myself alone beside the pool. I looked around in confusion but Max was gone.

As I stood up, I heard my Atlas ping in my satchel and pulled it out, expecting a message from Darcy wondering where I was. Instead I found a message from Max Rigel. Apparently waiting two minutes to speak in person was too much effort for the Water Heir.

Max:

Now we're even, little Vega. Let's get back to being enemies.

I rolled my eyes and didn't even bother to respond. I was more than happy to have mastered that skill so I wasn't going to complain about the fact that he'd felt the need to teach it to me. I'd be keeping his secret either way, just so long as he kept his Siren manipulations to himself too.

My Atlas pinged again and this time it *was* Darcy, wondering where the hell I was. I sent a quick reply, letting her know I was on my way and started jogging back to The Orb. I'd had more than my fill of Heirs for today but somehow, I'd come out unscathed. So maybe my luck was finally changing.

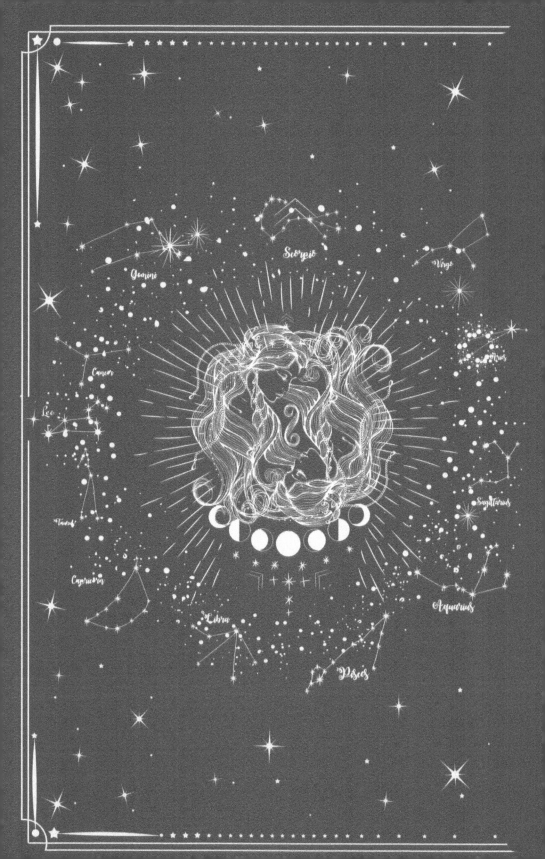

DARCY

CHAPTER EIGHT

Tory and I headed to our Earth Elemental Class after lunch, moving through The Wailing Wood at a casual pace. As we drew toward the northern edge of the forest a *pssst* caught my ear and we both paused. Tyler leaned out from behind a tree, frantically waving us over.

I frowned, drifting nearer a little cautiously. "What are you doing?"

He pointed up the muddy track and mouthed, *"Seniors."*

"I'm sick of Hell Week already," Tory muttered as we moved into the trees to join Tyler. A couple more freshmen wandered up the path and I spotted Kylie amongst them. Tyler encouraged us deeper into the shadows and we stepped out of sight.

They headed past us up the track and screams carried into the air as a trembling earthquake rocked the ground.

I braced myself on Tory's arm, my heart pounding a little harder.

Tyler started stripping out of his clothes, placing them into a backpack. "I'll carry you guys there?" he offered and my mouth parted.

"You don't have to do that," I said.

"I owe you one." He shrugged, pulling off his clothes and stuffing them into the bag before passing it to Tory.

I barely had a second to react to Tyler standing butt naked before us as he sprang forward and his body morphed into a beautiful silver Pegasus. He flexed his wings, arching his brows in a way which was so un-horsey that it made me laugh.

"Hey- did you hear that?" a voice called from beyond the trees. "Fresh meat!" A stampede of feet headed our way and I gasped. Tory and I hurried to climb onto him but something latched around my legs and my stomach lurched. I was yanked backwards, tumbling through the undergrowth with a shout of anger.

Tyler whinnied loudly, rearing up and Tory clambered onto his back, desperately holding onto his mane.

I kicked out at the vines binding my legs as I was dumped unceremoniously on the path before a group of older students in dark robes and creepy white masks.

"Prepare to suffer!" crowed the girl at the head of the group.

The sound of cantering hooves filled my ears and Tyler leapt over me with a furious neigh, his head bowed low as he aimed his shining horn at the seniors.

They scattered around him and started casting vines to try and snare him in a web. I severed the vines around my ankles with a blast of fire, scrambling upright as Tyler leapt into the air with two powerful wing beats.

"Darcy!" Tory yelled, thumping Tyler in the neck to get his attention.

One of the seniors turned toward me and I cast an air shield around myself just in time as more vines shot my way. Tyler wheeled around, his head grazing the canopy and sending a smattering of orange tipped leaves and a cloud of glitter tumbling down over the seniors. He swept toward me and Tory leaned down, holding out her hand.

I caught it with a whoop of triumph, forcing air beneath my feet so I was propelled up behind her. My thighs clamped around Tyler's belly as he broke through the canopy and the seniors started laughing as we flew to safety.

I was once again sailing away from harm on the back of a Pegasus and I grinned widely, clutching onto Tory's waist as we soared over The Wailing Wood towards Earth Cave. Anyone who thought the Pegasus Order were weak was absolutely deluded. Being beautiful certainly didn't make them any less badass.

Tyler swooped toward the rocky ground below, circling down to land outside Earth Cave where students were filing inside for the lesson, eyeing us curiously.

I spotted Kylie trudging up from the wood, covered from head to toe in mud alongside a few other freshmen behind her. Her hair was in full snake mode, her eyes two raging slits. Tory and I started laughing and Tyler neighed, trotting on the spot to show his amusement. She shot a glare our way and the snakes on her head hissed at us before she stalked into the cave, a stream of curses leaving her lips as she went.

I slid off of Tyler's back and Tory passed him his backpack as he changed into his Fae form, leaving nothing to the imagination as he stood stark naked before us. He grinned broadly, taking his bag and starting to dress.

"Thank you," I said.

"Yeah seriously, if you ever need a favour just let us know," Tory said as Tyler buckled up his belt.

"Well…there is something you could do for me actually." He pushed a hand into his blonde-tipped hair.

"Anything," I said with a shrug.

"Your friend Sofia…she's cute. Reckon you could, you know, big me up to her bit? Maybe you could mention how I soared in like a hero and saved your asses?" He eyed us hopefully, his soft brown eyes glittering.

"Oh, well she's seeing-" I started, about to tell him about Diego but Tory elbowed me in the ribs.

"Of course we will," Tory said brightly and Tyler beamed, his skin actually seeming to shine for a moment.

"I'll catch you up." He nodded to the cave as he continued to dress and we headed inside.

I linked my arm with Tory's, leaning in close. "Why did you say that? Diego and her..."

"Diego and her what? He's had plenty of time to define the relationship."

"I guess that's true...maybe letting him know he's got competition will make him ask her out officially."

Tory nodded. "Exactly. It's win-win for Sofia. She can take her pick."

I grinned conspiratorially at her. "Well we'd better let her know at dinner then while Diego's around."

Tory giggled softly. "She's gonna freak."

"Do you think she likes him too?" I glanced over my shoulder, but Tyler still wasn't following us.

"Who knows? Tyler's hot. Did you see those abs?"

I nodded, biting my lip to hold back my laughter. "He'd be a solid eight without those frosted tips. He looks like a nineties boyband member."

"I hope you're not talking about me," Seth's voice made my heart nearly stop.

I looked up, finding him standing at the end of the tunnel. Caleb stepped up beside him and they both started smiling. Like actually smiling.

Before I answered, Seth broke into song, cracking out the Backstreet Boys classic, I Want It That Way.

Caleb picked up the next line on cue and Seth started clicking his fingers to the beat.

They both started dancing, sashaying their way toward us and I stared on in surprise. Seth looked to Caleb and they both belted out the last line of the chorus together with their hands on their hearts.

"Oh my god, *puke*," Tory said and I blew out a laugh. "If you keep singing at us I'll throat punch you like I did to Max."

Caleb shot to her side in a blur of motion, slinging his arm around her shoulders. "Ohh what beautiful poetry you weave for me, sweetheart. Gets me so hard."

She ducked out of his hold and we both glared at him in a perfectly symmetrical *back off* stare. I knew Tory was into him, but she wouldn't let it be seen in public. Besides, I couldn't really blame her when I looked at that roguish smile and set of stacked muscles. I wasn't really one to judge considering my own fanged crush either...

As we drew closer to Seth, he moved to my side while Caleb kept to Tory's. I felt like we were being penned in and it made my heart tick a little faster.

"Can I have a word, babe?" Seth whispered to me, surprisingly not touching me yet.

"No," I said instantly.

He looked to Caleb and nodded. My heart lurched as Caleb picked Tory up, tossing her over his shoulder and sprinting away into the cave system, her scream calling back to us. My mouth fell open and Seth grinned at me, catching my hand as I went to run after her.

He twirled me around like we were dancing, pulling me into his chest and locking his arm around my waist. "Don't worry about her, you know as well as I do those two have been hooking up. She's gonna be more than fine."

"Good for her. I'd like to be fine too, so if you could just get your grubby paws off of me that would be swell." I pushed him and he released me. I backed up a step, then two, surprised when he didn't grab me again. I went to walk away, but his eyes softened and he gave me a heart-melting expression that made me pause.

"What is that look for?" I asked uncertainly, unable to help myself. *Damn puppy dog face.*

"I just wanna talk to you for one minute. If you don't like what I have to say, you can walk away and never talk to me again."

"I like the sound of that second part," I mused and his eyes grew wider. His hair was long and shiny around his shoulders and I frowned as I realised he wasn't scratching. "How's your fleas?"

"All gone," he said brightly. "Prestos ordered in the best flea dip in Solaria. My entire pack is clean." His face fell as he mentioned his pack and a low whine left his throat.

My throat tightened as I recalled the glassy eyes of his pack member Ashanti on the battlefield.

"I'm sorry about your friend," I said gently. No one had deserved to die that day. And I could see how much it was hurting him, asshole or not.

"Yeah…" He cleared his throat, glancing away.

I sighed. "One minute?"

"One minute." He turned to me, smiling again as he stepped forward, drawing back his muscular shoulders.

I raised my brows, waiting for him to start and spotted Tyler heading past us, nodding to me as he went.

When we were alone again, I eyed the sharp lines of Seth's handsome face and he took a measured breath, preparing for whatever he was about to say. "I have a proposal for you."

"I'm not really looking to get married right now," I taunted and he grinned demonically.

"Not that kind of proposal. Although, now you mention it…" He smirked and I rolled my eyes.

"Thirty seconds are gone already."

"Okay so…don't say no to this immediately, but I want you to come and meet me tonight-"

"No," I cut over him. "No way."

He bobbed on his heels, reaching toward me like he longed to touch me but I jerked backwards so he couldn't. A frustrated growl left his throat and he pushed his roaming hand into his hair instead. "You're making this really hard on me, babe."

"I really don't care," I said with a shrug.

His eyes darkened. "Look, I'm giving you a choice in this before I have to force it. Don't underestimate me being an Alpha. It runs right through to my damn soul and you're in my pack. I *have* to initiate you. There isn't a way out of it, alright? If you keep making me wait, do you know what's gonna happen?"

"No…" I said, my heart thumping out of rhythm.

"I'll lose control. I'll put you in line whether you want me to or not. And it won't be the cuddly nice way."

"But I don't want to be a part of your pack," I said in horror. And I certainly didn't want to be forced into it.

"I know, I know. But we gotta jump through the hoops. First, I'll initiate you, then I'll work out the details to make sure I can kick you out and we can all go back to normal."

I frowned, considering his words. If he really was going to flip on me one of these days and force me into his pack, I didn't have much choice.

"What do I have to do exactly?" I narrowed my eyes and he gave me that hungry look which made fear flicker inside me.

"Meet me alone after dinner."

"Yeah, that's not gonna happen." I folded my arms and he gritted his teeth.

"Darcy," he snarled. "You're not getting the message here."

"I'm getting it loud and clear. I don't trust you, Seth Capella. Do you really think I'd be stupid enough to meet you alone after what you did to me?"

His brows drew together and he pulled his Atlas from his pocket. "I thought you'd say that, so…" He lifted the Atlas, tapping something on it then mine pinged in response to whatever he'd sent.

I went to take it out but he shifted forward, taking hold of my wrist with a serious look. "That email is for your eyes only. I'm desperate here, that's why I'm doing this. It will show you how serious I am about this. I don't want to hurt you. But if you refuse to meet me tonight, it will only be another day or two before I lose control." His grip on my arm tightened and my breathing quickened from the intensity of his tone. "That message is ammo against me. I'm trusting you not to use it. But if I screw with you tonight in any way, you've got it as a back up, okay babe?"

I nodded, falling still as his hand slid into my hair, fear dripping down my spine as I called on my magic, preparing to throw him off. He moved forward in a flash, pressing his lips to my forehead before darting away into class. The heated mark of his kiss turned cold as I swivelled around, staring after him and wondering what the hell he'd just sent me.

I sat in The Orb with my friends and a large group of the A.S.S at dinner time. I still hadn't looked at the email Seth had sent, not having had a moment alone to do so since classes had finished.

Diego and Sofia sat opposite us and Tory gave me a pointed look before resting her elbows on the table. "So, guess who we bumped into today, Sofia?"

"I dunno, the Heirs?" she said with a frown.

"Nope, Tyler Corbin. He swooped in and saved us from a bunch of Earth seniors who were about to go mega Hell Week on us." Tory beamed and Sofia nodded, seeming confused as to why Tory was telling her this.

"That's nice of him," she said with a smile.

"And he mentioned something that might interest you," I said with a grin.

"What?" Diego questioned before she could, frowning as he looked between us.

"He has a crush on Sofia," I whispered, glancing across the room to where Tyler was sitting with some of the Pegasus crowd.

"Liar!" Sofia squeaked, her cheeks flushing pink.

"Nope, it's totally true," Tory promised.

Diego looked over his shoulder, his eyes not-so-subtly narrowing on Tyler. "That pendejo?" he muttered. "I don't trust him."

"Well I do," I said brightly and Diego looked to me, his lips pursing. I sensed Tory holding back a laugh beside me and felt one bubbling in my own throat. Well if Diego wasn't going to define things with Sofia, why shouldn't she have other options?

"You should go over there," Tory said in encouragement.

Geraldine shifted closer, clearly having been listening in and I spotted Angelica smiling over at Sofia without blinking.

"Did I hear correctly?" Geraldine asked. "Do you have a suitor vying for your hand, Sofia?"

"I wouldn't put it like that," Sofia giggled, hiding her face in her hands.

"You must go to him! Your love awaits!" Geraldine said loud enough to draw attention from the Pegasus table and plenty of others.

Tyler glanced at Sofia hopefully then turned back to his friends who all started prodding and elbowing him.

"Oh my god," I said excitedly as Tyler rose to his feet.

"What?" Sofia hissed, her eyes Bambi wide.

"He's coming over," I laughed, schooling my expression as Tyler arrived behind her and Diego's hand curled tightly around his fork.

The entirety of the A.S.S fell quiet, looking at him expectantly.

"Hey Sofia," Tyler said, clearing his throat, turning slightly red himself with so many eyes on him.

"Hi Tyler," Sofia breathed as she turned around.

Geraldine was half out of her seat, her eyes sparkling as she stared at Tyler, totally absorbed in the moment.

"So um…there's a fair on in Tucana on Sunday. I thought maybe…after my Earth Trial in the morning we could head over there…together?"

"Say yes," Geraldine whispered as she cupped her mouth with her hand.

"Yeah, I'd like that," Sofia said, smiling shyly as Tyler sucked on his lower lip and nodded.

"Well I'll see you then, then." He moved backwards as if to leave then swooped down and planted a kiss on her cheek. The Pegasus herd started slapping the table and neighing as he headed back to join them, leaving Sofia bright scarlet and grinning her head off. Diego looked ready to skewer Tyler with his fork, but Sofia looked so happy that I couldn't feel too bad for him.

You should have asked her out then, Diego!

I sipped my orange juice, smiling as Tory started helping Sofia decide what to wear on Sunday. I sensed another online shopping delivery in the works and wondered if she might be forming an addiction.

"Well gravy on toast, this calls for a celebration!" Geraldine announced, jumping from her seat and heading off toward the spread of food and drinks on the other side of The Orb.

She returned a moment later with a huge pitcher of some bright pink cocktail, placing it down at the heart of the table and pouring out glasses for everyone.

"Hey, I know a drinking game we can play?" Diego offered, his mood taking a brighter turn. He looked to Sofia, nudging her hopefully.

She eyed the alcohol with a giggle. "I'm in."

"Me too." Tory picked up her glass.

Geraldine took a large swig of her own drink. "I must sadly decline. I'll stick to one glass or my wild and wicked side will come out. And as it's a Tuesday night, I'll keep her locked up tight."

"Boo, I want to meet her," Tory complained.

I sighed with disappointment. "I really wanna play but Seth begged me to meet him tonight and apparently if I don't he's gonna go wolf crazy on me."

"Nooo." Tory leaned against me dramatically. "Don't go."

"I'll come back," I promised.

She leaned in to whisper in my ear. "Okay but be careful. Me and the Ass club will be on hand for back up. Oh and you have to tell me what's in that email the second you open it."

I hooked her little finger with mine. "Promise." I rose from my seat. "I'll catch you later guys."

A chorus of goodbyes sounded from the Ass club and I waved as I headed away.

Part of me wanted to just stay here and open the email, but it didn't seem right doing it in front of the whole A.S.S. Not that I owed Seth anything, but the way he'd acted earlier made me think it was a good idea to open it in private.

As I jogged away from The Orb, I headed along a winding path which passed through Fire Territory. It was a slightly longer route to Aer Tower but I'd be less likely to meet any Hell Week opportunists along the way. I breathed in the night air with a smile on my face, taking my time as I headed north through Fire Territory, then curving east to avoid The Wailing Wood.

It was still another hour until curfew began but the sun was long set, the path lit by burning torches. My Atlas pinged and I took it out, wondering if it was Seth shooting me a reminder about tonight.

Was I really going to meet up with him alone? I guessed that depended on whatever he'd sent me.

Instead of finding a message from him, my heart pumped out of rhythm as I found one from Orion instead. I hadn't replied to his message last night, I just…couldn't. I didn't know what he wanted from me, it was too confusing. He said he couldn't think straight around me and I seriously reciprocated that feeling, but I also knew that I wasn't going to make some rash decision just because my libido went from zero to a thousand every time I was around him. If we went down that route, gave into that urge, it could end in absolute disaster.

But hell, it was the strongest temptation I'd ever resisted.

I took a steadying breath and opened the message.

Lance:

You do like keeping a guy in suspense don't you?

Darcy:

For someone who was very clear about what does and doesn't happen above swimming pools, I'm surprised you're still looking for the answer to your last question.

Lance:

What about the question before that then?
Green or blue?

A smile gnawed into my cheeks as I thought up my reply.

Darcy:

What difference does it make to you aside from being able to tell me and my sister apart?

Lance:

Blue means you like me.

A surprised laugh tore from my throat and I rolled my eyes to the sky as I closed in on Aer Tower.

Darcy:

That makes no sense. Besides, blue hair meant something to me once, but I don't need it anymore.

I reached Aer Tower just as my Atlas pinged again, but I stuffed it firmly away, casting air at the triangular symbol above the door and heading inside. I hurried upstairs with a burning need to read that message but I held out all the way until I got into my room.

I pushed the door closed, dumping my bag on the bed and fishing my Atlas back out. I stripped my blazer off, dropping onto my desk chair and switching on the lamp beside my sketchbooks. When I checked my messages, I found two from Orion.

Lance:

I know what it meant. Darius told me after the Fall Party. But I have my own (better) meaning and Solaria has one too.

P.S

I fully intend to break that guy's legs once you give me his name by the way.

Lance:

I guess you're about to go back to radio silence so for what it's worth…

In Solaria blue means royal.

And to me, blue means you.

I swear I reread that last sentence a hundred times, my ears ringing and my heart thrashing in my chest. *Blue means you.*

My eyes whipped back to the first message and pockets of heat burst in my cheeks.

A knock came at my door and I jolted out of my reverie, standing up and pulling it open.

Seth stood there with a vulnerable look on his face and magic automatically rushed to my fingertips.

"Yes?" I demanded, fire blazing in my palms.

"Have you watched it yet?" he asked with a strange smile pulling at his mouth.

"Watched what?" I frowned.

"The video I sent you. It's your ammo against me tonight."

"Oh… no I haven't." I glanced over at my Atlas and my heart smashed into my throat as I spotted the gleaming Aquarius Moonstone sitting beyond it. *Oh shit!*

"I'll watch it now." I slammed the door in his face, rushing to my desk and stuffing the Moonstone into the top drawer. If he ever found out what I'd done, he'd kill me. He'd lost his entire pack because of the fleas I'd summoned - which had been a definite bonus but now meant his fury would be tenfold.

"That hit me in the face you know," he said from the other side of the door and I answered with a laugh. "I'm just gonna wait right here."

"Do what you want, mutt," I said under my breath, navigating my way to the email he'd sent me and clicking the video to play it.

The recording was taken in Seth's room and I frowned as he stepped in front of the camera in his school uniform. You Can Leave Your Hat On by Tom Jones started playing and my mouth fell open as Seth tugged off his blazer to the raunchy music, swinging it over his head and tossing it onto the bed.

"Oh my god," I breathed, unable to stop watching as his strip show played out. He was over-dramatic on purpose, pulling out his hair and whipping it in a circle before ripping off his shirt and sending buttons flying everywhere.

I started laughing and heard Seth chuckle out in the corridor. In the video, he sprang onto the bed, looking like stripper Tarzan as he dove off of it and skidded across the floor on his knees right up to the camera. As he started unbuttoning his pants, I had the feeling this strip show was going to go all the way, so I tapped the screen to turn it off. I got to my feet, shaking my head with another laugh as I opened the door again.

I folded my arms, trying to school my expression as I leaned against the doorframe. "And what exactly was that video supposed to achieve? That's not ammo, you get naked ten times a day to change into your Order form."

"True, but did you watch until the end?" He quirked a brow and I shook my head. He nudged his way past me, his fingers brushing my arm as he went. He picked up my Atlas, sliding the video to the last frame and holding it out to show me.

"This better not be a freeze frame of your dick," I muttered and he snorted as I took it from him.

"You'd need a wide-angle lens to fit it all in if it was."

"Yeah keep telling yourself that." I looked at the screen and found he was now holding a sign over his junk that said *I renounce my claim to the throne of Solaria.*

"If you sell this image to the press, I'm royally fucked," Seth said with a grim smile.

"Seth," I gasped, looking up at him with my heart in my throat. "Why would you give me this?"

"Well it's only yours for the next..." He checked his watch. "Four hours. At midnight it will automatically delete. So you've got that long to destroy my life if you choose to."

My throat tightened and I stared at him for a long moment before finally nodding. This wolf pack initiation thing must have meant a helluva lot to him if he was willing to risk me giving this video to the press. So my instincts told me I was safe.

"Do you trust me then babe...just for tonight?" he asked hopefully.

"I'll never trust you," I said bitterly. "But so long as I've got this, I know you'll behave."

"Good, that was the plan," he said brightly.

"So what do I have to do?" I asked cautiously, recalling how he'd rubbed himself all over me the last time this subject had come up.

"Well like I said before, you have to challenge me or please me. You can't challenge me because I'll win and I can't hold back or it doesn't count."

"I think I'd prefer that to the other thing though," I said, wrinkling my nose.

He reached out to touch me again then withdrew his hand, shifting uncomfortably like it was really difficult for him to keep his paws off of me. "Well you don't have to screw me to make it work. As much as my particular pack like to go all the way with each other, that's not the only way to please me."

"Good, because like I said before-"

"You'd rather never fuck anyone again than screw me. Yeah I remember, babe. Kinda hard for a guy to forget something like that." He arched a brow at me and a laugh escaped my throat. That sounded even better being echoed back to me from his lips.

"What do I have to do then, buy you a present?" I jibed.

He barked a laugh. "Nope." He held out his hand. "Come with me, we're going on an adventure."

I ignored his hand, grabbing my coat and picking up my Atlas. I forwarded the email to Tory with the message *'if you don't hear from me by 11:30, send this to the press'*. Seth watched the whole time, making no move to stop me, then I tucked my Atlas into my pocket.

"Lead the way," I said, wanting to get this over with.

He grinned devilishly before snatching my palm and tugging me out of the door. I turned back, scrambling to lock up before he pulled me away, running into the stairwell and dragging me after him.

"It's nearly curfew," I warned as I tried to keep up.

"Sure is." He led me out of the exit at the bottom of Aer Tower and my Atlas pinged.

Tory:

Holy shit - be careful, Darcy!

We're still drinking in The Orb. Come join us when you're done.

I looked up with a grin, tucking my Atlas away and Seth tugged me into a run.

"What are we doing?" I laughed, unable to help it as the cold wind blustered around me and the lambent moon shone down on us, its bulbous form nearly full.

"Awooo!" Seth howled up to the celestial being above and the sound set my heart pounding and the hairs rising along the back of my neck. "You're coming on a run with me."

He released my hand, pulling off his clothes and stuffing them in his backpack before tossing it to me. I caught it, putting it on as he twisted away from me and tore into his huge white form, his fur rippling in the crazy wind that beat around us. He lifted his head and a true howl left his throat, the piercing sound sending a shiver right down my spine and setting my pulse racing.

He lowered down to let me get on his back and I climbed onto him with a little thrill dancing in my chest. With the weapon I had against him, for once I really believed he wasn't going to risk pissing me off.

I locked my knees behind his shoulders, winding my fingers into his silky fur as he rose to his feet. I clutched on tighter, having forgotten how large he really was as he bounded away across the sprawling flatlands that led to the eastern cliff.

The air swirled around us, bringing the briny tang of the sea under my nose. The sound of crashing waves grew louder as we neared the cliff edge and I gasped, clutching on tighter as Seth veered sharply right, racing alongside the sheer drop. The moonlight caught on the cresting the waves, making the wild ocean sparkle like rhinestones.

A whoop of excitement escaped me as I held on tightly, adrenaline bouncing through my veins like lightning.

Seth turned down the steep steps that led to Air Cove and my heart lurched upwards as he sprinted down them at high speed. I clutched onto him for dear life as he sprang from the final few steps and his paws smashed into the sand, spraying it up behind him as he bounded toward the sea.

"Woah woah woah!" I cried as he made a beeline right for the waves. "Seth!" I screamed and he released a bark which sounded an awful lot like a laugh.

He turned at the last second, splashing through the shallow tide as it drew in around his paws and racing for the other end of the beach. The world became a blur as he charged across the land, intermittently howling to the moon as he went.

He eventually slowed to a halt and I couldn't stop smiling as I slid off of him and leaned back against a large boulder, shaking with adrenaline.

Seth returned to his Fae form and I passed him the backpack of clothes, turning away as he got dressed. After a minute he cleared his throat and I glanced back to find he'd dropped down to sit on a flat rock jutting from the sand. "Are you gonna join me?"

"It must be almost curfew," I said hesitantly, vaguely wondering if Tory and the others might have headed back to one of our Houses so I could go meet them.

"Five minutes?" he asked with a soft whine. "We'll be back before any teachers find us."

I bit my lip, the thrill of the ride still running through my veins. I did have that video after all and I wasn't totally untrained these days. If he tried anything maybe I'd be able to blast him to smithereens with my newfound fire powers.

I moved to the edge of the rock, sitting a few feet away from him and gazing out at the dark ocean.

"Have I passed your initiation yet?" I asked, glancing at him.

"Not yet," he murmured.

"What else have I got to do?" I asked suspiciously, the high of the run starting to wear off.

"We need to bond a bit," he said stiffly.

I narrowed my eyes. "Like how?"

"Nothing sexual, babe. Jeez. I gave you my word, didn't I?"

"You've lied to me before," I reminded him.

"I know," he sighed. "This isn't like that."

"And what was that like exactly?" I asked coldly.

"That was business. This is pleasure." He grinned mischievously and some of my rage ebbed away a bit. But certainly not all of it. I'd kind of enjoyed the evening so far, but it was definitely easier to like Seth when he was a giant fluffy wolf who couldn't talk.

I waited for more of an explanation on what I was supposed to do and he slid closer so he was within arm's reach. I gave him a stare that warned him not to touch me and he didn't.

He sighed, looking up at the stars blazing above us. "Sex is so much easier than this."

I watched him in my periphery not sure how to respond to that.

"Do you want to hear a story?" he asked and my brows arched.

"Okay," I agreed and he dropped his head to stare at the sea.

"In my family we have this tradition called Forging. Every cub has to go through it to prove they're strong enough to be a part of the pack."

I turned to look at him, intrigued by that. "What does it involve?"

His throat bobbed and he didn't look at me as he continued, "You have to survive a week on your own on Fable Mountain in Northern Solaria." He glanced at me. "This will sound a little fucked up, but it's the way of wolves so don't judge my parents too hard."

"Alright," I breathed, my skin prickling at the tension in his voice.

"Cubs don't get named until after their Forging because a lot of them don't make it back. The idea is to weed out the weak to keep the pack strong. It's been done for generations but a lot of Werewolves have given up the custom because it's so ruthless."

I nodded, my mouth drying up at the idea of parents leaving their children to fend for themselves like that, knowing they might not come home.

"What was it like?" I asked in a strained voice.

"I was only five," he said quietly. "Dad told me to spend the week in my wolf form, he said it was easier that way. It was so long ago but I can still remember every day vividly." He cleared his throat, a vulnerable look gripping his features. "I remember my parents walking me up the mountain through the thickest snow I'd ever seen. I thought it was a game, I remember laughing and playing. I didn't really get it until they left me there in a cave with no food, no water, nothing." He swallowed thickly and my heart stung as I pictured him as a small white wolf cub abandoned to fend for himself like that.

"That's awful," I whispered, threading my cold fingers together.

"I don't blame them. I love my parents. They made me strong," he said fiercely and I could see he really meant that.

"How did you survive?" I asked.

"I nearly didn't," he muttered. "There was a blizzard that week. The snow was so thick I only had to step outside the cave to be blinded by the endless fog. So I holed up in there, frozen to the bone, starving and…alone." His jaw tightened. "I'd never been alone before. I've got a lot of family. We always slept together and I didn't realise how painful it would be to be cut off like that." He rubbed a hand over his face with a sigh. "Do you remember what you said to me the other week, how I didn't break you…I forged you?" He looked to me and my stomach clenched as I nodded. "It made me realise how much I've become like my parents. After I survived that week on the mountain, I vowed that if I ever had a family of my own that I'd never put them through that. But somewhere along the way, I forgot that promise I made to myself."

We sat in silence and I tried to imagine what it would have been like to grow up in this cutthroat world. *Would I be as hard-hearted as the Heirs if the King and Queen had raised me?*

"How did you survive that week?" I asked.

"Well…the snow packed up so high outside the cave that it eventually kept the wind out. I got water from the ice, but I didn't eat anything. I was weak as hell by the time my parents came back and dug me out. But I survived so… I passed."

I reached out, resting a hand on Seth's arm, my eyes watering at the horrible image he'd conjured in my mind. He looked to me with a taut frown, releasing a low whine. An instinct rose in me and I wasn't sure if I should act on it, but he seriously looked like he needed a hug. I shuffled closer as I decided to give in to the feeling and wrapped my arms around him.

He buried his face in my neck and as I tried to pull back, he held me there a moment longer, making my heart judder.

"Seth," I warned and he quickly released me.

I scooted away again with a lump in my throat. There really was something to this whole Alpha wolf thing. His aura was designed to dominate, to make me want to bow to his commands and please him. But I wasn't a wolf. And I wouldn't ever act like I was either.

He gasped suddenly, resting a hand on his chest. "Oh thank fuck for that."

"What?" I asked in confusion.

"Welcome to the pack, babe. You're officially initiated."

DARIUS

CHAPTER NINE

My head was ringing and my pulse was slamming into my eardrums loud enough to make me lose focus.

"Are you listening to me?" Lance asked and I realised I hadn't been.

I blinked a few times and shook my head, trying to force the dizziness away.

"Say it again," I asked, drawing in a deep breath and releasing it slowly.

Lance caught my arm and pulled me to a halt. We were at the top of the cliffs in Air Territory, walking along the path that led to The Orb. It was after curfew but that actually made it easier for us to meet. No one was around to see us.

"Did I push you too hard?" he asked, a trace of concern leaking into his voice.

"No." I shook my head and took another deep breath of the sea air rolling over the cliff. "I skipped dinner though, so-"

"I've warned you about that," he growled, concern shifting to anger easily enough. "You need your energy when we do this. If anything, you should eat *more* when you know we're going to-"

"Alright, I fucking get it. I just got caught up talking to Xavier and the time got away from me." I tipped my head back to the sky, looking at the black, star speckled blanket above us as I got my mind straight again.

"Are you going to tell me what's going on with him?" Lance asked.

I sighed. It wasn't my secret to tell but I needed to talk to someone about it. And Lance had been keeping my secrets for as long as I could remember. If I couldn't trust him with this then why the hell was I trusting him with my life every other night?

"His Order emerged," I said, my eyes on the stars as I searched for the constellation which must have been responsible for my brother's fate. "He's... a Pegasus."

To Lance's credit he only swore once.

"Lionel knows?" he confirmed.

"He does. I think he would have killed him to cover it up but Mother stepped up. She's put a plan in place to release the story if anything were to happen to her or Xavier so he's... well I wouldn't say safe but he's not likely to die just yet." I blew out a breath and forced myself to look at my friend.

"I know you want to protect him from this but it isn't your job," he began.

"It wasn't your job to protect Clara either but you did all you could, didn't you?" I asked.

Lance's jaw ticked. "Not enough."

"No. Not enough to save her from my father. And he didn't even want her to die... what chance does Xavier have?"

I blinked a few times and found that the dizziness had passed. Lance assessed me through narrowed eyes and reached out to clasp my neck without bothering to ask. The heat of his healing magic slid through me and I waited patiently for him to finish.

"Better?" he asked.

"Yeah," I admitted.

We started walking again, giving Aer House a wide berth in case anyone was looking out of the windows.

"You want to help Xavier hide what he is, but maybe that's the wrong way to look at it," Lance said as we walked. "Once the story is out there, it's out there. If everyone already knew then what could Lionel do? He'd have to just front it out."

"I thought the same thing but Xavier is terrified of what would happen if anyone found out. He thinks Father would punish Mother. He said he's already accused her of having an affair."

"Well neither of your parents have ever been faithful in their marriage but that's hardly a secret," Lance muttered. "And Catalina might be many things but she's not an idiot. She would have cast the spells to prevent pregnancy."

"I know. He knows that too or he would have ordered a paternity test. But you know how he is. The Acruxes are pure blooded Dragons as far back as anyone can count. That's why he wants to marry me to fucking Mildred even though she's his cousin's daughter and looks like a warthog made love to a dishwasher to conceive her. He can't bear the idea of us even risking bringing impure blood into the mix for this very reason. And poor Xavier... he's like the cutest fucking Pegasus I ever saw." I ran a hand over my face and groaned. "If it wasn't so goddamn serious it'd be hilarious."

We walked in silence for a few minutes as Lance stewed over that little nugget of shit.

"I take it Lionel won't let him join a herd either?" he asked eventually.

I snorted a humourless laugh. "He's pretty much shackled to the bed. I don't even think he sees daylight half the time. They trotted him out for half an hour at that goddamn party with the Vegas just in case the press made note of his absence but aside from that he's being hidden away."

"Fae of the Pegasus Order need a herd just like Werewolves need a pack. He needs to come to terms with who he is and embrace that part of him. He needs to meet others like himself," Lance said.

"It doesn't even look like he'll be allowed to attend the Academy next year. I honestly think Father is just planning to lock him away forever more and hopes the world will forget he exists. I don't know what I can do to help him and I just feel so... useless."

"I'll try and think of something," Lance said. "Perhaps a herd could be paid off and we could come up with some cover story for them spending time at your family's manor-"

"Can you really see Father allowing that? Think of the glitter on the lawn. He'd shit a brick."

"I'd like to see that," Lance laughed. "I'll think on it some more. Did Xavier happen to mention anything about Lionel's movements this week?"

"He said he's been away from the manor a lot but he had no idea where. He didn't know anything which might help us figure out who he's planning to use on the Lunar Eclipse for his shadow magic. I considered asking him to dig around but if Father caught him…"

"I understand. It's better not to put Xavier in the firing line if we can avoid it. Is there any chance you can come up with an excuse to visit the manor this week instead then? We need to find out who he's planning to use before it's too late."

"I already have actually," I said with a smirk. "I'll head there tomorrow night and try to find out more. He's got a big council meeting that night about the Nymph situation so I should be able to search his office. With a bit of luck it'll give us the answers we need. At the very least I should be able to get something of his that's personal enough to let us use it for a reading."

"Good," Lance replied and I could see the relief weighing on him. "We need to figure this out before the Eclipse."

We walked on in silence for a while, both of us considering the repercussions if we failed to figure out Father's plans. But I couldn't let myself get caught up in what ifs. I had to presume we'd stop him before he got that far.

We reached a fork in the path and paused to say goodnight.

"Get something to eat before you head back to your House. And if you get caught then I'm not covering for you. I already had that FIB asshole sniffing around, asking questions about us," Lance said.

"Anyone would think you were embarrassed about luring students out to sneak around after dark with you in your secret cave," I teased.

"I'm mostly embarrassed it's you," he replied scathingly. "You're not even hot."

"Bite me," I joked.

"Don't tempt me."

I looked at him a little more closely and noted the bags beneath his eyes. "Maybe you should go get your Vega out of bed," I suggested.

"What do you mean *my* Vega?" he asked, shooting me a sharp look as we paused where we were due to part ways.

"Gwendalina," I reminded him with a frown. "You know, your Source. Unless you really are planning on biting me tonight?"

"Oh, right. No, I'll just catch her in the morning," he replied, looking out into the trees. "If I bite you before I sleep I'll end up fucking dreaming of you again."

"Oh come on, Professor, we both know you dream of me anyway." I flexed my muscles at him as I began to back away and he rolled his eyes.

"You wanna lose two hundred and fifty House Points for disrespecting a teacher while breaking curfew?" he asked.

"You wanna tell me if that's a dagger in your pocket or if you're just excited to see me?" I taunted.

He flipped me off before turning away and shooting off towards Asteroid Place.

I grinned to myself as I took the path to The Orb. If I headed there now

I could grab some food before going back to the House and make up for the meal I'd missed while talking to Xavier. Although I didn't feel like I needed it so much now that Lance had healed me. He was right though, it was stupid of me to take extra risks like that unnecessarily. I'd be more careful to eat before the next time we met.

I shouldn't really have risked being seen by any more teachers after curfew like this, but being an Heir bought me a lot of leeway and it was doubtful that I'd incur any punishment even if I was caught.

The Orb appeared ahead of me through the trees but as I stepped out onto the path, a shadow peeled away from Lunar Leisure and moved into my way.

"Tut tut, Mr Acrux, breaking curfew? You *naughty* boy." Washer waggled a finger at me as he moved closer and I stopped before him.

"Just had a little business to attend to," I said, layering my voice with enough friendliness to get him on side.

"Of the female persuasion?" Washer asked knowingly, throwing me a wink.

I gave him a smile which let him believe that.

"Well, perhaps I can let this little transgression slide if you offer up a taste of that lust for me. I'm sure a peek at your exploits would see me through the night," he purred, slinking closer.

As if I'd give you a look at my sex life to jerk off over.

"Not tonight," I said firmly. "I'm a little low on reserves myself." Not true but he could fuck off if he thought he was getting into my head.

"Ohh come now, a taste to buy my silence. You've been having fun while I've been out here patrolling. We can keep it between us boys." I felt a wave of his power flowing towards me, trust and friendship mixing with some lust as he tried to twist my emotions to his desires.

I slammed a wall of heated energy up around me and squared my shoulders at him.

"That was a *no,* Professor," I snarled and he backed up a step, fear flickering through his eyes before he could hide it.

A tense beat of silence passed between us and then he tittered a laugh. I dropped the wall of heat and he visibly relaxed.

"Ah well, you can't blame me for wanting a piece of your power," he said, dipping his head to me just a little in deference. I didn't often have to pull the power rank on a teacher but a little reminder of who I was didn't go amiss every now and then. And I certainly wasn't going to be prey to any of the parasitic Orders outside of the other Heirs and even then it was only with my agreement.

"Scamper on back to your House then you scallywag and I'll waive the punishment for breaking curfew this once."

"Thank you, Professor," I said brightly, like we hadn't just had a face off which ended in my favour.

I walked around him and Washer headed off into the trees to continue his patrol with a slight pout on his face.

As I strolled into The Orb to grab my late meal and a few beers to take back to my room, my mind focused on the conversation I'd had with Xavier again.

He'd overheard Father saying he might have a way to *fix* him and I was just as concerned about that idea as Xavier had been.

I glanced around as my skin prickled, sensing someone close by without actually seeing anyone. I frowned, drawing on my magic as I pushed back at the strange sensation and suddenly a glamour fell away, revealing three figures at the back of the huge room.

Raucous laughter drew my attention and I looked into the far corner, spotting Roxy Vega clambering up onto the table while two of her powerless little friends watched excitedly. She still had her uniform on and I wondered how long they'd been here, hiding themselves with that spell. It was a pretty clever way to avoid the Hell Week chaos going on back at the House even if they were being stupid by staying out after curfew. But then I could hardly talk on that front

"Far be it for you to not go through with the... for *me* to not to go through to do the daring..." Roxy was slurring and she stumbled, almost falling from the table even though she was only wearing flat pumps.

The guy leapt up and caught her waist to steady her and my gut lurched irritably as his hand skimmed her ass. I bit my tongue, turning away from them as I crossed the room in search of my drinks. I didn't think I'd seen her that wasted before and a Tuesday evening in The Orb seemed like an odd venue to choose for a bender. But that was her business.

"I only came up with that dare because I didn't think you'd actually lose!" the girl protested.

"I am not usually one for losing, Sofia," Roxy agreed. "*But* I will never back out of a dare and you ordered a strip show."

I paused a few meters from the ice chiller, fighting against the urge to look back over to them again. Roxy Vega might have been the most irritatingly rude and stubborn girl I'd ever met but she was fucking hot. And with the stupid games we played together while I was tutoring her in her fire magic I had to admit that I'd imagined her stripping for me more than once.

The guy muttered something in Spanish and the tone of it made me think she'd started to pull her clothes off.

I fought the urge to turn with clenched teeth then continued my mission for beer, deciding to skip the food in favour of sleep. I snagged a six pack from the chiller and turned back, meaning to head for the exit.

Of course my goddamn dick wasn't going to let me leave without looking over at Roxy again, it didn't care that I had to get rid of her or that she irritated me more than any woman ever born.

Her blazer already lay in a heap on the floor and she was fumbling with the buttons on her shirt, her inebriation obviously slowing her down. But the way she was swaying her hips and tossing her long, black hair still made her look sexy as hell. Her pleated skirt fell to her mid thigh, giving me a look at several inches of bare flesh between it and the top of her knee length socks, but the elevated angle of looking up at her on the table made it seem like her bronzed legs went on forever.

"Why don't you do another dare?" the boy protested. "Go for a run in The Wailing Wood?"

"Don't be crazy," Sofia objected. "There could be a Nymph out there!"

"Stop doubting my amazing stripping skills, dude," Roxy teased as she continued to struggle with her buttons.

I was about to force my eyes away from her when she cursed and yanked on her shirt hard enough to rip every button off of it.

Beneath it she was wearing a gold push up bra which accentuated her perfect tits and made her look like something out of a Dragon's wet dream.

She tossed her head back with laughter, taking a playful bow for her friends but her foot slipped and she tumbled off of the table instead.

I took a few running steps towards her before I could stop myself but the guy had leapt up to catch her before she could hit the ground.

"Tory?" he asked as she slumped against him, seeming to have fallen unconscious. "Oh, shit! Help me."

The girl Roxy had called Sofia scrambled to help him with her and they struggled to move her towards one of the cushioned chairs close to where they'd been sitting.

I shook my head to clear it of the image of her in that gold bra and spun on my heel, striding towards the exit and quite possibly a cold shower.

Just as I made it to the door, a loud scream halted me. I turned back to see Roxy's friends backing away from her in a panic as a thick sheet of ice spread across the ground away from her, tinting everything in its path a frosty blue.

"Wake up, Tory!" Sofia yelled desperately.

"Maybe you should run for a teacher," the boy said. "I'll try to get through to her."

Sofia turned to run for the exit and her eyes widened in panic as she found me striding towards her instead.

"What's wrong with her?" I asked, my tone clipped.

"She err..." Sofia hesitated, clearly not wanting to trust me with her friend's condition while battling against the inclination to do whatever I told her. "She passed out and now she's using magic in her sleep and we can't get close to help her."

Roxy whimpered behind her and I stepped around Sofia to inspect the damage for myself. I'd dealt with this kind of thing with the other Heirs once or twice when our powers had first been Awakened. We were just so powerful that if we got too drunk, sometimes we'd lose control over our magic in our sleep and Roxy had seemed wasted to me.

"It's fine, we'll look after her," the boy said firmly but I ignored him as I walked closer to Roxy where she was slumped in the chair.

Ice crunched loudly beneath my boots while the temperature around me plummeted and I hadn't even gotten close to her yet.

I drew on my fire magic, pushing it against the ice and melting some of it but Roxy's power fought back as she whimpered again.

"Roxy," I growled as I made it to stand before her. The ice was still spreading and thickening. She was trembling in the chair and I noticed a few tears sailing down her cheeks.

"Not again," she breathed, her fists balling as she curled in on herself.

"Roxy, wake up!" I snapped, moving forward to grab her arm and shake her.

She didn't wake but the ice around me thickened even more and her friends cried out as they were forced to back up again. My breath rose before me and I dropped the six pack beside her chair, crouching down before her so that I could shake her more firmly.

She started coughing and water burst from her mouth like she'd been drowning. I pulled her forward, slapping her back to help her get it all up and the tremors rocking her body reverberated through mine as she pressed against my chest. More cold water flooded from her, drenching her as she cried out in panic and I pulled her against me more firmly.

"You need to wake up," I commanded.

"I don't want to die like this," she breathed and my heart lurched as the ice thickened around us again.

This wasn't a dream she was having. It was a nightmare. And I got the sinking feeling that I knew exactly what it was about.

The ice kept thickening and I was shivering now too. If she didn't snap out of this soon she could really hurt herself and it would be my fucking fault.

"Shit," I breathed, taking her hand in mine and squeezing her cold fingers as I pushed my magic into hers.

For once the well of her power didn't burn with overwhelming magic and I thanked the stars that she'd obviously gotten through a good amount of her reserves today. The display she was currently putting on was clearly burning through her power and I'd only topped mine up after class so I was confident that I could wrangle hers under control.

I pressed my magic into her body, expecting the fight she'd put up when we trained together but to my surprise, her power welcomed mine like greeting an old friend. The surge of excited energy I felt when power sharing with her zipped through me but this was even more intense than usual because she wanted it. On some base level, at this moment in time, she fully trusted me.

I tried not to focus on how good that felt and shifted my attention to helping her reshape her magic instead. I had to fight to pull her away from her water magic which clearly wasn't helping anything right now but she started to writhe in my arms, looking for an outlet for this panic that gripped her.

My natural inclination was to encourage her towards fire but if she managed to overwhelm my control with that Element then it could be disastrous. I'd had a little practice with the other Heirs in power sharing and had managed to help them wield the Elements I didn't possess more than once even though it wasn't as easy. Essentially as I wasn't the one shaping the power, it was doable, so all I had to do was encourage her towards it. I decided that Earth magic was probably the safest bet while she was so out of control and fought to push her towards that.

My grip on her tightened and I ground my teeth as I twisted my power in the unnatural direction but all of a sudden, Roxy grabbed onto my suggestion and I felt the magic flooding from her.

I opened my eyes, glancing around to find the entire Orb springing to life with flowers of every colour imaginable.

I kept my leash on her magic intact as she slowly relaxed in my arms and released a juddering sob. She pressed her face to my chest and my heart leapt a little as she leaned into me like I was someone who could protect her.

Once she relaxed completely, the flood of magic stopped pouring from her and I pulled my own power back, releasing her hand.

Her hand shot out and caught my arm, her fingers gripping my bicep as I tried to pull away.

"Don't leave me," she begged and I cleared my throat as I looked down at her.

Her eyes were still closed and she was pretty much unconscious. I very much doubted she had any idea who was holding her. If she did she would likely be telling me to get the hell off of her. But she asked me not to leave and I found that I didn't want to. Besides, she'd only had that nightmare because of what me and Max had done to her in that swimming pool. So maybe I owed her my help with this if that's what she wanted.

"I won't," I replied as I shifted her against my chest and scooped her into my arms.

I stood and headed for the exit. The Orb was absolutely filled with ice and flowers and I guessed that the faculty wouldn't be overly impressed when they had to come and clean it up tomorrow so I couldn't just leave her here to get caught. Besides, she'd be easy prey for a Nymph in this state too and even with the extra security in place after the attack we couldn't be sure one wouldn't slip past the defences. I hadn't spent the last few weeks trailing her around campus to protect her from them just to quit now and leave her vulnerable. If the Nymphs managed to get hold of a power like hers it could be disastrous. And that was the only reason I'd admit to for getting her out of here. The way my heart was beating as I held her close had nothing to do with it.

Her friends had been forced to retreat all the way to the door by the onslaught of magic but they moved forward as they saw she was alright.

"I can take her now," the boy said firmly.

I eyed his scrawny arms and raised an eyebrow at him in disbelief. There was no way in hell he'd be able to carry her any distance.

"Not necessary," I replied dismissively. "I'll take her back to our House. You're not even from Ignis anyway so why don't you trot along home?"

I made a move to pass them but Sofia stepped into my way, squaring her shoulders as she prepared to argue with me. I vaguely knew her from around the House and seeing her with the Vegas but her power was practically irrelevant to me so I'd never paid her much attention. She was also barely over five foot tall which meant I was looking down on her by over a foot and a half but she still didn't back down.

"Thank you for your help but Tory wouldn't want you to be holding her like that," she said firmly. "Diego and I will manage to-"

"I said I'm taking her back to the House," I replied flatly. "Diego and you can try to stop me if you think you can." I snorted dismissively and tried to sidestep her.

She shifted right back into my way and her skin began to glow a glittery pale pink as her Order tried to push its way from her skin with her anger. She had pretty big balls for a low powered Pegasus, I'd give her that.

"What is it you think I'm going to do to her?" I asked. "I'm not a goddamn monster."

Sofia scowled at me like she didn't agree with that statement and I released a breath of frustration before pushing past her anyway.

I set a fast pace back towards the House and their footsteps followed close behind me, punctuated with hissed fragments of conversation as they tried to figure out what to do. As we closed in on the glass building, the boy declared that he was going to seek out Darcy and left us, his feet hitting one path at a thumping pace as he ran. I ignored them both and kept going all the way back to the House, taking the stairs two at a time before striding through the common room.

I received several curious glances as we passed but most people had headed to their rooms already and the look I threw the others was enough to stop them from taking photographs or asking questions.

I made it to my bedroom door before Sofia caught up to me again and she was even brave enough to grab my arm to halt me.

"What?" I asked, lacing my voice with a bit of threat.

Sofia blanched at my tone but didn't back down and I found myself equally surprised and impressed by the devotion of this nothing little Fae to the girl in my arms.

"Why are you taking her to your room?" she demanded. "I've got her bag right here with her key and-"

"And while she's in this state she could lose control again and burn the whole House down," I replied. "I'll have to stay with her tonight until she sleeps off the alcohol you watched her consume." There was more than a hint of accusation in my tone but the girl didn't even flinch this time.

"And that's all you're going to do?" Sofia demanded. "You're not going to play some trick on her or hurt her or..." She didn't finish that accusation but her gaze flickered to the point where my hand was gripping Roxy's bare thigh as I held her.

"I'm not a fucking rapist," I snapped. "I can have any girl I want in my bed any night of the week, why would I want to molest an unconscious one who hates me?"

Sofia backed off instantly, seeming satisfied by whatever she'd seen in my eyes as her shoulders sagged a little.

"Okay, I didn't mean to imply...just...look after her," she said, frowning at Roxy again with concern as she passed me her bag and backed up.

I made to turn away from her then an idea occurred to me.

"Wait...Sofia, right?" I asked, trying to sound vaguely friendly. It wasn't something I attempted often and the frown she gave me said I was terrible at it.

"Yes..."

"I er, have this... cousin. *Third* cousin actually, who just emerged as a Pegasus..."

"Good for her. Why are you telling me this?" she asked suspiciously.

"It's a him. He's called...Phillip."

"*Phillip*?" She looked at me like no one in the world was actually called Phillip and I had to admit I'd never met one. *Dammit. Why did I pick that fucking name?*

"Yeah. Well, as you can imagine in a family of pure blooded Dragons, Phillip isn't coping so well with the shame of-"

"Shame of *what?*" she asked, a clear challenge in her eyes for me to dare to finish that sentence. And in hindsight implying her Order was shameful probably wasn't the best way to get her to help me.

I shifted Roxy in my arms and sighed, wondering if I should just abandon this idea. But this girl had impressed me tonight despite her weakness and I didn't really have anyone else to ask so I barrelled on.

"I'll level with you. Me calling your Order shameful is about the closest to a compliment he'd get from a member of my family on the subject. He's been locked in his house, hidden away from the world, his father has actually considered *killing* him to conceal his true nature. He's...alone. And he could really use someone of his Order to talk to..." My throat felt tight, I didn't know if this was a terrible idea but Xavier had sounded so broken on the phone earlier, so desperate, I just wanted to try and help him. And maybe having another Pegasus to talk to would help him see some good in what he was.

Sofia just stared at me and I shook my head, turning back towards my door as Roxy mumbled something against my chest.

"Forget it," I muttered, my gut twisting as I failed him again.

"You know," Sofia said softly behind me. "Everyone says Darius Acrux is heartless and cold blooded just like the Dragon he turns into. But you're not, are you?"

I gave her a flat look over my shoulder but she carried on anyway.

"You actually give a shit about other people, don't you? You want to protect them, look after them..." Her gaze fell on the unconscious girl in my arms like that was proof and I growled at her.

"Is there a point to your inaccurate analysis?"

Sofia had the nerve to roll her fucking eyes at me. "I'll message you my number. You can tell *Phillip* to message me whenever he likes."

I raised an eyebrow at her in surprise and she threw a final look at Roxy in my arms before turning and heading away from us.

I unlocked my door awkwardly while still holding her and headed inside, kicking it closed behind me as I dropped her bag and crossed the wide space towards the bed.

Roxy's head lolled back against my shoulder and her hair hung over my arm. She was still soaking wet and I hadn't realised how much she'd been shivering as I'd walked here but now I could feel the tremors of her body where it was pressed to mine. I quickly used my water magic to pull every bit of moisture from her clothes and hair then pushed some warmth from my body into hers.

She drifted near to consciousness as she stopped shivering and shifted in my arms, mumbling something incoherent as she pressed her cheek to my chest.

My heart thumped a little harder than usual and I cleared my throat uncomfortably as I lowered her down onto the bed. Her brows pinched and she started mumbling something again as I released her.

I pulled her shoes off and tossed them on the floor and she kicked out at me, forcing me to step back.

"I can do it myself, Darcy," she muttered, still slurring. "You shouldn't have to look after me like this."

Before I could stop her, she lifted her hips up, pulled her skirt off and threw it at me. She still hadn't opened her eyes and I didn't think she was really awake at all. The gold panties she wore matched the bra which I could still see as her buttonless shirt had fallen open.

I tried not to stare at her, I *really* tried but I couldn't stop looking at her bronze skin, her narrow waist, the swell of her breasts as they rose and fell in time with her deep breaths...

Fuck it's like someone picked apart my deepest desires and brought every fantasy I've ever had to life.

Why did it have to be her? Why did I have to lust after one of the only people in the whole of Solaria who I could never have? I knew I was going to have to marry a Dragon Shifter one day but that didn't stop me from having other women. But this one would never be mine in any way. She hated me more viscerally than I thought anyone else ever had. And I couldn't even blame her. I'd hate me too if I was her. What we'd done to her, what *I'd* done... it was necessary but I still didn't like it.

I was supposed to be working with the other heirs to get rid of them and instead here I was protecting her like I'd lost my fucking mind.

I took a step away, pulling my sheets over her and intending to take a position in the armchair by the fire for the night but she caught my hand before I could leave.

I looked at her in surprise and found her eyes open, her gaze locked on mine.

"Don't go," she breathed, her grip tightening.

"I don't think you really-"

"Please don't leave me alone," she begged and the vulnerability in her voice broke down any further protests I'd been going to make.

She sat up a little and tugged on my arm, trying to pull me down into the bed with her. And I couldn't really deny the fact that I'd thought about getting her in my bed more than once before. Not that I'd lay a finger on her in her current state but even seeing her here, surrounded by gold and half undressed was sending zips of turbulent energy right through me.

She pulled on my hand again and I gave up trying to talk myself out of it as I kicked my shoes off and got in beside her.

She smiled at me and it wasn't sarcastic or taunting, the difference that made taking my breath away for a moment.

I settled back against the pillows and she rolled against me, pressing her nearly naked body flush to mine. I could feel myself getting hard just from that small amount of contact. I tried to prise her away from me but she wriggled closer, pressing her full breasts against me and giving me a clear view of them trying to break free of the confines of her bra.

"Fuck, Roxy, I cant sleep next to you while you're dressed like that," I said, rolling her away from me more forcefully.

She blinked up at me in confusion for a moment before pushing herself upright and looking down at her undressed state.

"Oh, sorry," she mumbled before pulling off the unbuttoned shirt and throwing it to the floor. "Better?"

My mouth dried up and a growl escaped me as the Dragon writhed beneath my skin.

"You need to be putting more *on,* not taking things off," I said tersely.

She huffed like I was the one who was being ridiculous. "Give me your shirt then," she demanded, reaching out to pull at my black t-shirt.

"I don't think it will help if I start taking off my clothes too," I said, catching her wrist to stop her.

"You're so fucking bossy," she muttered, a bit of her usual fire rising to the surface. "Just do as you're told for once."

Before I could respond to that, she shoved my hand aside and moved to straddle me in one quick movement. I was so surprised that for a moment I couldn't even react as she yanked on my shirt and pulled it over my head.

My hands found her waist, my thumbs brushing against her hip bones as she looked down at me with her dark hair tumbling around her shoulders and that sexy as sin underwear begging me to touch it.

She laughed as she waved the shirt at me triumphantly, doing a little victory dance which meant she was grinding right against my hard-on and sending my body haywire.

Before I could say or do anything, she pulled the shirt over her head and covered herself with it. I was so much bigger than her that it fell right down to pool around her thighs, trapping my hands beneath the material where I still held her.

Her gaze locked with mine and for a moment it was like none of the shit that had passed between us had ever happened and we were just us, alone...in my bed.

"Do you want to know a secret?" she breathed, her voice lowering seductively.

"What?" I asked, wanting to hear anything and everything she might ever want to tell me.

She leaned a little closer and her long hair tickled my skin.

"I think," she breathed slowly. "That I'm going to puke."

She leapt off of me so quickly that the bed bounced beneath me as she darted to the en-suite.

My dick was straining so hard against my fly that I thought it might actually burst and I had to rearrange myself before I could follow her.

By the time I got there she'd already emptied her stomach contents into the toilet and she flushed it before stumbling towards the basin where she washed her mouth out. She proceeded to steal my toothbrush like a goddamn animal and I leaned against the doorframe as I watched her, trying not to look at her ass too much as she bent forward over the basin but I was clearly failing at that.

I should have been pissed at her for intruding on my space like this but somehow I didn't mind at all.

When she'd finished, she sauntered back towards me, pushing a hand into her hair as she fought to walk in a straight line. She failed.

I caught her as she almost face planted into the tiles and hooked her into my arms before returning her to the bed again. She tugged me down too and I was past the point of protesting.

The moment her head hit the pillow her eyes fell shut but she turned towards me, draping an arm across my waist.

I flicked the lights off and the room was only illuminated by the fire which was burning low in the grate.

"You're unbelievable, you know that," she mumbled.

"In what way?" I asked, wondering if she just might be about to admit that she felt this heat between us too.

She shifted nearer to me and I pulled her close as she laid her head on my chest. My heart was hammering wildly and I couldn't quite believe the strange turn of events that had led us here. For the longest moment she didn't speak and I began to wonder if she'd fallen asleep but then she carried on.

"You have the *biggest* goddamn jacuzzi I've ever seen in your bathroom," she said and I couldn't help but laugh at the way that conversation had gone.

"Do you like it?" I asked.

"No. It's just unbelievable. Like you. You're just... such... a dick." Her breathing grew heavier and I was sure she'd passed out again.

A smile pulled at my lips in response to her comment. It might have been nice for my ego if she'd started declaring how attractive she found me, but in all honesty she just wouldn't have been herself without her smart mouth.

And I was beginning to realise that I might like that, and a few other things about her, just a bit too much.

TORY

CHAPTER TEN

When I was a kid I used to have the same dream over and over again to the point that I could almost convince myself that it was real. It wasn't anything special by most people's standards. I just used to imagine myself curled up in bed between the loving arms of my mom and dad. The parents I'd never known. Warm and safe and loved. It had been a secret I'd never even shared with Darcy because I didn't want to admit to her that I'd believed we were missing something in our lives. Having a twin was a blessing which meant I'd never been truly alone but growing up without knowing you had people there to love, nurture and protect you no matter what was hard on a kid.

As I grew up, I grew out of the dreams, steadily learning to rely on myself and my sister for support and love, growing a thick skin in the knowledge that I'd never have that kind of endless protection from a parent. And I'd certainly never looked to claim it from any man.

So this dream seemed oddly familiar and yet completely alien to me at the same time. Once again I was tucked in a bed, being held and protected against anything and everything the world might have to throw at me.

But instead of the soft embrace of parents I'd never known, my head lay on the chest of a man whose strong arms were wrapped around me like he never wanted to let me go.

His heartbeat thumped beneath my ear. My arm and leg were coiled over him while he held me against him, his hand resting on the curve of my thigh. He was warm unlike anyone I'd ever known, his skin almost seeming to hold a fire within it which filled my soul with strength and peace.

My eyes were closed so I couldn't see him but I just felt oddly at home. Like this was where I was meant to be.

My hand lay on the hard muscles of his abs and I slowly started tracing the lines the muscles created with my fingertips, not wanting to shatter the peace of the dream by opening my eyes.

He inhaled deeply, his chest rising beneath me while the arm holding me pulled me a little closer still.

I continued my sleepy exploration of his stomach, my fingers tracing the lines lower and lower until they suddenly skimmed against the edge of a rough waistband. I frowned to myself at the sensation of denim against my fingertips. Who would sleep in a pair of jeans? What kind of weird dream man had I conjured up?

I ran my fingers along the top of the jeans, the rough material tickling at the edges of my memory but my head was too foggy to place it.

"If you keep doing that I'm going to stop being a gentleman about this situation."

My hand fell still and I froze at the sound of that voice. There was no way even dream Tory would be deluded enough to feel safe in *his* arms.

My heart pounded a panicked rhythm against my ribcage and I peeled my eyes open, blinking a few times against the darkness I found waiting for me. Pain thundered through my skull and my tongue was thick in my mouth.

I cringed against the headache, trying to focus on something around me as I slowly realised that this wasn't a dream at all.

I spotted the fire burning low in the grate across the room first. There was a black fire guard standing before it and a plush cream chair beside it. I knew this room. I'd burned it down once. And somehow I'd ended up right in the centre of Darius Acrux's goddamn golden bed.

I was too horrified at myself to move, my brain hunting for answers in a foggy sea of alcohol infused memories. I'd been drinking in The Orb with Sofia and Diego while she shielded our presence with a spell to deflect attention so that no one would spot us and play any Hell Week pranks on us. Or notice the fact that we'd stayed out after curfew. I remembered playing a strange Fae version of truth or dare with them while we worked our way through too many shots and Diego came up with ideas to retrieve his hat from Orion. Then... nothing. Certainly nothing that could explain to me how I'd ended up in Darius Acrux's arms.

My gaze slid across the wide armchair where I spotted my academy skirt hanging over one arm. I swallowed a thick lump in my throat, turning my attention to what I was wearing...or wasn't wearing. I plucked at the huge t-shirt which clearly wasn't mine, pulling the neck wide so that I could look down inside it. A moment of relief found me as I spotted my bra still in place but he hadn't released his hold on me so I couldn't be sure my panties were still there too.

Darius slid his hand from my thigh, running it up my side over the fabric of the t-shirt until he found my hair where he began twisting it through his fingers. This was too damn weird. Why was he touching me like that? What the hell had we done last night to make him think he could? And why the hell was I letting him?

I still hadn't moved, my head still lay over his pounding heart, my fingers still rested on the edge of his waistband.

"Please tell me we didn't..." I couldn't actually bear to say it but I had to know because my memory was turning up blanks.

"I prefer my girls a little less blind drunk and a little more eagerly responsive," he replied. "Besides, you wouldn't forget it if I'd fucked you."

Heat rose along my spine at that insinuation but I ignored it in favour of focusing on the relief his words provided.

"Thank heaven for small miracles," I sighed but for some reason I still hadn't moved.

"No need to sound so pleased about it," Darius muttered but he sounded kind of amused at the same time.

"So why am I here?" I asked because this still made no damn sense to me and for some unknown reason I seemed to be frozen in place.

"You got yourself so wasted that you passed out and started using magic in your sleep."

I frowned at that. I'd been drunk, yeah, but I could handle my alcohol. Passing out in a public place was pretty full on even for me and I was fairly sure I wouldn't have drunk *that* much... would I?

Darius kept explaining when I didn't respond. "I had to use my power to bring yours back under control and then I brought you back here so that I could make sure you didn't set your bedroom alight in the night or anything."

At his words, I noticed the feeling of his magic coiling around mine where it had obviously been all night. He hadn't actually pushed it to merge with mine but it was dancing along the edges of my power as if it was asking to join it. On instinct I let the barrier around my power drop, welcoming his in.

Darius sucked in a sharp breath as his magic tumbled into mine and a breathy moan escaped my lips before I could stop it as the thrill of his magic caused every muscle in my body to tighten for a moment. The ecstasy of our magic combining was kind of addictive, like I could feel the heat of his power filling every dark space in my body and I had to fight to make sure it didn't burn me.

I pushed his magic back out before I could get lost in the feeling of it and we lay in silence for a few long seconds, neither of us commenting on what I'd just done. I was glad he didn't ask me about it because I really didn't know why I'd done it. But now every inch of my skin was alive with the memory of his magic filling me.

His fingers kept moving in my hair and I frowned, wondering why he was doing that. And why the hell I still hadn't moved. It was like we were under some spell where peace existed between us and we both knew it would be broken if either of us made any sudden movements.

"Did you undress me?" I asked slowly, heat clawing along my spine at the idea of that.

Darius released a breath of laughter and I inched back a little, moving so that my head was on the pillow beside his instead of resting on his chest. He rolled towards me, moving onto his side and shifting so that his hand rested on my bare thigh. He didn't move his hand once it landed there but the heat of his touch was burning through me like magma.

"You don't remember putting on a strip show for your friends in The Orb?" he asked, looking into my eyes.

I frowned a little. I could remember playing some Fae drinking game and forgetting the rules so that I lost a hell of a lot and consumed more than my share of the drinks. I had to admit that I wouldn't have shied away from a dare like that but it didn't really explain our current situation.

"No," I said eventually.

"Well you ripped all the buttons off of your shirt right before you passed out. I brought you back here to keep an eye on you - much to the disgust of your little Pegasus friend I might add."

"Sofia?" Yeah, I could imagine she wouldn't have wanted Darius Acrux taking me off to his room after all the shit he'd put me through. He obviously hadn't listened to her complaints though.

"She's pretty loyal to you," he said. "But as she couldn't exactly challenge me, she had to accept that I was just going to look after you. You took care of stripping off the rest of your clothes after that. Right before you straddled me and stole my shirt."

I opened my mouth to protest against the idea of that but it actually sounded vaguely familiar.

Darius was just watching me like I was somehow fascinating to him and I couldn't help but stare back into his deep brown eyes. His thumb shifted, painting a line of fire across my thigh and my heart thumped a little harder in response.

"And then we just... slept?" I confirmed.

"I wouldn't have touched you while you were wasted like that," he said, his gaze travelling over my face and landing on my mouth.

But I'm not wasted now...

I reached out slowly and pressed my palm down on his chest so that I could feel his heart pounding to the same fierce tune as my own. I dropped my gaze to the back of my hand so that I didn't have to see the way he was looking at me anymore.

His skin was flaming hot beneath my palm, the depth of his fire magic burning within him like an inferno. I wanted to look up again and catch his gaze with mine but if I did then I was fairly sure that I knew what would happen. And this dark temptation before me was so much more monster than man.

I'd never had an opportunity to really study the tattoos which marked his flesh before and I let myself look at the patterns which wove their way over his shoulders and chest in the dim light. A wing swept across his ribs from some design on his back, the feathers burning like they were made of fire themselves. The red Libra symbol on his forearm began a network of constellations and star signs which formed a sleeve over his bicep, though it stood out starkly as the only image with any colour in it.

Flames climbed over his left shoulder from the tattoo covering his back which I knew spurted from the mouth of a dragon. I was sure I could have lost myself in the art on his back if I could see it and I itched to ask him about them but it seemed too personal somehow and I held my tongue.

I shifted my gaze back to my hand above his pounding heart where his skin was bare of any marks. I cast about for something else to ask him as the silence spread and a kind of expectant energy seemed to build between us. I could still feel him watching me, waiting for me to look up and give him the answer to the question which was hanging between us.

"So what was I dreaming about that made me use magic?" I asked as I tried to piece together the missing lumps from my evening. "Was I trying to grow a fairy forest or create a tornado filled with cupcakes?"

"No... it was more of a nightmare than a dream," Darius admitted slowly.

"Well I only ever have one nightmare so..." I frowned as I stopped myself from going on, wondering why I'd been going to tell him about that. This hangover must have been making my brain fuzzy, or maybe I was still drunk and honestly that seemed like the only reason to explain why I was keeping company with him instead of leaving.

But if he was right and I'd been having a nightmare then I wouldn't have been growing trees or playing with wind. There would have been water and ice and panic...

"You were freezing everything around you," Darius said quietly. "And then you started coughing up water."

"Right." I pursed my lips as I nodded.

Suddenly everywhere that had felt hot between us felt cold and that same ice slithered through my veins as I tried to push myself out of his hold. He wrapped his arm around me more tightly, stopping me from rising.

"Don't go," he breathed and there was a strange kind of plea in his voice.

I pushed harder, my limbs growing cold with the same ice he said I'd been casting last night and he flinched where my hand pressed to his chest before releasing me.

I managed to sit upright and Darius pushed himself up too, catching my hand as I started to scramble backwards, having every intention of getting the hell out of here.

"Tell me about it," he begged. "Don't just leave."

"Tell you about what?" I demanded, meeting his eye again and thankfully finding the spell between us broken.

"Your nightmare. You said you only ever have one, so you must know what it was about." His grip tightened on my fingers.

"It's not the same as it used to be anymore," I said coldly, wondering why I was even bothering to have this conversation. But I wanted him to know. I wanted him to see exactly what he'd done to me even if I didn't really believe he was capable of feeling bad for it. "I used to relive that car crash again and again. I'd be stuck in the car as it sank to the bottom of the river and the cold water raced up over my head... My ex, Zane, just swam away and left me there to die. I used to think he was the worst person I'd ever met. But really he was just a coward. He saved his own ass and didn't risk it for me. He left me there to die but he didn't put me there intentionally."

Darius scowled darkly, a low growl rumbling in the base of his throat as I told him about Zane like the idea of that asshole pissed him off. Which was about the most ridiculous thing I'd ever heard because I was sitting in a bed with someone a thousand times worse than him.

I snatched my hand out of Darius's grip as he continued to hold onto me like he thought he was comforting me or something.

"*Now* when I have that nightmare, I manage to get myself out of the car and swim for the surface," I breathed, forcing myself to hold his eye. "But when I get there it's frozen over and there's no way for me to get out. I'm stuck, drowning, holding my breath while the last of my energy fades away and I know that I'll die as soon as I take another breath... And when I wake up screaming, I know full well that there are people a lot worse than Zane in this world."

Tears were burning my eyes and I scrambled backwards, getting to my feet and wincing against the banging in my skull as I moved. I began hunting for my clothes in the dark, wondering if I should just abandon them and run back to my room as I was. I'd had a newspaper article published about me claiming I had a sex addiction so I doubted looking like I was on the walk of shame could hurt my reputation much more than that anyway.

"When Max pulled that fear from you I don't think he looked at it as closely as he should have," Darius said slowly from the bed. "If I'd known that-"

"What?" I snapped, looking up at him angrily. "What is it that you think you can possibly say about that night that might make me see you any differently at all? Why do you even care anyway?" I demanded.

"I don't know," Darius replied on a breath and the way he was looking at me made me pause for a minute. "But for Fae, fear is weakness. Our parents force us to face our fears and overcome them to make us stronger. If we can't then it's just proof that we aren't good enough. We only wanted to show everyone that you weren't strong enough to face yours... I guess we didn't really think through all the repercussions for you though."

"Good enough for what?" I demanded, ignoring that last part because I didn't care if he realised he should have thought through the repercussions more, that didn't help me now. "Everyone has fears. And yeah, maybe facing them is good sometimes but what you and your friends did to us wasn't out of some sense of trying to make us stronger. It was cruel and calculated and it was fucked up."

"I know."

Points to him for not trying to excuse it but I didn't want to see the pain it was causing him. He didn't have a right to be looking at me like that.

"Well good for you, you know exactly how much of a dick you are. Next time I'm having a nightmare feel free to leave me to it. I don't need help from the monster who gave it to me in the first place." I managed to locate the light switch and flipped it on before wincing heavily as a knife drove right through my skull in response.

I spotted my satchel by the door and moved to grab it with relief, flipping it open to make sure my key was still in there.

My fingers brushed against the stolen dagger and I gasped as its presence washed over me, filling me with the desire to wrap my fingers around its hilt and take it into my grasp. I froze for a moment as its power called to me, begging me to wield it. I'd brought the stupid thing out with me last night because for some reason I'd thought it might be helpful if we were attacked by Nymphs again. But that thought kind of felt like it had come from the blade instead of me and as I looked at it now I wondered why the hell I'd brought it with me.

Darius got out of the bed and moved into my personal space, making my heart leap with fear as I quickly released the dagger and flipped my satchel closed again.

"My powers were Awakened three years before I came to this Academy so that I could spend that time mastering them with various tutors alongside the other Heirs," he said slowly like he thought he might spook me if he said too much at once. "During that training, my father did a thousand things to me to make me face my fears. He'd make me walk through fire, jump from cliffs, lock me in tight spaces, beat me, drown me, whip me, pretty much anything and everything he could think of so that he could forge me into a man who showed no fear. It's what we do. It's who we are."

"Well congratulations," I muttered as I backed up, my hand closing on the door handle. Yep, I was abandoning my clothes because there was no way in hell I was staying here for another second. "Now you're just like him."

Darius's face fell like I'd just punched him and the door spilled open behind me.

I turned and darted out into the corridor, jogging away from him and heading straight for the stairs. I didn't stop until I made it into my room, miraculously avoiding any of my Housemates on the way.

I locked the door behind me and pressed my back to the smooth wood as I released a long breath. I didn't know what Darius had been trying to prove by taking me back to his room last night but if he thought I was going to thank him for it then he was insane. The only reason I'd needed his help at all was because of what he'd done to me in that swimming pool. And maybe a little because I needed to learn when enough drink was enough. But I had no intention of altering anything at all about the way I felt about him.

He may have been strangely nice to me for one night but it didn't change anything between us. The past spoke for itself. And there wasn't anything that he could say to me to justify that.

I just wished my racing heart would agree.

I locked my door, then dragged my nightstand in front of it too, needing a solid barrier between me and the outside world.

"Fuck," I breathed as my pounding heart finally began to settle. Why did I let myself get into these situations? I could only be grateful that nothing else had happened between us because that would have been goddamn catastrophic.

I grabbed my Atlas from my satchel then dropped the bag on the floor. I tapped the device but found it dead and sighed as I plugged it in to charge before heading for a shower.

The bright lights in the bathroom drove more daggers through my skull and I groaned. It had been a goddamn school night, what had I been thinking getting wasted like that? I'd wanted to have a drink but the stars only knew what had pushed me to have so much. I could remember feeling buzzed and then it just went black. How had I managed to hop from tipsy to blackout without seeing it coming?

I set the water running in the shower and looked at myself in the mirror. My hair was a mess of curls and eyeliner had smudged beneath my eyes a little but the most horrendous thing in the reflection was the look in my eyes. It wasn't even shame. My eyes were alight with the thrill of Darius's magic.

"Hopeless," I mocked myself before pulling his t-shirt over my head.

The scent of cedar and smoke coiled around me like a caress and for half a second I was back in his arms.

I tossed the shirt away from me with disgust at myself and it landed back in my bedroom. My underwear quickly followed and I dove into the shower to wash Darius Acrux off of my flesh. I cranked the heat up to scalding for good measure and washed my hair twice. The feeling of his hands on my skin didn't wash off though and eventually I had to leave the imprints there.

I dried myself quickly, dressing in a fresh uniform before realising my shoes were missing. I cursed Darius and applied makeup while squinting against the harsh lights of my bedroom. Cardinal Magic with Orion was gonna be a goddamn nightmare with this hangover.

My Atlas started pinging like crazy as it came back to life and I reached for it with a groan, needing that noise to stop. The first thing to flash up was my horoscope.

Good morning Gemini.
The stars have spoken about your day!
After a turbulent start, you may begin to see things in a new light today.
Sometimes things aren't just black and white and though you may be tempted
to stick to original assumptions about certain situations, if you open your
mind to the possibility of change you might be pleasantly surprised.
A Libra and Pisces will work to dampen your flame today but keep heart, if
you can make it through the hard part, you may just find your luck changing
as the day wears on.

Well if a Libra was going to dampen my flame then I had a fair idea that that would be Orion. Peachy.

As I closed down my horoscope I found multiple messages from Sofia, Diego and Darcy all in a panic about Darius Acrux kidnapping me and wanting to know I was alright.

I sent a quick reassuring message to our group chat telling them I'd survived the Dragon and would fill them in on everything over multiple coffees in The Orb ASAP. The one thing I did know was that I wanted to get the hell out of Ignis House before I ended up running into Darius again.

I snagged a pair of black stilettos from my wardrobe, cursing the fact that I'd left my shoes in Darius's room. But I'd sooner spend the day in the ridiculous heels than have to go knocking on his door in search of my pumps. The mere thought of that made me want to curl up in a ball and scream. Nope. Crippled feet from heels were far preferable to the agony of that interaction.

Why had I let myself begin to forget all the things the Heirs had done to us? We hadn't even made anymore moves against them since the Pitball match.

Time to change that.

I grabbed the bag I'd hidden in the bottom of my closet and stuffed it into my satchel with a surge of determination.

I slid the nightstand away from the door and wrapped a thick jacket around myself before opening the door.

I almost tripped over the pile of folded clothes sitting outside my door and my heart pitter-pattered as I snatched them up. I quickly switched out the stilettos for my pumps, trying not to think too much about the Dragon who'd returned my things. Perhaps Darius was five percent not an asshole. Still ninety five percent a dickwad who'd tried to murder me though so I wasn't going to be sending him a thank you card.

I pulled my headphones on but my pounding head couldn't take the hell of music so I didn't turn any on. I just wanted to discourage anyone who might want to talk to me from doing so.

I needed coffee, Darcy and coffee in that order. My stomach was churning and just the thought of all the food at The Orb made me feel like I might puke but I had to get out of here.

The common room was filling up as I crossed it and I spotted Darius instantly, sitting in his usual spot, surrounded by his fan club. His hair was wet and he'd dressed in his uniform with one of those black robes over it already. His eyes followed me as I crossed the room but I pulled my hood up, withdrawing into the darkness within it as I tried to banish the painful light which wanted to split my head in two.

"Fresh meat!" The sound of approaching footsteps followed the yells as I was spotted and my gut dropped dramatically.

Fuck no! Do not mess with me right now!

I threw my hands up, automatically sending a shockwave of air magic tearing away from me in every direction. People and furniture went flying everywhere as I threw way too much force into the attack and only Darius and the people around him were spared the hit as he shielded them just in time.

Half a smile tugged at his lips but I looked away from him, jogging straight for the stairs to escape before the Hell Week assholes could come at me again.

"Let her go," Darius's voice followed me out and heat raced down my spine but I refused to even wonder why he'd done that. Probably just didn't want me to puke on the carpet.

The day was beautiful, the sky pale blue and clear of clouds as the sun rose to fill it and birds cried out joyfully. I scowled at it.

Stupid sun.

I needed a grey day to go with my grey mood and all of that bright light was going to cause me serious issues. I fished a pair of sunglasses out of my satchel and placed them on with a groan.

Why did I have to drink so much? Why did he have to be the one to find me? Why did he have to look so damn good in the mornings with his hair all mussed up and his shirt off...

As I finally made it into The Orb, I paused in surprise, looking around at the flowers which covered every available surface in every colour imaginable. As I looked closer, I realised they were growing through a thick layer of ice which sparkled in the shimmering lights which burned around the curved walls.

I guessed that this was the result of my out of control magic and I marvelled a little at what I'd managed to create.

My lips parted and awe almost drove my headache away until the smell of food sent my stomach tumbling over itself instead.

There weren't many students here yet but a couple of teachers were looking at the ice and flowers and discussing them in low voices.

"I say we leave the decorations up for a while, enjoy the change!" Washer said, rubbing his hands together enthusiastically.

"The choice is really between burning the whole thing away or trying to encourage the ice to melt and the plants to wither," Pyro disagreed. "We can't leave the place covered in ice and flowers. But the magic is so damn strong that it doesn't want to budge. I'm guessing this prank is courtesy of the Heirs, we should figure out which of them did it and dock House Points. At the least they should have to clean it up."

"Oh those rascals would never admit to it even if it was them," Washer said, waggling a finger. "Do you want me to give melting it a go then? I might get everyone wet though..."

I passed them by before hearing Pyro's response and glanced around to check no one was paying me any attention before casting the spell Sofia had taught me last night. My skin tingled as the glamour fell over me and I was hidden from the sight of anyone looking my way. It worked by simply making people look past me and could be broken if someone concentrated hard enough so I needed to hurry.

I crossed the room straight towards the red couch where the Heirs always held court and smiled to myself as I pulled the bag from my satchel. I grabbed a glittering purple Pegasus horn vibrator out first and quickly wedged it between the cushions. Next, I pulled out a riding whip which we'd gotten personalised so that *Caleb Altair* stood out in silver letters along the length of it and laid it at the edge of his usual spot with my heart pumping adrenaline into my limbs.

I headed straight for the coffee machine with a smirk playing around my lips and dropped the glamour again as I looked around to make sure no one had seen through my spell. I grabbed a tray and quickly made six coffees before carrying them to a set of curved couches in the corner where we'd have a good view when the Heirs arrived.

I shot Darcy a message to let her know what I'd done so that I wouldn't have to risk telling her while people might overhear us then reached for my coffee in desperation.

The first mouthful of my hot drink drew me a little closer to feeling human again and I released a soft moan as I drank it down.

"Holy shit, Tor, what the hell happened to you last night?" Darcy demanded as she jogged towards me. I barely managed to deposit my coffee on the table before she wrapped her arms around me. "Diego practically broke my door down looking for me and then Sofia called me and told me Darius Acrux had kidnapped you but there was a teacher lurking outside the exit to Aer House because of the curfew and I couldn't leave to find you!"

"It's alright, he didn't do anything bad," I reassured her. "The reason I look like shit is purely self inflicted."

Darcy plopped down into the soft armchair opposite me and claimed her coffee as I started on my second. I still had my sunglasses on like a total douchebag but I couldn't bear to lower them.

"I can't believe you got wasted on a school night," she said, rolling her eyes at me.

"Well you ditched us so I had to have your drinks too," I joked.

"So what happened with Darius?" she pressed.

I let out a heavy breath. What the hell *had* happened with Darius? I filled her in on all of it and she gave me a report of what Sofia and Diego had told her too. By the end of it I still didn't really know what to make of the Fire Heir's behaviour.

When she told me what had happened with Seth, my eyebrows practically got lost in my hairline.

"Maybe the stars are doing something weird at the moment," I said eventually. "Because that now means all four Heirs have managed to behave in less than asshole like ways in the last twenty-four hours. And that sure as shit isn't natural."

Darcy barked a laugh and relaxed back into her chair with a shake of her head. "You're right. Maybe Neptune is twisting their personalities into those of non-jerks for a while."

"Long may it last," I murmured over my third coffee.

"Well I'll drink to that," she agreed.

We clinked coffee cups and I winced at the sharp sound. Whatever the hell was going on with the Heirs, I just hoped it was going to stay this way.

As that thought occurred to me, the four assholes in question appeared. I raised an eyebrow at Darcy to draw her attention and she slid from her seat to take a place in the chair beside mine which offered her a better view of them as they drew closer to their couch.

"Maybe pissing them off again wasn't the best idea," I muttered, though it was too late to back out now.

"Pfft, this is nothing compared to what they did to us," Darcy replied, taking a long drink from her mug.

Seth dropped down into his seat, tipping his head back and howling in that way he did to make sure everyone noticed he'd arrived. Like his ego just needed the hit of having all eyes on him for two seconds every morning or he'd self combust.

Darius looked my way as he took his seat but I didn't react, knowing he couldn't tell I was looking back at him with my sunglasses shielding my eyes.

Darcy busied herself with pretending to scroll through something on her Atlas as she watched them through a veil of her hair and I had to fight to keep the preemptive smirk off of my face.

Max dropped into his seat the same moment Caleb did and he instantly shifted to yank the horn vibrator out from under his cushion. Geraldine was walking past them and stopped to point, calling out loudly as she spotted what Max was holding.

"For the love of sanitary sausages, please tell me you aren't bringing your depraved hobbies in here where we all eat our meals!" she cried. "It's bad enough you paid a griffin to take a dump on your chest without bringing your randy rocket out with you for breakfast!"

Darcy and I nearly choked on our laughter at what she'd accused him of - it was goddamn genius.

Silence fell as everyone looked at Max whose mouth had fallen open in shock. In the seconds it took him to scramble for a response, Geraldine swept away, heading for us with mischief glimmering in her eyes as laughter broke out around us.

"This isn't mine!" Max shouted, getting to his feet.

"No, that looks like it must be Caleb's!" someone called from the back of the room and the rest of the Heirs were suddenly on their feet too.

A laugh burst from my mouth and Darcy gripped my arm as she fought to hold her own laughter back. Geraldine dropped down opposite us, a restrained smile on her lips as she took a coffee from the table.

As Caleb got up, he knocked the whip with his knee and it fell to the floor with a clatter.

Darius bent down to retrieve it, his grip tightening on it as he held it up for the others to see.

"What the fuck is this?" Darius growled, his eyes shooting around the room though thankfully not lingering on us.

"Did you really pay a griffin to take a dump on your chest, Max?" a girl shouted. "Because I'd do it for free!"

Max's face turned a violent shade of purple and a wave of anger slammed through The Orb from him a second before he launched the horn vibrator across the room. It hit the metal wall with a dull thunk then fell to the ground where it promptly started vibrating and bouncing all over the place.

"When we find out who's behind this shit, you're going to wish you were never born!" Caleb bellowed as he snatched the whip from Darius's hands and snapped it in half with a loud crack.

My chest was hurting as I fought against my laughter, biting down on my lip almost hard enough to draw blood but it was a losing battle. There were more than a few sniggers breaking out from all around the room and I clutched onto Darcy as I lost control.

The Heirs stormed from the room and a cascade of laughter followed them as they went.

"Galloping gargoyles, that might have been the best one yet," Geraldine gushed and even though the laughter was definitely making my headache worse, I was pretty sure I had to agree.

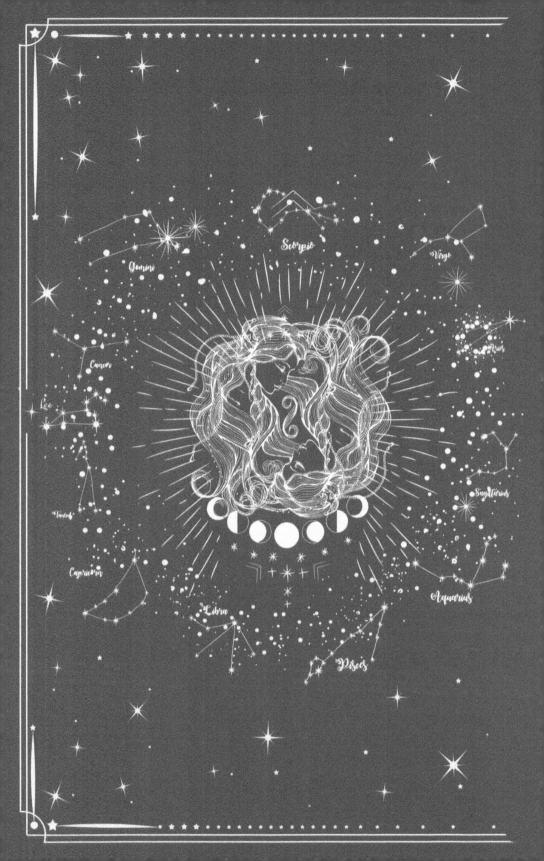

DARCY

CHAPTER ELEVEN

Orion arrived at Cardinal Magic with bags under his eyes and a pale look that said he was running low on magic. He shot toward me in a blur and two thoughts collided in my head. One: that I kind of wanted to give him the energy he needed and two: that I was Fae and I needed to start fighting back.

He dragged me out of my seat and my heart stuttered as I made my decision and slammed the heel of my palm into his chin to throw his bite off.

Tory whooped and Orion laughed as he locked his arm around my waist, tugging me close. Adrenaline scored through my blood as I flexed my fingers to cast fire but he snatched my wrist at speed, sinking his fangs into my skin, his venom immobilising my magic in an instant. *Damn.*

His heated mouth on my flesh and the way I was pressed right into the arc of his body sent electricity skittering through my veins. A noise left my lips that was bordering on sexual and I was just glad the whole class were still chattering loud enough not to hear it. My free hand lay flat against his chest and the solid thumping of his heartbeat drummed against my palm.

He didn't take as much magic as I expected, extracting his fangs and brushing his thumb over the wound to heal it. Without a word, he sped away from me toward the head of the classroom, stripping off his suit jacket and tossing it over the back of his desk chair. I sank back into my seat, my emotions all over the place as I came down from the high of his hands and mouth all over me.

Orion cleared his throat, a mischievous grin pulling at his lips as he wrote today's inspirational quote on the board.

YOU ARE ALL A BUNCH OF HORNY TEENAGERS.

My eyes widened and it sounded like someone actually spat out their drink behind me.

"Yes!" Tyler bashed his palm on the table excitedly as Orion turned to look at us all with a smirk on his face.

I sank lower in my chair, glancing at Tory as she gaped at what he'd written.

"Please tell me this isn't a sex ed class," I said under my breath.

"This is sexual education for Fae," Orion announced and I sank lower, wishing I could use my air magic to turn myself into a breeze and slip out the window.

Of all the professors to teach this, why did it have to be him?

I thought of my horoscope this morning and a line in it suddenly made perfect sense, but not in the way I'd hoped. *A Libra will make you blush harder than you ever have before today.* I'd maybe spent an extra ten minutes in bed daydreaming about how said Libra might achieve that. But not like this. Why did it have to be *this?*

My eyes drifted to Orion's desk and I noticed the watermelon wearing Diego's hat now had lots of friends around it consisting of bananas, peaches and one pineapple.

Orion folded his arms, moving to stand in front of the fruit selection, looking thoroughly amused. "With the coming Lunar Eclipse-"

"It's coming so hard!" Tyler cried out and Orion shot a blast of water at him that sent him crashing to the floor, his seat flipping over with him.

Orion looked back to us all with a challenge glittering in his eyes. "Anyone who makes a joke in this class will get wet. Just like Tyler got wet. So is anyone else getting wet?" he baited us and I covered my face with my hand, unable to bear looking at him. A few stifled giggles sounded around us and I felt one rising in my throat, desperate to break free. I simply could *not* adult my way through this.

I glanced out from behind my hand and found Orion barely concealing a grin as he looked my way. "As I was saying. With the Lunar Eclipse coming on Monday, we will all be under the powerful influence of its sway which tends to bring out the more carnal side of our Orders."

Holy shit. I hope that means I'm safe as I don't have an Order yet.

"Principal Nova has deemed it necessary that you are all prepared in case your libidos get out of control. And I'm sure none of you want any accidental pregnancies before the first term is even up." He tapped the board and the class sat up straighter as the title sprang onto the screen.

Sexual Education for Fae.

"This is *so* not good for my hangover," Tory groaned quietly and Orion whipped around to face her.

"Hungover, Miss Vega?" he growled and she sighed, realising her mistake.

"Yes, sir. If you fancy sending any of your healing magic this way, that would be swell."

Orion gave her one of his darkest smiles that said he definitely wasn't her friend right then. "Oh I won't be doing that. If you turn up to my class hungover you can deal with the consequences." He shot to her side at a fierce speed and bellowed, "CAN'T YOU?!" in her ear. It even made me flinch, but Tory winced with pure pain.

"Ah no shhhh." She covered her ears and Orion stalked back to the board with a chuckle.

He tapped the screen and the strangest list I'd ever read sprang up on it.

Pegasus Glitter

Pink Crystals

Moon Rock

Enchanted Birthstones

"My cousin said Pegasus glitter is the only way to kill Werewolf sperm," Kylie piped up and Orion gave her a hollow look.

"Well your cousin is a moron," he deadpanned.

"It works for me," Kylie insisted. "Me and Sethy have never had any issues."

"Ew, where does she get the glitter from?" Sofia whispered, gathering her hair over one shoulder and wrinkling her nose.

Orion pressed his fingers into his eyes for a moment then dropped his hand. "Miss Major, that is a myth. I assure you the reason you're not pregnant is because Mr Capella is protecting himself from any accidents, but it isn't a hundred percent effective unless you protect yourself too. So listen attentively unless you want to be carrying a litter of puppies the next time I see you."

Tyler started laughing. "Kylie's got a glitter muff!" he shouted across at her and Orion smacked him over the head with a slap of air.

He gestured to the board again. "What do these all have in common?" He pointed at a girl in the front row who shook her head and buried her face in her Atlas.

Sofia raised her hand but Orion pointed at Diego. "Mr Polaris?"

"Um, they don't work?" he guessed.

"Correct," Orion said brightly. "In fact, there's only one spell you need for contraception." He started passing out the bananas to the boys and peaches to the girls. He tossed one to me with a smirk and I fumbled the catch, but held onto it, placing it down on my desk with a blush lining my cheeks.

"You need to perform it every thirty days to keep the spell working. Boys must face the direction of Mars and girls the direction of Venus which you can calculate on your Atlases. It is only one hundred percent effective if both parties – or more - are protected by the spell. I highly suggest you don't rely on your partner to maintain contraception as the spell will also protect you from STIs like Faemidia, Centyphilis, Grifforrhea and Manticrabs."

"I hope he gives us a live demonstration of this spell," a girl whispered behind me and several giggles sounded in response. Heat rose in my blood and my hand tightened around my peach.

Orion picked a banana off of the desk and he suddenly had everyone's full attention as we waited to see what he was going to do with it.

"What's the pineapple for?" I muttered to Tory.

Orion grinned as he overheard me, setting my pulse racing as he locked me in his gaze. "That, Miss Vega, is to go with my lunch."

"Oh," I giggled.

A knock came at the door and an air of disappointment filled the room as Orion placed the banana down and headed over to answer it.

My heart thrummed out of tune as I spotted the beautiful Francesca standing there, her full lips slanted into a heart-stopping smile. "Hi Lance, sorry to disturb you, I need to see those memories of yours from the Nymph attack – it really can't wait any longer. Can I borrow you for ten minutes? Professor Washer agreed to cover for you."

My heart lurched as Washer stepped overly close behind her and she moved further into Orion's personal space, resting a hand on his arm as she escaped him.

I looked between the two of them with my heart in my throat, trying to figure out if this seriously hot woman meant more to him than I knew. Those thoughts weren't helped by Tyler who hollered, "Is that your girlfriend, sir? I hope she knows her way around your banana."

Orion knocked him out of his chair again with a gust of wind, not even glancing in his direction as he did it.

Francesca's gaze slid across the fruit on everyone's desks then to the title on the board.

"Oh sorry guys, I'll bring him back to you as soon as I can." She beamed, taking Orion's hand and tugging him out of the room. There wasn't a single drop of moisture left in my mouth.

Have I been a complete idiot in thinking he was single?

"I'll only be ten minutes, Brian, it's not necessary for you to oversee my class," Orion growled loudly out in the corridor.

"Nonsense, it's my pleasure," Washer replied. "Franny told me she'd be stopping by this morning so I came prepared to cover for you. I used to teach Sex Ed long before you worked here, remember? I taught you all the *ins* and *outs* of the physical act, so I'm sure you have a lot to thank me for."

Washer swept into the room and shut the door firmly behind him before Orion could reply. He had a large bag under his arm and he surveyed us all with a keen enthusiasm that made my skin crawl.

Oh please god no.

My stomach churned and Tory grimaced as he moved to the front of the class, his leather pants creaking as he went. His white shirt was tucked into those awful trousers and several buttons were open at the top, revealing his sun-baked chest beneath.

His tongue swiped out to wet his lips as he gazed hungrily at the class and I had the urge to run for the exit.

"With the Lunar Eclipse fast approaching, I'm sure you're all getting a lot of *urges* already."

"Pervertido," Diego breathed.

"So I'm sure you all want to know how *best* to deal with those frustrations whether you have a partner or not." He laid his bag down on the desk, slowly unzipping it in a way that seemed somehow suggestive.

"Actually, sir," Kylie called out. "Professor Orion was just about to show us the contraceptive spell? And then we were done to be honest." She sounded as desperate for him to stop opening that bag as I felt. I did *not* wanna know what was in there.

"Well that's quite simple. I'll show you that in due time," Washer said, taking something from the bag which appeared to be a spiralling black horn made of plastic. I turned to Tory in horror as I realised what that must have been for.

"Is that a Minotaur horn?" Sofia breathed, her mouth wide as she stared at it.

He started laying all kinds of strange sex toys out on Orion's desk including a fake Werewolf tail, a bunch of feathers, a scaly clawed glove and a set of fake Vampire fangs.

"Fetishes are perfectly normal," Washer purred. "We don't tolerate Order shaming at Zodiac so if anyone has a particular fondness for Werewolf fur or Vampire bites, no one's judging you here. In fact..." He moved into the aisles, his pants creaking as he walked up the row toward us with the Minotaur horn in his hand. "You can use this time to get comfortable with your desires." He placed the large horn down in front of Diego, pressing a button which made it start twirling vigorously so it rolled across the desk.

"Don't be shy. Pick it up and pass it along," Washer encouraged and Diego snared it between two fingers before tossing it onto the desk behind him like it was infected.

Washer proceeded to pass out more of the sex toys, brushing his hands over our shoulders as he moved. When the fake Dragon foot glove landed on

Tory's desk, she prodded it away from her with a pencil.

"I bet they're his," she whispered to me and a new level of horror invaded me.

Washer made a beeline for us and I looked away, desperate not to catch his eye but he moved in front of me and Tory so we were eye level with his bulging crotch.

I leaned as far back in my seat as I could, looking up at him as I kept my hands firmly under the desk where he couldn't get hold of them.

"Sexuality is perfectly normal. It's best we're all open about what we like. Let's all share some of our deepest desires." He reached for Tory and she shrank away but not fast enough as he caught hold of her wrist. "Maybe Mr Altair likes to use that Earth magic of his to tie you up with vines, hm?" He wiggled his eyebrows and magic tingled in my hands, my hackles rising as he sifted through my sister's memories.

"We like to play a game where he hunts me. It's so hot," she said, her voice husky and I lurched forward, catching her arm to tug her away. With my hands free, Washer caught me in his snare next, his fingers winding between mine as he smiled down at me.

"And what's your naughtiest memory, eh?"

Panic flooded me. He couldn't find out about Orion. I felt Washer sifting away my panic, pushing against my will and hunting for my darkest secret. I held onto it as hard as I could, desperate for him not to see it, but he dug in deeper, sending a flood of calm into my body to try and coax it out of me. He pushed harder, but I somehow kept up my walls against him through sheer desperation, a burning sensation flooding my veins.

"Well if you *really* don't want me to see it," he sighed, releasing me and I took a deep breath, overwhelmed with relief as he walked away, moving further into the classroom.

"Did you just fight him off?" Tory whispered, her eyes wide.

"Yeah," I said in relief. "I have no idea how though."

"Dammit. When you figure it out, you've gotta teach me." She held her pinkie out to me and I hooked it with mine to bind the promise.

Washer trailed through the class, closing in on Kylie who looked anywhere else as she tried to ignore him. His hand landed on her and she winced for half a second before his power slid over her. "That Seth Capella must be an animal in the sack. Give the class some insight so they can all learn a thing or two about Werewolf copulation."

Much as I disliked Kylie, no one deserved to get perved on by Washer and I cringed as she opened her mouth to speak. "He likes to do it doggie style and sometimes...he makes me howl for him."

"Do you enjoy that, Miss Major?" Washer purred and I glanced at Tory, wondering if we should lead an intervention, though I was sure we'd only end up in detention with him for it. And nothing in the world was worth that.

"Yes," Kylie sighed. "I like it even more when he howls back."

Washer released her, sweeping through the classroom while everyone desperately tried to avoid his eye. He approached Elijah who was standing behind his table with a nervous look on his face. Washer's hand wrapped around his and he smiled keenly as Elijah relaxed. "Tell me about your sex life, Mr Indus, any troubles?"

"Well..." Elijah clenched his jaw as he struggled against Washer's power and my stomach churned with sympathy.

"No need to be shy," Washer urged.

"When me and my boyfriend have sex...he only wants to do one thing-" Elijah blinked hard, trying to fight back.

"Which is?" Washer pressed.

"He asks me to dress up like- like-" Elijah was turning red and I bit into my lip with discomfort. "Like Darius Acrux," he gasped. "I have to use a smoke machine and growl like a Dragon while I boss him around. And he asks me to call him..."

"Yes?" Washer pressed.

"I can't," Elijah said in horror, gaining some self control back as he shook his head.

"You're in a safe space," Washer promised. "What does your boyfriend ask you to call him?"

"Prince Caleb," Elijah choked out and Tory descended into stifled laughter beside me.

My mouth was wide open and Washer grinned, leaving Elijah ghostly pale as he walked away from him.

"Roleplay is perfectly natural," Washer said, strolling up the aisle toward the front of the class with a grin.

Tyler was furiously tapping away on his Atlas and I had the feeling FaeBook was exploding with everyone's darkest secrets right now. So I couldn't feel particularly bad for him when Washer's hand landed on his, halting him mid-post. He glanced up in horror before his eyes glazed and a dreamy look took over his expression.

"Pegasuses have a reputation for being wild in the bedroom. I'd know of course, I've had my fair share of glittery companions. I'm still washing the glitter out of my sheets in fact," Washer chuckled and some part of my soul withered and died. "Who is it you lust for, Mr Corbin?"

"Sofia Cygnus," he said without missing a beat and Sofia turned bright red, covering her face with her hand.

"I see," Washer purred, glancing over his shoulder at her. "And what is it you'd like to do to Miss Cygnus?"

"Seriously dude?" Tory said, but Washer ignored her.

"I wanna make her feel so good she glows," Tyler sighed and I glanced at Sofia, unable to fight a grin.

"And does she want that back I wonder?" Washer walked away, making a beeline for her and Sofia sat up straighter.

"I do," she blurted before Washer could force the answer from her and he raised a brow, moving on past her.

Tyler shot her a look over his shoulder, biting down on the inside of his cheek and she gave him a shy smile in return. *Go Sofia.*

Washer continued on through the room and when he'd pulled memories from half the class, passed out all of his sex toys like they were part of some sick show and tell and run his hands all over us in the process, he finally returned to the front of the room. I now knew way too many details about the sex lives of my classmates and I wondered if we had any grounds to complain about this to Principal Nova or if this counted as acceptable because of his Order.

"Now I'll teach you how to do that contraceptive spell for all your naughty escapades on the Eclipse." He picked up the banana Orion had left on his desk and held it against his crotch, wrapping his hand around it.

I grimaced, wanting to crawl under my desk just so I didn't have to watch as he started rubbing it.

The door opened and a genuine breath of relief seemed to leave the lungs of every class member in the room as Orion strode back in looking fierce. He took one look at Washer holding the banana and started snarling like a wild animal. "Take your sex toys and get out of my classroom." He pointed them out on students' desks and Washer rolled his eyes as he moved to gather them up.

"Oh you need to loosen up, Lance. Your students would benefit from my years of experience. I can just finish up here for you."

"*Out*," Orion growled, sending a quiver through me.

Washer tucked the toys into his bag and headed out of the door with a huff. Exhales rippled through the room and my shoulders sagged as we were finally relieved of his company.

Orion slammed the door behind him with a blast of air, facing us with a deep scowl. "I got back as quickly as I could," he sighed, glancing around at the horrified faces of his pupils. "Let's move on to that spell." He scooped up the banana Washer had left on the desk, holding it way above his crotch. "Don't let your magic take any form. Especially if you have fire," he warned and some nervous laughter sounded around the room. "Face Mars if you're a guy which is that way… and Venus is that way for the girls." He pointed.

Heat rushed up my neck and I just wanted to fade away and not have to watch this anymore. *Isn't there just a pill we can take, dammit?*

"Cast your magic into a shield like this. And you're done." A vague glow ignited beneath his hand and ran down the length of the banana. He placed it back on his desk and folded his arms. "Now you try."

I picked up the peach with a frown, looking to Tory for backup but her forehead was pressed to the table.

"Ohhh it's so cold and nice," she sighed.

"You need to cast a shield on your peach," I said, nudging her. She lifted her head, showing me her hand which had a juicy pit in it. "I ate it."

I started laughing, looking to Orion to get her another one as she struggled to survive. He was standing in front of Tyler's desk, frowning while Tyler kept accidentally wrapping his banana in vines.

"No one is to cast this spell on themselves until you can do it on fruit," Orion demanded and no one complained about that.

"Sir?" I called and he looked over, raising a brow. "Can Tory have another peach?"

He headed to his desk, picking up another one and shooting over to Tory's desk at high speed. "HERE YOU GO, MISS VEGA!" he boomed and she covered her whole head with her arms.

"Whhhy?" she moaned.

I couldn't fight a laugh and Orion threw me a wink, remaining where he was.

"Let's see it then."

Oh no. No no no. Go away.

He chewed the inside of his cheek, his eyes firmly on me and I knew he was purposefully trying to unsettle me.

I sighed, dropping my eyes to my peach as Diego fiddled with his banana in the corner of my eye.

I took a breath, trying to ignore the hot teacher staring at me while I held my hand over the peach and shut my eyes.

"You're not facing Venus," he pointed out and I opened my eyes again, biting my lip as I glanced up at him.

"Right...yeah." I got my star chart up on my Atlas and swivelled in my chair, placing my peach at the edge of the desk and summoning magic to my fingers. The different Elements kept rising in my veins, trying to interfere with the pure energy beneath it. I pushed them back again and again, readying to cast the spell.

I imagined a shield into existence, willing it to surround the peach. The fruit pinged off of my desk as air exploded from my palm and it smacked right into the centre of the board, bursting into a cascade of orange pulp.

"Woops," I breathed while Tory fell apart beside me.

"Oh my god, Darcy, do *not* try that on yourself," she laughed.

"Again," Orion commanded, speeding back to his desk in a blur before returning to me and placing another peach down. "Concentrate."

I swallowed the lump in my throat. "Could you just look away or something?" I ushered him back and his brows lifted in surprise.

"No, I'm happy right here." He smiled cruelly and I clenched my jaw.

Is this because I didn't reply to your messages again, Professor Unprofessional?

"Fine," I said, pushing my shoulders back. *Screw him, I'll do this whether he's here or not.*

I focused once more, drawing back the other Elements and shutting out everything around me as I released the power from my palm. A light shimmered in my hand and floated down around the peach. I smiled victoriously but I was too cocky. Fire exploded from my palm and disintegrated the entire thing into a gloopy puddle.

Orion barked a laugh, running off to get me another peach, while tossing out more fruit to other students who'd destroyed theirs. As he returned, Diego sent his banana shooting out of the skin and flying over Orion's head.

He folded his arms, gesturing for me to try again and I narrowed my eyes at him.

Could he seriously go and watch someone else now? Why is he so intent on monitoring me?

When Orion finally left me to practise, I started to get the hang of it. By the end of the lesson, I'd attempted it successfully a couple of times but I was still nervous about trying the spell out on myself. It was *so* not worth any accidents. Besides, I was definitely not going to be having sex any time soon anyway. Lunar Eclipse or not. The moon was not gonna control me.

The classroom was a mess when the bell rang and everyone started filing out of the door.

"Miss Vega." Orion caught my wrist as I headed for the exit, pulling me back and heat scattered through my body. "Stay and help me clean up."

My heart tripled its pace as I nodded, terrified and thrilled about spending time alone with him.

"I'll catch up," I said to Tory and the others and they waved goodbye as they left the room.

I still had my peach, intending to practice on it later and I tucked it into my blazer pocket as the final students exited. Silence descended and I decided to play innocent as I picked up the trash can and moved to the board, cleaning up chunks of fruit which were splattered all across it. I felt Orion's eyes burning into me as I continued cleaning up just like he'd asked and my heart pattered excitedly.

"You didn't reply to my message," he said and a smile pulled at my mouth.

"Is that your new catchphrase?" I asked airily, placing the can down.

He was behind me in a flash, one hand on my throat and one on my stomach as he jerked me back into his chest. His teeth grazed my ear and my whole body convulsed with pleasure.

"You're supposed to fight back," he growled.

"I will if you try to bite me, but that's not what you want." I turned in his arms, gazing up at him under my lashes as my heart fell into a rampant beat. "Is it?"

He swallowed and his Adam's apple rose and fell. "The Lunar Eclipse is approaching. All Fae act crazy when that happens. I can't be blamed." A smile danced around the corners of his mouth, revealing the dimple in his right cheek.

"That sounds like a very convenient excuse to break the rules," I accused, my eyes flipping to the door and back. "And what would your girlfriend think?" I gave him a stern expression, my gut knotting tightly as I waited for his response to that.

"What girlfriend?" he asked lightly.

"Francesca," I said, trying to step away from him but he held on tight.

He grinned wickedly. "You're jealous."

I inhaled sharply as he scooped me up, turning around and planting me on the edge of his desk. He stepped between my knees and desire rippled through me.

"She's not my girlfriend." His thumb skated across my inner thigh, feather-light, lasting only a moment, but the reaction was pure chemical. His skin was weaponised and I was the victim of his lethal touch.

"She's not?" I asked and he shook his head.

He released a measured breath, his gaze falling down, down all the way to that place where my skirt rode up and his fingers lay against my flesh.

He glanced at the door with a taut frown. "You should go," he said, his tone deep and soft, like he'd meant to say the exact opposite of those words.

I nodded, leaning forward to get up, but he didn't move and I fell into the trap of his scent. I was too close and his hand was still between my thighs.

I'm going to get up, push him aside and walk out of here before I do anything stupid.

I pressed firmly against his chest and the heat of his skin flooded into my own. I applied more pressure but he still didn't budge.

"This is a bad idea," I warned.

I let my hand glide down his body, taking in the firm press of his muscles, the soft rise and fall of his chest, every line and plane I'd studied in class. *Gah, why does he have to be so irresistible?*

"I'm going to go now," I said with about as much conviction as he'd used.

"Are you?" he asked, his free hand sliding around my waist, his fingers curling, reeling me in as he stepped further between my legs.

"I am," I said, breathless, desperate. And not to leave. But to touch him without fear of what would happen if we crossed this line on school property. Of the trouble we'd both be in if anyone ever found out.

"Yes," I whispered a lie and his eyelids lowered half way, his seductive gaze drawing me in even further. We were baiting each other. This was inevitable. He knew it. I knew it. And frankly, we were fooling ourselves to believe we hadn't already crossed a threshold into forbidden territory on multiple occasions.

Our movements were slow and so delicate as if the softness of them meant this wasn't happening.

I shifted my hand to his right bicep and let it ride the swell of his muscles all the way to his bobbing throat. I reached up to the crook between his neck and his ear where heated skin met rough stubble.

My gaze lingered on the spot where my fingers brushed his flesh, but I felt his eyes on me like a hawk's.

"If you don't kiss me I'll go mad," his voice rumbled through his chest and a magnetic heat tugged me toward him.

It was my call. Kiss him and bring the world down on our heads, or let go, walk away and never look back.

I'm the sister who makes sensible decisions.

I don't play games with the devil.

And yet here I am tempting him with my own two hands.

The drumming beat of his heart matched mine. It seemed to sing my dilemma. *Walk away. Stay. Walk away. Stay.*

A knock came at the door and I scrambled backwards over the desk in my haste to put distance between us, dropping down over the other side of it. If my heart had been beating hard before it was nothing in comparison to this rioting panic. I flattened my skirt, my cheeks flushed as I tried to hide any evidence of what we'd just been doing.

Orion straightened his tie and gave me a look that said, *don't tell.* Did he really think I would?

He cleared his throat, dropping into his desk chair. "Come in," he called, sounding bored.

The door swung open and Principle Nova stepped in, barely seeming to notice me as her eyes locked straight on Orion. "I've called a faculty meeting in my office about enforcing curfew. The students are totally ignoring it. You don't mind giving up your lunch to sit on it, do you?"

Orion's jaw ticked – the only sign this irritated him beyond belief. "Very well. Miss Vega was just leaving."

Nova nodded, looking to me with the barest hint of acknowledgment. The lines under her eyes spoke of little sleep and she kept wringing her hands together in a way that said she was on edge. I guessed the Nymph attack was causing her a lot of sleepless nights. No doubt the FIB were on her case and the press too.

She nodded to me, turning and hurrying back out of the door. Orion moved to follow, sweeping me along with him by pressing a hand to the base of my spine.

His fingers circled for half a second, then he shot away after Nova at double speed. I felt him everywhere for a lasting moment, then he was painfully absent all at once.

TORY

CHAPTER TWELVE

We made it into The Orb for lunch while managing to avoid any Hell Week pranks and I slipped through the tables towards Geraldine and the Ass Club with my sunglasses back in place and my stomach rumbling. The idea of food still made me feel a little queasy but it was time to bite the bullet and go for something greasy.

"Oh my, Your Majesty," Geraldine gasped as she spotted me. "Whatever is the matter? You look positively frightful! Like the cat took a dump on your pillow!"

I snorted a laugh and dropped into a soft armchair with a sigh. "I'm suffering, Geraldine," I admitted. "Though it's through no fault of the cat. I can only blame Mr Jack Daniels and his friend of the Comforting Southern variety. I spent a little too much time in their company last night and I'm suffering the consequences."

"Oh! Well holy banana bread, why didn't you say? I have a home remedy for what ails you. I can whip it up in three shakes of a Manticore's heiny! Just you wait there and I'll see if I can find the salmon slugs and whispering onion dew..." She hurried away from me and I grimaced.

"I'm not consuming anything with slugs in it," I groaned. "I just need something nice and greasy."

"Let me see what I can find," Sofia offered, getting to her feet. "I feel responsible anyway."

"I'm a big girl, I can make my own terrible decisions," I said dismissively, though I was still surprised at just how drunk I'd ended up. I guessed I'd just lost track somewhere and let it get out of control though that wasn't usually like me. "But I will love you forever if you feed me so I'm not protesting that idea."

I looked around for Darcy but she still hadn't appeared. I guessed Orion was making her find every exploded bit of peach and banana in the classroom and I was just glad that he hadn't singled me out for that task. If I'd had to scramble about on my hands and knees looking for manky bits of fruit I was sure I'd have hurled.

A blur of motion shot towards us and my heart leapt as Caleb appeared in the chair beside mine, kicking his feet up on the table and leaning back as if he'd been there the whole time.

"Morning, sweetheart," he said with a grin.

I guessed he was over his embarrassment from this morning already. *We'll just have to work harder next time.*

Diego straightened in his chair opposite us, eyeing the Earth Heir warily.

"No, no," I said, waving Caleb away from me. "I can't do perky this morning. I'm in a decidedly down-beat mood. Please take that sunshine smile away from me."

"Ouch," Caleb said, clutching at his heart like I'd wounded him but I only tipped my head back against my chair to close my eyes for a moment.

"I'm unaffected by your pain," I assured him.

Caleb lowered his voice seductively but made no effort to stay quiet enough not to be overheard. "But I was going to ask if you want to play a game with me..."

Diego spat a mouthful of his coffee out and it sprayed the table between us.

"Shit, man! Watch out!" Caleb snapped, giving him an ounce of attention as he wiped at his uniform, though I was fairly sure Diego hadn't gotten him.

Diego apologised, hurrying off to find some napkins and Caleb watched him retreat through narrowed eyes.

"Washer dropped in on our sex ed class," I explained before Caleb decided to seek vengeance against my friend. "He's taken a bit of an interest in you and me and he got me to admit to our hunting game in front of the whole class." I couldn't hide the grimace which followed those words and Caleb leaned towards me with a frown.

"When you say he's taken an interest in us, do you mean he's been looking at your memories?" Caleb asked darkly.

My heart thumped a little harder in response to the threat laced in his voice and I could only nod in response.

"I'll sort that out, sweetheart. That old pervert needs to remember who he's spying on." He got to his feet suddenly and I reached out to catch his hand before he could speed away.

"What are you going to do?" I asked and he looked down at me in surprise.

"I'm going to make sure he stays out of your head," he promised. "And in the meantime, you can have your lunch and get your energy up for our game."

Caleb leaned down like he was going to kiss me and I shifted back. "I can't play today," I said, shaking my head even though it made the ringing in my ears get louder. "I'm half dying here. I drank way too much last night."

"Oh, is that all? You were starting to make me think you didn't like me anymore," Caleb teased. He reached out to cup my cheek and my lips parted to make some protest about him touching me like that in public but before I could, the warm flow of magic slid through my veins.

The pounding in my brain retreated, quickly followed by the sick feeling in my gut and every other symptom of the hangover from hell which had been plaguing me.

I stared up at Caleb in surprise and he leaned down to speak in my ear. "Will you play with me now?"

His stubble grazed my cheek and I turned to look up at him as he drew back a few inches.

"What if I don't want to today?" I breathed.

Caleb pouted and a smile tugged at my lips. "Then I guess I'll just have to bite you here." He pushed my hair back over my shoulder and touched his lips to my throat. The contact made my skin tingle and I bit my lip.

He kissed my neck, shifting an inch higher and kissing me again.

I cleared my throat and pushed him back a step as I tried to hide the reactions my body was having to him. But as he could probably hear the fast pace of my heart, I doubted he was fooled.

"I want to eat first," I warned him. "I'll play with you at twenty to one, that way I'll have five minutes to get to class after I win."

"You won't win," he assured me, brushing his fingers over my knee for a moment before shooting away from me.

I glanced around from within the confines of my sunglasses to see just how many people had noticed that exchange. I didn't really want to be publicly marked as Caleb's somehow. I wasn't his girlfriend and I didn't want anyone to think I was.

As I glanced over at the Heirs' couch, I found Darius looking right back at me and my heart leapt in surprise. I couldn't really figure out the look he was giving me but something about it made me feel uncomfortable. I dropped my gaze and pulled my sunglasses off, tossing them back into my satchel as I ran my fingers through my hair, super subtly making a curtain out of it to block my view of Darius.

Sofia and Diego reappeared at the same time, and they placed a few big pizzas on the table with some bowls of fries. I thanked them with a wide smile as I dug in.

"Where's the bloodsucker gone?" Diego asked, not bothering to hide the sneer on his face. He hadn't seemed quite so keen to show his dislike of Caleb to his face though.

"I think he's actually gone to tell Washer to stay out of my head," I said. "Which I have no complaints about. If he can keep that sleazebag away from my dirty thoughts then I'm all for it."

"I imagine he'll want something in return for that favour," Diego said darkly. "The Heirs don't just do things out of the kindness of their hearts."

I shrugged, not wanting to get into it with Diego. I knew I should have been keeping my distance from all of the Heirs but Caleb kept drawing me in. And at least with him there was no confusion about what he wanted from me. My body and my blood. Though sometimes I wasn't sure which he desired more.

Darcy reappeared as I was tucking into my second slice of pizza and dropped into her chair with a sigh.

"Orion being an ass?" I asked, gauging her mood.

"When isn't he?" she replied, avoiding my eye as she grabbed some pizza for herself. I got the feeling she was holding back but decided not to push her on it with the others around. I imagined it involved Orion being a mega dickwad though.

"How are you feeling about the Air Trial tomorrow?" Sofia asked and I was pleased to jump on a subject which didn't involve my sex life.

We spent the rest of our meal discussing our theories on what the trial might involve and I kept an eye on the time surreptitiously.

Just before twenty to, I pushed my chair back and said goodbye to my friends. Darcy gave me a knowing look when I didn't really say where I was going and I promised to meet her outside Tarot class in twenty minutes.

Caleb still hadn't reappeared but I was sure he'd start the hunt on time. I wasn't going to make the same mistake as last time though; hiding inside made it easier for him to find me because he could pick out my heartbeat in the silence. There was a strong wind blowing today so I intended to hide in the woods where the creaking branches and wind whistling through the leaves should mask the sounds of my body from him.

I cut a quick path between the trees in The Wailing Wood, moving off of the main track until I found a huge tree which had half rotted out, leaving a hollow area in its base. I pushed my way inside, using the warmth of my fire magic to dry out the space before settling down to wait.

I took my Atlas from my bag so that I could watch the time and smiled to myself.

Let's see if you can find me now, Altair.

I opened up FaeBook and glanced through today's posts. Caleb had been tagged in several Pegasus porn videos which I refused to click on despite the amusement they caused me.

The hashtag #getdumped was trending too alongside multiple pictures of Max Rigel, my favourite of which included a badly photoshopped image of him riding a Griffin and wearing a cowboy hat. The rumour Geraldine had kickstarted about the Griffin poo he'd been coated in at the Pitball game was catching on like wildfire.

As I was scrolling, a new post popped up and as the comments came in I had to battle not to laugh out loud.

Max Rigel:
Anyone entertaining bullshit lies about me on here will find themselves
waterboarded the next time we meet.
#rememberwhoiam #vengeanceissweet

Comments:

Tyler Corbin:

Yeah guys, don't dump on him #trueaboutthepoo #stoptheplop
#haveyouheardabouttheturd

Katie MacKenzie:

Don't be ashamed of who you are! Love and support with you always Max.
#sniffinthegriffin #bepootoyourself

I had to stop reading them or I was definitely going to give myself away by laughing loud enough for Caleb to hear me.

The minutes ticked by achingly slowly but the closer we drew to the end of the deadline, the more my excitement built. There was just one minute left and I still hadn't heard any sign of Caleb drawing close to me.

Just as I began to think I had it in the bag, the sound of my name carried to me on the wind and I spotted Caleb stalking through the trees ahead of me as he searched. I was deep within the shadows in the hollow trunk and I was confident he wouldn't be able to see me unless he got a lot closer.

My heart was pounding and I fought desperately to stay completely still. The wind blew wildly through the trees, making the leaves rustle and the bows creak and groan. I was sure it was enough to hide the soft sounds of my heartbeat and light breaths. He was right there but I'd definitely managed to hide well from him and the timer on my Atlas was down to its last few seconds...

Three, two, one...

"For fuck's sake!" Caleb yelled from the direction of the path.

A huge crash followed and I peeked out of the hollow trunk I'd been using to conceal myself just in time to see a tree go crashing to the ground. I flinched at the tremor which rocked through the earth at my feet and hesitated short of drawing attention to myself. I stepped out slowly, unsure whether I should approach him yet or not. He seemed really angry. Like, insanely upset for someone who had just lost a silly game.

Before I could decide whether or not I wanted to find out how much of that anger was directed at me, Caleb turned and spotted me.

I offered him a victory smirk.

His eyes were burning with fury but triumph flared in them at the sight of me.

Before I could say anything, he shot towards me using his Vampire speed and I gasped as he drove me back against the huge trunk of a tree before claiming my mouth with his. A flare of pain shot along my spine at the force he'd used to slam me into the tree and I jerked away from his kiss to swat his arm.

"Ow, you asshole," I grumbled and a flash of excitement filled his face for a moment before he dipped his head in apology.

"Sorry," he breathed, leaning in to trail kisses along my neck and speaking between them. "But I've been thinking about doing this all morning and then when it looked like you'd escaped I just lost control for a moment and-"

"It didn't *look like* I would escape," I corrected. "I *did* escape. Time's up, I win. So you don't get your prize."

I placed my hands on his chest and forced him back a step though he resisted for a moment.

"But..." Caleb's brows pulled together as he looked at me and the hunger in his gaze made me bite my lip. As much as I wanted to hold firm and refuse him anything at all, the call of his flesh was really making me doubt that choice.

"You don't get to bite me," I said firmly, the rest I wasn't quite decided on yet.

"C'mon Tory, I almost had you-"

"Not good enough. Almost doesn't get you your prize." His gaze drifted to my neck anyway and I narrowed my eyes. "If you bite me after I won I won't play with you again," I added to drive the point home. "If we don't stick to the rules then there's no point in it at all."

Caleb scowled and for half a second I thought he was going to lunge at me and drain me anyway.

Instead he turned suddenly, scraping his fingers into his hair as he started pacing. He released a groan of frustration and my smile widened with victory as he paced back and forth before me like a caged beast. I watched his motions with my heart hammering, feeling the frustration pouring from him and wondering if I might have to try and fight him off. It certainly looked like he was battling with the decision of whether or not he was going to stick to the rules.

He stopped as suddenly as he'd started, turning to look at me with a wicked smile.

"Okay then. What do *you* get for winning?" he asked, his voice deep and alluring.

My lips parted but I didn't have an answer for him. All I'd ever thought about when we'd played this game before was the fact that I could avoid a bite. I'd never considered claiming a prize myself.

"Seems like you need a reward," Caleb pressed, moving right into my personal space.

He kissed me slowly, his lips moving against mine in an achingly soft dance. He pressed me back, parting my lips gently and pushing his tongue into my mouth to stroke across mine. A groan of longing escaped me as I gave myself to the kiss, his hand moving to cup my cheek as he pulled me closer.

Caleb drew back and looked into my eyes for a moment, a smile pulling at his lips as he slowly lowered down onto his knees before me.

"What are you doing?" I breathed, looking around in alarm. We were in the middle of The Wailing Wood and I could see the path which led from The Orb to Aer Tower not more than ten meters behind him. If anyone came along they'd see us for sure and it was a pretty popular route.

"What's the matter, Tory? Are you afraid?" Caleb breathed as he placed his hands on my knees and started to skim them up my thighs beneath my school skirt, keeping his gaze locked with mine the entire time.

The sensitive skin on my inner thighs came alive as his fingers trailed higher and sparks raced to my core, making my heart thump harder. An ache of longing built in me as he moved, a wild part of me wanting to give in to him.

My breath hitched as he made it to my panties and he caught the sides of them before slowly tugging them down.

My gaze flipped back to the path again and I caught his wrists to halt him.

"Someone could see us," I said hesitantly.

"Don't worry, sweetheart," Caleb replied. "I promise to stop if I hear someone coming... aside from you of course."

I couldn't help but laugh at that and he took that as confirmation, pulling my panties down to my ankles until I stepped out of them.

My heart was pounding and I looked around again nervously, opening my mouth to protest. We were close enough to Terra House, we could just go back to his room and-

Caleb caught my knees and pushed them apart half a second before his mouth landed on me and I sucked in a breath in shock.

Any objections I'd been thinking of making were driven from my mind as he dragged his tongue right up the centre of me and I released a breathy moan.

He repeated the move a few times before switching to circling, sucking even a hint of biting. I fought against the impulse to cry out, gripping the rough bark of the tree at my back as I fought to remain upright while he pulled me apart.

"*Fuck*, Caleb-"

The pressure of his tongue increased as his hands shifted up my thighs, pinning my hips in place to give him better access. My eyes fell shut, my head lolling back as he pushed me closer and closer to the edge, my whole world circling around the movements of his tongue.

I was losing control on the noise I was making and Caleb released a dark laugh, the noise of it echoing right through the centre of me.

I shifted a hand to his hair, fisting his golden curls between my fingers as I urged him on. Pressure was building between my thighs and I was falling captive to him, my body bowing to his demands as he coiled me tighter and tighter.

His grip on me tightened, and I could feel myself falling apart as he moved his mouth with expert skill, pushing me towards ecstasy.

I swore as he slowed his pace, keeping me hanging in the final moments of this torture as he devoured me.

"*Please*," I moaned, needing him to put me out of my agony and with one final drag of his tongue, stars burst before my eyes and his name spilled from my lips.

Caleb got to his feet, gripping my waist and pinning me to the tree as he kissed me, hard.

"You are so fucking hot, Tory," he growled, kissing me again.

I gripped the front of his shirt as I drew him closer, my body aching for more of him even though I knew we must be late for class by now. I could feel how hard he was as he ground up against me and I was gripped with the desire to demand more from him. All of him.

His lips moved to my throat and I could feel his fangs resting against the skin there as he toyed with the idea of biting me.

"Are you really going to break the rules?" I teased as I managed to regain control of my breathing.

Caleb hung there, his muscles tight and his teeth oh so close to piercing my skin.

He groaned longingly and forced himself away before looking into my eyes.

"Next time, I'm going to win," he promised me.

My eyes sparkled with the challenge and I reached between us to run my hand down the hard length of his arousal beneath his pants. I leaned closer to him as I rubbed against him a few times, drawing a growl of desire from his lips. "Maybe then I'll return the favour."

Caleb groaned again, stealing another kiss for a long second before drawing back. He shook his head like he was trying to clear it and I laughed.

"Can I have my underwear back now?" I asked, holding my hand out.

Caleb pulled my red panties from his pocket and gave me a teasing smile. "Hmmm, I think these would make a good consolation prize for me," he objected.

I rolled my eyes and tried to snatch them from him but he used his speed to shove them back into his pocket.

"See you later, Tory." He kissed me for half a second then shot away so quickly that he was out of sight before I could even say a word in protest. He'd made me late for Tarot class and now I was going to have to show up with no underwear.

Damn Vampire.

I let out a shaky breath and ran a hand through my hair self consciously as I pushed away from the tree and started hurrying towards my Tarot class.

I was nearly fifteen minutes late by the time I got to Mercury Chambers and I steeled myself as I opened the door to the underground classroom, ready to face whatever punishment Washer decided to give out.

"Sorry Professor," I began as I pushed the door wide and he looked around at me as I clearly interrupted a talk he'd been giving. "I got held up by-"

"Mr Altair informed me you'd be late to class, don't worry about it. Please feel free to tell him that I was accommodating to his... ah... use of his Source," Washer said quickly, glancing at me then dropping his gaze as he clasped his hands together in front of him. For a moment I could have sworn his hands were trembling but he curled them into fists before I could be sure.

"Oh... erm, okay then." I headed towards my seat beside Darcy, frowning at her in confusion.

"*Sir!*" Kylie Major piped up, her face written in outrage. "You took ten House Points from me for arriving one minute late! How is it fair that-"

"As I said, Mr Altair had need of his Source. I'm hardly going to deny one of our most promising and influential students a favour when he requests it so... nicely. Do not forget that the Heirs are the future leaders of Solaria, Miss Major. Now, can we please return to our lesson?"

Kylie scowled but dropped it and I slipped into my seat.

Darcy raised an eyebrow at me and I shrugged in return. I'd known Caleb was going to tell Washer to back off but it kinda seemed like he'd scared the shit out of him in the process.

I pulled my books and Tarot deck out of my bag and sat back to listen as Washer went on with whatever he'd been saying before I interrupted.

"Um, so... yes. This will be the final Tarot lesson I'm covering for you I'm afraid," he said and I didn't even bother to hide the grin on my face in response. "Principal Nova has just confirmed that next week, those of you who survive The Reckoning, will be taught by Professor Nox who has recently decided to take up a profession in teaching. He has the gift of true sight which means he *sees* actual glimpses of the future from time to time and despite his young age he qualified at the top of his class so I'm sure he will be an adequate replacement for me. Though of course many people value experience over youth so maybe you'll all be begging me to come back and satisfy you before long." He winked at us and I recoiled, though thankfully his gaze wasn't on me.

"I'd take anyone over him," I whispered to Darcy and the others in an undertone.

"If he's young, maybe he'll be nice to look at like Orion," Sofia joked.

"No way we'd end up with two teachers that hot," Darcy scoffed.

"And you call Washer a pervertido?" Diego grumbled and I rolled my eyes at him.

211

"As if you'll be complaining when we start Physical Enhancement with Professor Prestos," I said. "You've just got a bug up your ass because you still haven't got your hat back."

"My abuela knitted that hat for me before she died," Diego growled.

"Well lucky you, my parents died before they got around to making me a hat," I snipped back.

Darcy bit her lip on a smile and offered me a raised eyebrow to say I was treading the line of bitch. I sighed. I was treading that line most days and I didn't usually adjust my personality to suit grief over stolen hats.

"Today, I think you're ready to start learning how to read the cards properly," Washer announced. "If you pair up then shuffle your deck I'll come round and instruct you on how to lay them out and read them in relation to each other. There are many ways to interpret the cards based on the order in which they're drawn and the energy you exude while shuffling the deck."

Washer headed off to the far side of the class and I leaned back in my chair as Darcy began shuffling her cards.

Diego muttered something in Spanish before getting up and asking Washer if he could go to the bathroom. The door clicked shut behind him and Sofia let out a long whistle.

"He's been in such a bad mood since Hell Week began," she commented.

"Yeah, he really needs to sort out his hattitude," I said, snorting a laugh at my own joke. Sofia laughed too and Darcy smirked but she was clearly trying to rein in her amusement.

"He's touchy about Orion ever since he broke that trinket box," she explained.

"Well I don't have the energy for his mood swings," I sighed. "They exhaust me."

"I thought that was Caleb," Sofia teased and I laughed again.

"He wishes." I crossed my legs beneath the table though, pursing my lips at the memory of him stealing my panties. I was less than impressed with that stunt.

"I think that if Diego just gets the hat back, he-" Darcy gasped, her fingers curling tightly around one of the cards in her deck as she tugged it loose.

"Don't tell me that's another one," I hissed, leaning close as she laid the card on the table between us.

The Empress looked up at us from the card, reclining on a chair in a dress covered in red roses while wearing a crown of stars. I reached out like I had no control over the impulse to do it and ran my forefinger down the centre of the card. A shudder ran along my spine as the magic in the card called out to me and I exchanged a loaded look with Darcy.

"How did Astrum set all of this up before he died?" I asked. "It seemed like he was caught out when he was killed by the Shadow, but every time one of these cards appears I have to think he planned on us finding them before he was murdered."

"Not necessarily," Sofia piped up. "Objects of special significance can stay linked to spirits after they pass. There are plenty of examples of powerful Fae managing to send messages back to the living from beyond the veil."

I let out a long breath, absorbing that.

"So why make the messages so cryptic then?" Darcy sighed. "Why not just say things clearly rather than giving vague warnings about things or snippets of information we can't possibly put together ourselves?"

"Maybe it gets lost in translation?" Sofia suggested.

"So all we need is to find a ghost who wants to translate for us and we're all set," I deadpanned. "What does The Empress even mean anyway?"

"She's associated with all things maternal," Sofia explained instantly. "She often represents the creation of life, pregnancy, romance-"

"Well let's hope this isn't a prediction," I said with an exaggerated shudder. "The last thing I need is a little vampire baby nipping at my ankles."

Darcy laughed. "You'd better make sure you learn that spell Orion taught us before you go near Caleb again. I'm not babysitting a kid that bites."

"You have to admit my big brown eyes and Caleb's blonde curls would make for a damn cute baby though," I teased.

"Urgh, and then we'd be stuck with the Heirs forever." Darcy mimed puking into her satchel and I laughed.

"Point taken. I'll do the spell twice to make extra sure. Shall we see if the message shines any light on The Empress then?" I suggested, eyeing the card suspiciously.

Darcy nodded, reaching out to flip the card over.

In the Palace of Souls, rests a secret untold.
Find the light who burned on after the fire...

"Clear as always," I said, leaning back in my chair irritably. What was the point of sending us these messages if they were always so damn cryptic?

"Do you think we'll ever get one that just says 'there's a folder full of answers sitting beside you'?" Darcy asked.

"Here's hoping, because that means nothing to me," I said, tossing the card away from me in disgust. It caught on an errant breeze, flipped over and landed right back on the desk in front of us. I scowled at it.

Damn ghost card.

"Well the first half is pretty self explanatory," Sofia said, raising an eyebrow at us.

"No it's not," I disagreed.

"Well, the Palace of Souls is your family's palace," she said slowly. "You know, where the Savage King and the Queen lived before they were killed..."

"I didn't know that," Darcy breathed, leaning back in her chair.

"We don't know much of anything about them," I added, twisting my lips. "But maybe it's time we found out... Who owns the palace now?"

"Well..." Sofia looked between the two of us. "I'm assuming *you* do."

I snorted a laugh and Darcy blew out a breath as she picked the card up. "I keep forgetting we're actually princesses," she said, shaking her head.

I looked at her and a smile hooked up the corner of my mouth. "Yeah, we're motherfucking princesses and we own a goddamn palace. Maybe it's time we went and visited it?"

"Do you really think we can?" Darcy asked, her eyes lighting with excitement for a moment at the idea. "Maybe some of our parents' stuff is still there..."

I swallowed thickly at that idea, a frown pinching my features. I hadn't really considered that. I'd been thinking more about vaults of gold than something that might link us to the people who brought us into this world. Suddenly my chest felt a little too tight at the idea of going there and I had to fight against the idea of backing out of the plan before we'd even made one.

"Perhaps we should just focus on getting through The Reckoning this week first?" I said, hoping it wasn't obvious that the idea of finding out more about our parents made me uncomfortable.

Darcy gave me a look that said she'd seen right through me and I offered a tiny shrug in response. "I guess you're probably right," she agreed but I didn't miss the hint of disappointment in her tone. "But maybe afterwards we can ask Nova about us taking a visit to the palace?"

"Sure," I agreed with a nod. I'd just have to suck it up and go. It wasn't like it mattered anyway. The King and Queen were just two dead people I'd never known. Even if all of their stuff still filled the palace it wouldn't change that fact.

The rest of the class passed quickly, though Diego stayed in a mood with me after he returned from his bathroom break. I half considered apologising to him then realised that I might have been being a bitch - but he was too so I was pretty sure we were even. No doubt he'd get over it soon enough.

We left the class without Washer coming over to me at all and I couldn't help but let some of my irritation with Caleb go in response. He might have been a damn underwear thief but if he'd actually managed to scare Washer away from me then I'd happily pay the price in panties.

That said, our next class was Fire Elemental and I had no intention of spending it without my underwear.

We said goodbye to Diego and I forced Darcy and Sofia to hurry down the path to Fire Territory, explaining my problem to them on the way. When they stopped laughing, they started running with me and we got to the Fire Arena early to wait with the full intention to retrieve my panties from Caleb before it started.

I waited outside for him to arrive with a very amused Darcy by my side. She kept trying not to laugh and I tried to look annoyed at her.

"Here comes the panty thief now," she said in an undertone as Caleb appeared on the path ahead.

"I shouldn't have told you," I muttered, rolling my eyes as she snorted a laugh.

"Do you think he'll give them back?" she asked.

"I'm going to make him," I said confidently, striding forward to meet Caleb who broke a smile as he spotted me.

"You have something of mine," I accused, folding my arms as I blocked his path.

"Really?" he asked, feigning surprise. "What's that then?"

I glanced around at the other students who were filing past us into the locker rooms and fixed him with a death stare.

"You know what."

"Remind me," Caleb challenged, stepping a little closer.

At that moment, Darius appeared. He strolled straight towards us and heat rose in my cheeks as his gaze landed on me. I felt ridiculously awkward around him after last night and I had zero intention of talking to him now.

"Forget it," I said quickly, turning away from Caleb before Darius made it to us.

"You can have them back if you promise to spend tonight at Terra House with me," Caleb called.

I turned back to him with a scowl. "No," I said flatly, flipping him off for good measure. I turned away before he could say anything else and headed into the locker rooms with Darcy.

"Oh my god, you should have seen his face when you turned your back on him," she said on a laugh. "I think you just really pissed him off."

"Whatever. He's shouting about us hooking up in front of the whole damn school. I'm not his girlfriend and it's no one else's business what we get up to. Plus he stole my underwear so..." I shrugged, not wanting to admit that Darius was actually the one who'd rattled me.

"Well you always knew he'd leave you for a Pegasus in the end anyway. He's got the horn for the horn," she said and I smirked in response. That joke would never get old.

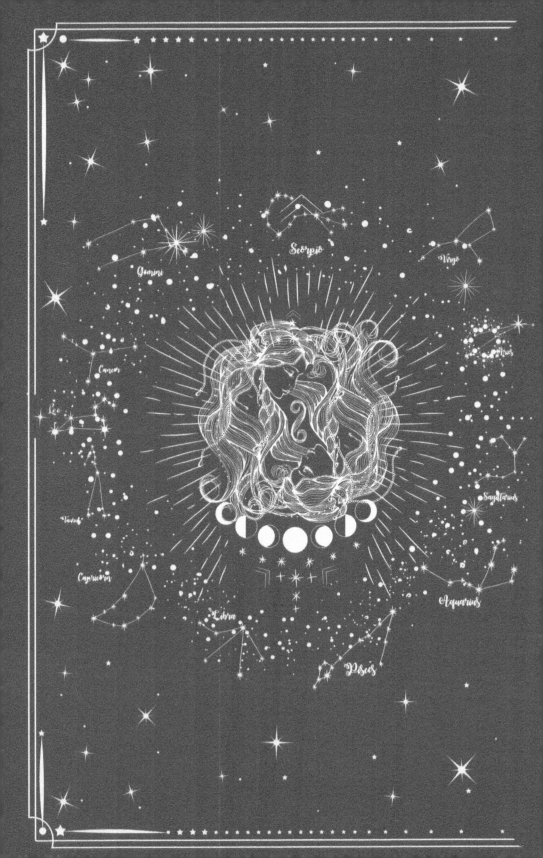

DARCY

CHAPTER THIRTEEN

I ducked into Pluto Offices out of the pouring rain after my final class of the day, pushing back my hood as water dripped off my coat to the shiny floor. The storm had rolled in from the sea and was picking up strength with every passing hour, but a package had arrived for me that I simply couldn't wait to get my hands on.

I headed into the postal area where the tall machines were humming and flashing, stretching high up above me right to the ceiling. I tapped in the code on my Atlas and the units shifted around until the one containing my package stopped before me and I snatched it out.

"A la mierda esta lluvia," Diego's voice caught my attention and I turned to find him hurrying into the atrium dripping wet with a scowl on his face. "Oh hey chica, this rain sucks huh?" he said, his eyes brightening as he spotted me.

He hurried to my side, pushing his hand into his dark curls to stop them dripping onto his cheeks. "I hate the rain. Where I grew up it never rained."

"I quite like it," I said with a shrug. "Something about a storm feels kind of... exciting."

"You're crazy," he laughed, glancing at my package. "What did you get?" he asked, heading toward the machines and taking his Atlas from his backpack.

"It's a secret," I said mischievously, tucking the box firmly into my bag.

"I like secrets," he urged, tapping in the code to retrieve his own package. He took the small box from the unit as it arrived and ripped it open.

"What did *you* get?" I asked and he pulled out a small tube with the words *Minotaur Strength Glue* printed on the side of it. "What's that for?"

"Mi abuela's trinket box," he said with a dark frown. "I'm going to try and glue it back together, but that bastardo professor broke it pretty good."

"Maybe there's a spell for fixing things. Have you asked Sofia?" I suggested gently, my heart pinching at the memory of Orion doing that to Diego. He really could be a total asshole sometimes.

"No..." Diego pocketed the glue then stepped toward me. "So come on, chica, I showed you mine, let's see yours." He lunged forward playfully and I laughed, dancing away as I held my satchel behind my back.

"No! It's a surprise," I laughed as he wrapped his arms around me, trying to reach my bag. My laughter echoed off of the ceiling and I stumbled back into the counter as he tugged at the strap.

"Come on! Let me see your package, Darcy," Diego insisted, grinning in my face as he stuck his hand into my bag.

"*Diego*," I warned, but not with actual annoyance. If he really wanted to see it, it didn't matter that much.

As his hand closed around the box, he was suddenly torn away from me and thrown forcefully onto the hard floor. The box went skittering away across the lobby and shock replaced my amusement as I found Orion standing beyond him.

"What the hell?" I demanded, hurrying forward to help Diego to his feet. He rubbed his head, scowling at Orion with a dark fury in his eyes.

Orion looked slightly confused by his own actions, backing up and scooping my package from the floor - which was thankfully still in its delivery box so he couldn't see what it was. I moved forward to take it from him, but Diego caught hold of my hand, pulling me back protectively. Orion eyed the interaction with a burning intensity in his gaze, his muscles twitching as if he was about to lunge at my friend again.

"He's not going to hurt me." I looked to Diego in surprise but he didn't seem convinced.

"Ten points from Aer," Orion growled, tossing the package at my feet.

"What for?" Diego balked. "We didn't do anything wrong."

Orion glared at him like he was trying to melt him with his stare. "Are you back-chatting me, Polaris?" he snarled.

I shook my hand free of Diego's, bending down and picking up my package. My face felt overly hot as I tucked it into my bag and stood upright, pursing my lips at him. Orion stalked away, heading to a long row of mailboxes which were evidently for the professors. He tugged one open marked *Orion, 3 Asteroid Place*, and grabbed a fistful of letters from inside.

"Come on," Diego muttered. "Let's leave the sanguijuela to himself."

We nearly made it to the door before Orion spoke in a deadly voice. "What did you call me?"

Diego stiffened, glancing over his shoulder and shifting closer to me.

Oh shit.

I turned around, finding Orion right behind us, his letters crumpling in his hand.

"I called you a bloodsucker," Diego said, sounding slightly less confident than before. "It's not an insult, just a fact."

Orion bared his fangs and I moved to put myself between them. "Professor," I said gently. "He didn't mean anything by it, did you Diego?"

Diego was too stubborn for his own good. His lips twitched but he couldn't get the words out that would clearly have been a lie. I could see how much he hated Orion and I couldn't exactly blame him after what he'd done to his grandmother's trinket box right before reading his journal aloud.

Orion rolled his shoulders, releasing a slow breath. He stepped around me, leaning in close to Diego's ear and he visibly trembled, shrinking beneath him.

"Dear diary," Orion taunted. "Today I was almost murdered by my asshole Cardinal Magic professor. I won't backchat him ever again because the next time I do I think I'll end up in a body bag for real." He moved to step away then paused, leaning close once more with a calculating grin. "P.S. I have a major crush on Darcy Vega, but she doesn't seem to realise it. I wonder what she'll say when she finds out." He strolled out of the door into the storm and I stared after him in utter shock.

"Darcy, I-I don't," Diego spluttered, shaking his head.

"I know," I said quickly, sure Orion was wrong about that. "He's just being an asshole. You're into Sofia, right?"

"Si," he agreed with a heavy sigh. "But now she likes Tyler Corbin." He hung his head and I laid my hand on his back with a guilty frown. Diego was having a seriously hard time these last couple of days and I really wanted to do something to cheer him up. An idea sprang to mind and a wicked grin pulled at my mouth. "I know what we should do..."

"What?"

I took out my Atlas, typing a group message to Tory and Sofia, telling them to meet us at Jupiter Hall. "Come on," I said brightly. "Let's go get your hat back."

"But Orion," he breathed, his eyes widening with fear.

"He didn't head that way," I said. "Besides, he was the one who challenged you to get it."

"I guess so," he said, nodding as a little more courage entered his eyes. "Let's hurry up then."

I pulled my hood over my head and Diego zipped his coat up to his chin, following me into the rain. Lightning flashed above and my heart pumped harder as we started running through the downpour. I pushed the air out around us both, making a shield, but the rain kept slipping through every time I lost concentration. I gave up as we arrived at Jupiter Hall, hurrying inside and finding Tory and Sofia there already. Beyond them were Geraldine and Angelica, looking excited as lightning illuminated us all, flashing through the windows.

"Oh hi guys," I said to Geraldine and her friend, surprised at finding extra recruits.

"What are you doing here?" Diego asked like he was disappointed to see everyone gathered there. I so did not understand him sometimes. Maybe he was still pissed at Tory and still bitter about Sofia going out with Tyler. But they *were* his friends. I guess he hadn't realised I'd invited them.

Geraldine answered before the others could."We are here to assist you on your quest, young Diego. A friend from the stars is a dear friend of ours." She puffed up her chest and Angelica raised her chin in solidarity.

"As a loyal member of the Almighty Sovereign Society, I have pledged to help the true queens and any ally who follows them diligently," Angelica said proudly, bowing low to Tory and I.

"Riiight, well let's go before Professor Psycho shows up," Tory said with a grin, taking a couple of hairpins from her pocket. This was clearly her way of apologising to Diego and his expression softened at the sight.

We hurried up the marble stairway toward the Cardinal Magic classroom, our footsteps clapping loudly around us.

"Jam doughnuts!" Geraldine hissed. "I better cast a silencing bubble around us, we sound like a herd of Pegasuses wearing tap shoes." She opened her palm and the magic pressed out around our group. We reached the door and Tory knelt down while Sofia cast the spell that would divert attention away from us. It wouldn't hold if a teacher got too close and sensed it, but it would definitely help.

"Dammit, it's not working," Tory sighed. "I think there's magic on the lock."

"Figures. Orion's a total security freak," I said. "I had to blast his desk apart to get to the stardust that time."

"If we damage the door, he'll know it was us," Diego said, frantically pulling at his hair.

"No he won't." Angelica stepped forward. "I'm great at fixing spells. I can definitely do it."

Diego looked at her with a hopeful smile. "Okay, chica, if you're sure. Maybe you could help me with mi abuela's broken trinket box sometime too?"

"Love to!" Angelica beamed.

Geraldine barged us all aside, pulling Tory out of the way and planting her feet in a wide stance. She raised her hands and yelled, "No one can hold back the power of a Grus! We are the guardians of the royal bloodline!" Water blasted from her hands in a massive deluge, taking the entire door off its hinges and sending it crashing across the room.

We all sucked in air as several desks went flying under the onslaught.

"Holy blue tits," Geraldine breathed. "I don't know my own strength sometimes. Onward friends!" She ran into the room and I giggled, hurrying along with everyone as we headed toward Orion's desk.

The watermelon was waiting for us and Sofia reached out to grab it but quickly snatched her hand back like she'd been electrocuted.

"He's put some sort of protection spell on it," she gasped.

I moved closer then looked to Tory. "Fire?" I suggested, holding out my hand and she took it, grinning as our power merged immediately, flowing through us instinctively.

We raised our free hands and fire burst from our fingers, blending together and surrounding the shield encasing the watermelon. We blasted it until it was clear it wasn't going to work then dropped our hands.

"Crap," I sighed, glancing back at the doorway as Angelica hurried around fixing chairs and siphoning away the water drenching the floor.

We gathered closer to the desk, frowning as we tried to figure out how to get the hat.

"Maybe it needs to be me?" Diego suggested, stepping to the front of the group. He raised his palm, casting a gust of air at the shield but still nothing happened.

"It's almost curfew," Sofia said anxiously. "We need to hurry."

"Tiny Tim in a handbag, there's something written here," Geraldine said excitedly, pointing at the back of the watermelon. We all shuffled around and I read the message written in ink across the back of it

Fae bleed for what they want.
Prove you're Fae, Polaris.

He pursed his lips as he realised what he had to do and I looked to him with a frown. "You don't have to-"

He bit into his hand and I winced as he sank his teeth in so deep he drew blood.

That is so not the way I would have chosen to do it.

"Holy shit, Diego!" Tory cheered as Diego let the blood drip over the shield. It fizzled out of existence and he snatched his hat from the watermelon, pulling it onto his head.

"You are a true Fae, Diego Polaris," Geraldine said with tears in her eyes and Angelica hurried over to pat his back.

Thanks to our Dragon friend, the classroom was all clean and there was no sign we'd been here aside from the missing hat. Geraldine strode over to pick up the door, carrying it back into place as we all hurried out into the hallway. Angelica stepped forward to help, fixing it back onto its hinges and removing any signs of a break in.

"Thanks amigas," Diego said with the biggest smile.

"Any time," I said, nudging him as we jogged back to the atrium and out into the raging storm. As curfew closed in, we all said our goodbyes and I headed back to Aer Tower with Diego. He was practically skipping along beside me as we went. I'd never seen him so happy.

When we were in the dry stairwell of the tower, my heart started thrumming harder for an entirely different reason and I quickened my pace upstairs. We turned into the eleventh floor and I said goodnight to Diego before hurrying into my room and stripping off my wet coat followed by my uniform. I headed into my bathroom in nothing but my underwear with my package firmly in my grip.

It was time for a new me. A girl who was Fae. A girl who was royal. And a girl who wasn't afraid to trust anymore.

Fae hair dye was incredible. My hair shimmered like stars when it caught the light and was as deep blue as a twilight sky. I'd coloured it all over, every last hair. And as I ran my fingertips through my soft locks, my heart began to beat harder again.

Blue means you like me.

I did like him. And I boldly, proudly wanted him to know it. But that wasn't the only reason I'd done this. It felt right. Like I was claiming that deep wound inside myself and healing it at long last. It wasn't an injury anymore, it was a battle scar. And I was owning it like a warrior princess.

I took a steadying breath as thunder cracked overhead and goosebumps fled across my flesh. The urge to show Orion what I'd done was consuming me. My body was alive with need tonight and I wondered if that had something to do with the dawning Lunar Eclipse or if it was all me.

I headed back into my room, pulling on my strappy white pyjama top and shorts for bed and dropping down onto my mattress. I picked up my Atlas and lightning flashed beyond my window, igniting the room in a white glare for half a second.

I chewed on my lower lip, shifting my hips as this need grew wilder and wilder.

What the hell is in the air tonight?

I tapped on my daily horoscope to reread it, wondering if I could find any answers between the lines.

Good morning Gemini.
The stars have spoken about your day!
It's time for an important decision to be made, and with that decision will come a big change. This is a time of growth so embrace the side of yourself which has started to bloom and you will soon reap the rewards.
Your stars are in perfect harmony with a Libra today and now would be a good time to address any issues between the two of you. It will be almost impossible not to enjoy this day if you follow your intuition.

I placed my Atlas down on my bare thigh, mulling over that last line. *Follow your intuition.*

I rose to my feet, moving to the window and a shudder rolled down my spine. The rain pattered against the glass in thick wet drops and every time the lightning flashed, all of them lit up like tiny snow globes.

Water magic rose to the edges of my skin and some deep part of me wanted to be out there in the tempestuous world, throwing my magic into the sky to see if I could equal its power.

A light glowed far down on the path below and I spotted a teacher patrolling within a shield, an orb of blue light hovering above them. I spotted another light far out in The Wailing Wood, their shield lit up in purple. Everyone was still on high alert after the Nymph attack and the idea of those creatures still lurking nearby made my blood chill.

I moved back to my bed, fishing up my Atlas and tapping out a message to Orion, adrenaline crashing through me in waves.

Darcy:

What are you doing..?

I waited for a reply and he gave me one in the form of a photo which made my heart nearly give up on life.

He was propped up in bed with a Numerology book in one hand, shirtless and giving me that sideways smile that made me want to just...*gah*. A message swiftly followed.

Lance:

Reading...

I'm sure I don't need to remind you to delete that picture. What are you doing?

(photographic answers are highly encouraged)

I grinned stupidly, sighing as I deleted his photo along with the last few messages he'd sent.

What am *I doing? I'd like to figure that out myself. Because it feels like playing with fire and I'm one slip away from getting burned.*

For some unknown reason I trusted Orion. It didn't make sense to me, but it seemed the stars were firmly on board with that idea today too.

Darcy:

You don't deserve a photo because you were rude to my friend earlier.

Lance:

Polaris was asking for trouble. Plus he had his hands all over you so you can blame the Vampire Code. I have to protect my Source.

P.S.

What am I gonna have to do to earn this picture?

A flush of heat took over my body as I realised this was *so* not about the Vampire Code. Diego hadn't been anything of a threat to me.

Darcy:

You can have a picture if you tell me the real reason you attacked Diego.

I hit send, laughing as I hugged a pillow to my chest. *Why is this so exciting?*

Lance:

Fine.

Seeing another guy's hands on you makes me want to rip out their eyes so they never get to look at you again.

Darcy:

That is so dark.

I started laughing, knowing I probably shouldn't. Diego definitely hadn't deserved to be shoved to the floor, but I couldn't deny how good it felt knowing Orion was possessive over me like that.

Lance:

It's nature, baby ;)

Where's my photo?

I hesitated then whipped the pillowcase off and wrapped my hair up in it. I took a selfie, poking out my tongue and grinning as I sent it. He replied almost instantly.

Lance:

Shit, how did you know about my pillowcase fetish?

I reined in my laughter, tapping out my next message.

Darcy:

I made a decision about my hair.
You're not allowed to see it.

Lance:

Hang on, why am I not allowed?
Is it green or blue?
Or am I way off base?
Please tell me you haven't got a mohawk like Max Rigel. Although, I'd probably still want you just as much. I certainly did when that fuckwit Capella took your hair.

My breathing grew unsteady and the smile on my face was starting to hurt. It felt so natural when we were messaging each other like this. As if he was just a guy I liked who happened to like me back.

It made me think about my first boyfriend and how I'd been naive to believe what we'd had had been anything close to love. I was nowhere near falling in love with Orion, but I already felt a thousand times more chemistry with him than I ever had with my ex. Orion made me want to jump in the deep end of this desire head first without question. And though I was completely terrified of that, it also made me feel incredibly alive.

My fingers hovered over the keys and all I could think about was him lying in bed with that demigod body going to waste. *He really needs a little company for all of those muscles...it would be a travesty for them to be alone tonight.*

Oh holy shit am I really considering this?

He might turn me away.

But he also might not.

Ohmagod I know where he lives.

I recalled the mailbox he'd gotten his letters from and I just knew, in the depths of my soul that that wasn't a coincidence. It was exactly like my horoscope had said. The stars *were* aligning for us tonight and I was sure they'd stay on my side at least a little while longer.

I jumped out of bed, pushing my feet into my sneakers and tugging on my raincoat. My legs were bare but screw it.

I'm not going to think tonight, I'm just going to do. Regrets belong to tomorrow.

I crept out of the door and complete silence met my ears. With the teachers moving around campus in those lit-up shields I'd be able to spot them a mile off.

I jogged downstairs, not letting myself back out on this for one second.

As I hurried across the ground floor, I paused at the door, tugging it open a crack and peering out into the howling night.

Raindrops blew over me and I shivered as thunder boomed overhead, something about the rumbling noise urging me on. There was no sign of any professors close by so I slipped outside, pulling the door shut behind me.

I clung to the edge of the tower, circling around it toward The Wailing Wood. It was the quickest route to Asteroid Place even though it slightly terrified me to go in the forest when it was this dark.

By the time I thought to cast an air shield I was already soaked but I was running on adrenaline anyway so I could hardly feel the cold as I raced down the path into the trees. My sneakers squelched in the mud, splashing it up my legs as I ran on and I started to wonder if I was losing the plot. But if this was what going crazy felt like, I was more than happy to sacrifice my mind.

I ran on, my hair drenched and dripping, seeming to make the dye even brighter as if the rain was bringing it to life. *This dye is awesome!*

I ran with fear and anticipation crashing together in my heart, burrowing in deep.

This is insane - what the hell is he gonna think?

I finally slowed to a halt in front of the tall fence surrounding Asteroid Place. Students were strictly not allowed here, but I'd known that when I'd left. And there was no backing out now.

Through the raging wind and beating rain, it seemed like I was reborn as a new, powerful girl who ruled her own life. And she was damn well going to get over this fence.

I gazed up at the top and forced air into my palms. I launched myself skyward, stifling a yell as I propelled myself too high and crashed down toward the concrete path on the other side. I somehow landed on my feet which was a damn miracle and I smiled as the rain washed the mud from my shoes.

With a nervous exhale, I eyed the rows of chalets stretching away to my right and the alleys parting each one. In front of them was an enormous pool which was rippling under the downpour.

The windows I could see were shielded by curtains or blinds but fear still clutched my heart as I hurried toward the alley between the third and fourth house.

A porch light on number four placed a glaring target on my back and I could barely draw in air as I stepped in front of the door to number three.

Don't back out now.

You've come this far.

I raised a hand, standing entirely still as icy water trickled under my coat and sent goosebumps rushing across my neck. I knew if I hesitated a second longer I'd turn back, run away and pretend I'd never come here. But I was Fae.

And I was going to embrace this reckless side of me because it felt like pure ecstasy.

Do it, Darcy Vega.

I lifted my hand and tapped on the door, afraid of being too loud in case I disturbed any of the other teachers. With Orion's Vampire hearing, he wouldn't miss it.

A few agonising seconds passed where my stomach scrunched up into a tight ball and my whole body began to shake.

The door yanked open and Orion stood there bare chested in nothing but black sweatpants, looking ready to berate the person knocking on his door late at night.

He stared at me with his mouth parted, his throat bobbing as he processed me standing on his doorstep with soaked blue hair and raindrops clinging to my cheeks.

"Blue," I answered his ongoing question on a breath that rose before me in a cloud of vapour, knowing that it meant far more than that. That I'd just told him I wanted him. And in turn, agreed to this dangerous affair.

He said nothing as the rain continued to beat down on me and fear made a passage through my chest, clasping my heart with sharp claws. "I just...came to tell you that."

Oh shit he's gonna turn me away. I'm gonna have detention for a full year.

I took a step back and he finally moved, catching my hand and dragging me inside. He pushed the door closed, boxing me in with his arms and I couldn't breathe as he remained there, one hand planted on the door, the scent of cinnamon caressing my senses.

"I know this is crazy," I whispered, aware of how near the next chalet was.

Water dripped steadily from my hair and Orion reached out, brushing his fingers through it and casting heated air which dried it out in seconds, leaving it soft and shining around my shoulders. The air continued to travel down my body and my skin tingled with sensitivity as every inch of me dried out.

I eyed his athletic chest, craving to move closer and take what I needed. But he still didn't speak and I was starting to worry that I shouldn't have come here.

"Come in then." He turned away, moving into the kitchenette to my right.

Okay...

"Drink?" he called.

"Um, just water." I took my coat off, hanging it on the back of the door then kicked off my shoes. I stepped onto the soft carpet barefooted and took in the large lounge ahead of me. Everything was cream and grey, neat and tidy. I hovered near the huge L-shape couch, unsure what to do with myself. I'd only really planned up to knocking on that door, but now I was here this was all very *real*.

I brushed my fingers over the throw on the back of the couch, my eyes flitting to the open door across the room which gave me a glimpse of a large bed. My mouth became overly dry and I turned away sharply, catching sight of Orion leaning against the counter in the kitchen, his muscular arms firm with tension.

Shit, maybe I've made a serious mistake. I don't wanna put him in a compromising position.

I cleared my throat and the noise sounded like a gunshot.

I took a step toward the exit, my heart all knotted up in my chest.

I'm never going to live this down.

"Actually... I think I'd better go."

Before I could take another step, Orion shot in front of me in a blur, crowding me in against the couch. He had two tumblers of water in his hand and held one out for me.

"No," he demanded. "Stay."

I nodded, my throat tight as I took the glass from him and my legs brushed against his. I lifted the glass to my lips, unable to drag my eyes from his as I swallowed down the water in two gulps and he did the same.

When I was finished, he took my glass, reaching past me, his shoulder grazing mine as he leaned down and placed them on a table at the end of the couch.

"You're not drinking?" I breathed.

"No." He inched closer, resting his hands on the couch either side of me.

"And you haven't been drinking?" I raised a brow and a smile finally tugged at his mouth.

"No." His fingers intertwined with mine and he leaned in closer, his body so agonisingly close to pressing against me. Energy crackled between those tiny millimetres parting us, making it almost unbearable not to cross the distance. But I didn't want to make this decision for him. He hadn't said the words and I needed to hear them before we really did this.

"Are you angry that I came here?" I asked, trying to assess his mood as he kept that firm mask over his face.

He dipped his head to my shoulder, his lips brushing my skin and sending an arrow of heat right to the deepest regions of my stomach. "No."

"Is that all you can say now?" I asked, growing frustrated as he lifted his head and slid his hand onto my cheek, his fingers tangling in my hair.

"No," he said with a grin.

"Stop it," I begged, pushing against his chest, but he responded by pressing me back and closing the distance parting us. His heated skin moulded to mine and it felt *so* good.

"What would you like me to say?" he asked and I desperately tried to swallow down the lump in my throat.

"You haven't made any comment on me coming here," I said, growing hot all over and throwing a glance at the exit again. He caught my chin, tugging me back to look at him, sending my heart ricocheting through my chest.

"Give a guy a second. One minute I'm messaging you wishing I could have you right here and the next thing..." He leaned in, kissing the corner of my mouth and I melted. Or that was what it felt like anyway. As if there wasn't a single solid organ in my body. "Here you are."

Instead of giving me more of his mouth on mine, he painted a line of kisses up to my ear. He pushed his fingers into my hair, his touch like a drug bleeding into my veins and I shut my eyes to savour the high.

"I don't want to get you into trouble," I whispered, sliding my hands up his arms to rest lightly on his shoulders. It still felt like we were hovering on that line between doing this and not doing it. I could still walk away and I wouldn't put him at risk of losing his job and so much more. But this connection between us was undeniably powerful and I didn't think I could leave until he point blank refused me.

His hand wound around my waist, sliding under my top and pressing against my back, skin on skin. His teeth grazed my ear at the same moment and everything down south squeezed with need.

"*Orion*," I warned, determined to get my answer.

"Lance," he corrected. "And I know the risks." His hand trailed up my spine, driving my top up at the front too so even more of our skin united and made my thoughts hazy. "But do you?"

He shifted my hair over my shoulder, his lips making a more dangerous journey south. I tilted my head to one side with a breathy moan, his gentle torment more powerful than a hurricane.

"I do," I panted, desperate for him to put me out of my misery as I came apart under his wandering mouth.

He hooked his finger under the left strap on my shoulder then paused, lifting his head to look at me with a concerned frown. "If we do this, we can't undo it."

I slid my hand around the back of his neck, drawing him down to meet my lips. I gave him my answer with my kiss. I needed this like the grass needed rain. Without it, I'd wither and die.

He deepened our kiss, his tongue hesitantly stroking mine and the barriers suddenly came crashing down between us. Our magic merged at every point of contact and his tongue sank deeper into my mouth, a desperate groan escaping him. My legs trembled as he hoisted me up to sit on the back of the couch and he stepped between my thighs, his fingertips skating up to the edges of my shorts. His touch was as possessive as his magic swimming in my blood. He was claiming me and I claimed him right back.

"If you want me to stop, tell me to stop," he said breathlessly and I wrapped my legs around his waist.

"Okay, don't stop," I exhaled and a heady laugh fell from my lungs as he drew me flush against him, feeding on my desire.

"I want you to the point of pain, Blue."

His old nickname for me made a smile pull at my lips. I slid my hands over his shoulders, digging my nails in as that frustrated ache spilled into every corner of my body.

"Then have me," I commanded.

He scooped me into his arms, his hands on the backs of my thighs as he carried me into his bedroom and kicked the door shut, the sudden loudness making my heart jolt. He turned and pressed me against it, his mouth meeting mine so fast it took my brain a second to catch up.

The forceful magnet in my chest finally reunited with its other half and sent a rocket of pure pleasure down my spine.

I need him this close. I can't get enough of it.

His hands grew even hotter against the backs of my legs and desire blossomed at the base of my spine, growing roots and spreading deep into my bones. I knew we were picking up right where we left off in that pool. Like this all-consuming yearning had been ready and waiting to devour us as soon as we got close enough to fall prey to it again.

He pinned me more firmly with his hips and the hard press of his arousal made me moan, my hips automatically flexing to grind myself against him.

"Shit, Blue," he growled before kissing me harder.

I wanted to shed every layer I wore and every rule that kept us apart all at once. We were breaking the rules together, tearing them to pieces with our bare hands, every touch rebellious, every kiss defiant.

He drew back and planted me on my feet, making me ache for him all over again. He pushed his hand into my hair, admiring the way it glittered under the low light of his bedside lamp. When he released it, he moved his hand in a gesture I was coming to recognise as the silencing spell so no one could hear us.

My heart was firmly stuffed in my throat as he stepped back just enough for me to look at him and my gaze dropped to his sculpted chest then the bronzed ovals of his abs. I felt his eyes sliding over me too and he reached forward to toy with the drawstring on my shorts, tugging me closer by it with a hungry noise.

"You can still say no," he reminded me and I grinned, shaking my head at him.

He gave me a boyish smile which undid me and I planted my hand on his chest, pushing him back toward the bed, barely casting a glance around the rest of his room. There was only one thing in it that mattered right then.

He dropped onto the edge of the mattress and I pressed down on his shoulders as I knelt over him. He drew me down more firmly and I gasped as I felt every inch of him between my legs.

He clutched the back of my neck, drawing me into another slow kiss that resounded through the shell of my flesh.

"I hope you brought your peach," Lance said and a laugh tumbled from my throat as I leaned away.

"You're such an asshole," I thumped his shoulder and he chuckled, his hands sliding beneath the waistband at the back of my shorts.

"I know." He smirked and I moved to kiss him again but he leaned back to escape me, his eyes igniting with some thought.

He stood up suddenly, dropping me onto the bed. "Lie that way." He pointed and I frowned at him as I shifted diagonally across the bed.

"Why?" I asked with an amused laugh.

He grinned in answer and my eyes drifted down to trace his huge shoulders, the firmness of his chest and stomach, the red Leo tattoo on the crook of his right arm. My toes curled against the sheets and I squirmed beneath him as he surveyed me with a carnal look that suggested he was about to devour me.

He reached down, taking hold of my right foot and wrapping his large hand around my ankle. I wriggled like mad as he caressed the sensitive skin there, laughter rising in my throat.

"Ticklish, Blue?" he taunted, brushing his fingers over my heel and I yelped, my back arching as I tried to pull free of him.

He laughed, trailing his hand up the back of my calf and I sighed in relief as he left my foot alone. His hand sailed higher and he crawled up the bed, hovering above me and making my laughter die away as I met the intensity of his eyes. His knees pressed against the insides of my thighs and I could see that question in his gaze again.

"Don't stop," I answered it firmly, my heart hammering so loud he could certainly hear it. "I want this."

His eyes glittered at my words and he wet his mouth. "Show me how much," he growled and electricity coursed up my spine.

I steeled myself, taking his hand and drawing it to my lips, pressing a kiss to his knuckles. With heat invading my cheeks, I guided his palm down to my throat, over the swell of my breasts and stomach, inhaling deeply as I led him beneath my waistband right to where I wanted him most.

He swore as he felt me and I tugged my own hand free, reaching out to curl it around his neck. His mouth crashed against mine as his thumb circled against the most sensitive place between my thighs and pure pleasure radiated through me.

"Stay still," he commanded thickly as he continued his delicious torture.

I nodded then a tingling warmth spread out beneath the hot press of his hand, driving through me in a blaze. I gasped as the magic swept into me and his eyes locked with mine as I realised he must have done the spell he'd been teaching us in class.

Yes.

I couldn't wait any longer so I dragged him down against me and he gave in to my demand, laying his weight on me and pulling his hand free from my shorts. I tugged my top over my head and he groaned in delight, palming my breast and rolling his tongue over my hardened nipple.

His thumb skated over my other breast and I absorbed his touch like a stone dropped in a heated pool, the ripples of ecstasy chasing each other through to my core.

I lifted my legs either side of him, my hand riding the flex of his shoulder blades as his mouth descended to my bare stomach. His kisses were roaring hot, each one igniting a flame on my skin and leaving it there to burn forever as he moved lower and lower. His fingers hooked into my shorts and dragged them down my legs, his hesitation entirely gone as he fully committed to this decision.

We're actually going to do this.

The heated pad of his tongue slid over me and I cried out, bucking up to receive every ounce of pleasure he had to give. He wrapped his tongue around me like he'd done it a thousand times before, knowing exactly how to push me forward and draw me back. He had total control and it was driving me to madness as he continually held me right on the knife's edge of ecstasy while I craved to be sliced apart.

"*Lance*," I begged, unable to get any more words out than that.

He moved away and I shut my eyes, rolling my neck as he left me in complete despair. I was gifted something even better than his mouth as he shifted between my legs and possessed me with one powerful thrust of his hips.

I reared up, my nails clawing into his back as I adjusted to the fullness of him inside me. My teeth grazed his shoulder and he fisted his hand in my hair, tugging to make me look at him.

God if he doesn't move I'm gonna go mad.

His eyes blazed with the might of a supernova and I wrapped my legs around him, my nails still digging into his back.

"For god's sake," I gasped. "Move."

He laughed, his nose brushing mine. "Just checking."

"Stop checking," I panted, rocking my hips and he finally gave me what I wanted, drawing his hips back before taking me once more. I writhed beneath him, urging him on with hungry kisses. He drove into me again and I clung to his powerful shoulders, his mouth meeting mine as he rolled his hips.

Pressure quickly began to build inside me like it had been waiting for this moment for a long time, the type only his body could release.

I was thankful for the sound bubble protecting as I cried out louder and louder.

He hooked his hand around the back of my left thigh, slowing his pace and luring me closer to climax with the teasing movements of his hips. He shuddered as he struggled to hold himself back and the sight of this man falling to ruin because of me made my head spin.

"I'm gonna lose my mind over you," he gasped, burying himself inside me and everything became too hot. I was panting then falling, lost to nothing in the sweetest oblivion I'd ever known. I felt him follow me into it, his hands clawing the sheets either side of me, his body weighing me down and his hips firmly locked against mine.

Dizziness washed through me as the tide of pleasure pushed deeper then withdrew from me entirely, leaving me exhausted and happy, so damn happy.

His thumb brushed my lower lip and my eyes fluttered open. I fell into the deep well of darkness awaiting me in his gaze. I'd never noticed before but his eyes weren't quite black after all, they were deepest admiral blue, holding a galaxy of light in them.

Orion lifted a hand to my mouth, releasing a gentle flutter of air against my lips. I felt it moving all the way deep into my lungs and suddenly I wasn't breathless anymore. He rolled off of me and I stared up at the ceiling, resting a hand on my burning hot stomach. The longer I lay there, the more a knot of worry formed right beneath where my hand lay.

I've not even been here a term and I just screwed a teacher.

The silence grew thicker and I couldn't make myself look over at him, afraid of what I'd see when I did.

Panic?

Shame?

Regret?

What if he just got me out of his system and I have to spend the rest of my time at Zodiac trying to forget this ever happened?

Don't freak out. You're totally overthinking this.

His hand suddenly wound around mine and he reeled me toward him, making my fears flutter away on the wind.

"Talk to me, Blue," he urged and I leaned my weight on his chest as he curled his arm around me and held me close.

"Was this a mistake?" I whispered, hating the way he winced when I said it.

"Not to me," he said in an anxious tone. "Was it for you?"

"No," I said quickly, sliding my hand onto his cheek and grazing my fingers through his perfectly trimmed beard.

His hand trailed down to rest on my lower back and the tension in his body melted away. He slowly circled his fingers, raising goosebumps beneath them.

"If we're going to continue this, we have to be careful," he warned.

"I know." I kissed him gently and his hand slid into my hair to hold me there a moment longer.

"You can't tell anyone."

I nodded.

"Not even your sister," he impressed.

I sighed as I nodded again. I knew she would have taken this secret to the grave but I had no idea what this crazy thing between Orion and I even was yet. And if it stayed between just the two of us, I knew there was absolutely no chance of it getting out. So long as we didn't make any stupid decisions. *Like coming to the teacher's quarters with bright blue hair late at night.*

I groaned, hiding my face in his shoulder and soaking in the musk of his skin and the scent of cinnamon which was now branded on me too.

"If we ever get caught, I'll do everything in my power to ensure you don't get expelled," he said seriously, a deep crease forming on his brow.

I brushed my fingers across it as my heart beat a little quicker. "Let's plan never to get caught."

"Plans are the best way to make the stars laugh," Orion pointed out with a playful grin.

"Well let them laugh." I giggled and his eyes dropped to my mouth with a heady lust falling over his expression again.

"Stay," he breathed, tracking his finger down my arm.

"You know I can't," I sighed. "It's too risky."

He sighed, lifting his hips to tug out the duvet beneath us and drawing it around us like a cocoon. His Numerology book tumbled out from somewhere within it and I laughed.

He released a feral noise in his throat. "Five more minutes then I'll take you back," he offered and I gave in, unable to resist spending a little longer with him like this.

"You drive a hard bargain, Mr Orion." I dropped the 'professor' knowing he didn't like it when we were this close. Not that we'd been *this* close before.

He grinned darkly. "I can drive an even harder one if you want?"

"Very tempting, but I'm not sure five minutes is long enough for your *hard* bargain."

He laughed as I curled up against him, resting my head on his shoulder and drinking in the perfect peace between us.

The storm rattled the windows like it was threatening to get in. But nothing could touch us here. Not the rules which bound us, or the lines drawn in the sand between us where he stood with the Heirs and I stood with my sister. Here, we were nothing but two Fae who craved each other with a force that rivalled mother nature. And I could no longer resist the call of its power.

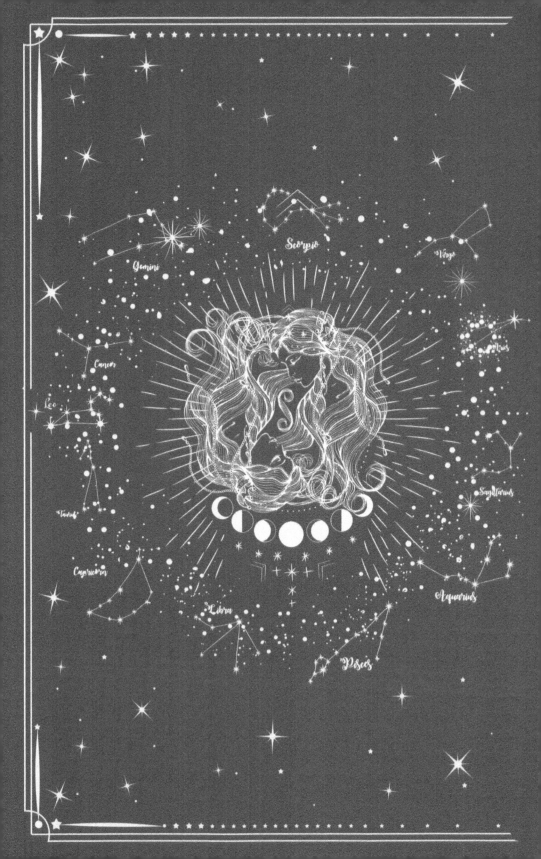

TORY

CHAPTER FOURTEEN

Darius:

I'll come to your room in half an hour. Be ready to ride.

Who the hell did he think he was to be sending me a message like that? I hadn't even heard from him all evening and I'd presumed he'd been joking about the whole race thing and now, at gone ten, he sent me a fucking summons?

I wrote out a rude as shit refusal then held my thumb suspended over the send button.

I should do it. I should tell him where to stick his middle of the night nonsense, especially the night before my Air Trial.

No doubt that wasn't accidental either. He was hoping that by keeping me up late he'd throw me off for the assessment. Little did he know that late nights were standard for me. Early mornings weren't my friend but with the trial at one o'clock, I'd have plenty of time to sleep in before it as lessons were cancelled. *If* I went with him. Which this message clearly said I wasn't.

I scowled at it then deleted it instead. He wasn't going to scare me off that easily. But I wouldn't play to his tune either. He wasn't coming to my goddamn room; I'd be going to his.

I got out of bed where I'd been listening to music while working on a Cardinal Magic assignment and headed for my closet, finding some ripped black jeans and a navy crop top. I threw them on then tossed my leather jacket over the top of it before lacing up the new boots I'd bought for the winter. They were strong and practical; the kind of thing I'd have worn on a job back in Chicago. And that was how I was seeing this little excursion. If I won this stupid race, I'd be claiming one of Darius's precious bikes as my prize. And I fully intended to win. So this job would actually end up with me owning one of those beautiful beasts instead of having to sell it on. *If* he kept his word about me keeping it. Which I actually got the feeling he would.

I decided to channel a little bit of 'Joey's bar Tory' tonight and went heavier on the eyeliner, added dark lipstick and messed up my hair on purpose so that the waves were untamed but wouldn't mind the addition of a motorcycle helmet.

I assessed myself in the mirror critically, scowling for effect. I wouldn't wanna mess with this bitch. I just hoped Darius would feel the same.

I stuffed my Atlas into my pocket and didn't bring anything else. That stupid dagger hummed with expectant energy as I brushed my fingers over it in my bedside locker but I forced away the desire to take it with me and headed out of the room.

I jogged up the stairs to the top floor and headed down the hallway towards Darius's room.

A door on my right opened before I got there and I cursed as Marguerite stepped out.

"Are you lost?" she demanded.

"I don't think so. I was looking for the hall of basic bitches and average assholes and it looks like I've found it now that I see you here." I smiled sweetly while quickly tossing up a wall of solid air around me and reenforcing my shields against Coercion.

"Tell me why you're here," Marguerite demanded, her voice laced with Coercion as I'd expected.

Her power crashed against my mental shield but I let the look of disdain slip from my face and widened my eyes so that she'd believe the next words from my lips were the truth she'd wanted.

"I'm here because I spend all of my spare time watching you and wanting to be like you but you're mean to me and won't be my best friend forever like I sooo wish you would. So I decided to become you instead. I'm starting off by creeping up here to seduce your precious Darius and screw him senseless just to make you cry. Then I'm going to dye my hair the cheapest, shittiest shade of red I can find and finally I'll become the head cheerleader because I fucking love being cheery. Mostly I'm going to do it because I'm obsessed with you but partly because I'm a psycho bitch who just wants to ruin your life." I smiled at her sweetly and flames sprung to life in her hands.

Marguerite shrieked as she launched them at me but they collided with the shield of air I was holding in place and ricocheted into the walls instead. "You cheap ass gutter whore!" she snarled at me, stalking forward with more fire in her hands. "You and your idiot sister think you can just stroll in here and act like you own the damn place when we all know that you grew up with nothing and no one. Two sets of parents died rather than be stuck with you and then you couldn't even find a mortal family to love you enough to keep you so they just bounced you from place to place like the unwanted trash you are. So why don't the two of you just realise that no one wants you *here* either?"

I took a step towards her, my eyes narrowing as rage built in my gut. All the things she'd said about the way we'd grown up was true and the low blows stung but there was only one thing in amongst her tirade that had really gotten a reaction from me.

"Did you just insult my sister?" I snarled.

Marguerite launched flames at me again and they crashed across the front of my shield in a blinding display of her power. I felt the air magic I was holding tremble with the force of withstanding her attack and I aimed more power into my defences while throwing out my other hand and directing a column of water straight into her chest.

Marguerite was knocked off of her feet and went crashing back into her bedroom which was flooded by the force of my magic.

I stalked after her and looked down at her on the floor. "You might want to remember this if you come at me again. Because I get the feeling you just threw the extent of your power at me but I barely even scratched the surface of *my* magic in retaliation."

Marguerite glared up at me from her puddle on the floor but she didn't respond. I swung her door shut between us and turned to find the rest of the hall's occupants standing in their doorways watching our exchange. More than a few of them gave me an appraising look and one guy even bowed his head a little before turning back into his room.

"I hope you meant the part about screwing me senseless." Darius stood leaning against his doorframe at the end of the hall and I mentally shrugged off the altercation with Marguerite as I stalked towards him.

I rolled my eyes at him. "In your dreams."

"Every night," he agreed and his tone was serious enough that it brought a blush to my cheeks.

I fought it off and came to a halt before him. "Are we going then?" I asked, not responding to his last comment.

"I told you I'd come and get you," he said mildly. He was dressed in jeans and a white t-shirt and looked ready to walk out of here to me so I didn't see what the issue was.

"Did you?" I asked innocently. "Your message was so long and detailed I must have missed that part."

Darius twitched a smile at that. "Well as you're here, we might as well head off." He ticked his head towards his room and walked inside, clearly expecting me to follow.

I stayed on my side of the threshold and folded my arms. "I can just wait here for you to grab your purse, dude. I don't really have any interest in visiting your bedroom again."

"We're leaving from here," he said, beckoning me impatiently and I reluctantly stepped inside.

Darius moved close and shut the door behind me, turning the key in the lock for good measure.

"What are you doing?" I asked, backing away from him as he turned to face me once more.

"We'll go via stardust. I spoke with Xavier and he confirmed that Mother and Father are away for a few nights in the city while he concentrates on the war effort with the rest of the Celestial Council so we don't have to worry about seeing them."

"Wait, what?" I asked. "You're taking me back to your fancy mansion in the middle of nowhere? I just thought we were going somewhere within walking distance-"

"What's wrong, Roxy? Are you afraid I'm trying to kidnap you?" Darius teased.

"I just think you could have been a bit more forthcoming with the information for this venture."

"Is this your way of trying to back out of the race so that you don't have to face losing to me?" he asked.

"*No.* But-"

Darius lifted his hand and threw a pinch of glimmering black stardust into my face before I could finish my sentence.

The world spun, stars blinked into existence all around me and my stomach plummeted right down past my feet. When everything came into focus again, my boots hit the gravel of the Acruxes' drive and I sucked in a lungful of crisp night air.

"What the hell?" I demanded while Darius smirked at me.

"You said you weren't backing out."

Thunder crashed loudly overhead and I flinched as I realised we were in the middle of a torrential downpour. Darius had cast a shield of heat around us and as the rain hit it, it sizzled out of existence without managing to reach us. My eyes widened slightly at his casual use of such impressive magic. If I tried to replicate that I knew it wouldn't work. But he'd gotten it into place the moment the stardust had dropped us off before even a drop of rain hit us and didn't seem to be paying it any attention at all.

"Are we seriously going to race in this weather?" I asked him, raising an eyebrow in disbelief.

"Are you afraid? You can always just forfeit the race and admit that I'm the winner. I'll still want my prize though," Darius warned me.

"You never actually told me what you want," I reminded him.

"I'll tell you when I win. Or when you forfeit..."

"Not going to happen," I said firmly. *Looks like I'm riding in this crazy ass storm then.*

"I need to head inside and see Xavier before we ride, are you hungry? I can just send Jenkins a message to wake him up and have something made for you? I need to let him know I'm taking a couple of the bikes out so that security don't come hounding after us anyway." He started tapping out a message on his Atlas and led the way along the drive towards the towering front door which led into the manor.

"I'm not really hungry." Why the hell was he offering to feed me? "Who's Jenkins?" I asked, mainly to make sure there wasn't any awkward silence.

"Our butler. I didn't give him advance notice because I didn't want to risk Father coming back when he tipped him off. With a bit of luck, he'll be far too busy to drop everything just to come and see me anyway. He's still pretty pissed about the whole Pitball fuck up. Luckily the Nymph attack dominated the news that day so the story didn't cause too much embarrassment and he hasn't felt the need to visit me about it. But if he knew I was home..." Darius trailed off when I failed to respond.

I didn't really know what he wanted me to say. Did I want Daddy Acrux to come back while we were here? Hell no. So I guessed I was glad he hadn't warned him about our arrival but other than that, I didn't think it was a good idea to start talking about his family with him. He didn't exactly seem super close to them but no one liked to hear insults aimed at their parents.

"Yeah that whole Pitball game was crazy," I said, agreeing with the only part of his rant that I could really weigh in on without causing an argument. "I was told you were the best academy team in Solaria but then you just lost like that..."

Darius's jaw ticked but he managed to respond in an even tone. "Well a few of us were off our game for various reasons," he muttered. "But that won't happen again."

Oh no! I wonder why? I forced myself not to laugh and responded with my eyes on my boots. "I'll look forward to watching you win the next match then."

"Maybe I should make you wear a shirt with my name printed on it instead of Geraldine's at the next match as my prize for beating you tonight," he suggested.

"That's what your want for a prize?" I scoffed. "While I'm racing for a shiny bike of my own?"

"What I'd like for a prize probably isn't on the table," he replied with a shrug.

I looked up at him, meaning to ask what he meant by that but the look he gave me in return made me unsure if I wanted to know.

Darius gave me a smile that made my gut clench and opened the door into the manor, holding it for me like he had goddamn manners.

I brushed past him and he followed so close behind that I could feel his breath on the back of my neck, sending a shiver down my spine.

I bit my lip as I looked around at the huge entrance hall and sweeping staircase in front of me. I felt like a pea in a bowl of peanuts. I didn't fit here. I'd grown up with less than nothing and he had so much money that he was actually too rich for me to have even attempted robbing in my old life.

Just as I thought I couldn't feel any more awkward, Jenkins appeared through a hidden door beneath the stairs like a goddamn phantom in a penguin suit.

"Can I take your coat, Miss Vega?" the butler asked formally, inclining his head to me.

"Oh, err... sure." I shrugged out of my leather jacket, handing it over as the butler's gaze swept over my exposed stomach with a frown so brief I might have imagined it. Either way I was guessing I wasn't the kind of girl the Acruxes would want their son bringing home. Although, as they were already planning on marrying him off to his cousin I guessed they didn't really have to worry about that.

"Where will you be entertaining the lady, Master Acrux?" Jenkins asked, bowing to Darius.

"We'll be in my rooms," he replied, hooking an arm around my waist as he drew me toward the stairs.

"I'll have refreshments sent up right away." Jenkins bowed again and withdrew, taking my jacket with him. I realised too late that my Atlas was in the pocket but he was gone. I guessed I didn't really need it anyway.

Darius stayed close to me as he urged me towards the stairs and his magic brushed up against mine like a question hanging between us.

I pushed it away as heat ran up the back of my neck and shifted out of his grip so he no longer held me in the cage of his arm.

"Why are you doing that?" I asked, shooting him a suspicious look.

"You let me in this morning," he reminded me in a low voice. "Why did you trust me so easily then and not now?"

I cleared my throat uncomfortably. "I didn't trust you then. I was half asleep and half drunk and for thirty seconds I forgot what a dick you are. You reminded me of the fact quickly enough though."

"But you still liked it. You still felt the rush when you let me in," he pressed and I couldn't really deny that that was true. Blending my magic with his was bordering on indecent; the rush I got when his power poured into me was heady and addictive. It lit up every inch of my flesh and awoke desires in me which I refused to admit to around him. Which was precisely why I wasn't going to be doing it again tonight.

"Seems like you're the one who liked it," I teased, following him down a long corridor without giving him the satisfaction of replying beyond that.

Darius let it drop but the smile playing around his lips said he didn't buy it.

Our footsteps filled the space around us as we walked on and on through the huge building and eventually I had to speak rather than let the silence build into anything more uncomfortable.

"What's it like growing up somewhere like this?" I asked, eyeing a huge portrait on the wall as we passed it. Daddy Acrux looked younger, fierce, sitting in a chair and glaring out at the viewer.

"When we were kids we spent a lot of time with nannies and private tutors, we mainly saw our parents for meals. It was pretty much the same as anyone's childhood I'd imagine; we stayed in our wing of the house and had anything we could ever want."

"Having anything you could ever want isn't pretty much the same as anyone's childhood," I muttered.

"I have no point of reference so I can't really say but I suppose you're right. We were happy enough anyway. While we were young."

"And then?" I asked because apparently you can't switch off being a nosey bitch even when the guy you're prodding at is a grumpy asshole who could flip on you at any moment.

"As we grew older we had to learn more about our responsibilities and I had to spend more and more time with my father learning what would be expected of me when I take his seat on the Celestial Council. So there was a lot less time for being a kid. What about you? What was the mortal world like to grow up in?" he asked, giving me a look that said he was actually interested.

"We didn't have much time for being kids either," I muttered, not really wanting to go into detail about the shit storm that was our childhood. Being bounced from place to place so often that our heads never stopped spinning. Promises from social workers that this couple or that couple were interested in adopting us and giving us a real home which never worked out. Christmases spent on extra chairs hastily added to the furthest end of the table where we could easily be cropped out of family photos...

Darius led the way up a curving staircase and I pointedly ignored the looks he kept shooting my way.

"Did you ever feel like you missed Solaria, without really knowing what you were missing?" he asked.

"How could we miss something we never even knew existed?"

"It's just that I've visited the mortal world and the whole time I was there I had this ache in my chest like deep down I knew I was in the wrong place. The lack of magic all around me was stifling and their cities were so big they made it almost impossible to see the stars at night..."

I pursed my lips as I considered that. Maybe he was right; I'd certainly never felt like I belonged anywhere growing up but I'd put that down to our situation. In fact, the only time in my life when that feeling had gone away had been since Orion brought us back to Solaria.

"Maybe. I never felt like I had a home before we came to the Academy," I admitted. And he'd done everything in his power to take that from us since we'd arrived. Everything with him always just circled back to that.

Darius opened a door for me and I found myself in a huge suite of rooms with curving walls. A king sized bed dominated the space and everything was decorated in tones of dark blue. It was an adult's room but something about it screamed little boy too. On a high shelf, a wooden train sat above a stack of books.

Another shelf held rows of Pitball trophies and I wandered towards them slowly.

My gaze caught on a collection of framed photos on the wall. The same group of four boys in each one. The Heirs were captured at every age; four little babies laying side by side in a crib getting older and older in each shot. My gaze snagged on a picture of them at around six years old, playing at the side of a stream in the blazing sunshine.

Caleb's golden curls made him look like a little angel as he laughed, knee deep in the water while Seth was grubby on the bank with smudges of dirt on his face and grass stains on his knees. Max smiled so widely I could practically feel the happiness pouring out of him and Darius looked so serious I had to laugh, his lips pouting as he pointed at something out of shot.

"You were the grumpy one," I said, gesturing to the picture and Darius moved close behind me to look over my shoulder.

He scoffed lightly. "Not always. But Seth had just destroyed a camp we'd been building all morning by shifting into a big fat werewolf pup right in the middle of it. He was so damn clumsy when his Order first emerged that he was constantly breaking everything, either by exploding into a wolf with no notice or by getting so hyped up he just fell over his own feet and caused chaos."

I released a laugh. "Tell me about it." I looked up at him over my shoulder and his dark gaze pinned me in his. "Darcy always..." I frowned, wondering why I'd been going to tell him about our childhood but he only shifted closer to me, refusing to release me from the trap of his gaze.

"Always what?" he breathed like anything I might say would be the most interesting thing in the world.

My lips parted and some deep part of me wanted to tell him. A frown pinched my features and I shook my head a little, unsure why I'd even been talking to him about any of this.

Darius reached out for me, his fingers brushing against mine and making my gut flip over as he hooked a finger around my thumb, grazing it up the centre of my palm.

A shiver of energy shuddered straight through my body at the tiny point of contact, my heart lurching in surprise as I failed to pull away from him.

He was too close to me, the scent of cedar and smoke overwhelming me as I looked up at him. I needed to move. I had to step back. I-

"I thought I heard you in here," Xavier's voice interrupted us and I flinched away from Darius like we'd just been caught doing something we shouldn't, whirling around to look at Xavier as he stepped through a door in the back corner of the room. "Oh, sorry, I didn't realise you had company-"

He started backing up but Darius strode straight towards him, pulling him into a tight embrace as I lingered awkwardly by the wall.

Xavier smiled up at his brother as he stepped back and the two of them turned to look at me.

"You met Roxy at the party for a bit," Darius reminded him briefly. "She's come to lose a race against me on my bikes."

I scoffed lightly, not bothering to respond to that.

"Yeah, I remember. You're not easy to forget," Xavier added, offering me a shy smile.

"Neither are you," I replied. "I still can't believe Darius is related to someone who's not entirely obnoxious."

Xavier laughed while Darius almost smiled, which was just too damn weird.

"Did you want a drink?" Darius offered, pointing at a table across the room which I hadn't noticed held the refreshments Jenkins had promised. That dude worked fast.

"Sure," Xavier headed across the room to claim one and I followed so that I didn't have to lurk.

"How's life in the mansion?" I asked him, not really sure what else to say as I claimed a coke.

Darius exchanged a loaded look with his brother before eventually shrugging.

"Father has been a bit preoccupied recently so I've been alone a lot," Xavier said.

"I guess you're looking forward to coming to Zodiac next year then?" I asked. "To save you from the boredom of life in your rich boy tower."

"Errr... yeah," Xavier said awkwardly, looking at Darius again.

"It'll be good to have you there," Darius said firmly.

"Sure," Xavier said but he seemed kinda deflated like he wasn't really looking forward to it.

"Don't you want to come to the Academy?" I asked curiously.

"Sure I do." Xavier chugged a whole glass of coke and Darius didn't look at me as I narrowed my eyes at the two of them, sure I was missing something.

"So, Father said there's a theory that you and your sister will emerge as Dragons any day now," Xavier said, forcing a subject change.

"Maybe," I said with a shrug, lifting my drink to my lips.

"If you're a Dragon maybe you can marry Darius and save him from Mildred," Xavier suggested casually.

I half choked on my coke and set it down quickly as I coughed. "Fuck no," I said once I could speak. "Mildred is welcome to him. I want a front row seat to their wedding so that I can laugh my ass off but that's the only reason I'll be attending."

Darius scowled at his brother, seeming unhappy with the turn of the conversation. "Even if Roxy wasn't the most annoying woman I've ever met and I could overlook her many personality flaws for long enough to consider marrying her, it wouldn't matter," he said in a flat tone. "She isn't pure blooded. Her mother was a Harpy and her father was a Hydra. Not to mention insane. I don't think Father would give her even a moment's consideration, do you?"

"He's right," I agreed instantly, finally finding something I could agree with Darius Acrux on; we could both absolutely agree that the idea of marrying each other was abhorrent. I eyed his tight t-shirt for a moment, the tattoos showing beneath the sleeves drawing my eye. I mean, yeah the sex would obviously be hot but the rest of it would be just awful. So there was no fucking way.

"I'm not pure," I said, driving my point home. "There's nothing clean and innocent about me. I might be a princess but my crown would be made of broken, dirty things, not gold and jewels. I'd never be good enough for Daddy Acrux. And that's just the way I like it."

Darius actually smirked in response to that and Xavier seemed amused too.

"I actually need to go and check something downstairs before we can head out for our race. Can you keep Roxy company for me?" Darius asked his brother, already edging towards the door.

"Oh, erm, well... do you really think that's a good idea?" Xavier asked nervously, shooting me a glance before looking back to his brother. "What if I..."

"You won't," Darius replied confidently. "You're in control. The more practice you have the better anyway. And I won't be long." He headed out of the door before either of us could say anything else and I smiled at Xavier a little awkwardly, wondering what that was about.

"So..." he said, trailing away from me across the room. "You and Darius are friends now, eh? I thought you hated him?"

"Ew," I replied, scrunching my nose up. "I do hate him. I'm purely here to win one of his shiny bikes off of him and laugh when he cries about it."

"It just seemed like I walked in on..."

I scowled at him hard enough to make him drop that line of thought and Xavier laughed.

"Okay, there's no you and Darius," he agreed quickly. "But you might be doomed if that's not what you want because I saw the way he was looking at you and Darius always gets what he wants once he sets his mind to it."

"Gross, dude, you're gonna make me hurl," I said, grimacing at him. "And I can assure you the hatred between me and your brother is entirely mutual. Neither of us want anything else."

Although as I said that, I couldn't help but remember waking up in his arms and feeling like I actually belonged there for several long minutes. Of course I'd been hungover and confused so that didn't mean anything and I'd been reminded of why that thought was insane quickly enough.

I cleared my throat and set my drink down.

"So what are we going to do while we wait for Darius to go braid his hair?" I asked.

"Err, I dunno, do you wanna come play Xbox in my room?" Xavier took a step back towards the door he'd emerged through and I glanced over his shoulder at the dark space beyond.

"No offence dude but that looks like a total boy pit in there. I can smell the unwashed gym socks from here and I wouldn't really know where to begin playing Xbox anyway." I'd had the odd turn on games consoles growing up but it wasn't really my thing.

Xavier laughed and folded his arms as he leaned back against the wall. "So what do you suggest then? I haven't really left my rooms in a while and I'm running low on ideas for entertainment."

"You're like Rapunzel locked up in your tower," I teased. "But instead of long golden hair you've got an Xbox and too much time on your hands."

"You don't know the half of it," he muttered.

"Well what did you like to do for fun as a kid around here? Before the teenage angst kicked in."

Xavier looked at me for a long moment like he couldn't really think of anything then a smirk pulled at his lips. "We used to have tray races sliding down the stairs," he said. "But we're probably too big for that now."

"Pfft, Darius is probably too big with all his spare muscles and that big puffed up head of his but I'm sure *we* can manage," I said.

Xavier's eyes lit with mischief for a moment but then the dare faded out of them and he shook his head. "It's a dumb idea."

"Oh come on Rapunzel, let down your hair," I begged. "I've been dragged all the way out here with promises of a race just to be ditched. And you were tasked with making sure I had fun."

"I'm pretty sure I'm just supposed to keep you company-"

"The fun was implied," I said. "It was just hard to tell because Darius always has that serious as shit expression slapped on his face. But it was definitely in the small print."

Xavier cracked a smile and I beamed as he caved.

"Fine. One race. But I warn you, I'm the champion so you're about to lose."

"Bring it on," I taunted.

Xavier ducked back into his room and reappeared a moment later carrying two big silver trays which were probably worth enough to buy a small car.

"Luckily the servants haven't been up to collect my leftovers from dinner yet," Xavier explained with a grin as he held them out for me. He moved to Darius's bed and threw the duvet and pillows to the floor before yanking the mattress off of the frame. He might not have been as powerfully built as his brother but he was clearly strong in his own right and he dragged the heavy mattress across the room easily before heading back out into the hall.

I followed behind him and he told me to wait as he headed off down the curving stairs with the mattress.

Within a few moments he jogged back to me with a grin on his face, pushing his dark curls back before holding his hand out for his tray.

"I haven't done this in years," he said. "You're a bad influence."

"You have no idea," I agreed.

"I can see why Darius likes you."

"Ew, no, stop that," I said, faking a shudder. "You're just trying to put me off my game because you know I'm about to win."

We moved to the top of the stairs with the two trays and my heart started to beat faster in anticipation.

"Are you sure you wanna do this?" Xavier asked a little nervously. "I made a crash pad at the bottom with the mattress but we always used to end up smacking into the walls. You might get hurt..."

"Well just think how proud Daddy Acrux will be if you manage to kill one of the Vegas for him," I said.

Xavier smirked and moved his tray to the top of the staircase, sitting on it as he prepared to race. I quickly copied him, gripping the two handles on either side of me as I teetered on the edge of the top step.

"Three, two, one-" Xavier leaned forward and whooped as he sped away down the stairs.

I was a little more cautious but as the tray spilled over the edge, I couldn't help but scream in excitement as it shot down the spiralling staircase at speed.

I flew around and around, my hair pulled back behind me before crashing into the mattress at the bottom of the stairs and laughing as I tumbled across it.

Xavier snatched my hand, dragging me upright and grinning so widely that for a moment it almost looked like he was glowing.

"Again," he demanded. "This time don't be a chicken shit at the start line."

I barked a laugh and grabbed my tray, running back up the stairs at his side.

We rearranged ourselves on the trays again and my heart pounded with the fun of the game.

The second time, I threw my weight forward at the same time as him and we shot down the stairs side by side, whooping with laughter before spilling onto the mattress at the bottom.

"I won that one," I exclaimed while Xavier shook his head.

"You wish."

"Okay, cheater. Let's up the ante." I grabbed my tray and he grinned as he ran up the stairs at my side, his skin almost seeming to glow again. I frowned to myself, wondering if I was imagining it. I'd never seen a Dragon glow like that before.

We positioned ourselves at the top of the stairs once more and I raised a palm behind me.

"I'm gonna give us a push," I said, grinning mischievously.

Xavier smiled so widely that it made me laugh. Something about him just drew me in. He was so different from his brother it was untrue. Even though I hardly knew him, hanging out with him was like hanging out with an old friend.

"Hold on tight." I called on my air magic and directed it to push us down the stairs.

In my excitement I pushed a little too hard and I screamed as the magic slammed into my back, practically lifting us off of the ground as we shot over the top step.

Xavier yelled too and we zoomed down the spiralling stairs so fast they were a blur.

The tray skidded off of the final step, my scream rising in pitch as I flew straight towards the wall. I flung my hands up again and we bounced off of a cushion of air magic instead of going splat before falling back onto the mattress.

I was laughing so hard that I could barely catch my breath and as I turned to look at Xavier beside me I found him glowing so brightly that he actually lit up the space around him.

"Shit dude," I said between breaths of laughter. "You're sparkling."

"What?" Xavier gasped, scrambling up onto his hands and knees. "No I'm not!"

I laughed harder. "Yes you are! If I didn't know any better I'd say you were about to turn into a Pegasus!"

Xavier's eyes widened with panic and he tried to push himself to his feet as he shook his head but before he could manage it, tremors wracked his body and he shredded right through his clothes.

My mouth fell open as I stared up at the glimmering lilac Pegasus before me. He still had half a t-shirt hanging around his neck and his horsey eyes were wild with panic.

My smile widened as I looked up at him. He was probably the most beautiful Pegasus I'd ever seen.

"Well shit," I breathed. "No wonder I like you so much. You skipped the asshole Dragon genes!"

I pushed myself to my feet, grinning at him as he tucked his rainbow wings tight in the small corridor, stepping from hoof to hoof.

"I think my mortal is showing because I really just wanna tickle your horsey ears right now," I teased, drawing closer to him.

Xavier looked at me cautiously, his ears twitching as he lowered his head, slowly moving into my personal space.

"Seriously?" I asked as he seemed to be offering me the chance to do as I'd said.

He whinnied softly and I could only grin more as I reached out and ran my hand straight up the centre of his nose.

Xavier released a heavy breath, his eyes boring into mine in a way that almost broke my heart.

"Why do you look so sad?" I whispered as my fingers slid down the side of his head, tickling his ear like I'd promised.

He nuzzled his nose against my shoulder and it was like he was aching for this contact. I wrapped my arms around his neck and squeezed him, trying to figure out why the hell I wanted to cry.

"Shit," Darius murmured behind me and I turned my head to look at him in surprise. "Roxy..." His lips parted and for a moment he just stared at me, his eyes filled with the same panic I'd seen in Xavier's right after he'd shifted.

"What?" I asked, brushing my fingers over Xavier's mane.

"You can't...please promise you won't tell anyone you saw him like this," Darius begged, reaching out towards me then dropping his hand again like he didn't know what to do.

"Like what?" I asked in confusion.

"Trust you not to even notice when you've stumbled upon a secret that could get you killed," he muttered. "No one can know that Xavier isn't a Dragon."

"Why?" I asked incredulously. "He's beautiful. And I'd much sooner be a Pegasus than a grumpy ass Dragon."

Xavier suddenly shifted back into his Fae form and I squeaked in surprise as I found myself in the arms of a very naked boy. He squeezed me against him so tightly that I could hardly breathe.

"Thank you," he whispered in my ear.

"For what?" I asked in complete confusion, not really hugging him back because he was really fucking naked. I opted for awkwardly patting him on the back as he refused to release me.

"For not even batting an eye. For actually thinking there's something good about this." Xavier leaned back and I looked up into the eyes of someone who was completely broken.

"Xavier," I breathed, laying a hand on his cheek for a moment, unsure how to even begin to respond to the pain in his eyes.

He pressed a kiss to the top of my head and released me, hurrying away up the stairs before I could say anything else. The door to his bedroom clicked shut and I was left standing with Darius who was looking at me like I'd just summoned the moon to come and sing us a lullaby.

"Stop looking at me like that," I said, folding my arms in case he got any weird ideas about hugging me too because it actually looked like he might for a moment.

Darius took a deep breath, letting it out slowly.

"You can't begin to imagine the difficulty Xavier's been going through since his Order emerged. My father..." He shook his head, obviously deciding against elaborating on that but it wasn't hard to imagine Daddy Acrux would have been a total dickwad about the situation. "Thank you," he added. "Xavier really needed to see that someone could just accept him for who he is."

"No problem," I said, looking away from him because in that moment it didn't really feel like he hated me at all and it was too weird. "So have you finished reapplying your lipstick? Can we go race now?"

Darius snorted a laugh and turned away, beckoning me after him.

"You're ready to lose now then?" he asked.

"Whatever you wanna believe." I shrugged. I didn't need to trash talk him, I'd beat his ass easily enough and then he'd eat his words while I rode away on my shiny new bike.

We headed down the corridors in silence as Darius seemed lost in thought and I wondered if the storm had eased up at all since we'd been inside.

"I meant what I said about keeping Xavier's secret," Darius said as we headed down the stairs to the front door. "Father would-"

"It's fine," I said quickly, not needing him to threaten me into agreeing. "I don't see why it matters but I won't tell anyone if it would hurt Xavier. I actually like him and I wouldn't want him to suffer because of me."

"Thank you," Darius murmured and I could feel his gaze on me but I just shrugged, not looking back. I wasn't doing it for him anyway.

Jenkins was waiting with my leather jacket at the foot of the stairs and I took it from him with a word of thanks.

Darius didn't head back through the front door but led me to a door on the other side of the space where a staircase led down to the underground parking lot.

Lights flicked on around us as we headed out into the cold space. He strode through the echoing lot filled with luxury vehicles and I couldn't help but imagine just how rich I could get by robbing this place. Hell I could probably be set for life by stealing a few golden picture frames and things from the unused parts of the house and they'd never even realise they'd been robbed.

I followed Darius to a metal key cabinet to the left of the elevator and he punched in the code to unlock it while I watched and memorised it. *1678#43.*

I yawned like I had zero interest in what he was doing and pulled my Atlas from my pocket, adding the code into the notes section before casting an eye over the messages I'd received in the last hour.

Caleb:

My power is running low tonight, sweetheart. You wanna help me out?

Caleb:

I'll make it worth your while...

A picture followed that of him lying shirtless on his bed in Terra House and I smirked as I tapped out a reply.

Tory:

Sorry, I've had a better offer tonight. But feel free to bite someone else, I don't mind at all. Besides, you lost our game today so you can't get your fangs in me until you win...

Caleb:

What better offer? And if you won't let me put my fangs in you, how about something else? ;)

I bit my bottom lip to keep my smile contained before responding.

Tory:

Can't tonight. But you can always try to catch me tomorrow...

Caleb:

You're killing me. Why don't I just come to Ignis now and I can help you relax before your Air Trial tomorrow?

Tory:

I told you, I got a better offer. I'm not even on campus.

I shoved the Atlas back into my pocket and looked up to find Darius watching me.

"Am I keeping you from your friends?" he mocked.

"That's one of *your* friends actually. He's very persistent."

Darius's jaw tightened as he looked me over. "Which one do you want?"

"What?" I asked with a frown.

He nodded towards the other end of the lot where the bikes were parked up. "Pick a bike."

"Oh right." I pursed my lips and walked towards the super bikes, eyeing their gleaming perfection with a little adrenaline trickling along my limbs in anticipation.

My Atlas started pinging in my pocket again and again and Darius released a low growl of irritation. He raised his own Atlas and started typing something but my attention was fixed on the bikes.

It was tempting to pick the most valuable bike in the lineup but my gaze fell on a pitch black Hondusa which I knew had one of the highest top speeds of any super bike ever made. A smile tugged at my lips and my heart started beating faster as I headed straight for it, tracing my fingertips along the sleek bodywork.

I turned to look at Darius, unable to even try and hide the wide smile on my face as I thought about riding this beauty.

He returned his Atlas to his pocket and mine kept pinging but I ignored it as I looked up at him.

The frown he'd been sporting fell away and he smiled back at me, stepping closer.

"You like this one?" he asked, his gaze sweeping over the bike before coming back to rest on me.

"I do," I replied, holding his eye as I perched on the saddle, claiming it as my own. "I'm going to really enjoy winning it from you."

"I'm going to really enjoy wiping that smile from your face when you lose," he replied, his tone teasing.

He drew even closer to me, placing his hands on the chassis either side of where I sat and caging me in with his body.

"Are you going to tell me what you want if you win?" I asked.

"Something I can't buy," he replied, leaning a little closer. "Which I don't think you'd give me if I just asked."

"What?" He was so close to me now that I could feel the warmth of him dancing in the air between us.

His gaze fell to my mouth for the briefest of moments and my heart leapt of its own accord. "You'll have to wait and see when I win."

Darius stepped back and turned away from me as he chose his own bike.

I took a deep breath as I tried to clear my head of the fog he'd placed around me and my Atlas pinged again.

I pulled it out of my pocket and glanced at the messages I'd received. There were several shirtless pictures of Caleb and promises of things he'd like to do with me then there was another message, demanding I confirm whether or not I was out with Darius. I raised an eyebrow in surprise and glanced at Darius, finding him looking back at me with a smirk on his face.

"Problem?" he asked, sounding amused as he rolled a red Yamaharpie out of the line up.

"Did you tell Caleb we were out together?" I asked.

"Were you planning on keeping it a secret?" he asked in response.

"No," I replied. "I'll be telling everyone and anyone about how I won one of your precious bikes from you by tomorrow. But I get the feeling you might have annoyed him."

Darius held a hand out for my Atlas and I handed it to him, not really caring if he read the messages Caleb had sent.

He cast an eye over them for a few seconds then tossed it back into my hands before taking his own Atlas from his pocket again.

Darius caught my hand and pulled me upright, before throwing his arm around my shoulders as he held his Atlas in front of us and took a picture while pressing a kiss to the top of my head. I couldn't help but laugh as he took the picture which he instantly sent on to Caleb.

"You're an asshole," I said halfheartedly as I ducked out from under his arm.

"At least I'm consistent," he replied with a laugh.

I couldn't really hide the smile which was trying to fight its way onto my lips and with a jolt of surprise I realised I was actually enjoying Darius's company. I switched my Atlas off and shoved it back into my pocket. I'd just have to deal with Caleb tomorrow.

"Are you ready to lose a bike then?" I asked.

"I'm ready to see what you've got, Roxy," he confirmed, hooking two helmets from a shelf above the bikes and tossing me one.

"That storm is going to make this interesting," I commented.

"I could use magic to keep the rain off of me but I'm guessing you can't yet?" he asked.

I shook my head, turning the helmet over in my hands. I knew I wouldn't be able to give enough concentration to maintaining an air shield while trying to win the race. "I don't need magic tricks to beat you anyway."

"Then I won't use any either. I don't want you thinking I only won because I had an advantage." Darius pulled his helmet on and I followed suit. The visor lit up with a little display in the bottom left corner and I frowned in surprise as I looked at it.

"There's a built in GPS which I've programmed with the track circuit," Darius's voice came through an earpiece in the helmet and I flinched a little. "Just follow the directions in the bottom left. I set it to a random route so that I won't be at an advantage but we can take a ride around the main ring first if you want to get a feel for the track?"

"I'm used to following random routes. I don't need a practice round," I assured him. No need to add that that was because I was often fleeing the police and taking back alleys and sidewalks to escape them.

"Okay then. It's a fifteen mile route, I'll lead you out to the start point. First one back to the drive wins."

"I hope you're not a sore loser," I teased.

Darius tossed me the key to my bike and I caught it neatly. "I wouldn't know. I've never lost."

I rolled my eyes as I kicked my leg over the saddle and started the engine. It was actually something of a novelty to use a key to do so.

The engine roared with the promise of the rush I'd been missing and I sighed with pleasure, letting my eyes fall closed for a moment as I just appreciated this metal creature beneath me. "*Fuck yes.* I've missed this feeling so much."

"What bike did you leave behind in the mortal world?" Darius asked and I opened my eyes to find him watching me like I was the most interesting goddamn thing he'd ever seen.

"I've never owned my own bike," I said before realising that I probably shouldn't have admitted that.

"Then how did you learn to ride?" he asked in confusion. I could only hear him over the roar of the engine because his voice still came through the speaker by my ear but somehow that made it easier for me to talk to him.

"I had a boyfriend with bikes. A few actually. That tended to be my type, particularly after I lost my trust in cars."

"Because bikes don't have a roof, so you can never get stuck in one?" he guessed.

"I suppose that won't help me if I get caught beneath ice again though will it?" I snapped. I didn't want him digging around in my head and I certainly didn't want to be chatting to him like we were friends or something. Why the hell did I keep on letting myself forget what he was and what he'd done to me? "Are you done stalling or are you ready to lose a race?" I asked.

Darius nodded at me and though I could only see his eyes through his visor, I got the impression he wasn't pleased that I'd put an end to our little chat. But what the hell did he want from me? I wasn't going to be spilling all of my secrets to the guy who had treated me like shit from the second he met me just because he'd suddenly decided to take an interest in who I was over *what* I was.

I revved the engine and dropped the clutch, shooting forward and up the ramp.

The rain slammed into me the second I made it onto the drive and I slowed as I guided the bike across the gravel.

Darius came up beside me and I let him take the lead as he headed along the front of the house before turning onto a concrete track which wound into the shade of woodland to the west of the manor.

He pulled up, placing his foot on the ground as he waited for me to take my place beside him on his left.

Thunder crashed through the sky overhead quickly followed by a flash of lightning which lit up the trees around us and the track which led away from me.

I must be absolutely insane to do this in this weather.

The GPS at the bottom left of my visor said my first turning was going to be a right in half a mile which meant I was going to need to make the most of the straight shot before that turning.

"Ready, Roxy?" Darius purred.

"Prepare to lose, asshole," I replied darkly, my gaze fixed on the track ahead of me, or at least as much of it as I could see in the dark.

"Three. Two. One-"

I dropped the clutch and pulled the throttle, shooting forward with the force of a rocket launch as I ducked my head low and sped into the storm.

Darius was right beside me and a wild grin pulled at my lips as I increased my speed. Raindrops speckled my visor but the speed we were travelling at meant they were swept away again as quickly as they landed.

Darius laughed in my earpiece as he took the lead and my smile widened as I watched his exhaust edge ahead of me.

The second he was clear of me, I threw my weight to the right, swinging my bike that way as I dropped a gear and opened the throttle again, sweeping into the inside lane just as we hit the turn.

My knee almost skimmed the ground and puddle water splashed up against my jacket as I leaned all the way into the corner before righting myself again and opening the throttle wide the second I hit the straight. I flew into the lead and Darius cursed through my earpiece.

The track left the woods and I followed the GPS directions with Darius right on my tail as the track wound through a sweeping meadow which was being battered by the storm.

My heart was pounding and the bike roared with hungry energy beneath me, tearing up the course as I fought to keep control of my lead.

We swung a right then a left and my elbow brushed against Darius's as he sped up the inside lane, struggling to regain his position.

I threw half a glance at him, changing gears and leaning low as I fought to hold him off. He fell back for a moment then gained on me again, managing to keep the inside track as we hit a hairpin turn.

By the time I'd navigated it, he'd taken the lead back and I growled at his back as his excited laughter reached me through the speakers.

Thunder boomed overhead again and I flinched as lighting forked through the sky instantly. The storm was right on top of us and the track was slick and deadly as we pushed the bikes to their limits.

We sped around the track, the engines roaring and my heart hammering to a tune of pure, unbridled joy. This was freedom. There was nothing in the world that compared to this feeling.

We shot back into the woods and I was so close to Darius's bike that I was sure my wheel almost touched his once or twice. He was good. I'd give him that. But I was better.

I gritted my teeth as we came upon a long straight, flattening myself as much as I could so that the bike could cut through the wind at top speed.

I closed in on Darius, my front wheel making it in line with his back.

The manor was ahead of us, the display on the GPS telling me I had less than a third of a mile to the end of the track. I couldn't let him win.

I could feel the water beneath the wheels threatening to unbalance me as I pushed the bike harder.

Thunder echoed through the heavens so loud I could have sworn the earth trembled. A great arc of lightning shot down from the clouds, slamming into the trees ahead to our right and fire sprung to life.

I couldn't spare the burning glow any attention as I drew the throttle back even further, my bike finally speeding past Darius's as he yelled something which I couldn't concentrate on.

The finish line was looming ahead, the gravel driveway calling me home for the win as heavy rain splattered my visor so thickly I could barely see.

Movement caught my attention on my right just as the huge, burning tree which had been hit by the lightning crashed across the track in front of me.

I squeezed the brakes, pulling way too hard for the wet conditions and feeling the back wheel slide out behind me instantly.

I screamed as the bike spun out, ducking my head as I clung to the handlebars for dear life. I caught sight of Darius's bike spinning out of control too half a second before my bike collided with the fallen tree and I was thrown into the air.

My heart slammed into my ribs as blind panic consumed me and I flung my arms out, magic pouring from me in a wave which I had no control over. I only begged for it to save us.

I was tossed about in a vortex of wind which managed to slow me down somewhat and threw me towards the sweeping lawn to the front of Acrux manor.

I hit the ground hard but it felt soft and spongy beneath me as earth magic cushioned my fall. Darius slammed into me a second later, the impact of his massive body hitting mine causing more pain than hitting the ground had. His helmet smacked against mine and a crack was scored through my visor.

We tumbled across the ground in a tangle of limbs before jarring to a halt with him on top of me.

I groaned as pain danced through my body, drawing in a ragged breath which my ribs protested to with a blinding flash of pain which made half a cry pass through my lips.

"Roxy?" Darius asked, pushing himself back as he yanked his helmet off and tossed it to the ground. "Are you okay?"

I groaned in a noncommittal way. I was alive which was pretty damn miraculous all things considered but okay was pushing it. I was in a whole world of pain and it was taking all of my self control not to start screaming, especially as I took another breath and blinding agony ripped through my ribs again.

Rain slammed down on Darius, plastering his dark hair to his forehead but he ignored it as he reached out to pull my helmet off too.

I ground my teeth together as I tried to ignore the agony in my chest but as he touched my side, a line of curses spilled from my lips potent enough to make him raise his eyebrows at me.

"Hang on," he said, reaching out to cup my cheek in his rough palm.

The warmth of his magic pushed into my body and the tension coiled in my limbs relaxed as he took the agony away.

I took a deep breath, raindrops washing over my cheeks as I lay with my face to the tempestuous storm clouds above, panting as the pain faded.

Darius finished healing me and caught my shoulder, heaving me up to sit facing him. I looked into his eyes as the rain pounded down on us and we both tried to catch our breath. My gaze slowly slid to the wrecked bikes and the fallen tree which should have killed us and my lips parted at the sight of the mangled metal.

"Well shit," I breathed. "How the hell did we survive that?"

"You should know," Darius replied, his eyes still on me as I stared at the flames. "I don't have air or earth magic."

I looked back at him in surprise. "*I* saved us?" I asked, needing confirmation because I sure as hell hadn't been thinking clearly enough to be able to do it on purpose.

"You did," he confirmed.

I looked back at the blazing wreckage of my bike and laughter burst from my lips. After a beat, Darius started laughing too and I leaned into him as my smile nearly split my face in two.

That had been fucking insane but it had also been one hell of a rush.

"We should get the hell out of here before Jenkins sees the mess we've made," Darius said, a wide smile on his face as he took my hand and pulled me to my feet.

"Won't your dad care that we wrecked those bikes?" I asked as Darius took the stardust from his pocket and held it ready, still keeping hold of my hand.

"I bought them with my allowance, he won't care about that," Darius said dismissively before throwing the glimmering stardust over us.

The storm and blazing wreckage disappeared in an instant, stars swimming in an endless galaxy around us before the world righted itself and I found myself back in Darius's bedroom in Ignis House.

We were dripping a puddle onto the floor, our muddy boots staining the new carpet while the two of us grinned like naughty school kids.

"That was insane," I breathed. "I can't believe we tried to race in that storm."

"I can't believe you almost beat me," he replied, stepping a little closer to me.

"Almost?" I scoffed. "We were at the finish line. I had you beat and you know it."

"I was about to take back the lead but it's cute you think you would have won." Darius caught my waist between his hands and I looked up at him in surprise.

His magic swept over my skin and he drew the water out of my hair and clothes before mixing it with that from himself and sending it all flying into the bathroom and down the drain.

I watched the water as it flew away from us, my throat bobbing as he kept his grip on my waist.

He stepped closer again and I stepped back. I looked up into his eyes and found a smile playing around his lips. He walked me back another step. And another. My thighs hit the edge of his golden bed.

Before he could move me again, my hand landed on his chest. "I should go," I breathed.

"Stay," he replied instantly.

Silence hung between us and my heart started beating faster as I looked at the perfect angles of his face, the rough stubble lining his jaw and the endless depths of his dark eyes. For a moment I felt like I wanted to know all of his secrets and give him all of mine but my hand was still on his chest, holding him back and I didn't remove it.

"I have my Air Trial tomorrow," I said. "I really need to get some sleep and-"

"So sleep here. Like last night. We don't have to do anything else."

I frowned at him, wondering why the hell he would ask me to do that and why the hell I wanted to say yes.

"I have a perfectly good bed downstairs," I replied, shaking my head just a little. "Why would you want me to stay?"

Darius frowned like he wasn't sure what to say to that but he inched a little closer all the same. "Because it feels right," he breathed.

I wanted to deny that but my heart pounded a little with the truth of his words. Hadn't I woken up feeling safe and secure in his arms this morning? Hadn't I wanted that feeling to go on and on? But I'd also been horrified and a little terrified to realise exactly whose bed I'd found myself in. That part hadn't changed. He was still the monster who had hurt me in more ways than I could count since I'd arrived here.

I shook my head slowly, increasing the pressure of my hand on his chest as I forced him back a step.

Darius's gaze dropped to my hand on him and he released his grip on my waist.

I moved out of his hold, breaking contact with him as I started backing away towards the door.

"Are you going to admit that I won?" I asked, a faint smile pulling at my lips again as I reached the door.

"Never," he replied, watching me go.

"Then I guess this is goodnight." I pulled the door open and stepped outside quickly, closing it between us before heading down to my room.

It was nearly two am and I needed to get some sleep in before the trial tomorrow.

I quickly changed into my pyjamas and slid into my bed, pulling the duvet up around me to ward off the chill left in my bones by the storm.

I flicked my Atlas on to set an alarm for the morning and it pinged just before I closed my eyes. I pulled it closer to read the message quickly and I bit my lip against the smile which wanted to break free in response to what I read.

Darius:

But maybe we could call it a draw?

ORION

CHAPTER FIFTEEN

Five minutes had turned into hours. And I was definitely to blame. Darcy wriggled out of my arms and I groaned as she stood up, tracking down her clothes. I traced the curves of her body, eyeing the deep bronze colour of her skin and the way her hair shone like starlight.

This girl is made for me.

"Just another hour." I shifted out of bed, standing and drawing her back against me.

"Lance," she laughed as I brushed my hands across the velvet skin of her stomach. I couldn't get enough of the way that felt. "I have my Air Trial tomorrow."

"Not until the afternoon," I said, though I was definitely not winning any awards for teacher of the year right now. It was after two in the morning and if I didn't let her go, I was going to have a serious problem getting her back to her House unseen. But the truth was, I feared that if she left, she might not come back. And even if she wanted to, who knew how long it would be until we got an opportunity to be together again? I wasn't exactly the most patient guy and every step I took with her would have to be carefully planned. It would be frustrating as hell and I wasn't ready to face it yet.

I curled a lock of her hair between my fingers while my other hand tracked along her collar bone.

Fuck, I *had* to let her go. For her sake. Definitely not mine. I was going to suffer the second she was gone.

She slipped away from me, tugging on her slinky white pyjamas, twisting her hair up into a knot on top of her head.

"Alright," I sighed, grabbing my boxers and tugging them on. "I'll take you back."

A knock sounded on my window and both of us froze like fucking snowmen in the dead of winter. There was only one person who would show up at my house in the middle of the night – barring Blue apparently.

"Who's that?" Darcy mouthed at me, her eyes wide in horror.

"Darius," I said, cursing under my breath as I hurried toward her. "He can't hear us, the silencing bubble is still in place."

"Oh," she breathed, still looking unsure. "What's he doing here at this time of the night?"

I didn't have an answer for that so I just shrugged. The knocking came again a little louder this time and I knew what was coming next. To get my attention he'd-

"Motherfucker," I hissed as he pinched himself hard enough to hurt me through the bond.

"Lance, I know you're up. Open the window," Darius hissed.

"I'll go out the front," Darcy breathed and I nodded, cursing Darius as I jogged after her out of the bedroom. She made a beeline for the front door, pushing her feet into her shoes and tugging on her coat. She reached for the door, but I caught her arm and tugged her through to the conservatory at the back of the chalet. I dropped my mouth to her ear as I unlocked the door. "It's a straight shot to the fence this way and there's no porch lights." I pointed and she nodded seriously, moving toward the door, but I dragged her back, stamping my mouth to hers, trying to say all the things I'd planned to say before she left. But now we were out of time.

I released her and she was gone, darting into the darkness and making my soul feel like it was being ripped in two. I loved Darius, but by the stars, did he have to come to me tonight of all nights?

Shit…what if he'd turned up sooner? He'd lose the plot if he knew what I'd been doing with one of his mortal enemies.

My throat thickened and I cast that thought aside.

When I was certain Darcy was gone, I stepped outside barefoot onto the rainswept pathway, casting an air shield around myself as I circled the house. Darius had his face pressed to my bedroom window with his hands cupped around his eyes, rain burning away around him as it touched the heated power emanating from him.

"Hey," I hissed. "Get inside peeping Tom."

He smirked, striding toward me and we quickly moved back into the conservatory before I locked the door and led him through to the living room. In the light, I realised he was wearing a bunch of gold medallions, chunky rings, two thick bracelets and a belt with a buckle that was a solid gold dragon.

I started laughing. "What the fuck are you wearing?"

"Ha. Ha," he said dryly. "I'm tapped out. I've gotta fill up my reserves and I'm guessing I'm not going to be getting much sleep tonight now so I can't just fill my bed with gold like usual."

"Right, but are you expecting me to call you Draggy D now because I don't think you can pull it off." I chuckled and he broke a grin.

I spied the two glasses I'd placed on the table beside the couch and my heart lurched, my smile falling away. *Shit.*

"What took you so long to open the door?" Darius asked, casting a silencing bubble then realising I already had one in place. He frowned. "Why would you cast a silencing bubble if you're here on your own?"

I folded my arms, trying to come up with an answer for that. "Well Washer is right next door. I don't want him listening in on…" I didn't have an end to that stupid ass sentence.

"On what?" Darius frowned then cast me a narrowed-eyed look before moving to the bedroom and sticking his head through the door. I used the distraction to send one of the glasses flying into the kitchen on a gust of air, landing quietly in the sink.

"What? Do you think I've got a girl here?" I snorted and he raised a brow as he turned back to me. My heart hit a frantic beat and I knew it was partly because I was lying to him. I didn't think I'd ever lied to him before about anything and I wished I didn't have to. The thought made me kind of ill and I hoped the bond between us didn't let him sense that.

"Apparently not. So I guess you were just in the middle of jerking off over your Numerology book. Again."

"Numbers are hot," I said with a smirk. "But I was actually busy jerking off over your mom. She sent me some dirty pictures. Again."

Darius barked a laugh, throwing himself down on the couch. "Hey whatever man, I wasn't the one jerking off alone at two in the morning. I thought your hot FIB girlfriend might be here."

That might have been a better lie.

"No…and she's not my girlfriend." I dropped down beside him and instinctively drew him in for a hug. He pressed against me, sighing as the bond became keener for a moment and made me need him that close.

He sat back with a content smile and combed a hand through his hair. "So I got something tonight." He pushed a hand into his pocket and tossed an object to me. "Which you would have known if you answered your messages."

"I like to jerk off undisturbed." I picked up the ornament he'd passed me, inspecting the carved emerald dragon with gold eyes. "What's this?"

"I told you'd I'd get something of Father's, didn't I? Something he gives

286

a shit about. Well that tacky piece of crap is a paperweight he had made in his image. And a life sized version is currently under construction in the backyard."

Shit, I'd totally forgotten Darius was going home tonight.

I rolled the heavy thing in my hands. "Yeah that sounds about right." I sat up straighter as something occurred to me. "Your father didn't see you tonight did he? About half an hour ago I felt like my whole body had been punched." Darcy must have thought I was *really* fucking enjoying myself when I'd cried out mid-sex - which I seriously had been, I just didn't tend to get that vocal about it.

"That wasn't Father," he said and the tension ran out of my body. "I fell off my motorbike."

I instinctively reached out to him, resting a hand on his knee. His hand brushed across mine, then I pulled away, clearing my throat. *Damn Guardian bond.*

I picked up the Dragon ornament, swiftly changing the subject. "Are you sure he won't miss this?"

"He won't be home for a few days. I'll put it back when we're done."

"Perfect." I stood, fighting a yawn. Fuck I was beat. But this couldn't wait. "I'll get dressed." I shot to my room, pulling on some clothes and grabbing my Atlas.

Darius:

I'm heading home, maybe catch you later?

Darius:

I took Roxy Vega.

Darius:

I'm coming over. Text me back asshole.

Darius:

I'm outside.

Darius:

It's raining.

I blew out a slow breath. Tory Vega? Holy shit.

I glanced over my shoulder, finding Darius drifting into my room, looking slightly lost.

"You took Tory Vega home?" I questioned, putting my Atlas down and doing up my shirt. "Are you screwing her?" *Please say yes so I can tell you about Darcy.*

"Fuck no," he said but not nearly as fiercely as he should have. He ran his hand down the back of his neck. "She came over to race me on my bikes that's all."

"So you lost when you fell off?"

"No, we both fell off so it was a draw… or okay maybe she sort of won." He smiled like that didn't actually bother him then sighed. "She spoke to Xavier and he burst into a Pegasus in front of her. They seem to get on pretty well and she said she won't tell anyone, but you should have seen her face. She was surprised and actually happy about it."

"Do you trust her?"

"Yeah," he said stiffly. "Dunno why but…" He shrugged and stepped closer.

I get it.

A beat of silence passed between us and for a second it felt like the Vegas were in the room. Tonight had been unashamedly one of the best of my life and I wanted to tell my goddamn best friend about it. But it wasn't that simple. In fact, it was the complete opposite of simple. And from the look on Darius's face I guessed he was dealing with some not-so-simple shit himself.

But neither of us said a word.

"Let's go." I pulled a coat on and took out the Pitball card collectors box I kept at the base of my closet. "I'll carry you so we can get down there quickly." I took out a backpack, stuffing it inside and passing it to Darius. "Put this on."

He did as I said and we headed to the back door, slipping out into the persistent rain. I cast an air shield around us and the night kept us hidden well enough. I turned away from Darius and he jumped onto my back, locking his legs around my waist. "Giddy up pony."

I laughed then took off at high speed, launching myself over the fence with the power of air and running flat out as I hit the other side. My heightened vision picked out every prick of light there was to be seen so we didn't need to create a light orb. I sped through The Wailing Wood toward the eastern cliff in Air Territory, the wind battering against my shield.

I was soon racing down the steps to Air Cove with Darius gripping me tighter as I took the steep path as fast as I could. I reached the cove and tore up the sand while Darius blasted away my footprints behind us with a gush of water magic.

My magical wards tingled against my skin as I drew closer to the hidden cave and I slowed to a halt, dropping Darius to his feet. He reached into the backpack, taking the draining dagger from where it was hidden in the Pitball box and passed it to me. I nodded in thanks, moving to the cliff wall as the waves crashed behind us, splashing against the dome of air I continued to cast.

I raised the dagger, feeling out the wards and cutting through them to gain access to the concealed cave. The wall appeared to dissolve, though anyone else would still see it as intact. We headed inside and I expanded the shield around us to block the wind from following us inside.

Darius cast a large fire, lighting the cave in a warm red glow. We knelt at the heart of the space and Darius placed the Pitball box between us alongside the emerald dragon. I flipped the lid of the box, popping the secret compartment beneath the rows of Pitball cards and taking out the four Elemental bones which would assist me with the magic I was about to cast. I placed them in a row, pushing the box to one side then sitting the dragon between them.

A thrill flickered in my veins; the call of dark magic always set my blood pounding.

My movements were familiar as I pressed the tip of the dagger to my wrist and dragged it up the centre of my palm. Pain gave way to pleasure as the whisper of the shadows gathered around me. The dagger sang a sweet tune, delighted we'd given it the blood it craved. I could feel its draw, its power demanding I give it more blood, but I pushed the feeling away and passed the blade to Darius.

I held myself on the verge of bliss as I focused on Darius mimicking my actions. Blood slid from his palm and I reached out, clasping his hand so our wounds met and the blood dripped down between us. The second the blood hit the bones, the pull of ecstasy took over and I was dragged out of my own body, plunging into the depths of the shadows.

Dark magic felt like the best drug in the world, but it always wanted more. Training Darius in its ways had taken a long time, but he'd mastered the art of pulling away from the lure of the shadows. Even after all my years of practising it, I still wanted to go to them. Every damn time. That would never go away, but controlling my own mind was the key to using them to my advantage.

I hung in a chasm of darkness, the whispers filling my head and begging me to give in to them. They wanted more than blood, they wanted my body, my soul. My heart yearned to go to their outstretched arms, the sensation rolling over me like the sweetest caress.

I drew on my training, turning away from them and tugging Darius's presence along with me. With an object of Lionel's in our midst, I could latch onto the essence of him, seeking him out in Solaria. Past, present, future, it was difficult to control which we'd see. But I focused on what I needed to know, desperate to hear more of his plans for the Lunar Eclipse.

I felt my lips moving, the dark and ancient language I spoke guiding me closer and closer to what I wanted.

The veil of blackness slid aside and my feet met solid ground. Darius appeared beside me and I nodded to him as we arrived in a massive atrium with golden floors and a huge stairway at the far end that split off in three directions. Pillars of onyx flanked both sides of the hall, holding up a huge balcony which ringed the floor above us beneath an expansive ceiling of shining glass.

This was the Court of Solaria; the parliamentary building for the Celestial Council. Men and women in professional clothes strode up and down the atrium. An ornate, cubic clock hung from the centre of the ceiling, the date stamped beneath it telling me we'd landed in the past. Just yesterday.

A huge man marched right through us, our bodies not corporal in this place and I instantly recognised Lionel Acrux.

We hurried after him, the edges of the vision becoming shadowy as we moved. Lionel climbed the staircase, heading right and swinging around onto the long balcony with its mahogany railing and black doors along the wall.

He marched all the way to the end before opening a door and stepping inside. It shut before we reached him, but it didn't matter. I stepped through the door itself, finding a desk barring our way with a prim receptionist behind it. Lionel had already moved onto the staircase beyond her and we hurried after him, following him up to an office which was the size of an entire apartment.

A long window on the far side looked back down over the atrium far below and a huge desk made entirely of gold sat before it. Everything in the room was as gaudy as it was in his home, he even had a golden bust of his own head. A dark green dragon had been painted across one wall, inlaid with emeralds which glinted under the light of a chandelier.

We moved to where Lionel was standing by the window, his hands clasped behind his back as he gazed down on his subordinates.

A shrill noise sounded and Lionel moved to his desk, picking up the phone. "Yes?"

My heightened hearing caught the words on the end of the line. "Ms Orion is here to see you."

"Send her in," Lionel said, placing the receiver down. He shrugged out of his robe, laying it over the back of his desk chair and my spine prickled as he loosened his tie a little.

"If my father starts screwing your mom, I'm out of here," Darius said with a grimace.

"Agreed," I said, mirroring his expression.

Stella entered the room in a fitted black dress that accentuated her curves, her short dark hair angled to points by her chin.

"Lionel," she said with a wide grin. "I have wonderful news."

Lionel smiled but it looked eerie on his face. "Tell me over a drink." He headed to a cabinet across the room, taking out a bottle of port and pouring two small glasses.

He handed one to Stella as she approached and his fingers brushed against hers, making my insides coil with disgust. He could have any woman he wanted, did he really have to screw my mother? Not that she was objecting, the lust in her eyes was evident enough.

Lionel cast a silencing bubble and they moved to sit on a golden couch side by side.

"I've had a reading done by Madam Monita," Stella said brightly and my ears pricked up at the name. She was the best astrologer in Solaria; it would have cost a fortune to get a reading from her. "The stars are firmly in our favour for the Eclipse, Lion, so long as we choose well. We must pick someone who is truly pure. It seems my daughter wasn't good enough last time and for that I am so deeply ashamed…" She dipped her head and fury burned inside me with the heat of the sun.

Lionel caressed her cheek, drawing her up to look at him again.

"I am grateful for the sacrifice you made for our cause, Stella. And I want you to know that I am willing to make just as great a sacrifice as you."

Stella nodded, dabbing her eyes then resting a hand on his chest. "We can't choose wrongly again."

"Xavier is pure blooded," Lionel growled and my heart turned to stone. "Despite his recent emergence, I can guarantee his Order is due to whichever constellations he was linked to at birth. It has nothing to do with my blood or Catalina's for that matter."

Darius growled and I glanced at him with fear burning a hole in my chest.

"I will go over the scriptures again," Stella said, nodding decisively. "I won't risk Acrux blood if I'm not sure."

"I trust you," Lionel purred, drawing her closer. I thought they were about to kiss, but he rolled his zipper down like that was the most intimate thing he could offer. Before my mother bowed to his whims, I dragged Darius out of the vision with a force of energy.

We'd heard enough and hell if either of us wanted to stand there a moment longer.

I jerked back into my own body, my hand still clasped around Darius's as he returned too. I dropped his palm, panic swimming in my chest, but it was nothing in comparison to the dread in Darius's eyes.

"He's going to use my brother," Darius breathed, horror sprawling across his features.

"No," I growled, a promise in my voice. "We will do everything in our power to stop him. I swear on the stars, Darius, we won't let Lionel hurt Xavier like he hurt my sister."

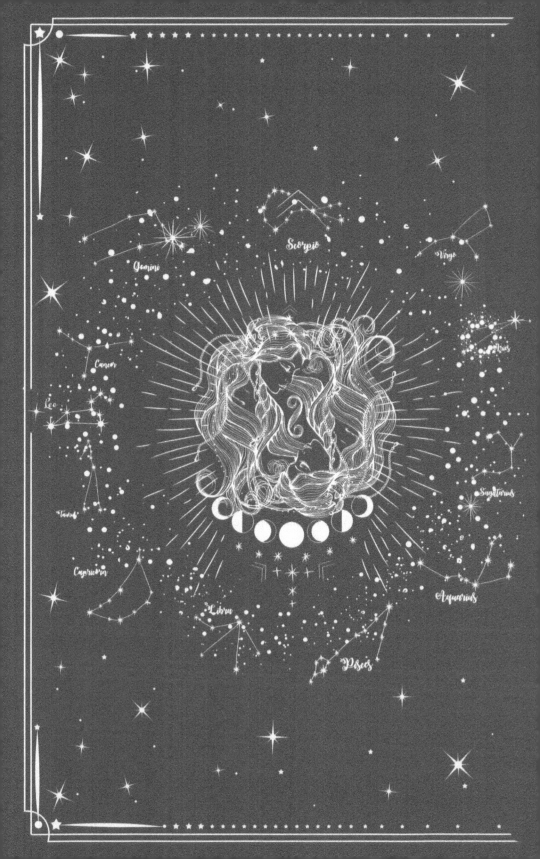

DARCY

CHAPTER SIXTEEN

I woke up late the next morning, reaching through the sheets in the hunt for warm muscles to pull me close but when I fully gained my senses, I remembered I was alone. My hand landed on my Atlas and the light wind-chime alarm jingled from it barely a heartbeat later.

I pulled my covers over my head and tucked my knees to my chest, brushing my fingers over the places Orion's hands had been and committing every touch and kiss to memory. The wild emotions inside me made my heart feel like it was going to burst. I'd never felt like this about anyone before and I was kind of scared of this powerful storm inside me.

My Atlas persisted and I rolled onto my stomach, tapping the screen to read my horoscope with a yawn.

Good morning Gemini.
The stars have spoken about your day!
You will be set a fierce task today but that might not be the only challenge you

have to face. The unpredictable and disruptive Uranus has moved into your chart, so you should expect the unexpected at all times.

Someone started hammering on my door and my heart lurched.

"Who is it?" I called but whoever it was just kept pounding their fist on the wood.

I jumped out of bed, unlocking the door and tugging it open in annoyance. I was nearly bowled over by Seth as he strode into my room, eyes roaming.

"What the hell are you doing?" I tried to shove him back out of the door, bringing air to my fingertips and throwing a gust at him. He blocked it with a simple flick of his hand, his eyes falling to me.

"Who are you fucking?" he demanded.

"What?" I blurted, my heart stumbling at his accusation. *Ohmagod how the hell does he know?*

"Don't lie to me, babe," he growled. "I had a Hell Week nightmare lined up last night and you weren't in your bed when we dragged all the freshmen out."

His eyes flipped over me then settled on my hair. He shot forward, gathering me into his chest and pressing his nose into it. "Mmm I could start up a whole bracelet store with all of this."

"Get off my hair!" A vine shot from my hand and slammed him into the door, wrapping around his neck. He was still goddamn smiling even when it started choking him and I smiled at the power I'd conjured against him. He severed it with a sharp whip of air, that dark grin of his growing wider.

"Calm down, babe, your Alpha's just checking in on you." He stalked closer again. "I always like to know who my pack members are screwing. But it's usually easier to keep tabs on that as they're either screwing me or each other."

"I'm not screwing anyone." I folded my arms, giving him a firm stare and his eyes narrowed suspiciously.

"Then where were you last night?"

"I was at Tory's."

"Liar liar panties on fire," he purred. "Darius told Caleb that she was with him and Caleb came to me ready to combust."

She was with Darius? Why?

"Yeah, she was," I said coolly, trying to cover my ass. "When she went to meet Darius I fell asleep at her place. I got back here an hour ago."

Seth ran his tongue across his teeth. "Alright, babe. Keep your secrets. If you want your needs met by a real man though, you know you can come to me. Caleb and Tory have a good thing going, we could have the same..." He stepped closer and I folded my arms.

"No thanks. I can meet my own needs."

"Hm, I'd like to see that some time." His eyes dragged down to my bare legs then back up to my eyes. "So my pack are still shunning me. Do you wanna come on a run with me again tonight?" He raised his brows, looking genuinely hopeful.

"No, Seth. You said you had to initiate me so you could kick me out. So get on with it."

"I'm working on it, little Omega. Or maybe I should call you little O-Vega." He chuckled and I gave him a blank stare. "Come on, I know you're tempted. Riding me is fun, isn't it?"

"Why don't you go bother your girlfriend with your innuendos? You know Kylie actually cares about you, right?"

Seth nodded, hanging his head. "I get separation anxiety." He started pacing. "Breakups are hard for wolves, especially for Alphas. I have to keep my options open until I find my mate. It's our nature, the best way to spread the gene pool, you know?"

"Surely you're not going to have kids with Kylie?" I said in disbelief.

"*I* know that, but my Alpha brain doesn't know that." He continued pacing, looking to me, whimpering as he went.

"Well it's not my business, but I don't think it's fair for you to keep her on the hook all the time."

"Are you jealous?" he asked hopefully and I snorted.

"No. Like really no."

"Oh." He sighed, resting back against the door. "So...do you wanna hang out for a bit?"

"No," I breathed in confusion. "Of course I don't."

"Right yeah..." He frowned, hanging his head and a whine sounded deep in his throat. "How about a hug then?"

"What part of 'I hate you' do you not get? You cut off my hair, Seth. And you knew what it meant to me when you did it." For a moment I was back there at Seth's feet, my hair clamped in his hand and my heart crumbling apart.

He nodded, his jaw tightening as he lifted his head. His eyes were as sharp as knives as they landed on me. "You don't know what it's like being one of us. I mean you really have no idea. A handful of hair is nothing for the sake of my throne, Darcy. Losing it would be the end of me."

"But you didn't just take my hair, you made me believe you liked me." I walked toward him, my shoulders quivering with rage as I closed the space between us. "You lied to my face, you tricked me into believing you were my friend. And maybe more than that."

He straightened as I got even closer, intending to try and make him leave even if I wasn't as well trained as him.

Flames flickered in my palms and he kicked off of the door, gazing down his perfectly straight nose at me with a penetrating look. "And what if I meant it? What if that part wasn't a game?"

My lips parted and I shook my head, refusing those words, but he caught my hand and tangled his fingers between mine.

"No." I yanked my hand back, trembling as I pointed at the door. "Get out."

He drew in a slow breath through his nose then turned and headed out of the door. A low howl filled the corridor which sent a ripple of discomfort through me.

Lying jerk.

Even if it was true I was minus five thousand percent interested. There was only one guy I wanted and he was of the bitey teacher variety.

I shot a text to Tory, checking in to make sure she was alright after her night with Darius. It wasn't long before our Air Trial started and I hoped she was ready for it. A yawn fought its way out of my throat and I wondered if *I* was ready for it.

She finally replied and I relaxed as I read her text.

Tory:

I'm okay. Raced Darius on his bikes. I won.

Darcy:

Woo! Do you wanna get breakfast and tell me about it?

Tory:

It's so early.

Darcy:

It's nearly 9!

Tory:

Shhhhhhhh.

I laughed, heading into the bathroom to get ready for the day, unsure what to wear. As we didn't have lessons and I didn't know what was required for the trial, I dressed in jeans, boots and a cami, tugging on a cream cardigan over the top. I stuffed my Atlas in my pocket, grabbed my coat and headed out of the door.

I hurried downstairs and into the cool air which was gusting around but the depths of the storm had moved on. Leaves tumbled around me, some of them still green, torn from their branches in the night.

I headed to The Orb, growing more nervous with every step I took. *What if Orion's there?*

I wanted to see him, but I was also slightly terrified of pretending last night hadn't happened. It meant so much to me that it made me kind of sad that I couldn't talk to anyone about it. And that led me to worrying about what the future held. Because how could this go on? Surely at some point we'd have to stop...

I'm just not going to think about it.

I stepped through the door, making a path for the large table full of A.S.S members, my eyes whipping to where the faculty usually sat. Orion was rarely ever at breakfast, so I didn't know why I expected him to be there today. My shoulders dropped a little when I didn't spot him and I headed over to sit between Sofia and Diego at the table. I didn't know if I was relieved or disappointed. Maybe a bit of both.

"Woah," Sofia gasped as she looked at me.

"What?" I whipped a bagel from a mountain in front of Geraldine.

"Babbling blueberries!" Geraldine exclaimed and I laughed, realising what the fuss was about.

"Oh yeah, I dyed it." I shook my head and my hair shimmered in my periphery.

"It's amazing," Sofia cooed.

"Fantastico," Diego agreed.

Geraldine wound her hands into her brown locks, eyeing my hair with delight. "Do you think my hair would agree with such an astounding colour?"

"I prefer red." Max appeared behind her, leaning forward and snatching a bagel from the mountain at the heart of the table.

Geraldine smacked his hand so hard, he dropped it back into the pile and he turned to glare at her.

My tongue grew heavier and magic tingled in my palms, but Geraldine was more than a match for Max Rigel. She was a force to be reckoned with on the Pitball pitch let alone what I imagined she could do when faced with a real fight.

She rose to her feet as Max stood back with a sneer, sizing her up.

Geraldine was eye to eye with him, almost the exact same height. "Your unroyal mits aren't fit to touch my buttery bagels," she hissed and it would have been funny if Max didn't look like he was about to rip her to shreds.

"Everything in that buffet belongs to me if I want it, Grus," he snarled. "Even your *buttery bagels.*"

"Well we'll see about that." She rolled up her sleeves and hoots and whistles sounded out as the rest of the students in The Orb realised a fight was about to break out.

"Are you sure about this, Geraldine?" Diego asked, looking anxious.

"Oh I'm as sure as a sugar loaf on a Tuesday morning, Diego," Geraldine said, lifting her chin.

"I guess that's sure," Sofia whispered to him and I couldn't fight a giggle.

"Take him out," Angelica encouraged, clapping excitedly.

The other Heirs appeared, muscling their way to the front of the crowd that had formed around Geraldine and Max.

Darius cocked his head to one side, evidently not having expected to find his friend facing off against Geraldine Grus. My gut tugged at the memory of him coming to Orion's house last night. What the hell had he wanted at two in the morning? I wondered if their bond with each other drew them together like that regularly, or if there had been another reason for him showing up there. It was extra annoying that I couldn't discuss it with Tory.

Seth rested his hand on Caleb's shoulder, bouncing on his heels and howling keenly.

"Show her who's boss, bro," Caleb said with a wide grin as Max and Geraldine squared up to each other.

Anxiety bubbled inside me as Max threw out his hands and water shot into the air in a stream, twisting up and around Geraldine to attack her from behind. She blocked it with a fierce slab of earth conjured from nothing then slammed her palm into the air, casting a splash of mud at his face. He whipped out a hand, blocking it with a shield of air and throwing the dirt back at her. She darted sideways and it slapped into the face of Milton Hubert amongst the crowd. He sighed heavily, wiping it from his cheeks with a disheartened expression.

I snorted a laugh as everyone started backing up and casting shields to protect themselves from rogue magic. Geraldine twisted through the air with grace, landing confidently and casting water beneath Max's feet. He ran through the puddle, looking like he was about to tackle her to the ground, but she froze it in an instant and he slipped and skidded, slamming to his knees with a curse.

"Vega *Ass*-licker!" he barked, using air to propel himself back to his feet.

"Griffin turd bather!" she shouted back and laughter rang out through The Orb which I was definitely joining in with.

Max threw a forceful vortex at her and she was caught up in it, spinning wildly around in circles. She cast water into the surrounding wind so it shot out from the tornado in a ferocious stream.

I gasped as water sprayed over everyone within range, wiping the splashes from my cheeks. Max increased the pressure of the wind, dumping her hard on the floor. She growled, whipping his legs out from under him with a shot of water.

He slammed down onto his back and she sprang forward with a battle cry, straddling him and pressing her weight down on his chest like they were in a Pitball match. He gazed up at her in shock as someone started counting down. "Five, four, three-!"

Max clutched her bare forearms and Geraldine drew in a sharp breath as his Siren gifts fell over her.

"Get off her!" Diego shouted, but didn't move to intervene.

My stomach writhed as Geraldine's eyes softened and her hands lifted from Max's chest, moving to caress his cheek instead.

"Slippery melons," she breathed. "You are a bad, bad beast, aren't you?"

Max shoved her off of him and rose to his feet, gazing down at her with a triumphant grin. Geraldine gazed up at him in confusion as the lust wore off. I frowned, annoyed on her behalf as Max kicked the puddle at his feet so it splashed over her. He leaned down as her features rearranged into a grimace.

"Yeah I'm real bad, peaches. Better not piss me off again, huh?" He stood upright, moving to the table and snatching a few bagels before moving off to join the Heirs at their couch.

Tory appeared, pushing through the dispersing crowd and dropping down beside me. "Shit did you just fight Max, Geraldine?" she asked and Geraldine nodded, her pride clearly wounded as she snatched up a bagel and took a ferocious bite out of it.

"Ooh that boy is six feet of rancid crustacean juice on a hot summer's day. What I'd give to see him fall from grace." Geraldine shot a glare over at the couch of Heirs, her eyes pinned on Max.

"Maybe we *can* do something," I said and Tory perked up as she sipped on a cup of coffee an Ass member had handed her.

"Like what?" she asked excitedly and Geraldine leaned in closer.

I bit my lip, gazing across the table to see what we had to work with, an idea coming together. I grabbed an empty bowl and lowered my voice. "Everyone pass me your scraps."

Geraldine scraped the last of her oatmeal into the bowl with a wide smile. "What are we making?"

"Griffin poo," I breathed and Tory giggled, splashing some of her coffee into the mix. Sofia sprinkled the remains of her pastry into the bowl and Diego added the last of his eggs with a low chuckle.

The rest of the A.S.S started surreptitiously passing down the remains of their breakfasts and I stirred in pieces of pancakes, croissants and various cereals. Finally, I grabbed the chocolate sauce and Tory grabbed the maple syrup from the centre of the table and we squeezed in a load before mixing it into a thick, brown gloop that I could barely extract the spoon from.

"How are we going to dump it on him?" Tory whispered with a grin, glancing over at the Heirs who were surrounded by a group of girls who giggled at everything they said.

"Umm…" I tried to think of a way and Geraldine slapped her hand on the table.

"If you are willing, Your Highnesses, then I would simply *love* the opportunity to volunteer. I can use my water magic to ensure this wonderful concoction finds its way to his head."

"Of course," I said, bobbing in my seat.

"Do it," Tory encouraged.

"I'll make everyone look away," Sofia whispered, concentrating as she cast the spell to draw everyone's attention off of us.

Geraldine poured the gloopy mixture onto the table, holding her hand over it and water slid into the liquid from her palm. She wiggled her fingers and the sludge moved like a slug under her will, crawling forward across the table.

"Oh my god *gross*," I giggled.

"If I could use a little of your air magic to elevate it to the ceiling, Your Highnesses?" Geraldine asked with glee in her eyes.

I took Tory's hand, knowing we could cast more accurately with our combined power and we focused on pushing air beneath the mixture. It peeled off the table with a schhhuuck sound then we propelled it toward the domed ceiling where it immediately got stuck. A laugh bubbled from my throat as we dispelled our air magic and the gloop remained stuck there.

"Get rid of the distraction spell, Sofia. We can't risk them sensing it," Geraldine encouraged. "Everyone act naturally."

The whole table fell into casual chatter around us and I leaned my elbow on the arm of my chair, fiddling with a spoon as Sofia's magic lifted away from us.

"Oh my god you are *so* funny," a blonde girl said to Max and he grinned from his seat beside Seth. "How'd you get *so* funny?"

"I practice in my bedroom," Max smirked. "You should come watch sometime."

I couldn't fight a glance up at the ceiling and a laugh battled to get free from my lungs as I saw the sludge slithering across the ceiling as Geraldine pressed her power into it. It wormed its way closer and closer to the Heirs' couch and I could barely contain my excitement as it drew to a halt above Max's head.

Geraldine's fingers curled into a fist as she stopped casting magic and anticipation rippled across the table as everyone waited for it to unstick itself from the ceiling.

Max leaned back in his seat, reaching a hand behind his head as he grinned cockily at the girl before him. "Maybe we should head to my room right now in fact."

"Right now?" she breathed, twirling a lock of hair between her fingers.

A spot of the sludge dripped down onto his face and he flinched, wiping it from his cheek with a frown. "What the-"

SPLAT.

Syrupy chocolate gloop exploded all over him, splashing Seth too and making him yelp as he lurched away. The girl he'd been talking to screamed and ran away with her friends.

"AH!" Max shouted, jumping to his feet followed by the rest of the Heirs who looked ready to take on everyone in The Orb. Brown muck slid down his face and Seth pawed at him to try and wipe it away.

"Who the fuck did this?!" Max bellowed, dislodging bits of food and sending them flying around him.

Laughter roared through the room and I lost control, leaning against Tory as tears swam in my eyes.

"Oh my god it's Griffin shit!" someone shouted and Max whipped around, trying to locate them amongst the crowd.

"It's not!" he roared, lifting a hand to cast water to wash it off but there was so much syrup in it, he had trouble getting it off. "It's not Griffin shit!"

Seth wiped some off of his shirt, lifting it to his mouth and licking it. "It's chocolate."

"Oh my god, Seth Capella is eating shit!" Tyler shouted and Seth looked up with a bark of anger as people started taking pictures and echoing what Tyler had said.

"For fuck's sake, let's go," Caleb snapped, taking hold of Seth's arm and Darius moved forward, pushing Max along. They hurried out of The Orb while Max threatened to kill anyone who took a picture of him and Tory and I fell apart.

I headed down to Air Cove with Diego and Tory, nerves rushing through me as we arrived at the beach with the other air Elemental freshmen. The fun we'd had in The Orb had given way to anxiety now we were faced with our first trial.

A set of bleachers had been set up further along the sand and the freshmen ran to meet their parents who had come to watch. As more and more students were wrapped up in the arms of their mothers and fathers, my heart filled with a long-forgotten ache. Tory and I were soon left with Diego, waiting awkwardly for the hugging to stop.

Diego shuffled in the sand, glancing hopefully toward the seats and a minute later a tall man appeared with short dark curls and a thin moustache. His suit was a murky brown colour and he wore a thick red woolen scarf against the chill. He had a frown on his face and the lines around his mouth said it was a life-long expression as he jerked his head to beckon Diego over.

"That's my uncle Alejandro," Diego said to us with a nervous smile then hurried away to greet him.

"Looks friendly," Tory muttered.

Alejandro patted Diego awkwardly on the shoulder then folded his arms and remained silent as Diego spoke to him.

"What's with that family and fugly knitwear?" Tory said under her breath and I started laughing.

"Don't let Diego hear you say that, I think he'd sacrifice a goat for his hat," I teased and she grinned like I'd just dared her to do it.

I dug my feet into the sand as we stood there waiting and turned my gaze to the sea to try and figure out what this trial might involve. Clouds had drawn in and the water was choppy and grey beneath it. I could just make out a wide wooden platform bobbing on the surface far out to sea.

A table was set up in front of the bleachers where Professor Perseus and Principal Nova were sitting. The wind didn't seem to tug at their clothes or hair and I assumed a shield was cast around them as they chatted lightly, unaffected by the cold weather.

"Daddy!" Kylie shrieked as she appeared on the beach, bounding past us before being drawn into the arms of a handsome man with dark blonde hair and deep green eyes. I looked for her mother but didn't see anyone nearby who fit the bill and Kylie didn't look for anyone else when she detached herself from her father's arms.

"Don't drown today, little Vegas," Max's voice hit my ears and I turned in alarm, spotting the four Heirs moving toward us with their fan club in tow. He was entirely clean and I realised all of them had changed their clothes as if in solidarity. Nothing about Max's expression hinted at what had happened to him, but rage seeped from him in waves. "We'll be watching."

"Yeah don't go dropping out of the Academy and doing us all a favour or anything," Darius taunted, but his tone was kind of hollow as his eyes slid to the crowd. He nudged Seth beside him. "Great. They're all gonna want autographs."

Caleb's gaze pinned on Tory and she bit her lip, looking uncomfortable as he walked towards her.

"Is your Atlas broken, sweetheart?" he asked, a slight frown pulling at his handsome features.

"Nope," she replied casually though I could tell she was putting it on. "Why?"

"I sent you a few messages and you don't seem to have replied. And then I find out you're off chasing around after one of my friends all night. So what am I supposed to make of that?"

Darius was smirking behind Caleb's back and Max shifted uncomfortably, folding his arms as Seth whimpered.

Tory's gaze hardened as all of them looked at her and I almost winced in preparation of her response. If Caleb expected her to apologise he was about to be severely disappointed because my sister never let guys back her into a corner and I could see her temper flaring as he tried.

"Honestly?" Tory asked, cocking an eyebrow at him. "I don't tend to date guys who are so needy they send me fifteen messages without a response. So if you're hoping for me to message you back you might wanna tone back the desperate vibe I'm getting. And secondly, I'm not your girlfriend so I don't have to check with you about where I spend my evenings or who I spend them with."

Caleb scowled at her, his fangs snapping out as he lurched towards her, clearly intending to bite. Tory stepped back but he jerked to a halt as Darius caught his arm, a low growl sounding from him as he did.

"If you bite her right before her trial then people will say you were trying to sabotage her by draining her magic," Darius hissed. "It'll make it look like we're worried about them passing The Reckoning."

Caleb opened his mouth to respond but Max got there first. "He's right, Cal, just leave it."

"Why don't we go and watch from down there?" Seth pointed to the other end of the beach, throwing a glance at Kylie and her dad. "Let's avoid all the bullshit."

"Yeah I'm sure you've had enough shit for one day," I said airily and Seth glared at me in fury.

"Sethy!" Kylie suddenly spotted him. "Come say hi!"

"Hi Kylie!" he waved enthusiastically.

"Come on over!" she beckoned him.

"What? Can't hear you! Good luck!" Seth headed in the opposite direction, tossing an arm around Caleb to make sure he followed and the others walked after him, shoulder to shoulder. Their friends trailed behind them and I spotted more and more of their groupies pouring onto the beach including Marguerite dressed in full cheerleader uniform with the squad behind her.

"I didn't realise other students could come and watch," I muttered to Tory. "We could have asked Sofia along."

"Well she's probably better off not being stuck on a beach with that bunch of dickwads," Tory reasoned.

"Tory, Darcy, would you like to come and meet my uncle?" Diego called and I was glad of the distraction as we headed over.

He stood awkwardly beside the man in question who looked like he was attending a funeral rather than his nephew's school assessment.

"Good day, my name is Alejandro Calabozo," he said in a faint spanish accent, his pebble grey eyes moving between us curiously.

"Nice scarf," Tory said overenthusiastically and it took everything I had not to start laughing.

Alejandro stroked it proudly. "Mi madre knitted it for me."

"Oh, Diego's abuela?" I guessed and Diego's eyes narrowed on us.

"Si, rest her soul." Alejandro kissed his fingers and pointed them to the sky. "She's with the stars now. But at least she isn't around today to be disappointed by her grandson." His lips tightened.

"I'm sure she wouldn't be disappointed," I said, but Alejandro didn't acknowledge that comment.

"So my nephew says you're friends. How much did he pay you to say that? I'll be sure to reimburse you."

"*Uncle*," Diego grumbled.

"Of course he didn't pay us," I laughed, but apparently Alejandro hadn't been joking as he fished out his wallet and starting to count out auras.

"No really, dude," Tory refused. "He's our friend."

Alejandro's expression barely changed apart from the corners of his eyes crinkling slightly. "Well, what wonderful news," he said hollowly. "Diego has finally done something worthwhile with his miserable existence."

"Being friends with us isn't really an achievement," I said, trying to fight Diego's corner, but I realised how it sounded a second too late.

"No, you're right. It isn't," Alejandro sighed then clapped Diego around the back of the head. "Are you going to disappoint your parents today? You know I'm only here to pass on the message of whether you pass or fail. I really didn't want to waste an afternoon, but your mother insisted so here we are."

Diego hung his head. "Is she mad?"

"Seething," he enunciated every letter.

"Why? He hasn't even done the trial yet," Tory said in disbelief.

"She's mad because I've been having trouble casting my magic," Diego said quickly. "I write to her every week to update her."

I glanced at Tory, feeling a little unsure of what to say.

"She wanted me to tell you that you don't have a room to come home to if you fail today," Alejandro said and my jaw fell slack. "Have you grasped *any* basic spells yet or are my expectations rightfully low?"

"I have. And I won't fail," Diego growled, his shoulders stiffening and his eyes filling with determination.

"That's right, you won't," I said firmly and he gave me a small smile.

"Air students – please make your way into the tents to change!" Nova commanded, pointing beyond the bleachers where two tents were set up for guys and girls.

The fifty or so air freshmen headed down the sandy beach toward the tents and I walked away from Diego's cold uncle with Tory, hearing Alejandro laying into him in Spanish before he could follow.

"I'm starting to think having no parents is a good thing in Solaria," Tory said, though as my eyes trailed over the many proud faces in the stands, I wondered if that was entirely true.

For a delusional moment, I pictured our mother and father up there, conjuring an image of them with our dark hair and deeply bronzed skin, calling our names as we headed into the trial. A bitter kind of sigh left me then I pushed the vision away and headed into the female tent with my sister. Sometimes it was better not to indulge in impossible dreams. And at least we had each other.

A pile of wetsuits were laid out in different sizes on a wooden bench and Tory scooped up two smalls for us before we moved into a corner to change. I folded my clothes as I stripped down and tugged on the wetsuit. Tory pulled up the long zip at the back for me and I gazed down at the tight-fitting suit with a frown. "I thought this was an air challenge."

"Looks like we're going in the sea though," Tory said with a visible shiver. "I'm already cold and I freaking hate the water."

"Will you be alright?" I asked with concern and she nodded firmly as I did up the back of her suit too.

"Max Rigel taught me that air bubble thing. I'll be fine."

I nodded, hoping that was true. "I wish I could do that hot air thing." I lifted my hand, drawing air to my fingers and trying to warm it but the magic only switched sharply to a roaring flame instead.

"Bit late to practice now," Tory laughed. "You'll set your suit on fire first."

"Yep, guess we're gonna get cold and wet then," I conceded, moving to follow the other girls as we headed back onto the beach barefoot.

The boys were already waiting in front of the judges' table and the girls grouped around them as we looked to the teachers for direction.

"Right," Nova said brightly. "We're just waiting for our final judge and we'll get started," She glanced up to the end of the beach with a frustrated look and I suddenly had a pretty good idea who we were waiting for.

My heart did something weird as I continually glanced at the path leading down the cliff, expecting to see Orion at any moment.

Nova checked her watch, shaking her head in annoyance before tapping something on her Atlas which I suspected was a message to hurry him up.

"You alright? You look kind of pale," Tory asked.

"Just nerves," I said. Which was true, but now my nerves had escalated to fidgeting hands and major dry mouth. The breeze pressed in around us as we waited and everyone grew impatient.

"Here he is, Professor Gives No Shits himself," Tory announced and I bit into my lip as Orion strode across the sand at a pace that suggested he wasn't late, maybe even early.

He was dressed in jeans and a t-shirt looking decidedly casual, but the second he drew near he tugged his shirt over his head and my eyes arrowed in on his chest. My throat closed up as I took in all of those hard muscles which had been firmly pressed against my naked body not that long ago. *What the hell is he doing?*

"Get up then Perseus, wouldn't wanna start late, would we?" he shot at the Air Elemental Professor with a smirk.

Professor Perseus got to his feet, looking a little flustered as he hurried over to join him. Orion kicked off his shoes and proceeded to unbuckle his pants, giving the whole audience a show.

What the crap is happening?

I glanced around and found most of the girls and several of the boys outright staring at him, waking a feral creature in my chest that growled *mine*.

I shook off the strange feeling with a frown. I was so not a possessive person but something purely animal awoke in me when I was around Orion. And I was kind of afraid of the certainty with which she wanted him. I'd struggled with my trust issues for a long time, but he'd slipped through my defenses like they didn't even exist. We'd power shared in the battle without a moment's hesitation and I'd only realised how impossible that was to do with anyone other than my sister after trying to do it with Caleb in Fire Elemental class.

Perseus pulled his own shirt off followed by his trousers, giving a show of his body which was surprisingly toned. I only had eyes for Orion though as he stepped out of his pants and socks, then walked straight into the sea like a goddamn backwards bond moment.

"Fuck me...that body," Tory whispered, watching him and a small laugh escaped me.

Dammit, I wish I could tell her about last night.

Perseus headed out after Orion until the two of them were up to their waists in the sea about twenty feet apart.

Nova rose from her chair, looking stern. "Right, you will all have one hour to make it to that platform out there." She pointed far out to sea. "It's a three hundred foot stretch over very deep water. You must only use air magic to get there, but you can do so in any form you please, and you must not get wet once you pass the starting line." She lifted her hand and a glowing green line appeared in the sea just ahead of Orion and Perseus.

"Will we fail if we do?" Kylie balked like that seemed impossible and I had to agree with her.

"Of course not." Nova clucked her tongue. "If you touch the water on your way out there, Professor Orion or Professor Perseus will bring you back to the starting line where you will try again. If you cannot make it to the platform before the time is up, you will fail the exam. You may work together or alone, it's entirely up to you. And if you *do* make it to the platform, you will be graded by both myself and the other professors based on your skill, how many failures you had and how long it took for you to make it there. Any questions?"

"What happens if we use magic that isn't air?" Kylie asked as pink petals danced in her hand.

"You will be disqualified," Nova said firmly and Kylie quickly dropped the petals to the ground.

"Is there a water Elemental here who's going to warm up the sea?" Diego asked, looking genuinely hopeful of that and Nova threw back her head on a laugh.

"Okay. Question time is over." She raised her hands and a huge timer burst from her palms, travelling up high above the water and showing sixty minutes on the clock. It glowed red just like the Pitball timer and I marvelled at the magic for a moment before setting my eye on the horizon.

"Line up at the sea's edge!" Nova commanded and the parents behind us started cheering excitedly. I was sharply reminded that no one here was cheering for us and dug deep to summon my courage.

We'll cheer for our damn selves.

Tory and I hurried along the shore to the furthest end of the line. "We're doing this with each other, right?" she asked.

"Of course," I said then frowned as she eyed the water. "Are you sure you're gonna be okay?"

She nodded firmly. "We'll get through this together."

"Together," I echoed, pulling her into a quick hug before facing the sea again.

"Any ideas how though?" she breathed, but a whistle blared in my ears and the clock started running down.

Students poured into the sea and we ran forward too. The second the waves splashed up my legs, I winced as the cold water sank into my wet suit, chilling me instantly. We hurried out toward the starting line and I shot a glance at other students as they drew to a halt in front of it too. Goosebumps spread out across my flesh and I clenched my teeth as I tried to focus.

"Let's just try to fly over there," Tory suggested, raising her hands above the sloshing waves.

A shriek caught my attention and I spotted Kylie casting herself haphazardly into the air. She lost control and immediately sank under the waves on the other side of the line. Perseus lifted a hand, ripping her backwards through the sea and depositing her at the starting line again. She spluttered, pushing her golden hair out of her face with a grimace.

Several more students made their attempts and I turned to Tory, focusing on our own plan.

"Okay let's do it," I said.

We both cast air from our hands, pushing ourselves out of the water to hover above the sea. I angled my palms to try and float forward and grinned as I managed it, moving slowly over the start line. Tory went up way higher than me and I glanced up at her as water streamed from her feet all over my head.

"Go on Tor!" I cried, pushing more air beneath me.

I spotted Diego being yanked out of the water by a whip of wind and thrown back beyond the starting line at high speed, his arms and legs cartwheeling as he hit the waves and sank under.

Several other students were trying out our tactic, but others were casting small pockets of air, hopping from one to another as they progressed toward the platform.

I pushed the wind from my hands and too much energy rushed from me at once. I cried out as I shot sideways. The second I panicked, I was done for. I lost control and sucked in a breath at the last moment as I crashed into the water beneath me.

Icy salt water assaulted my senses and I kicked hard to breach the surface.

A tight coil wrapped around my middle and I jerked backwards violently as I was yanked out of the water by the whip of air.

I flew backwards above the sea and my stomach swooped violently as I was dropped unceremoniously back over the starting line. Someone's arm curled around my waist, dragging me upright and I found myself face to chest with Orion. My hand was pressed to his bicep and I immediately withdrew, cursing my racing heart.

I gave him the hint of a smile then turned and ran back to the starting line just in time to see Tory being dumped into the water beside me. She came up spluttering, shaking her head violently and a stream of curses left her lips as she blinked the salt water from her eyes.

Screams filled the air as students were dragged out of the water left right and centre, but a few had made it almost half way to the platform and determination filled me as Tory and I moved closer to the glowing green belt of magic.

Adrenaline started to keep the cold at bay and I set my eyes on the platform with my jaw clenched. The crowd was cheering behind me and someone got overly excited as a girl far out to sea almost reached the platform. She started running across the air she'd cast beneath her, but suddenly stumbled, her arms wheeling, her scream carrying back to us. She plummeted into the ocean and Perseus tore her from the water, dragging her all the way back to the starting line at a ferocious speed. A huge splash crashed over us as she was dropped beside us then came up for air with a huge breath. My eyes widened as I realised it was Jillian.

She huffed, moving back to the line to start again and Tory grabbed my hand, her power flowing into mine.

"We're stronger together," she said and I nodded, my heart dancing at the feeling of our magic merging.

"Cast air beneath us and run like hell?" I suggested and she grinned.

"Worth a shot."

With our free hands, we pushed ourselves out of the water with a blast of air, hovering a foot above the surface. I clutched her hand tighter and she squeezed my fingers in reassurance.

"Ready?" she asked.

Before I could answer, a howl hit my ears followed by a chant from the Heirs. "The Vega Twins are out of luck, it's time for you to give it up!"

"Shitbags," Tory growled as the crowd of their friends took up the chant so it echoed off of the cliff walls. Even some of the parents joined in.

"Let's show them what we can do," I hissed and Tory nodded.

We glided forward across the starting line then Tory counted, "Three, two, one-"

We continued to cast air beneath our feet and started running, sprinting for the platform out to sea. We moved faster and faster, the shield beneath us growing almost solid as we raced along it in perfect time with one another.

The chant grew deafeningly loud, following us over the water so we couldn't possibly escape it. "THE VEGA TWINS ARE OUT OF LUCK, IT'S TIME FOR YOU TO GIVE IT UP!"

I tried to focus on the magic at my fingertips, forcing it beneath our bare feet as we pushed ourselves even faster. The platform was in sight and no other students were even close. Cheers and boos tangled in the air as we got nearer and nearer to finishing this trial before anyone else.

"No one wants you to win, losers!" Max's voice rose above the crowd followed by another of Seth's piercing howls.

"I guess losing is in your blood, Roxy!" Darius called and I felt her concentration falter a little.

"Don't listen," I panted, trying to block them out and Tory nodded.

"Whoever you were screwing last night is having hashtag regrets right about now, Darcy!" Seth bellowed.

My blood turned to ice. Tory glanced at me and the air gave way beneath us the moment we lost concentration. We plunged into the ocean just ten feet from the platform and the icy water enveloped us once more. I was barely under for a second before magic snared my waist and I was ripped backwards through the waves. A scream got stuck in my throat as I ascended from the sea, flying through the air and crashing into the water in front of the starting line. I coughed heavily as I tried to force the briny water from my throat, staggering as I found my bearings. My hand pressed to firm, warm skin and I looked up, finding Orion right next to me.

His jaw was tight and I gave him a look that I hoped communicated the fact Seth was just baiting me and didn't really know anything.

"Focus," he growled, pushing me back toward the starting line.

I stumbled toward Tory as she slogged away from Perseus with a scowl.

Diego suddenly crashed into the water between us, rising to his feet with a desperate look on his face. "I'm not gonna get through this," he panted, pushing his sopping wet hair out of his eyes.

"You will," I said firmly, looking to Tory. She shook her head as she realised what I was about to offer, then stopped the second Diego glanced over his shoulder at her.

"We'll do it together," I said and Tory gave him a tight smile.

"Yeah, Diego," she said, prodding him toward the starting line. "Together." She threw me a concerned look and I couldn't help but return it as I hoped Diego wouldn't hinder us. We couldn't hesitate any longer though; the timer was already halfway down. At least no one else had made it to the platform yet so we weren't the only ones struggling.

"The Vega girls are super lame, go ahead, renounce your claim!"

I turned, spotting Marguerite heading a line of cheerleaders in navy and silver, waving their pom poms at us. They all flipped backwards in the sand, bending over one at a time to reveal the phrase '*Vega Whores*' spelled out across their asses on their white underwear.

"Screw them." I turned to face the sea, gathering air between my fingertips.

"How about a shield?" I suggested and Tory nodded.

"Yeah, maybe we can use it like an inflatable ball," she mused.

"I missed the class on shields, chicas," Diego said sadly, hanging his head.

"We'll help," I said immediately and Tory nodded. Her gaze drifted back to our enemies on the beach then she moved closer and rested her hand on Diego's arm.

"Just stay close," she said firmly.

"Okay, if you're sure?" he asked and we nodded. We couldn't just leave him here to fail. He was our friend.

Tory and I caught hold of his hands and we cast air at the same time. Diego helped but our combined magic was obviously doing the heavy lifting as we rose above the water once more. A tumult of cheers fell over us and I gazed out to the platform where several students were stepping onto it. Jealousy hit me as I took in the line up. I was fairly sure Kylie Major and her friend Jillian were amongst them.

"Come on, let's finish this," Tory growled, casting a firm shield around us.

"Vega whores are such a bore!" Marguerite led the next chant, but this one only fuelled my determination. "The boys they screw don't come for more!"

I pushed my magic out to join my sister's and the wind halted as we created a solid sphere around us. The noise around us dimmed so we could barely hear the chanting over the intensity of our shield.

"Three," I breathed excitedly.

"Two," Diego said.

"One!" Tory cried and we charged forward, making the shield spin around us like we were in a solid ball. I whooped as we all fell into a rhythm, moving in perfect synchronization as we raced for the finish line.

"Keep going!" I encouraged and we picked up speed, moving across the sea with complete ease.

We made it over the water so fast that I was shocked when we suddenly rolled onto the platform. We dissolved the magic and dove on each other in a three-way hug, bouncing up and down in excitement.

The timer still had twenty minutes left on it and I beamed as pride swelled in my chest. We'd made it through the first trial.

"We did it!" Tory cheered and Diego looked between us guiltily, but I didn't acknowledge it. So what if he'd gotten a free ride? He deserved to be in this academy as much as we did.

We waited for the trial to end and soon thirty eight others joined us on the platform. When the timer went off, a horrible feeling scraped through my stomach. A girl just two feet from the finish line wailed in horror as she realised she hadn't made it in time. She'd have a low score when it came to The Reckoning. My heart juddered as I looked to Tory, seeing the same feeling reflected in her eyes.

"We can't fail any of these trials and risk not making the cut," she said and I nodded seriously.

"We won't, Tor. Zodiac is where we belong."

TORY

CHAPTER SEVENTEEN

The high I felt after completing our Air Trial was simmering through my veins as I stood beneath the steaming hot water in my shower.

I closed my eyes, letting the water ease some of the knots out of my shoulders as my mind began to wander. I kept thinking back over last night and the way that Darius had made me laugh when I'd let my guard down a little. Sometimes it was like he was a completely different person to the dick who had done so many awful things to me from the first second I'd arrived in this academy. My mind drifted to the way it had felt to wake up in his arms and how my fingertips had trailed over his sculpted muscles. I wondered what it would be like to trace the lines of all of his tattoos and how he might react to me doing it. I bit my lip as my mind started to wander in the direction of where that might lead and I had to curse my luck for the thousandth time that he was such a damn asshole.

But if he wasn't then there were more than a few things I'd like to have done with him. I thought about the way he'd looked at me when he'd tried to convince me to stay with him last night and my heart started to beat a little faster, my breaths coming a little heavier-

"This is your worst attempt yet, sweetheart," Caleb's voice came through the door to my en-suite and I half leapt out of my skin. A scream escaped my lips and I stumbled back a step, knocking the shower door open with a loud bang.

"What the fuck are you doing in my room?" I shouted, snatching a towel and wrapping it around me tightly before I stormed towards the door.

I threw it open with another bang and found Caleb lounging against my desk like he owned the goddamn world. His blonde hair was dishevelled and he was wearing a pair of jeans and a red t-shirt which hugged his muscular figure and made him look good enough to eat. Or at least it would have if he hadn't just broken into my room and scared the crap out of me.

"I messaged you," he said innocently. "Fifteen minutes. You had time to run." He pushed himself upright, moving towards me but I glared at him in response, making him hesitate.

"New rule. If you haven't had a reply then the game isn't on. I was in the shower. I didn't even get your damn message. And how did you get in here?"

Caleb seemed to realise that I was genuinely pissed off and he stopped his advance on me, raising his hands innocently.

"Your door was unlocked. I thought you left it open for me."

I opened my mouth to protest, but he might have been right. I'd come back here in a hurry and it was possible I hadn't locked the door.

"Well I didn't. And I was under the impression you were pissed at me anyway?"

"I thought I'd give you the opportunity to apologise," Caleb raised an eyebrow expectantly and I scoffed.

"Not likely. You're the one acting like you own me because we hooked up a few times. How would you respond to a girl who did that to you?"

Caleb sighed dramatically, his lips twitching like he was amused. "You could give it a try and I'll see if I like it?" he suggested.

I gave him a flat look and he drew closer to me.

"Okay," he said, raising his hands in defeat. "Point taken. Let me make it up to you."

He leaned in and pressed a kiss to the corner of my mouth, slowly carving a trail along my jaw and down my neck as he pushed his fingers into my wet hair. Heat spread beneath my skin and a small smile tugged at my lips as he broke through my irritation with him.

"Are you going to give me some space to get dressed?" I asked as he pressed his body against me more firmly, my heart beating faster in response.

"Don't you want me to stay?" he murmured.

"I'm meeting Darcy and my friends in The Orb. And I'm starving. So no," I pulled back and pointed him towards the door but he resisted.

"I thought-"

My door opened again and we both looked around as Darius stepped into the doorway.

"What are you screaming about in here? I thought you were being murdered." His eyes took in my wet hair and towel and the fact that I was trying to push Caleb out of the room and a low growl rumbled from his chest. My skin suddenly felt altogether too hot.

"Well now you can see no one is here to murder her you can leave us to it," Caleb replied, moving closer to me instead of further away.

"No. Now that both of you have let yourselves into my room without knocking, you can both fuck off," I snapped, embarrassment clawing at me.

"I was just making sure you were alright," Darius said softly, his eyes on me but the tension in his posture was all for Caleb's benefit.

"I will be when you're both gone." My heart was pounding something chronic and blood was heating my cheeks. There was one thin towel dividing my body from these two gorgeous men and my blood was pumping like mad with a mixture of mortification and something a little less respectable.

The two of them looked at me and I fixed a scowl on my face as I waited for them to do as they were told.

"Sorry for crossing a line, sweetheart," Caleb said softly, pressing a brief kiss to my cheek before heading towards Darius. "Come on Darius, let's go get a drink."

Darius's eyes stayed on me for a long moment and I couldn't really do anything but stare back at him, caught in the snare of his gaze.

Caleb clapped him on the arm as he reached him and he nodded, turning away quickly and pulling my door shut without so much as another word to me.

I moved forward to lock my door, blowing out a shaky breath as my frantic heart settled.

Geraldine had messaged to say the Ass Club were making a celebration out of dinner for us in The Orb so I pulled a blood red skater dress out of my closet and spent a bit of time styling my hair and doing my makeup before I headed out.

The sun was low in the sky but it wasn't cold out so I grabbed my leather jacket and threw my Atlas into my pocket.

I still felt a little jittery after having a Vampire and a Dragon Shifter break into my room while I was showering and I quickly scoured my desk for something sweet to take the edge off of my nerves.

I checked my bedside locker when I couldn't come up with anything but instead of finding candy, my fingers brushed against the hilt of the dagger I'd stolen from Darius's room.

A deep longing coiled its way through my chest and I pulled it into my grasp, letting out a soft sigh as I held it. I closed my eyes for a moment, almost feeling like I was in the presence of an old friend, someone who wanted to protect me...

I bit my lip as I looked down at the silver blade, running my thumb over the swirling design engraved on the hilt.

My horoscope had warned about troubles as night drew in today and as I glanced out of my window at the sun which was already beginning to set, I wondered if taking the dagger with me wouldn't be the worst idea. If I ran into any Nymphs then I could use it to defend myself if my magic was paralysed, especially as I hadn't been able to summon the blue and red flames again since the attack...

With a shrug of my shoulders, I slid the dagger into my pocket and zipped it up. I could still feel the call of the blade through the material which divided it from my skin and there was something oddly comforting about having it close like that. It wasn't like I was going to use it anyway. It was just backup. Just in case.

I headed out of my room to meet Sofia in the common room so that we could head for The Orb together.

She wasn't there when I arrived and my gaze lingered on Milton Hubert who was sitting in the back corner of the room by a window. No one was looking his way or talking to him. He was completely isolated just as he had been every time I'd seen him since I'd let him take the fall for stealing Darius's treasure and he looked utterly miserable.

My gut twisted uncomfortably. Milton was an ass who had taken naked pictures of me and spread them around the school but he'd never been outwardly hostile to me aside from that. I'd known that Darius would be pissed at him for stealing his treasure and I'd wanted to throw a bit of discord and mistrust into Darius's inner circle but I hadn't realised he'd become a total pariah. This shunning stuff was pretty twisted.

I pursed my lips and decided that it was probably on me to do something about this situation if I didn't want it to go on.

I crossed the room with purposeful steps and came to a halt behind the chair opposite Milton. He looked up at me in surprise, glancing around as if he thought there must be someone else here I'd been meaning to talk to.

"Can I help you?" he asked hesitantly.

"Mind if I sit?" I asked, taking a seat anyway.

He raised a bushy eyebrow at me and looked around nervously again.

"Darius won't like it if he sees you talking to me."

"Pfft. I don't give a crap what Darius likes," I said dismissively. "You may not have noticed but he's done some rather unpleasant things to me too. So I'm thinking that we're in the same boat as far as that goes."

"I didn't steal from him though," Milton said with a frown. "I swear I-"

"And *I* don't want his stupid throne but he doesn't really care about the truth, does he? Anyway, this isn't really about him. I was just thinking that maybe you and me could have a fresh start? You've done things to me and I've done things to you..." *Like putting you in this shitty position...* "But we could just draw a line under all that now if you want? Start over as friends?"

"Why would you want to be my friend? Darius has made it clear that anyone who's seen with me will-"

"I don't care what Darius thinks, dude. And I've got my own friends who he already doesn't like. I assure you the A.S.S. won't shun you if I say you're cool by me. And I promise you won't even have to wear a shiny Ass badge to hang out with us."

"I dunno..." Milton looked around nervously like he was expecting a pissy Dragon to appear at any moment.

"Your choice, dude, but the offer is there. At this point what more can he really do to you anyway? Seems silly to shun yourself into a corner when you're being offered an olive branch." I shrugged and got to my feet as I spotted Sofia entering the room.

She grinned excitedly as she showed off a new slinky black dress she was wearing and I moved to join her.

"So is that for Diego's benefit or Tyler's?" I asked.

"If I say both does that make me a terrible person?" she asked and I laughed.

"Hell no. Let them fight it out for you," I encouraged with a grin and we headed across the common room for the exit.

I glanced back at Milton to see if he'd decided to join us and with a determined look, he got to his feet and crossed the room. I offered him an encouraging smile and Sofia widened her eyes at me, dropping her voice to a whisper.

"Is he coming with us?" she hissed. "If Darius sees-"

"I'll deal with Darius," I replied. "Besides, the enemy of my enemy and all that."

Sofia still didn't look convinced but she didn't say anything as Milton joined us and we made our way to The Orb.

We headed inside and I could practically feel the tension rolling off of Milton beside me as he looked towards the centre of the room where the Heirs were all sitting on their red couch.

I caught his arm and guided him through the crowd towards the left of the room where the Ass Club had congregated.

Milton ducked his head, clearly not wanting to draw the attention of the Ignis House Captain but as I glanced Darius's way it was clear that that tactic hadn't worked. Darius got to his feet and prowled towards us like a pissed off tiger who had just broken free of its cage.

"Shit," I muttered, pushing Milton a bit to encourage him into the safety of the Ass Club.

Geraldine perked up as she spotted us and leapt to her feet. "Good golly lolly, what a tremendous day!" she exclaimed. "Please let me be the first to offer-"

"Sorry Geraldine but I've just got a little situation to deal with," I interrupted. "Can you look after Milton here for me while I do?"

"It will be my honour to take on the task!" she gushed, pulling Milton towards her as I turned back to face the Dragon asshole who was burning a hole into the back of my head.

I turned and set a quick pace across the room, ignoring Darius as he closed in on me and heading straight for the ice cooler to grab myself a drink.

My hand closed on a bottle of pink lemonade just as Darius grabbed my wrist and spun me around to face him.

"Hi," I said innocently as he pinned me in with his huge body.

He frowned as that threw him off and I slowly unscrewed the top of my drink and took a swig.

"What are you doing coming in here with Milton?" he asked in a low voice as he recovered from his surprise.

"Are you jealous?" I teased.

A queue was forming as people tried to get to the ice cooler and I stepped a little closer to him, encouraging him to move. Darius didn't seem to give a shit about holding people up but he drew me away all the same, placing a hand on my back to make sure I didn't escape.

"I made it clear that Milton is being shunned," he snarled as we made it into a corner beside one of the fires which burned around the edges of The Orb. He placed a hand on the wall beside my head as I pressed my back to the golden wall but I arranged my features into a mask of mildly bored rather than giving any reaction to his intimidation tactics.

"And I made it clear I don't do as I'm told," I replied with a shrug, looking up at him as I toyed with the lemonade bottle in my hands. "Are you going to punish me?"

Darius growled at me and I smiled despite the shiver that ran down my spine in warning.

"Do you growl at everyone like that or do I get under your skin more than most people?" I asked.

"I find you particularly frustrating," he replied evenly. "And I think you sometimes forget what lies beneath my skin."

I gave him a sweeping look, my eyes trailing from his feet all the way back up to his eyes as he continued to lean over me and I shrugged.

"I haven't forgotten," I replied. "I'm just not going to let you push me around because you're scarier than me. Trying to avoid your wrath didn't do me any favours anyway, so why shouldn't I just do as I please?"

"Your smart mouth is going to get you into trouble with me one of these days," he warned.

"Is that a promise?"

Darius held my eye, inching closer to me like he wanted to see which of us would blink first. I held my ground, looking right back at him as my heart started pounding with fear and something a little more intoxicating. I couldn't back down now but I was sure he wasn't going to either.

"I want you to send Milton away again," he breathed, a dark warning.

"Are you really so unforgiving that you won't even let him have other friends?" I asked softly. "Isn't it enough that he's lost his social group and your affection? Let him hang out with the outcasts..."

"Why? I thought you hated him for sharing those pictures of you. Why do you even care what happens to him?" Darius asked, his voice lowering.

"Maybe I don't enjoy hating people," I replied. "Maybe I just want to forgive him and move on."

"Do you mean that?" Darius frowned at me and I shrugged.

"Why not? He only shared a few photographs. I made him delete them and I punished him for it. It's not like he's the one who burned my clothes off or like he did anything else to hurt me, is it? I might as well save my hatred for those more deserving."

"Do you hate *me* then, Roxy? Or do you still not care about me enough for that?"

"Why do you care if I do or I don't?" I asked in response because in that moment I didn't even know anymore. The heat of him was coiling around me again and instead of leaning away from him, I was shifting closer. He was danger and power and the worst kind of temptation but I almost wanted to find out just how close I could get before I got burned.

Someone cleared their throat beside us and I flinched away from Darius as if we'd just been caught doing something wrong.

"Forgetting something, Mr Acrux?" Orion asked mildly, his gaze sweeping over me where I was still pinned in against the wall.

"I'm not finished here," Darius replied without looking at him and I swallowed a lump in my throat as I looked back into his dark eyes.

"Do you want me to add time to your detention then?" Orion asked, his tone darkening.

Darius let out a breath of frustration, leaning in closer to me so that he could speak into my ear. "We aren't done, Roxy." His chest brushed against mine and the rough bite of his stubble grazed my jaw. He started to shift back but I caught his arm before he could, meeting his gaze as he looked at me curiously, barely a breath dividing us.

"I know we aren't," I replied, a smile tugging at the corner of my lips. "Because you still owe me a bike."

Darius let out a breath of laughter before drawing back and releasing me from the cage of his body. The heat of him retreated too and I watched him walk away with the faintest twinge of regret that we hadn't quite seen that altercation through.

Orion raised an eyebrow at me and I offered him a scowl in response to the judgment which he smirked at before leaving with Darius.

I quickly headed back across the room to find my friends and smiled as I spotted Darcy at our usual table.

I glanced over at the Heirs' couch and noticed a pretty girl with dark hair braided down her back sitting on Caleb's lap as he ran his fingers along her neck. He caught my eye and smiled provocatively and I smiled right back. If he thought he could make me jealous by biting some other girl then he was way off base. I was more than happy to give over the biting part of our relationship to someone else to endure.

I dropped down into my spot opposite Darcy and fell on my meal without any further distractions. The Air Trial had been exhausting and I was already dreading having another one tomorrow.

"Just imagine how tired we'll be by the time this Reckoning stuff is over," I groaned, shovelling creamy pasta into my mouth like the Italians might run out of it.

"Do you think all the trials will be that hard?" Darcy asked.

"I remember almost wetting my britches during my Earth Trial," Geraldine offered. "It was so darn hair-raising I almost had a perm by the end of it."

I sniggered a laugh and Milton hesitantly joined in. He was sitting beside her while she introduced him to every member of the Ass Club and tried to convince him to join up officially. To say he looked like a fish out of water was an understatement but he hadn't left to go sit alone in a corner so I guessed our fan club was preferable company to no company at all if nothing else.

"What did Darius want with you?" Darcy asked in an undertone as everyone returned their attention to their food.

"I dunno. He never really got to the point. Mostly he doesn't want me being friends with Milton but it always feels like I'm only getting half the story with him." I shrugged because I wasn't sure what else to say and Darcy nodded in understanding.

Caleb appeared between us in the blink of an eye, perching on the edge of our table and inspecting his fingernails.

"We have a problem, sweetheart," he said to me, though he continued to inspect his nails.

"I know. There's a Vampire sitting on our dinner," I replied and Darcy giggled in response.

"You're killing me, you know that?" he asked, dropping his hand and pinning me with his navy eyes. "You're ignoring my messages, you won't play our games, you won't visit me when I ask and to make it worse you're going on secret dates with my friends."

"What secret dates?" Sofia asked.

"Didn't she tell you she went out with Darius last night? He took her back to his manor and they got up to god knows what," Caleb said.

"I don't believe one of the true queens would spend her free time with that ruffian," Geraldine said proudly and I cleared my throat uncomfortably. I had been planning on telling them about my late night adventure at Acrux Manor especially if I'd won a shiny new bike but I hadn't gotten around to it yet with the madness of the Air Trial today. And it wasn't like it was something I could easily explain in a few short sentences either.

"He sent me a picture of them together to prove it if you don't believe me." Caleb pulled his Atlas from his pocket and flashed the picture Darius had taken of the two of us around at everyone.

I glanced at it and was surprised at how much we looked like a happy couple in the snapshot. I was looking straight into the camera, a laughing smile on my face while Darius pressed a kiss to my head, the corner of his mouth hooked into a grin and his arm wrapped around me.

"That is a pretty misleading picture," I said lamely as Darcy mouthed *what the hell?* at me behind Caleb's back.

"You look like you were having an absolutely marvellous set of shenanigans, Your Majesty!" Geraldine gushed, changing tact in an instant. "I didn't know you'd become so friendly with the sexy Dragon Heir!"

"Did you just call Darius Acrux sexy?" Sofia asked in surprise and I snorted a laugh as Geraldine blushed.

"Well I have *eyes*!" she said defensively. "That's not to say he's the *most* attractive of the Heirs."

"Obviously," Caleb said cockily.

"No. Clearly the title of the most drool inspiring hunk of handsome goes to Max Rigel even if he is a blackhearted fiend. But Darius isn't a bad second," Geraldine said, a faint blush lining her cheeks. Sofia started laughing and Darcy covered her mouth to hide her grin. Diego looked like he'd like to be absolutely anywhere else.

"What?" Caleb asked, his brows pinching with irritation as I snorted a laugh. "You're ranking me *third*?"

"No! Of course not!" Geraldine said loudly, seeming horrified. "Seth Capella would be third."

I fell back into my chair, clutching my stomach as my laughter grew out of control and Caleb tried his hardest not to look as disgusted as he clearly was.

Caleb seemed lost for words for a moment before obviously deciding he'd be better off not responding to Geraldine's assessment of him. He swung the photo back around to me and arched a brow instead.

"You care to explain your little date then, sweetheart?" he asked me as I reined in my amusement.

"It wasn't a date," I said, rolling my eyes. "And I'm sure he told you what we were doing anyway so why do you need me to confirm it?"

"Then why do you look so damn happy in this photo?" he asked.

I gave the picture another look and I had to admit he was right. Taken out of context it did look like we were really enjoying each other's company.

"You're right, I do. Maybe I should make it my profile pic?" I suggested.

"Are you aiming to break my heart, sweetheart?" Caleb asked me, placing his hand on his chest as he tucked the Atlas back into his pocket.

"Don't be ridiculous. You don't even have a heart," I teased.

Caleb leaned closer to me, smiling knowingly. "If I hadn't heard you scream my name with such vigour multiple times, I'd be thinking you're not into me at all."

Diego started choking on his spaghetti beside us and Sofia patted his back as Caleb raised an eyebrow at him.

"Do you always hang out with frigid virgins or do you make an exception for this specimen?" Caleb asked me in a whisper shout which carried to everyone.

"My main criteria is non assholes so really you're the one who's out of place." I shrugged at him and he smiled.

"Come and stay with me tonight," he said boldly, holding my eye as he waited for my answer.

"I need to get a good night's sleep before my Water Trial tomorrow. I don't think what you have in mind would include much rest."

"Do you enjoy making me run around after you like this?" he asked.

"I don't entirely hate it," I admitted.

Caleb smiled widely and got to his feet. "Then I'll be sure not to stop. You might want to watch out for Hell Week pranks tonight - though I could keep you safe if you take me up on my offer." He winked at me and was gone as quickly as he'd appeared. Darcy leaned over the table to talk to me again.

"Do you think we should get out of here?" she asked, glancing over at Caleb as he rejoined Seth and Max on their couch. "I swear they're plotting something."

The three Heirs had all shifted close together, talking in low voices while they shot glances around the room. The looks on their faces did seem pretty suspicious.

"You could have the right idea there," I agreed.

We said goodbye to our friends and headed out through the back of The Orb. As we went I glanced back at the three Heirs and found them watching us leave. I exchanged a look with Darcy and we upped our pace to escape them. This Hell Week stuff was getting out of hand. I was really looking forward to making it past The Reckoning and getting back to normal again. Whatever the hell that was around here.

A howl sounded from inside The Orb quickly followed by a cry of, "Gather the freshmen!" from Max Rigel.

"Oh shit," I breathed as Darcy snatched my hand and we started running.

We made it to the dark space between Earth Observatory and Mars Labs just as a flood of freshmen ran screaming from The Orb. Older students chased them with the hoods of their black cloaks pulled up and white masks in place.

My eyes widened as a wall of fire flared into existence beyond Jupiter

Hall, blocking the escape in that direction just as the ground started to tremor beneath our feet. The earthquake sent the freshmen crashing to their hands and knees where vines grew from the mud to trap them.

"Quick," I urged, turning away again as the older students started to move closer to us. "Let's get the hell out of here before they spot us!"

"Good plan!" Darcy raced away between the buildings, heading straight for the cover of The Wailing Wood.

Adrenaline surged through my veins as I hounded after her and the freshmen continued to scream as the Heirs and the other students carried out their Hell Week prank.

"Where did the Vegas go?" Seth yelled and I upped my pace even more.

"Where to?" I begged as we raced up the trail towards Aer House. "If we go back to our rooms they'll find us." I wanted to think the Heirs would accept us escaping them but I doubted there was much chance of that. We would be at the top of their hit list and they'd want to humiliate us more than anyone else.

"How about the beach?" Darcy panted as we ran on. "We could go to Air Cove where no one will be able to spot us and we can wait out the chaos."

"Sounds like a plan," I agreed.

A cry went up behind us and we both wheeled around in panic at the sound of footsteps racing along the path towards us.

We didn't dare say another word, simply upped our speed as we sprinted away.

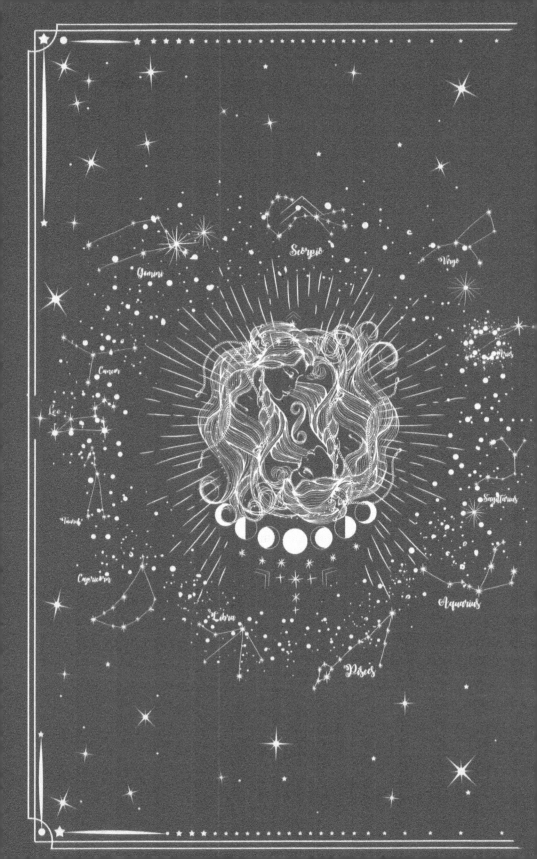

DARCY

CHAPTER EIGHTEEN

We darted down the steep pathway to Air Cove and I battled the urge to glance over my shoulder, needing to watch my feet in case I fell. With the pace we were moving at, even Tory stumbled more than once, but somehow we managed to remain upright, tearing onto the beach at the base of the path and finally pausing to check if we were still being followed.

"Did they see us?" Tory panted and I shook my head, dragging in a few lungfuls of the cold sea air.

"Don't think so," I gasped, a laugh tumbling from my throat. "We'd better keep moving just to be sure. There's another path up to Fire Territory at the far end of the beach that way." I pointed and Tory started in that direction.

The sand crushed beneath our feet, leaving a trail behind us and I paused, frowning at our footprints which led straight back to the path.

"Tory, we'd better cover these somehow."

She didn't answer and I looked over my shoulder, finding her heading off down the beach at a purposeful stride.

"Tor!" I called after her, but she still didn't look back.

What the hell? The wind wasn't *that* loud.

I jogged to catch up, having to abandon the footprints and just hope we'd lost the Heirs for good. I raced to my sister's side, catching her arm, "What's up?"

I glanced down at her hands, spotting that strange silver dagger she'd stolen from Darius's room in her grip.

"It's guiding me, I think it wants to show me something," Tory said, nudging me away and hurrying on down the beach.

My heart beat harder as I followed her. "Do you realise how crazy that sounds?"

"Yeah but…" she trailed off, picking up her pace.

My gut twisted as I jogged after her. "I really don't think it's a good idea to follow the urges of some creepy knife."

She didn't answer, moving to the cliff wall and running her fingers across it. "I think it's going to let us see," she murmured.

"See what? You're starting to freak me out." I tried to stop her again but she moved on methodically, seeming to search for something as she traced her hand along the cliff wall.

She halted abruptly and I caught her wrist, planning to pull the blade from her hand.

"Here," she whispered, lifting the dagger and scoring lines across the rock that were eerily deliberate, like the knife was guiding her hand.

My mouth parted as the wall completely disappeared. We were looking right into a cave with a domed roof; glistening stalactites hung from the ceiling and glinted like diamonds. But that wasn't what shocked me most, it was the two people standing inside who made my heart tumble into my gut. Darius and Orion didn't appear to see us standing there as they spoke with one another, the battering sea air not ruffling their hair one bit.

"They can't see us," Tory confirmed in a whisper and I noticed her pupils were overly dilated. I still wanted to get that dagger from her hands but I also couldn't resist the urge to find out exactly why Orion was here with the Fire Heir.

Sweat was beading on Darius brow and he swiped a hand across it, starting to pace in front of Orion. "I'll get it next time."

"You need to relax," Orion said patiently. "You can't control it through sheer rage. You must exert your will."

"I know, I know," Darius spat, kicking a stone at his feet and sending it skittering across the floor.

Orion shifted forward, pulling him around to look at him and leaning close to his face. "You want him gone, don't you?"

"Yes," Darius sighed, the tension in his shoulders running away. "You know I do."

"Then focus." Orion pushed him back a step and Darius rolled his neck, setting his feet as he faced him.

Orion moved back a few paces and scooped something off of the floor. It was white and shining and looked suspiciously like a bone, the sight of it making my skin prickle. "You can harness this Fae's strength. I know you can, you've done it before."

"Only for a minute," Darius said and I frowned, trying to work out what they were talking about.

"A minute might be all you need to give you an advantage," Orion muttered and Darius's eyes became hooded with darkness. For a second I couldn't tear my gaze from him. He looked more than angry, he looked vengeful, full of a deep, cold hatred that seemed to tangle with the air itself.

"Show me again," Darius breathed and Orion nodded.

He looked detached as he traced his hands across the bone and spoke in a whispered language I guessed was latin. "Chiedo al buio di disturbare questo corpo dalla pace e di mettere la sua magia nel mio sangue."

The air chilled and the shadows seemed to thicken in every corner of the cave. A shudder seized my spine and I instinctively moved closer to Tory as Orion raised the bone in front of him, wielding it like a weapon.

Darius's face was fixed in complete concentration as he watched and I sensed this was some kind of one-on-one tuition. But the way they were hiding down here made me certain this was definitely not part of Zodiac's curriculum.

The bone glowed as if a fire burned within it and flames suddenly burst to life along the length of it. Orion released a hiss of pain, but held it firmly in his grip as the flames licked his skin. They receded along the bone and Orion dropped it, twisting his hand up so the fire continued to ripple in his palm. His jaw set, and his eyes flickered with the shadows that closed in around them. My heart pattered uncontrollably but I couldn't tear my gaze away.

"Do it," Darius said, seeming excited as he shifted from foot to foot.

Orion closed his hand around the fire and snuffed it out. I waited, glancing between the two of them as they seemed to be preparing for something.

Heat was emanating from Orion in waves but that didn't make any sense. He didn't hold the Element of fire. His hands shot up and Darius threw out his palms at the same moment to cast an immense shield of water around himself. Fire exploded from Orion's palms and I stumbled back a step, completely shocked as the raging, twisting Element cascaded over Darius's shield. The flames battered it with a terrifying force then finally fizzled out, leaving plumes of steam in its wake.

Orion dropped his hands, rubbing his eyes, his shoulders shuddering. My heart twitched and I had the urge to go to him- if it hadn't been completely crazy.

Darius went to him instead, cupping the back of his neck. "Here." He shut his eyes and I sensed they were sharing magic as Orion cast some spell I could feel but couldn't see. The result was the shadows receding and the darkness in his eyes passed away too.

I shared a look with Tory and we wordlessly decided to stay a bit longer.

To find out what the hell we were watching. *How had Orion just wielded the Element of fire? Did he take the Element from the bone of some dead Fae? And where the hell did he get that bone?*

"Now you." Orion passed Darius the bone and he nodded, looking determined. "This Fae only had fire but they were strong. It will add a lot of power to your own flames."

Darius nodded, mimicking what Orion had done as he ran his hand across the bone and muttered the Latin words. The shadows rushed in again and my heart clenched as that same darkness fell over Darius, seeming to seep beneath his skin. Fire flared along the bone and he drew it into his palm, his eyes snapping shut in concentration.

Orion eyed him with his hands raised as if expecting something bad to happen.

Darius convulsed once, his shoulders trembling.

"Hold it in. Let it merge with your power, no matter how unnatural it feels," Orion instructed.

Darius looked like he might throw up as he clutched his stomach then dropped the bone with a clatter.

"Darius?" Orion stepped closer.

Darius held up a hand and his eyes flew open, revealing a swirling storm of darkness within them. A smirk twisted his features and Orion cast a dome of air around himself just as Darius released a huge blast of fire in the shape of a cobra. It coiled around the edges of the cave, filling it up, its huge body slithering and undulating, its eyes blazing red.

Orion gazed up as it reared its head and true fear found me as it lunged down and crashed against his shield. Orion started laughing and I relaxed as the flaming beast coiled tighter around his shield then flitted away into a thousand embers.

He rushed to Darius's side, laying a hand on his shoulder as they did whatever spell was necessary to end this crazy process.

"You fucking did it." Orion dragged him into a hug and I could see the strength of their bond shining from them as Darius curled his arms around him too. A Dragon and a Vampire bound together. And I was sure this was deeper than just that Guardian mark linking them.

Darius released a cheer which echoed off the walls, tipping his head back to the roof as Orion released him.

"Let him try and beat me now, huh Lance?" He whooped again and Orion laughed, dropping down to the cave floor and tugging a backpack in front of him.

"You did it once. I want to see that fifty times before I agree you've mastered it," Orion said with a grin. Darius puffed out his chest as he moved to join him on the floor.

"Easy."

"Yeah, it only took you three months," Orion jibed, taking something out of the backpack. He placed a wooden box between them, flipping it open and revealing a display of cards with the *Solarian PitBall League* printed across the top of them. I frowned as he reached into it, opening a secret compartment at its base. My breathing quickened as he took a slim silver blade and four small bones from it. The blade was exactly the same as the one in Tory's hand and I turned to her with a questioning look.

She offered a shrug in response and my tongue grew heavy as I turned back to watch.

Orion pushed the box aside and placed the four bones down between them in a line. Then he took something from his pocket and I frowned as he placed an emerald dragon ornament between the bones.

He toyed with the blade in his hand, looking to Darius with a terse expression. "Still no luck finding the one I gave you?"

My heart jerked. *Orion gave it to him? What was it even for?*

"No. Milton must have stashed the rest of my treasure somewhere. But he's still sticking to his lame-ass story that he didn't do it."

"Maybe he didn't?" Orion suggested and my gut prickled uneasily.

"He did say someone sent him it. His grandma or some bullshit. I figured he was lying but..." A contemplative look crossed his features and Tory shifted nervously beside me. "Maybe someone did send it."

"Well whoever stole that dagger is gonna pay the price when we find them," Orion growled and fear laced my gut. *Holy shit they can't ever find out.*

Darius nodded then gestured to the knife in Orion's hand. "Come on, let's find out what my doting father is up to."

Orion rested the tip of the blade to his wrist then carved a line up the centre of his palm, making me gasp. Blood oozed and he curled his hand into a fist, passing it to Darius who immediately copied the process. They held their hands above the bones, squeezing to make the blood drip onto them. They both dragged in a breath of pleasure then their eyes fell closed and their hands dropped into their laps.

"What's happening?" I breathed in confusion.

Tory released the same noise of ecstasy beside me and I turned to her in alarm. Panic clutched me with sharp claws as I spotted the long gash on her hand. She was still cutting herself with the blade, her eyes shut and a picture of intoxication on her face as she carved a deep line up her inner arm. I lunged forward, trying to seize the knife as she sliced a second gash along the inside of her forearm, blood spilling to the sand at our feet.

"Tory!" I yelled as she passed out completely, crumpling to the ground. I caught her just before she dashed her head on a rock and clamped my hands over the wound to stem the bleeding. There was so much of it, red coating her skin, her clothes, me.

Fear raced through my veins and drowned me entirely. "WAKE UP!"

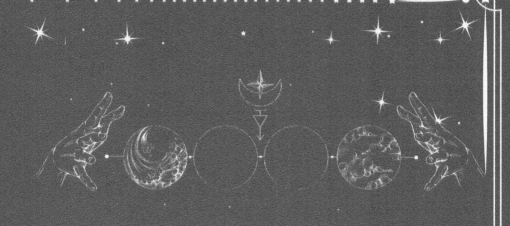

ORION

CHAPTER NINETEEN

*F*uck, blood magic felt good. Every time I did it, I swear the high got better. It was focusing that was the problem. Using dark magic was deadly. I could bleed out here before I'd even realised what was happening.

I drew my magic into the darkness surrounding me, pushing at the wall of shadow which wanted to take me with it. It tugged and lured and sang promises of pure bliss, but if I went that way, I'd never come back.

I felt Darius follow me through as I broke the barrier and a strange tickling feeling made me think for a moment that there was some other presence with us too.

As the sweet edge of the euphoric feeling in my veins eased off, my vision cleared and we found ourselves standing on a dark cobblestone street beside a tall fence. My heart ticked with recognition. I knew this old road. We were to the east of the Acrux manor, just beyond its walls. Which meant Lionel was expecting a visitor by stardust.

I could sense we were in the recent past, guided here by the connection he had to that tacky dragon ornament and the will of us both to find out what he was up to.

This was nothing but a shadow of time gone by. The edges of the world blurred like a haze and if I focused on one spot too long, it faded from my grasp. We only needed to wait here to find Lionel though. Darius stepped up beside me the moment his father rounded the corner ahead. Lionel marched along, his dark cloak whipping out behind him as he moved, his powerful frame haloed by the moon.

The atmosphere shimmered before him like stars and a tall man stepped out of it, sweeping a hand over his wavey black locks. I committed his face to memory in an instant; everything from his thin moustache to his curling upper lip. He wore a dark green overcoat and a knitted red scarf which spoke of a severe lack of fashion sense. He dipped his head, although the gesture came off slightly mocking. "Mr Acrux."

"*High Lord* Acrux," Lionel snarled. "Have you brought it? I didn't get you into that school just to waste my time." He held out his hand expectantly.

"And I didn't strike up this alliance to waste *my* time," the man growled in an equally dangerous tone.

"This is getting rather one-sided, Alejandro. What use are you if you and your worthless family don't do as I ask?" Lionel sneered and Alejandro reached into his pocket.

He took out a thick envelope and my eyes narrowed as I recognised the Vega Twins' personal file. I'd read it back to front before I'd gone to Earth to find them. It even had a coffee mug stain on it that I'd left there myself. Everything about their birthright was in that document. And it certainly didn't belong in the hands of Lionel Acrux. It had been locked up tight in Nova's office.

"Here." Alejandro thrust it at Lionel and I wished I could step into this memory for real and intervene before his hand closed around it. I didn't know what he could learn from it that would assist him, but my gut said it was nothing good.

I looked to Darius and my heart hit top speed as I spotted Tory goddamn Vega standing behind him.

Her eyes locked with mine, her face as pale as a ghost's. She stared at me, then looked to Darius and the men beyond, looking totally baffled as to why she was here. *That makes two of us!*

"WHAT THE FUCK!?" I bellowed, making both her and Darius jump. The memory swirled like mist then something crashed into my cheek, sending a spike of pain blooming through my skull.

Another blow came and I blinked, jerked violently out of the vision, finding Darcy on top of me, her reddened palm raised to slap me again.

"Fucking – what? What is happening?!" I roared, snatching her hand before she could hit me again. Her eyes sparkled with tears and some of them had spilled down her cheeks. A thousand terrifying worries crashed through me as I realised she was straddling me in a cave she had absolutely no way of getting into. Not without-

My mouth parted in complete horror as I saw it on the ground. The dagger. *Darius's* dagger. And beside it was Tory, her arm wrapped in Darcy's jacket surrounded by a huge puddle of blood.

"Help her!" Darcy begged, scrambling off of me and dragging me over to her sister. I threw a glance at Darius, the Leo mark on my arm pulsing strangely as he awoke from the vision.

His eyes snapped to Tory and he swore, diving forward and pulling her into his arms. "Lance!" he demanded.

I dropped to my knees beside him, cursing between my teeth as I snatched Darcy's jacket away and found the deep wounds on her hand and arm.

"How did this happen?" I barked at Darcy, resting my hands to her sister's skin and healing her with every ounce of magic I had.

A royal Vega Heir is not going to die in my hands. Not here. Not in this fucking place. And not with a wound that can only be explained by one goddamn thing.

Darcy held her other hand, pressing her fingers to her neck to feel for a pulse. She buckled forward when she felt one, but I could hear it anyway, drumming softer and softer by the second. My stomach yanked and tugged as I tried to block out the desperate pain on Darcy's face and focus on saving her sister.

"That dagger did this," Darcy said, shaking her head at me. At. *Me.*

"She did it to herself. Do you have any idea how dangerous that dagger is?" I snapped and Darcy glared back at me, setting her jaw.

"Clearly, you asshole," she snarled and I bit down on a retort. When Tory was sound and fucking well, then they'd get the full force of my rage. And they were going to seriously regret laying a finger on that dagger.

If they were the ones who took it, that means...

"Focus!" Darius shouted at me and I looked up to find sheer panic in his eyes, his mind clearly not on anything but the girl in his arms.

"I am," I promised, healing magic pouring from me in waves and digging out the last of my power reserves.

Tory dragged in a breath as her wounds healed beneath my hand. I looked up and my gaze rammed into Darcy's.

"Where did you get the dagger, Blue?" My voice was a deadly soft trap to lure her in and she nervously avoided my gaze, leaning down to check on her sister. Darius hugged her to his chest, his eyes shut as he concentrated on pulling her consciousness back to her body, clearly unaware of what we were saying.

"Where?" I snarled and her gaze finally flipped up to meet mine again, her lower lip quivering with anger or fear. Maybe both.

"You know exactly where," she whispered. "But are you really in a position to punish us after what we've just seen you doing, *Lance*?"

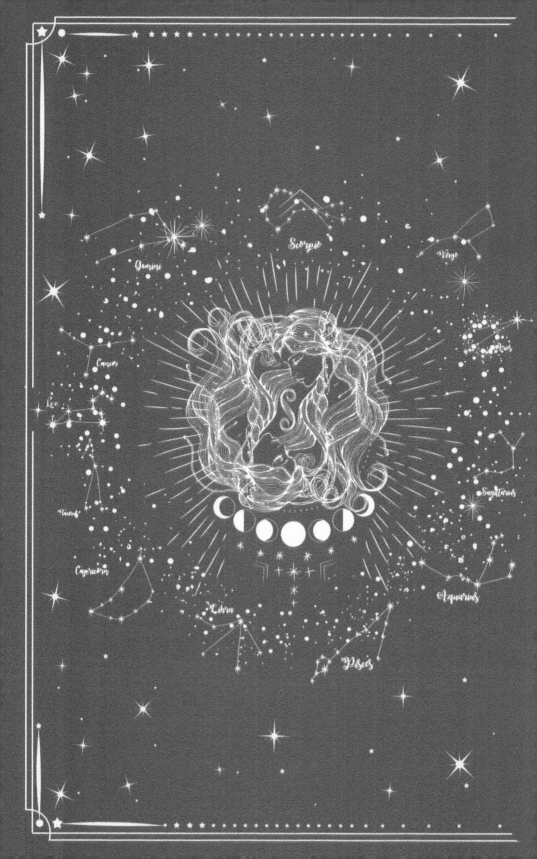

TORY

CHAPTER TWENTY

I was trapped in a cage of terror so all consuming that I couldn't breathe, couldn't think, couldn't even scream for help.

My heart was slamming against my ribs, rushing to a deadly crescendo as I trembled on the edge of the void.

Darkness was calling to me, whispering my name on the back of a rancid breath. It wanted me. It yearned for me. And some deep, hidden part of me wanted it too. It was evil and terror and eternal flames but down in the lowest part of my soul there was a piece of me which wanted to be just like that as well. There was a promise of power floating on the taste of the air, drawing me in, urging me on.

I reached for it and my arm flared with an agony so intense it was blinding. It was as though the very essence of who I was was being drawn out through the deepest cut along my flesh.

Something was waiting for me in the shadows. Something which knew my name. Something which wanted to own me.

The agony grew as I tried to withdraw from it but when I paused, it lessened. I inched a little closer to the terror in the dark and a writhing power slipped beneath my skin.

I was flirting with the shadows and some base part of me liked it, wanted it...needed it.

I reached out, losing any sense of why I wouldn't as the shadows coiled around my fingertips, wanting to be one with me, needing me to join with them, to go to them. And for a moment I couldn't see why I wouldn't answer their call willingly...

As I made a move to slip between the edges of the darkness, a deep heat grew at my back and something danced along the surface of my mind.

I fell still and the shadows writhed and wailed, desperate to have me. But the fire drew me back.

I turned, wrenching my gaze from the dark until I saw the flames at my back burning bright and fierce in the shape of an enormous, golden Dragon.

My eyes widened as I reached for him and a breath of pure, salty air tumbled past my lips as the world came crashing in on me again.

I groaned as pain assaulted me, the agony in my arm sharpening as reality closed in.

Darcy was sobbing somewhere close by. Someone was holding my hand and pressing healing magic beneath my flesh. But almost all of my attention fell upon the man holding me in his arms.

Darius was looking down at me, his eyes wild with panic as he brushed my hair away from my face.

He was saying something and it took me a moment to push aside the echoing in my ears so that I could listen to him.

"-would fucking break me. So don't you dare give in to them. I'll follow you into the shadows if I have to and drag you away from them kicking and screaming. Because they can't have you. They fucking *can't*."

"Darius?" I asked in confusion, frowning up at him as he seemed to realise I was awake and his tirade came to an end.

"You're back?" he asked, his voice breaking as he ran his fingers over the lines of my face.

I frowned at him, trying to remember how I'd gotten here. I glanced beyond him, finding Darcy and Orion staring down at me with concern.

The tide was crashing against the shore beyond them and I was laying half on the wet sand and half in Darius's arms.

"What the hell *was* that?" Darcy demanded, her voice panicky.

I fought to remember how I'd gotten here and I suddenly recalled the two of them in the cave, the words they'd spoken and the way the dagger had whispered in my ear, begging me to use it. I vaguely recalled seeing two other people in the vision, but it had only lasted a moment. "Why was Lionel with Diego's uncle?" I mumbled in confusion and Darcy frowned with concern.

Darius and Orion shared a look, some silent conversation passing between them, but said nothing to me.

I lifted my arm and winced at the tenderness I felt there. My flesh was bloodstained but the wounds were gone.

"I...that thing made me cut myself," I said, frowning at how crazy that sounded but I knew it was true.

"What thing?" Darius demanded. "How did you manage to cast black-"

"She had this," Orion said, speaking over him and holding out the silver dagger I'd taken from Darius's bedroom the night I'd burned it down.

"A knife can't just make someone cut themselves like that!" Darcy growled. "What the hell is it?"

"Where did you get that?" Darius asked, his grip on me tightening from comforting to restraining.

"I..." I looked between him and Orion, wondering how the hell I was supposed to explain that without giving away what I'd done but from the heat that was pouring from Darius, I got the feeling he was figuring it out already.

I scrambled backwards and Darius let me sit up but he didn't release me, catching my wrist and pinning me with his dark gaze.

"Tell me where you got that dagger, Roxy," he growled.

His grip on my wrist tightened to the point of pain and I winced at the rough treatment, trying to draw back. He yanked on my arm to keep hold of me and I was suddenly reminded of the way he'd held onto me when he'd dragged me to that swimming pool.

My heart leapt with fright as I tried to pull away from him again, slivers of ice driving through my chest as I found myself back at the mercy of this monster. Why had I woken feeling safe in his arms? He was the one who had done this to me. That dagger was his and whatever the hell it was, it was dark. I had no doubt that if those shadows had taken me I'd be beyond help by now.

"Let me go," I demanded but Darius just caught my other wrist as I tried to prise his fingers off of me.

He pulled me close, his breath mingling with mine as a deep growl resonated through his chest and his eyes shifted into reptilian slits.

"Where did you get that dagger?!" he shouted and fear washed through me on a tide.

"Let her go!" Darcy demanded but Orion caught her waist, holding her away from us as he waited for my answer too.

But I wasn't just going to cave to fear and tell him what he wanted to know. I'd just come within inches of death and it was his fault yet again. I had some goddamn questions of my own.

"What the fuck is that thing?" I snarled. "It made me do that. It made me cut my damn arm open and tried to give me to the fucking nightmares to devour. Why the hell do you own something like that? What the fuck is wrong with you?"

Darius's grip tightened on me so hard that a gasp of pain escaped my lips but I didn't back down.

Darcy was trying to struggle out of Orion's grip but he was glaring at me intently and just kept her locked in his arms like he couldn't even feel her fighting him. Some brilliant teacher he was, leaving me to the mercy of a Dragon.

"I want my fucking answer, Roxy!" Darius yelled. "Did you steal that from my room? Did you light that fucking fire?!"

I flinched away from his rage and threw magic from my body in a wild attempt to get him off of me. The wave of air crashed into him with the force of a tornado and Orion and Darcy were knocked from their feet too. Somehow Darius managed to keep his hold on me and I screamed as we were flung through the air.

I landed on top of Darius as we fell back to the ground but he didn't miss a beat, whipping me around and slamming me back down into the wet sand as he moved to straddle me.

He caught both of my wrists in one of his huge hands and pinned them to the sand above my head. Coils of fire leapt from his free hand, winding their way up my arms and locking them in place above my head as he snarled down at me.

My heart was pounding a desperate, panicked rhythm as I looked up at him, his features shadowed by the bright moon which hung low in the sky beyond him.

Darius pushed his weight down on my hips as he sat over me, driving me down into the wet sand and curling a hand around my throat. He didn't exert any pressure but his grip was enough to let me know that he held my life in his hands and pure terror washed through me, pinning me in place more effectively than his magic.

Darcy was shouting at Orion to release her but I couldn't look away from the pissed off Dragon who was currently looking like he might actually kill me.

"Did you break into my room and steal that dagger?" he demanded, his voice low and predatory.

My heart was pounding, fear licking through my limbs like a living thing but a spark of defiance burned strong in the depths of my soul. Yes he had me at his mercy. Yes he had me beaten. But he would never break me. And after everything he'd done to me, I refused to cower beneath him now.

"You burned my clothes off of my body on my first day here. You encouraged every asshole in this school to make my life hell. You tortured and tormented me every second you got the chance and you laughed while you did it. You took my deepest fear and dragged me to that pool so that you could force me to relive it and you almost fucking killed me," I hissed, all the venom of all the hatred I'd ever felt for him pouring out of me like it was an open wound. "So yes. I broke into your goddamn room and I stole your precious fucking treasure and that psycho dagger while I was there. And then I melted every other piece of gold you owned and begged the flames to burn the rest. And I fucking laughed while I did it. It was the least you deserved. And I'd do it again in a heartbeat."

Silence rang out as a deathly rage flooded through Darius's body. His fingers tightened around my throat an almost imperceptible amount but my limbs tensed in anticipation of what he might do. Terror came writhing through my body, devouring me whole and spitting me out to lay at his mercy in the sand but still I glared up at him. There was nothing I could do to stop him anyway and I wasn't going to let him see my fear.

Darius bared his teeth at me, smoke spilling between his lips as a deadly snarl escaped him.

"*Darius,*" Orion warned but I could see the violence building in the eyes of the creature before me and I knew he was beyond hearing him.

A huge roar escaped him and his grip on me tightened half a second before Darcy screamed in defiance and he was thrown off of me.

I gasped in surprise, fighting off the bonds of Darius's fire magic as he lost control of it and was sent crashing into the cliff wall with the force of Darcy's air attack.

He got to his feet instantly, a ball of deadly flames springing to life in his hands. Orion cursed and I felt his magic slipping over me as he threw up a shield half a second before the flames collided with it, bursting over us in a blazing arc of red and orange.

"Stop!" Orion commanded, shooting forward to place his hands on Darius's chest to hold him back.

Darcy was at my side in moments, dragging me to my feet and casting a concerned eye over me. We stood together, raising our hands defensively as we waited to see what would happen next.

Darius was actually shaking with rage and I got the feeling he was having a lot of trouble containing the Dragon beneath his skin.

His gaze was locked on me and I matched the pure hatred I found there with even more of my own. Why had I even begun to consider that there could be anything more to him than this? After everything he'd done to me, I should have known that he could never be any different.

Darius tried to step around Orion but he refused to move, using his Vampire strength to hold him back.

Darius growled and I flinched, drawing closer to Darcy as we joined hands and let our magic flow between us, ready for whatever he might do next.

Orion snarled right back at him and the two of them glared at each other for an eternal moment.

"Think about this, Darius," Orion warned. "We have the dagger back now, she can't tell anyone about it because she'd have to admit what she did to your room. This has worked out in our favour."

"In our favour? She burned my fucking room down and stole from me!" Darius bellowed. "I can't just let that stand!"

"In light of what you did to her, you probably should have expected some payback," Orion snapped. "I'm surprised all of the Heirs haven't found themselves at the end of their retaliation yet!"

I exchanged a glance with Darcy and my heart pounded a little faster.

Orion looked around like he'd heard it and Darius pointed an accusatory finger at us. "I'm not just going to let her get away with doing this. I'm Fae! I'm a Celestial Heir! I can't just-"

"You can and you will! If you want Tory to hide her knowledge of that dagger then you'll have to let this anger go. Let everyone keep on believing Milton did it. We have the dagger back and-"

"Milton," Darius interrupted suddenly. "You set him up?"

"He spread naked photos of me around the school," I hissed. "And I wanted to see you lose faith in your little group of followers."

Darius tried to lunge at me again and Orion grunted as he fought to hold him back.

"You made me shun my friend!" he shouted. "How the hell am I supposed to explain-"

"You're not!" Orion snapped. "You can't admit that Milton didn't do it without exposing her. And if you do that then she will have no reason to stay quiet about the dagger!"

"You still haven't told us what that dagger is. It almost killed Tory," Darcy hissed. "We want some answers."

"All you need to know is that that dagger and what we were doing aren't the kinds of things you mess around with," Orion warned darkly.

"So you just expect us to keep quiet about your shady little secrets without giving us any real information?" I asked with a scowl.

"Just like we'll keep quiet about you, yes." Orion's tone held no room for negotiation and I exchanged a look with my sister.

"We need better answers than that," Darcy demanded.

"Well you aren't going to get them, Blue. Just keep your mouths shut and so will we. That's the best you're going to get." Orion looked back at Darius who offered me a glare filled with poison before pulling off his shirt and tossing it to Orion. His pants and the rest of his clothes followed suit and he turned away from us, releasing a roar as he shifted into his Dragon form.

We stood our ground as the giant, golden reptile, stalked away from us across the sand but thankfully he didn't look back. He ducked low, spreading his wings in anticipation of a flight and Orion looked at us one last time before shooting after Darius and leaping onto his back with his Vampire speed.

Darius took off instantly and we watched as they flew out over the sea, a great arc of fire spewing from Darius's mouth as he delivered an earth shattering roar to the heavens.

I slowly released my grip on Darcy's hand, biting my lip as some of the terror leaked from my limbs.

"What the fuck?" I breathed.

"My thoughts exactly," Darcy echoed and the two of us exchanged a look filled with all the horror of what had just happened before turning and starting our walk back off of the beach and away from Air Cove.

I didn't understand half of what had just happened but one thing was completely and utterly clear to me and I was going to make sure I never forgot it again. Darius Acrux was not my friend. He was cruel and mean and ruthless and he wouldn't bat an eye at hurting me a hundred times in a thousand different ways. I never should have tried to see him as anything other than what he was. And I wouldn't be making that mistake ever again.

DARIUS

CHAPTER TWENTY·ONE

I raced through the sky, flying hard and fast with Lance on my back. I bellowed flames all around us for a good half an hour before my rage finally started to simmer down enough for me to consider landing. We'd flown well beyond the confines of the school and out to sea but I didn't head back, scouring the dark waves beneath us until I found what I was looking for.

I banked hard as I spotted the little island we sometimes came to, circling as the sea breeze fought against my movements. Lance cast his power over the air around us to make it easier for me. I tucked my wings as we dove towards the sandy cove on the south side of the island which was the only place open enough for me to land.

My claws dug into the sand as I brought myself to a halt and I sank a little with the weight of my Dragon form pressing me down.

Lance leapt from my back in well practiced movements and a shudder ran down my spine from the tip of my snout to the end of my tail as I shook off the scales and fire of my Dragon form and retreated back into my Fae flesh.

It was harder to do than usual as my rage fought with the desire to stay in my Order form but I forced it back, needing to vent about this situation to Lance while we were able to talk in private.

The second my bones had realigned I turned to him and started on a rant which I wasn't sure would ever end.

"Can you believe the balls of that fucking girl?" I snarled, scraping my hands through my hair so hard that I was fairly sure I'd drawn blood along my scalp.

"Put some pants on before you kick off, will you?" Lance muttered, tossing my clothes at me as he turned away and began pacing along the shore.

I bit my tongue as I forced my legs into my pants and he set to work casting the familiar spells of silence and repulsion just in case anyone was trying to spy on us. Though out here that seemed more than unlikely. But he never let his guard down, even when we could be sure of privacy. His movements were tense but the rage I was still feeling seemed to have burned out of him a little during our flight here.

I didn't have the patience to do any more than pull on my sweatpants before I started up again.

"How did she even get into my room? It was still locked when I went to put that fire out. And I followed her back to Ignis House right before we found it too. She was right ahead of me in the crowd so I don't even see how she could have managed to-"

"The Vegas never made it to the assembly on Astrum's death," Lance interrupted. "Darcy broke into my office while she should have been there and tried to steal some stardust so that they could go home. I'm guessing Tory went to your room to get some gold. I don't know how much I told you about how they were living in the mortal world?"

"Why would I give a shit about that?" I snapped.

"Because it might help you understand Tory's motivations. It's obvious that you're more than just pissed off about this because she got one up on you."

"What's that supposed to mean?" I demanded, prowling towards my friend while he looked back at me like I wasn't a goddamn Dragon capable of biting his head off if he pushed me the wrong way.

"It just seems like you're taking it a bit personally," he replied with a shrug. A fucking shrug.

"Of course I'm taking it personally - she stole from me and set my whole room alight!" I yelled.

Lance snorted a laugh and I snarled as I ran at him, fully intending to punch that stupid look off of his face. He shot away from me using his Vampire speed and I spun around, finding him behind me and out of reach again.

"My point *is*," he continued like I hadn't just tried to attack him. "That the two of them were living in this shitty apartment which was really just one tiny room with mold on the walls and a broken window which made the whole place cold and fucking miserable. I'm pretty sure they were sharing a beat up couch for a bed and they could barely even afford to pay the rent. Tory was stealing motorbikes for money and they were both the kind of skinny which spoke more of a lack of food than a dietary choice."

"Do you expect me to feel sorry for them?" I asked incredulously, though I couldn't quite fight off the mental picture he was painting for me. I couldn't even imagine living like that. Money had never been something I'd even thought about. I took it for granted, it was the least important thing in my life because we had way too much of it. To think of the Solarian Princesses living in squalor like that was absurd but I knew Lance wouldn't lie to me either.

"No. I don't expect you to feel sorry for them, but it makes sense for you to try and understand them. The only real reason they came to Zodiac Academy in the first place was to claim their inheritance. And then you and the other Heirs did everything in your power to drive them out. But without graduating from the Academy, they can't claim their inheritance and they'd be back to having nothing. So when you all did what you did to them on the night

365

of the party and they wanted to run, they needed two things. A way to leave. And money." He sounded so fucking reasonable in his argument that I felt some of my anger melting away.

"So, what? I'm just supposed to give them a free pass because they were desperate?" I asked incredulously.

"They're Fae, it's in their nature to fight back just like it's in yours. Question is, do you think that what she did to you shows she's more powerful than you? Especially if you line it up to the various things you've done to her..."

"Obviously not," I spat. "But how am I supposed to just carry on like she didn't do it?"

"I think she got a good grasp on your rage when you realised what she'd done," Lance continued in a low voice. "For a moment there I felt like I was looking at Lionel instead of a man who swore never to be like him."

This time I didn't give him a chance to escape me as I swung towards him. I slammed my palms against his chest and forced him back a step, glaring right in his eyes in a clear challenge.

"Say that again," I snarled.

Lance didn't even fucking flinch which only pissed me off more. "How did it feel when you pinned her to the ground by her neck?" he breathed. "Did that make you feel good? Did you put her in her place?"

I swallowed hard against a lump in my throat as shame prickled up my spine. "I wasn't going to choke her. I didn't even tighten my grip. I just..."

"You just wanted her to think you *might*. Sound familiar?"

I turned away from him suddenly, not wanting to see that accusation in his eyes. I refused to admit I was anything like my father but a small voice in the back of my head was telling me he was right. Roxy had stopped fighting back by the time I put my hand around her throat. My magic had already immobilised her and I'd known that I'd already won. The rest of what I'd done to her hadn't been about winning it was about rubbing it in. Just like my father

366

always did to me. Driving salt into the wounds.

"Fuck." I started pacing, scraping my hands through my hair again as I tried to force away the image of her glaring up at me as I pinned her to the ground. "I can't...she drives me insane, you know that? She challenges me at every goddamn turn. No matter how thoroughly she's beaten she still gets back up and looks me right in the eye again. Every. Damn. Time. And she hates me, it's obvious, she says it right to my face but then every now and then she looks at me like..."

"Like what?" Lance asked curiously, drawing a little closer.

I dropped to the sand with a heavy sigh, my anger burning low as all kinds of unnamed emotions swirled to the surface instead.

"I dunno. Like she's trying to work me out. Or maybe she wants to. But then she goes right back to calling me names or standing in opposition to every little thing I do or screwing *Caleb...*"

"What does that have to do with anything?" Lance asked, taking a seat beside me.

"Nothing," I said instantly. "It just pisses me off. It's like she gives him a free pass for all his bullshit but expects me to grovel at her feet for just being Fae."

Lance didn't say anything in response to that and I raised my head to scowl out over the water.

"Enough about the fucking Vegas," I muttered.

"You were really only talking about one of them," Lance pointed out.

"Well Roxy is always in my face. She lives in my House, I have to help her with her fire magic, she's screwing my friend, so-"

"That's the second time you've brought that up."

"What are you, my fucking critic or my friend?"

"Both most of the time," he joked.

"Well right now I just want a friend. Stop pointing out my flaws and just agree with me while I rant about the situation."

"Okay, if you think it'll make you feel better," Lance agreed. "Tory Vega is such a bitch. You went way too easy on her and I really hope she's off somewhere crying right now because she knows how wrong she is."

A faint smile tugged at my lips and Lance leaned back on his elbows as he went on.

"I also heard that she's fucking awful in bed and Caleb is only screwing her because he feels sorry for her. Besides, everyone knows she really wishes she could fuck the Fire Heir but he's way out of her league so she just cries herself to sleep over it every night instead."

"Fucking Vegas," I muttered, half a smirk tugging at my lips.

"Fucking Vegas," he agreed.

We sat in silence, listening to the waves crash against the shore for a few moments and I tried to stop thinking about Roxy Vega and all the things I hated about her. Plus some of the things I didn't.

I let out a long breath, closing my eyes for a moment as the Dragon finally fell back asleep within my chest. Roxy's brown eyes found me in the dark, the way they'd widened slightly as my fingers gripped her neck. The flicker of her pulse against my thumb, which gave away exactly what she thought of me in that moment. She thought I might kill her. She'd believed it. I'd wanted her to fear me and succeeded in painting myself as a monster in her eyes.

So why did that suddenly seem like a bad thing?

I swallowed thickly and opened my eyes again, not wanting to look at her in my mind. Which was where she was. Too fucking often.

I shook off the feelings of guilt before they even had a chance to surface. She'd stolen from me. Burned down my room. Looked me in the eye and made it beyond clear she hated me. I didn't care what her reasons were. I didn't care if I'd pushed her to it.

She hated me. And I hated her.

Simple.

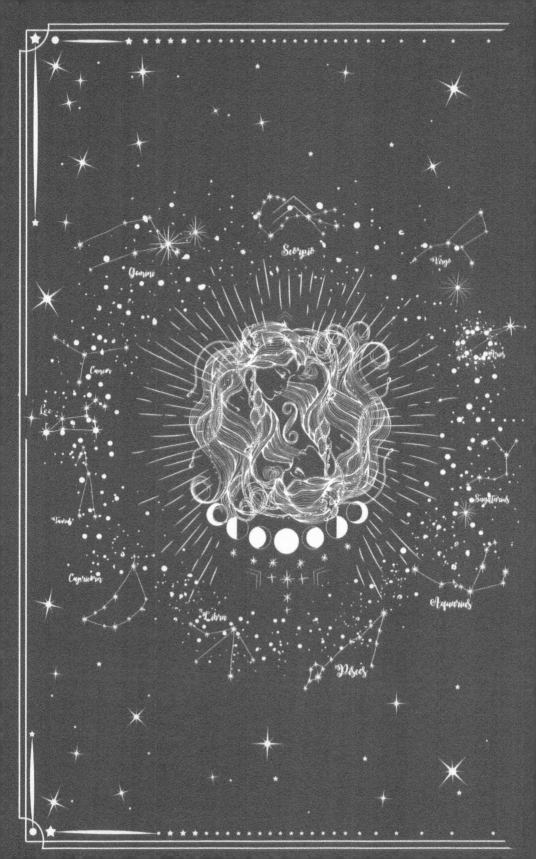

DARCY

CHAPTER TWENTY TWO

Good Morning Gemini.
The stars have spoken about your –

You have a new private message, Darcy!
You have a new private message, Darcy!
You have a new private message, Darcy!

"Is this broken?" I muttered to myself, sitting upright with a yawn and pushing my bed covers down as I blinked hazily at the screen. It was earlier than I'd usually get up, but I'd kept dreaming about Tory on the beach, blood everywhere, waking in a burning sweat. I tapped on the private messages and my lips pursed as I found they were all from Orion.

Lance:
Come meet me in my office before breakfast.

Lance:

And if we're lucky, through breakfast.

Lance:

And I'm always late anyway so after breakfast too ;)

I scowled, shaking my head. Was he serious right now?

I tapped out an answer to shut him down, my gut writhing and squirming as hurt niggled at me. He didn't even realise I was pissed at him. How could he think we were on good terms? That I'd actually go and screw him?

I let out an actual growl, hitting send on my message.

Darcy:

Obviously not

I didn't even give him a full stop, let alone an x. I really didn't want to think the other night had been a mistake but Orion had held me back whilst his goddamn Dragon friend had threatened to choke my sister to death. But not before he smacked her around like a lion toying with its prey.

I was fuming. I wanted to tear out both Orion and Darius's eyeballs for it. I wasn't usually the outwardly feisty twin, but today I was on a warpath.

I lifted my Atlas to read my horoscope like I'd intended, trying to slow my breathing.

Good morning Gemini.

The stars have spoken about your day!

Mars is firmly backing you today so if you feel like going in to battle, that may be because of its presence. Now is a good time to face your issues head on. So long as you have faith in the red planet's guidance, you will win any argument you strike up. But be careful, you will collide with a Libra today

who also has Mars in their chart. If you clash too hard, the results could be
disastrous.

"Good, I fancy a disaster," I murmured just as another message flashed up from Orion.

Lance:
Is this about your sister?

I rolled my eyes, turning the Atlas off so I couldn't even be tempted to reply. I dragged my butt into the bathroom and had a shower that lasted nearly half an hour, trying to drain away some of this furious energy. But it clearly wasn't going anywhere. So by the time I pulled on my ripped skinny jeans, a fitted black sweater and painted my face for the day, twisting my hair up into a Viking braid that said war, I was ready to take on the whole damn school.

I grabbed my satchel on the way out of the door, tossing it over my shoulder. I headed into the stairwell and spotted Seth trotting toward me in my periphery. I quickened my pace but he circled around me, stopping me and several other students in the process.

"Move," I demanded, trying to file after the other students as he let them by.

His brows jumped up. "Shit, babe, which stars spat in your cereal this morning?"

"All of them," I huffed. "Now move."

"Is that a challenge?" His eyes sparkled and I pursed my lips.

I cast air from my palm which crashed into his shoulder and shoved him aside. But he didn't miss a beat, turning sharply and sliding his arm around my waist. I didn't even care to throw him off, I just continued along at my own fast pace and hoped he'd fall behind.

"I think I like this angry side of you, do you want to take it out on me?"

Seth murmured in my ear as we stepped out of the door onto the pathway.

My gut did a skydive as I found Orion standing outside, docking House Points from students for various offenses. I tried to walk away, but his eyes landed on me like lightning, shifting between me and Seth.

"Hey Professor," Seth called. "What brings you out of bed before midday?"

Orion came at him so fast, I nearly fell over as he dragged Seth off of me. He threw him back through the door, bellowing, "Ten points from Aer!"

My heart somersaulted as I made my escape, marching into the crowd and trying to meld in. *Damn my beautiful hair.*

Orion was in front of me in a blur, moving so fast I walked straight into his chest.

"What the hell?" I demanded. "Get out of my way, asshole."

Horrified inhales sounded around me and for some unknown reason Orion's mouth curved up into a triumphant smile. "My office. Now, Miss Vega."

"No!" I gasped, realising what he'd managed to do. Give himself a damn excuse to haul me away like a misbehaving student.

I tried to duck past him, but he caught my arm. The students around us had scattered and I gazed up at him, venom pouring from my eyes.

"Let me go," I said icily.

"Make me," he spat, dragging me along the path at a ferocious speed. I knew he would just toss me over his shoulder and carry me there if I made any further protest and I wasn't going to deal with the humiliation of that.

He marched me up to Jupiter Hall like I was a prisoner of war about to be thrown into a firing line. My heart ricocheted off the walls of my chest as we arrived at his office and he unlocked the door, pushing me inside.

I took a deep breath as he stepped in after me and slammed it behind him. I fought the wince I knew he expected, clenching my jaw and glaring at him.

He raised his hand, casting a silencing bubble and I lunged forward, grabbing his wrist to try and stop him. It was already too late, which meant we were having this conversation now, whether I liked it or not.

"Screw you," I hissed. "You had no right-"

"I have every right," he snarled, stalking closer and sending a shudder rolling down my spine. "I'm your teacher."

"Handy that," I laughed dryly. "You didn't act like one the other night, *sir*." He cornered me against his desk, placing his palms down either side of me so I was enveloped in his scent and the taste of coffee on his breath.

"This is about your sister," he echoed his message from earlier. "Isn't it?" His fangs were on full display and I tried not to pay them attention but it was difficult with him so close.

"Of course it is," I snarled, collecting my thoughts and preparing for the argument which I was clearly going to be forced into having on his terms. "You held me back while that bastard hurt her. Do you have any idea what that feels like? How would you feel if someone hurt your sister right in front of you?"

He jerked away as if I'd scolded him, turning his back on me and raking a hand down his neck.

My heart thumped out of tune and my mind wheeled as I wondered if that actually *had* happened to him once.

"So you do know how it feels," I said darkly, moving away from the desk with my heart in my throat.

He grunted in affirmation, still not looking at me. "But you can't intervene in a fight between two Fae," he said in explanation. "You should know that by now."

"She's my family," I said in disbelief. "I don't care what I'm *supposed* to do, Lance. I'll always look out for her no matter what the cost."

Orion nodded, scraping a hand over his face then moving to sit behind his desk. He opened the lowest drawer and took out the predictable bottle of bourbon. Tears suddenly pinched my eyes. Tears of rage, but mostly of sadness that he needed that stuff. That he thought it would help whatever it was he was trying not to feel.

I stormed forward, snatching it from the desk before he could pour a glass. "Deal with your emotions." I pointed the bottle at him. "Drowning them doesn't make them go away."

He stared at me as if no one had ever pointed out his drinking habit before (especially with the actual bottle). And as if no one had ever told him to stop. Well I was telling him now and he was going to goddamn listen.

I stormed to the window, wrenching it open and holding the bottle out by the neck, staring at him with a threat in my eyes. He was up from his seat, his expression contorted in a mixture of confusion, anger and disbelief.

"Blue," he whispered, but I didn't know what he was asking of me. To drop the bottle or to not drop it.

I gasped as he ran at me, my heart sinking, knowing that this alcohol meant so much to him. He grabbed hold of my hand and prised the bottle from my fingers, dropping it himself. The smash hit my ears, but I didn't see it because he dragged me against him, his mouth crashing into mine with the heat of a volcano.

I was still angry, so damn angry, but I couldn't stop kissing him. I clawed at his arms then wrapped my hand around his tie and pulled hard enough to choke him. He dragged me away from the window, shoving me up against the door instead, every part of us colliding. Our bodies, our teeth, our souls. It was sloppy and desperate and *everything*.

I groaned, still trying to hurt him as I dug my nails into his forearms and he bit down on my lip in response. He suddenly caught my chin, wrenching my head sideways and sinking his teeth into my neck. My magic immobilised, but I didn't need it. I wanted to claw at him until I shredded right through to his heart and made him feel how I had when I'd seen my sister hurt by Darius.

His arousal ground against my leg but there wasn't a chance in hell we were going *there* right now. I was still furious and wanted a proper apology.

When his hand took a turn south, I slammed a palm to his chest and he extracted his fangs from my throat, releasing a frustrated sigh. His pupils were dilated and I could see the excitement burning beneath them as he dipped his head for another kiss.

I pressed my hand to his mouth, shaking my head as anger grew deeper roots inside me. "No."

His brows drew together and he gently removed my hand, kissing the back of it. "Was I too rough?"

"No." I fought a blush but it scorched right through me.

"Not rough enough?" he teased and I battled a grin, refusing to meet those hungry eyes of his.

"I'm still mad at you," I said, folding my arms and willing away the burning need between my thighs. But I wasn't going to ignore all of my principals and let him have me. I'd imagined it so many times in this office, but not like this. Not with a pit of rage in my chest which just kept widening and widening.

"You'll get over it." He brushed his thumb across my neck to heal the bite mark and I glowered at him.

"That's all you have to say? I'll get over it?" I hissed.

"Well...yeah." He shrugged, seeming kind of out of his depth for a second.

I pushed my way past him, ignoring the craving in my soul that begged me to stay as I strode toward the door. He beat me to it, barring my way with an anxious look in his eyes.

"Wait," he commanded and I lifted a brow. "I need you to do something for me."

"Are you serious?" I balked, completely baffled by him.

"Blue, please. It's important," he pressed, his brows raising hopefully.

I tsked at him, reaching for the door handle, but he caught my hand and drew me into his arms instead. His palm pressed flat to my back and he nuzzled against my head in a way that was almost like Seth. "I'll make this up to you. But nothing I say right now is going to make it right."

Sorry would go a long way. But hell if I'm going to spoon feed you.

"What do you want?" I demanded and he held me tighter, his mouth falling to my ear.

"I need you to talk to Diego Polaris. I believe his Uncle Alejandro is up to something criminal that involves Darius's father."

"Like what?" I breathed in alarm, leaning back to search his eyes.

He shrugged. "I don't know yet. But Diego would never trust me or Darius. I need someone close to him to ask about his uncle. Where he lives, what he does for a living, whether he's involved in anything suspicious. Anything you can learn at all that could help."

I chewed on my lip, unsure what to say. "Diego's my friend, I don't want to lie to him."

"Then don't lie." He traced his thumb across my cheekbone. "Just ask."

I glanced at the door, uncertain if I should agree. I didn't want to offer anything to Orion right now, but this sounded like something bigger than us.

"Please, Blue. I wouldn't ask if I wasn't desperate. Lionel is a danger to us all." His eyes bored into mine and I knew I couldn't refuse this request. Darius's father terrified me so if he was up to something shady, I had to do what I could to stop him.

"Alright, but what is it you think him and Lionel are even up to?"

"Bad fucking shit, that's all. I have to protect Darius and I need to know what Lionel's planning."

"How do you know he's planning anything?" I tried to pull away but he held on tight.

"I overheard him at the party."

"Saying what?"

"Darcy..."

378

"You can't expect me to help you if you're not honest with me," I said firmly.

He sighed, leaning back against the door. "He's planning something bad around the time of the Lunar Eclipse. That's all I know."

I thought of Astrum's warning in the card I'd found at the Acrux manor and my gut knotted.

Do not underestimate the beast who shadows you.

He is the ultimate power, ruling over your lives and the lives of many others.

Had those words been referring to Lionel?

The school bell rang out shrilly and we moved instinctively apart as reality came crashing down on us. His hand circled around the doorknob as he surveyed me.

"Good luck with your Water Trial," he said earnestly.

"Thank you." I moved forward but he didn't open the door.

"Are you still angry with me?"

"Yes," I replied, but a part of me wished I didn't have to be. I wanted to rewind two nights and fall into his arms all over again. But everything was messed up between us and I couldn't forgive him for holding me back from helping Tory.

"Let me go," I whispered when I could see he wasn't planning on moving.

His eyes hardened as he tugged the door open and the sound of chatter and movement of students filled the halls. I stepped past him and glanced back over my shoulder but he was already shutting the door. I swallowed hard and walked away, wondering if we were done before we'd even started.

I headed out of Jupiter Hall onto the path and spotted Seth lingering beside the door. "Hey is he hassling you?" He strode toward me, his brows drawn low.

"I can handle Orion." I started walking, meaning to head past him but he caught my arm. I raised my brows, giving him a hard look that told him to let go.

"I'm starting to see that, Omega," he said with a sideways smile. His hand lingered on my arm, sliding higher and inching toward my hair. "But I'm still your superior."

I stepped away, narrowing my eyes. "You might be better at magic, Seth, but you're not superior to anyone."

"You really haven't grasped how Fae work yet, have you babe?"

"I've grasped it," I said in a low voice. "But more power doesn't equal better."

He frowned as if he was struggling to understand that.

A loud growl made my heart lurch and I turned, spotting Seth's pack walking down the pathway toward us, brushing their hands over each other and nuzzling as they moved.

A girl with dark hair and bright eyes headed the line. "Still betraying us, Seth? We'll have to hold fights for a new Alpha soon." Her tone was void of warmth and her eyes as hard as steel as they fell on me.

Seth moved closer to me, a deep growl rumbling in his throat. "You're the one betraying me, Alice. All of you are." His eyes swept across the group and a few of them dipped their heads.

"Maybe we'll deal with the problem ourselves." Alice stepped toward me and I raised my hands, fire bursting to life in my palms. If she wanted a fight, she'd caught me in a bad enough mood to get one. Besides, Mars was backing me today so hopefully I had the upper hand.

Some of the pack started howling in anger and my blood chilled, but I refused to back down. Seth moved in front of me, squaring up to Alice. "Accept her or get out of my sight," he snarled.

"I don't even want to be in your pack," I said, frustrated but it was clearly the wrong thing to say as Alice snarled at me.

"Are you going to let her speak like that?" Alice snapped.

"Don't you dare question me." Seth drew himself up to his fullest height, glaring down at her with his teeth bared. She held his eye for a long moment before bowing her head with a growl of annoyance. She jerked her head to beckon the pack, leading them away from us and Seth released a low whine as they went.

Pain emanated from him, but I tried not to feel bad. He deserved to suffer like this after what he'd done to me. But I still didn't want to be his Omega and maybe I was starting to feel one-percent shitty about his situation.

"Just cut me from the pack, Seth, then this will stop."

He turned to me with a desperate look in his eyes that cut right into me. "It's not that simple."

"Well make it simple," I said with a shrug. Before I could react, he wrapped me in his arms, nuzzling into my hair with a groan.

"Maybe I don't want to let you go." His mouth grazed my temple, then he drew away and headed off down the path, my heart beating frantically as I watched him leave.

I didn't like to admit it but I was starting to accept that Seth had feelings for me. And for some reason that terrified me far more than him hating me ever could.

TORY

CHAPTER TWENTY THREE

I ran through The Wailing Wood with my headphones on and the music pumping loud enough to bust an eardrum or drown out the echoes of the shadows which were still whispering on the verges of my mind.

I'd barely slept. Each time I drifted off, the darkness had been waiting for me, thick with promise and expectation.

I didn't know if I was more afraid of it taking me or of me choosing to go willingly.

I knew it wasn't real, just a memory of what Darius's dagger had exposed me to but the goosebumps lining my flesh were still in place since the moment I'd woken up on that beach. I felt cold. All the way down to my bones. And even the fire magic in me couldn't do much to fix it.

My heart was pounding against my chest, my breaths coming hard and fast as I pushed myself to my limit. I had twenty minutes until my Water Elemental Trial and I intended to use each of them up before I arrived. If I could pound the shadows out with a heavy bass and hard exercise then I'd do it.

I took a turning south towards Water Territory, increasing my pace as I hit a downhill.

The lake shimmered between the trees as they began to thin and I took a turn quickly, gasping as I spotted someone standing right in my way. I couldn't stop in time, my sneakers skidded in the mud and I slammed straight into Darius Acrux's chest.

My headphones were knocked loose, falling to hang around my neck and the world came crashing back in on me.

He caught my forearms to stop me from falling and looked down at me in surprise.

I fought to catch my breath, some kind of violent death metal song clashing out of the headphones hanging around my throat as I stared up into his dark eyes.

Darius looked at me in surprise, his lips parting like he had something to say but he hadn't quite decided what. His grip on me tightened a little, just like it had on my throat last night.

"Get the fuck off of me," I growled, yanking my arms back.

His eyes darkened instantly like a wall had slammed into place behind them.

"Gladly," he snapped. But instead of releasing me, he shoved me hard and I fell back onto my ass in the mud.

Pain ricocheted through my hips and tears stung the backs of my eyes as something in my chest twisted sharply.

My mouth fell open in shock as I looked up at him, the cold of the ground burrowing into my bones quickly and banishing what little warmth I'd managed to glean from my run.

For a second I remembered laughing with him after we'd crashed his motorbikes and somehow survived and I swallowed thickly against the sensation that I'd lost something with him now. It was like that had been someone else. Not this cruel, hard shell who stood over me, only looking to cause me pain.

"Whoops!" Caleb said cheerily as he shot onto the path beside us. I caught the sounds of Seth howling somewhere in the trees too. "Did you fall down, sweetheart?" He offered me a hand to pull me up but I looked away from him, pushing myself upright instead.

"She was just getting used to the feeling of being where she belongs. Beneath our feet," Darius growled.

Caleb looked between us, a frown pulling at his brow for a moment as he seemed to realise he'd walked in on some kind of altercation.

I didn't bother to respond to Darius, sidestepping him quickly as I made to continue my journey to my Water Trial.

"Did you just shove her in the mud?" Caleb asked incredulously.

"What does it matter to you?" Darius snapped.

"It's just a bit..."

"What?" he snarled.

"Weak," Caleb snapped back and I paused, glancing over my shoulder as I looked between the two of them.

Darius moved to square his chest against Caleb's, rising up to his full height and making the most of the few inches he had on him.

"You wanna say that again?"

"Any asshole can push a girl in the mud, it's got nothing to do with your power or hers," Caleb snarled. "And it's a petty fucking thing to do to her."

My heart beat a little faster at his words. Caleb had made it clear that he stood with the Heirs always, I'd never expected to hear him standing up for me against one of them. Even if it was just because he didn't like the *way* Darius had gone about belittling me rather than objecting to the idea as a whole.

"Petty?" Darius growled. "Well I'd sooner that than be a pathetic little puppy, begging for every moment of her time. You literally let her run away from you rather than just taking what you want from her. What kind of Vampire are you?"

"The kind who's overpowered *you* more than once," Caleb hissed, his fangs lengthening.

I backed up a little as the air between them crackled with the promise of violence.

"Wanna put that to the test?" Darius baited.

Max crowed like a cockerel as he made it to the path behind me with Seth at his side but the two of them fell still as they looked at their friends in a stalemate. I wasn't sure if Darius would bite Caleb's head off first or if he'd get his throat ripped out instead.

I glanced at the other two Heirs but they weren't offering me any attention.

"What's going on?" Seth asked, a whimper escaping him as he took in the spiralling tension in the air.

"Caleb's crying because I pushed his little whore about," Darius taunted and for some reason those words stung more than him shoving me had.

Max looked at me with narrowed eyes and I backed up further. Whatever the hell this was, I didn't need to stay around and watch it play out. I had a trial to get to and the fewer assholes I had around me during it the better.

"Darius is just pouting because she won't look twice at him," Caleb retorted.

Seth turned to look at me, a snarl aimed my way through bared teeth like this was my fault. All I'd wanted to do was go for a run. He couldn't expect me to be on asshole patrol at all times, just in case I ran across one. They were freaking everywhere in this place.

"Or maybe the two of you just want a dick measuring contest but you can't find a microscope to judge it," I snapped.

Darius and Caleb turned away from each other to glare at me instead.

Yeah, I'm out.

I turned away and started running again. Mostly because they were making me late, partly because I just wanted to get the hell away from them.

From Darius.

"Come stay in Terra House with me tonight, Tory!" Caleb called after me but I didn't respond to that either, I just kept running.

A crowd had formed alongside the lake, slowly moving up onto the bleachers which had been erected for them to watch the challenge.

I circled them, heading straight for the tents which had been set up for the freshmen to change in. One glance at the magical timer hanging suspended beside the bleachers told me I had six minutes until it started and I upped my speed in response.

Darcy's eyes widened in relief as I pushed my way inside the tent.

"Where the hell have you been, Tor?" she demanded, holding out a black swimsuit for me to put on as I quickly tossed my headphones off of me and used water magic to wash the mud from my hands and face.

"Fucking Darius," I muttered, dropping my leggings. "Doesn't matter, I'm here now." I hadn't told her about the shadows yet. I would. But she needed to focus on this first and foremost and there really wasn't any time now.

I dropped all of my clothes in a heap and dragged on the bathing suit, noticing a belt around it with a large, metal hoop hanging over my right hip, before hurrying out of the tent at Darcy's side.

She was still eyeing me with concern but I set my jaw, raising my chin. That seemed to be good enough for her and she grinned at me.

"We got this," she said firmly.

"Let's show that asshole who he's fucking with," I growled.

"*Those* assholes," Darcy teased. "There's four of them, remember."

I snorted a laugh. "Five really. Orion just licks his ass too."

"Yeah," she agreed, a frown pinching her brows.

We reached the group of freshmen assembled before the lake and moved to take our places alongside them.

Professor Washer strolled along the lakeshore in a fluffy red robe and I glanced at Darcy, exchanging a 'thank god he's covered up for once' look with her.

"The trial!" Washer called, gaining silence from the onlookers as well as the freshmen. "Is simple. There are coloured keys hidden in three different forms of water. One is a block of ice. Another, a relentless waterfall. And the third, the depths of the lake itself-" I suppressed a shudder at that one. "- to succeed in passing this trial, you must each claim a red, blue and yellow key and make it to the platform in the centre of the lake within the allotted hour. Only use water magic - no sneaky Siren transformations, *Julian,*" he purred the guy's name and threw him a wink which made me gag.

"They should make the challenge to escape from Washer," I breathed to Darcy. "I'd run so fucking fast I'd have it won in five seconds flat."

She slapped a hand over her mouth to stop her laugh and Washer looked our way, offering a cheeky grin.

"I'll be on hand alongside several other Sirens to monitor your progress, make sure no one is cheating and that no one drowns. The ice is that way-" he pointed over a bridge to our left. "The falls over there-" He pointed right. "And if you just want to go ahead and get wet with me right now, you can all see, the big, blue..." Washer dropped his robe to reveal his blue scales covering his body and wriggled his hips suggestively. He was wearing the smallest fucking red speedo I'd ever seen. It was practically a thong. My mouth opened in horror. "Lake!" he finished, throwing his hands up just as a claxon sounded the start of the challenge.

"What first?" Darcy asked as the freshmen all started running in different directions, most of them going for the falls and ice.

I stared into the lake, nightmares shifting beneath my skin.

"I hope you don't drown, Roxy!" Darius shouted from somewhere in the crowd.

"Again!" Max added.

The sound of hundreds of students laughing filled my ears and blood flooded my cheeks.

"Fuck them," I spat. "Let's do the lake first!"

"Hell yes," Darcy agreed and we both started running straight for the water.

We'd done a fair bit of work in our Water Elemental lessons on controlling water. The trick to it was in giving it somewhere else to flow. You couldn't just cut through it, you needed to carve a hole into existence and encourage it to flood on by.

The cold liquid splashed across my legs and the slick feel of reeds pushed between my bare toes in a way that made my skin crawl but I didn't slow.

We kept wading until we started swimming, aiming for a ring of blue lights which sat in a circle on the water's surface, marking the spot where we needed to dive.

As the water got deeper, we began to swim. The endless depths beneath me made my heart beat faster but instead of caving to that fear, I used the energy to fuel my weary limbs.

We made it to the ring of lights and I looked down into the darkness of the blue water. I could see my legs but not much beyond.

Washer was bobbing in the water before us, a smile playing around his lips. "How long can you hold your breath?" he teased, though for once he kept his Siren magic the hell away from us.

I openly sneered in disgust at him as I drew on my water magic.

"On three?" Darcy asked, her eyes glimmering with the depths of her power.

"Three," I said, just before I dove beneath the water.

I pressed my hands out in front of my face as I kicked down and worked my hardest to channel the water around me.

A flood of air hit my face and I gulped it down before it slipped away. I tried again. And again. Each time I succeeded, the longer the air stayed around me, the water sliding by as if I were in an arrow-shaped cocoon.

Blue lights glimmered ahead and I kicked harder, trying to ignore it every time the water cut back in and hit me in the face. Each breath I managed was a success, the glowing blue lights signalling this win.

Darcy's leg skimmed mine and I was glad to find her right beside me. It was hard to make her out in the gloom beneath the water but just knowing she was there leant me strength.

As we neared the bottom of the lake, the blue lights revealed themselves to be keys. I cried out in triumph, bubbles spilling through the water around me as I snatched one into my grasp.

I caught Darcy's eye for a moment as I hooked the key onto the loop at my waist and she did the same.

She pointed at the surface far above us and I nodded my agreement as I started to kick towards it.

Rising was easier than diving and the air slid over my lips less and less often as I chose speed over wielding the water away, the promise of oxygen waiting so close above.

My head breached the surface and I whooped in triumph, sparing a moment to high five Darcy as Washer grinned at us.

"You're the first to make it to the base," he said and for once I didn't flinch away from the suggestive tone he used, I just laughed.

"Ice next?" Darcy suggested and I agreed quickly as we started swimming for the shore.

A chant had started up from the crowd but I couldn't make out the words. I probably didn't want to anyway.

We kept going until we were dragging ourselves up the bank and started running towards the bridge Washer had pointed out.

"Vegas gonna take you down! Vegas coming for the crown! Watch out Heirs you'd better bow! Vegas gonna take you DOWN!"

I looked around, my eyes widening in surprise at the chant which was taking place and my gaze fell on Geraldine in full on conductor mode as the Ass Club all screamed their lungs out in support of us. She had a baton and a white shirt with *Vega Royals!* scrawled across the front of it and was grinning her damn head off. I couldn't spare her more than that quick glance as we ran on but we both let out a laugh as we went.

We crossed the bridge quickly and my eyes widened as I spotted the huge block of ice before us. I felt the freezing cold air coming off of it before we even made it within ten feet. Inside it, red lights were glowing which I knew had to be the keys.

"Shit, how will we get one of those out?" I asked desperately. I'd created ice more than once, though not really on purpose and I hadn't ever tried to melt it with water magic. My natural inclination would be to use fire for that.

A girl with bright blue eyes was standing a little way along the block of ice, both hands pressed to it and sinking in. With a cry of success, she drew back, yanking a red key with her before she turned and sprinted away.

Darcy sprang forward and I followed her lead, ignoring the bite of cold that came at me as I moved towards the ice.

I laid my palms against the frozen block right over a glimmering key which looked to be about a foot inside it.

I took a deep breath, closing my eyes and trying to feel for the sensation of water moving between my palms, willing the ice to take on that form for me.

A bead of moisture raced down the back of my hand. Then another. And another. I pressed on, refusing to open my eyes in case it broke my concentration as water began to spill between my spread fingers.

My palm finally hit metal and I snatched the red key out with a whoop of triumph, hooking it onto my belt and looking to Darcy as she did the same.

"One to go," I said excitedly.

"Oh I'm gonna rub it in the Heirs' faces so hard when we make it through The Reckoning," Darcy announced and I laughed at the fire in her voice.

We ran back across the bridge, past the bleachers and the crowd who were still screaming encouragement for us under Geraldine's guidance.

We crossed paths with students racing in the opposite direction, one guy smacking straight into me and earning himself an elbow to the ribs in response.

When we made it to the waterfall, I stumbled to a halt, staring up at it in shock. It slammed down on the path in an endless torrent, the water cycling back around and around magically with so much force that I knew we wouldn't be able to stand beneath it much less pass through it without magic.

I bit my lip as I raised my hands and stepped forward, the spray crashing over me.

My magic was beginning to feel a little empty, the well inside me running lower than usual at all the power I'd exerted. But we needed more. Just a little more.

We'd figured out how to make it through the waterfall which led into our Water Elemental class in our second week and I guessed this was just a more extreme version of that.

I took a deep breath and pressed my influence into the torrent as I raised my hands, willing it to part in the centre and convincing it that the routes to the left and right of me were easier. Darcy threw her own magic at the same spot and all of a sudden the water parted like a curtain, revealing a pedestal covered in glimmering yellow keys.

We darted in and grabbed two, hooking them to our belts before dropping the magic and sprinting back towards the lake.

The crowd screamed as they spotted us and adrenaline surged through my shaky limbs as I caught Darcy's hand so that we could run together.

The platform in the centre of the lake seemed impossibly far out but I also noticed that no one stood on it yet. We were in the lead, the first of the freshmen to have collected all three keys.

I grinned as I ran straight into the water, swimming as soon as I could, using my water magic to carve an easier path for my aching body along the surface.

There were a lot of other students in the lake but they were all still in the process of diving for the blue key. I was so glad we chose to do that first now that the exhaustion was pounding through my limbs. It had taken the most magic and I was sure more than one of the students in the water were struggling on low reserves now.

It seemed like we swam forever, the sound of the crowd lost to the swoosh, swoosh, swoosh of water around my ears before finally, my hand hit the wooden platform.

My arms trembled as I dragged myself up onto it, catching Darcy's arm to help pull her over the edge at the same time.

We pushed ourselves to our feet and the screaming crowd went wild on the lakeshore, a grin almost cleaving my face in two as I looked out over everyone.

"We did it," Darcy said, partly in relief, part shock, part pure goddamn joy.

"Hell yeah we did!"

I threw my arms around her and we squealed like little kids who'd just turned up at Disney Land. After the horrors of the night before, a win was exactly what I'd needed and holy crap did it feel good.

Geraldine threw us a celebration of ridiculous proportions in The Orb over dinner, laying out plate after plate of food for us until we were so full we were fit to pop.

By the time it got close to curfew, I'd joined Sofia and the members of the Ass Club who lived in Ignis House and headed back to my bed.

Exhaustion had tugged at my body and I'd managed a few hours of sleep before a nightmare had woken me. I scrubbed a hand over my face as I tried to fight it off but I could still hear whispering in the dark corners of my room.

I snatched my Atlas from my nightstand and scowled as I realised it was only half eleven.

My heart was beating a little too fast and my mind was whirling with crazy ideas which wouldn't let me rest. I tried closing my eyes to block them out but gave up as the nightmares drew close again.

I let out a breath of irritation as I rose, trying to figure out who might be awake to keep me company.

I slipped out of bed and decided to investigate the common room. Maybe Sofia or even Milton would still be up.

It was chilly out of the comfort of my bed and I quickly dressed in a pair of jeans and a red sweater before kicking my sneakers on and heading down to the common room.

I thumbed through FaeBook posts on my Atlas as I walked and one caught my eye.

Tyler Corbin:

Watch out Griffins. I've personally dealt with an Heir lusting after me for my sparkly tail. Here's a few tips to you Griffins if Max Rigel peer pressures you into joining his turd herd with his Siren powers.

1. Don't look him in the eye too long (Caleb Altair started touching himself when I did this)

2. When in your Order form, take dumps in private. If Max catches you, charge him down. (He's not as fast as a horny Vampire)

3. If all else fails, shit on him and shit on him good. He might enjoy it but at least you'll get even. (Caleb's still washing the glitter out of his hair since I did this – I'm starting to think he wants it there)

#pooboo #dungchum #maxlikescracks

Comments:

Milly Badgerville:

Ewww is this true?

Amy Sawyer:

Oooh where can I sign up to the turd herd?

Max Rigel:

You are so fucking dead.

Geraldine Grus:

If you lay a finger on him you foul faeces enthusiast, you will face the wrath of the Almighty Sovereign Society!

Milton Hubert:

Hahaha Geraldine

Darius Acrux:

@Miltonhubert Ghosts don't have FaeBook profiles. Delete it before the end of the day.

Caleb Altair:

I'm going to Pegassassinate you.

Angelica Luevano:

The A.S.S protect all friends of the true queens! Hail the Vegas! Hail their friends! #downwiththeheirs

I laughed to myself as I continued to read the comments and only looked up as I reached the common room. I stilled, looking around for a friendly face. I didn't find any. Instead I spotted Darius Acrux and his fan club taking up a huge circle of chairs by the biggest fireplace in the room. I almost turned and walked straight back out but he looked up at that moment, his gaze fixing on me.

I pursed my lips, refusing to scurry from the room but no longer having a reason for being there.

"Sneaking out to go screw Caleb again?" Marguerite mocked as she spotted me too. "You realise he's just using you for your power, right?"

I lifted my chin and stalked towards her, silently thanking her for the brilliant idea. Caleb was exactly what I needed to take my mind away from my nightmares.

"You're wrong, Marguerite," I said sweetly. "He's not just using me for my power: he gets my body too."

Darius growled and a wall of flames sprang into place before the doorway, blocking my way out.

"It's after curfew," he snapped, daring me to go against him.

"Yeah," I agreed, pausing before the flames. "There are lots of silly rules in this place. They even frown on people hanging out down at Air Cove with tea-"

"I don't give a shit what you do but I don't want you getting caught and losing us House Points," Darius snarled, cutting me off as he dropped the barrier of flames.

I offered him an insolent look and headed for the door. Darius got out of his chair before I made it though, stepping into my way. He snatched my Atlas out of my grip and I fought against the urge to try and snatch it back, clenching my teeth instead.

"What are you doing?" I demanded.

"I just wanted to make sure you've seen the latest story about you. Wouldn't want you to miss it," he said with a shrug, tapping away at something on the screen.

His fan club were all watching us expectantly and they fell silent while they waited to find out what would happen next.

"Unlike you, I don't jerk off over the sight of my name in the press so don't bother," I said, holding my hand out for my Atlas.

"Oh but it's such an accurate piece, I'm sure you wouldn't want to miss out."

Marguerite laughed excitedly and I narrowed my eyes on him, wondering why it was taking him so long to search for a single news story.

Darius twisted my Atlas in his hand and pushed it back at me. Unsurprisingly the story had been written by Gus Vulpecula and the title was less than complimentary.

Are the Vega Twins cheating their way through school exams?

I instantly shut down the page, having no interest in reading more bullshit that guy had invented about us.

"Can I go now? My sex addiction needs an outlet." I looked up at Darius like he was boring me and his jaw clenched.

"You might wanna give Cal some notice if you're planning on surprising him. Last I saw of him, he was heading back to his room with Milly Badgerville, it might be embarrassing for you if she's still there," Darius taunted as he stepped aside.

I snorted dismissively. "Let's hope you're right and the three of us can have fun together."

I moved towards the door and Darius called after me, unable to just let me go and escape his aggravatingly boring company.

"If you get caught you'll be fucking sorry."

His fan club laughed appreciatively and Marguerite gave me a look that suggested she thought she'd won something.

I rolled my eyes at him and continued towards the door. "I hope you have a great night too," I muttered. "And your friends don't end up suffocating from shoving their heads too far up your ass."

Once I was outside, I wrapped my arms around myself and set a quick pace to Terra House, slipping off the main paths to avoid being caught by patrolling teachers. I probably should have been more worried about coming across a stray Nymph but I really needed a distraction from the shadows which would be waiting for me if I tried to sleep again now. Besides, with so many teachers out patrolling and the FIB still maintaining a perimeter around the school grounds, I found it hard to believe a Nymph could get in again. Even so, I decided to run so that the trip would be over as quickly as possible.

It didn't take me long to get to Terra House and I swerved around the back of the large hill, tiptoeing up to the very highest window where Caleb's room lay.

As I got closer I dropped to my hands and knees, slowing my movements in the hopes that even his Vampire senses wouldn't detect me.

I lay on my stomach and inched forward until I could see down into Caleb's room through the window in the grass. He was laying in bed, one arm hooked behind his head as he watched TV with his shirt off and the duvet wrapped between his legs.

I bit my lip and carefully pulled my Atlas from my pocket, tapping out a message with feather light movements in case he detected me.

Tory:

15 minutes...

I heard his Atlas ping through the glass and he reached for it slowly, dragging it out of the folded duvet while his attention stayed fixed on the screen at the foot of his bed. He lifted the Atlas to read the message and I grinned as he sat up straighter, tapping out a response instantly.

Caleb:

I'll find you in five ;)

He leapt out of bed and flicked the TV off without a second glance, snatching a hoodie from his wardrobe and shrugging it on before pushing his feet into his sneakers and heading straight out of the door.

I counted to thirty to make sure he was well down the corridor then carefully jimmied the latch on his window using a pen I had in my pocket so I could open it. It was easily done now that I was familiar with the catch after we'd broken in to plant the Pegasex doll and within moments I had the window wide.

I shoved the pen back into my pocket and shuffled around so that I could lower myself into his room. I hung from the window frame before letting go and falling down to land on my ass in the centre of his bed with a laugh.

I quickly got up and kicked off my shoes as I moved to sit on his bed. My heart pounded with adrenaline as I lifted my Atlas into my grip and typed out another message for him.

Tory:

You're getting colder... do you want a clue?

Caleb:

Watch out sweetheart or I'll start to think you want to lose.
But of course I want a clue...

I held my Atlas up and took a selfie of me sitting on his bed before sending it to him. I knew that it would mean I lost the game, but I wanted him enough tonight not to care about being bitten. I just needed to get out of my own head and lose myself for a few hours and what better way to do that than in Caleb Altair's arms? Plus I probably owed him some kind of thanks for sticking up for me with Darius.

I waited for a reply but none came and I drummed my fingers against the side of my Atlas impatiently.

A moment later the key sounded in the lock and Caleb swept into the room with a wide smile on his face.

"How?" he demanded, looking around at the door as he closed it again.

I smirked at him and pointed to the window above my head. "You left it open," I replied innocently, though I was fairly sure he knew that was a lie.

Caleb didn't seem to care much about the truth to my claim as he stalked towards me instead, his gaze fixed on me where I sat in the centre of his bed.

"I thought you were pissed at me?" he teased.

I shrugged. "I decided to give you a pass in light of you sticking up for me with your friend."

Caleb paused, a crease forming on his brow. "You know my loyalty is still with the Heirs though, right? I just happen to think shoving girls about isn't the best way to show strength."

"Yeah, I got that. Don't worry, I don't think you've suddenly turned into a knight in shining armour. And I wouldn't want you to either; I can fight my own battles." My gaze trailed over his mouth and my pulse hitched a little.

"I don't know about that, you promised to punish me for my involvement with that shit at the pool but I'm still waiting for you to come at me," he teased.

"Are you, now?" I couldn't help but smirk to myself at that. He had no idea we'd already hit him solidly in his reputation with those Pegasus rumours, but if he liked the idea that he still had one up on me then I wasn't going to burst his bubble. "Well maybe I'm building up to it," I said, dropping my voice as I looked over his body slowly.

Caleb smirked at me and hounded forward, closing in on me with intent.

"Wait," I said as he drew closer, shifting up onto my knees as I moved to meet him at the edge of the bed.

"Why?" he breathed, his gaze roaming over me intently.

"Because I made you a promise," I said, offering him a sly smile.

"What promise?"

I stepped off of the bed and bit my lip as I caught his waist and walked him backwards a few steps until he bumped against the wall.

Caleb caught my jaw in his rough palm and guided my mouth to his possessively. My heart pounded at the heat in that kiss as his body begged for me like I was aching for him. I needed to push the shadows away and forget everything else and his kiss was a promise of oblivion. Even if it couldn't last forever.

I kissed him hard, my tongue sweeping over his as I tugged at the drawstring which secured his sweatpants, loosening it so that I could have access to every hard inch of him.

Caleb groaned as my hand gripped the smooth length of him and I smiled against his mouth as I slid it up and down a few times slowly.

I broke our kiss as I reached up to unzip his hoodie, sliding it off of his broad shoulders so that I could have access to more of his flesh. He wasn't wearing a shirt beneath it so I was instantly rewarded with what I'd wanted.

He pushed his hands into my hair as I moved my mouth down his neck, over his collarbone and down the firm ridges of his abdominals before I dropped to my knees before him, pushing his pants down as I went.

"*Shit,*" Caleb breathed, his word a curse and a prayer as he realised what I was going to do with him.

Caleb swore more forcefully as I took him into my mouth, my tongue sweeping around the length of him as I drew him between my lips, sucking and teasing as his hands fisted in my hair.

He groaned as I found a rhythm, moving my mouth over him as I pushed his body closer and closer to release.

Caleb gripped my hair tighter in a desperate movement and drew me back off of him. His hand slid to my chin and he pulled me upright again, claiming my lips with his as he peeled my sweater off. He tossed it aside and quickly unbuckled my jeans, his fingers swift and urgent with his need until he had me in my underwear.

"You always surprise me, Tory," he breathed, turning me suddenly so that my back was to him and his arms wrapped around my waist, drawing me close. "I never know what to expect from you and it drives me fucking insane."

I moaned as his teeth skimmed along the line of my jaw, arching into him as his hands moved across my flesh.

He kissed my neck and I pushed my ass back against him, moaning as his fingers pushed beneath my bra and he began a sweet torment on my hardened nipple.

"Just when I think I've got you figured out, you do this to me and I could just about lose my mind over it."

Caleb's other hand shifted beneath the fabric of my panties and he groaned with desire as he pushed a finger inside me, feeling just how much I wanted him. His dick was so hard against my ass that my mouth was drying up with desire to feel every inch of him inside me.

Caleb kept moving his hand and started walking me forward towards the bed. I went willingly, my breaths laboured with need as he kept up his sweet torment, his fingers giving me a taste of what I needed from him while keeping me hanging in suspense at the same time.

We reached the foot of the bed and I caught the bedpost, leaning forward over it without needing any more encouragement. Caleb withdrew his hand, catching my panties in his grip and shoving them down. He lined himself up behind me and I panted breathily, needing this from him more than I'd realised when I came here.

He groaned with desire and claimed me with one hard thrust of his hips. I cried out, bucking forward as I gripped the bedpost to stop myself from falling.

Caleb swore under his breath, gripping my hips as he drove himself into me again and again, each powerful thrust forcing a moan from my lips as he pushed me closer and closer to a climax which my body ached for so desperately.

The headboard was slamming into the wall and my nails were gouging lines into the wooden post which was the only thing stopping me from toppling over beneath the strength of his desire.

Caleb's hand slid from my hip, pushing down until his fingers were riding the perfect place at the apex of my thighs, the power of his thrusts meeting with a circle of his fingers on that sensitive spot.

I sucked in a breath, my head spinning as he drove me closer and closer to the edge, drawing so much pleasure into my body that I could barely even meet his thrusts with the rocking of my own hips.

Caleb drew back one final time, his fingers pressing down a touch harder as he slammed into me and sent me careering into a mind blowing wave of pleasure with a cry which was punctuated by his own gasp of release as he followed me into ecstasy.

He fell forward over me for a moment, our bodies slick with sweat, chests heaving as we fought to recover from the impact of what we'd just done.

He pressed kisses to the back of my neck and shoulders, little shivers tumbling through my sensitised skin at the feel of them.

After several minutes where neither of us could do much more than try to catch our breath, Caleb eased off of me and drew me upright into his arms.

He turned me around, his hand sliding into my hair as he kissed me sweetly, righting his pants which hadn't even made it off of his body in his haste to have me.

I smiled into his kiss, my flesh humming with satisfied energy as I ran my hands along the firm muscles of his biceps so that I could hold onto him.

"You have no idea how much I needed that," I murmured, kissing him again as he guided me back to his bed.

"You've been keeping me in suspense for days, sweetheart," he replied with a laugh. "I think I know how much."

I sank down onto his mattress and he offered me one of his shirts which he snagged from a chair beside the bed. I shrugged into it, fastening the buttons as he watched me intently, following me back onto the bed.

"You wanna stay and watch Rambo with me?" he offered with a shy grin which was so unlike his usual cocky smirk that I couldn't help but stare at it a little.

"Yeah," I replied, moving to lean against his pillows as his smile widened. "That actually sounds really... nice."

Caleb flicked the TV on and pulled me under his arm so that I could rest my head against his shoulder as the classic action film got underway. It was about a third in already but I shook my head when he offered to restart it for me, happy to just sit and let the noise of it wash over me while I stole a little comfort from his arms.

Caleb held me loosely, his fingers toying with my hair as we watched the film before inevitably falling back into the temptation of each other's bodies and I soaked up all the pleasure I could take from his flesh.

While he held me, the shadows seemed to stay a little further from my mind and I couldn't really ask for much more than that.

He was the perfect escape from the mayhem of everything else that was going on in my life. And I was more than happy to lose myself with him for a little while.

DARIUS

CHAPTER TWENTY FOUR

I circled through the sky above the Academy grounds for about the hundredth time, beating my wings occasionally before just gliding on the currents.

I was angry enough to spit fire. Which I had. Multiple times. So much that even my Dragon throat was beginning to feel raw with it.

My gaze narrowed on the huge mound of earth which contained Terra House. She was in there now with Caleb. I knew it. And the anger it lit in me wasn't something I could put out easily.

It was almost dawn. I'd been out here all night and she hadn't left. At first I'd been meaning to confront her again, force her to bow to me and make her learn her place beneath my feet. But as my rage simmered, I'd realised that that would only be a short fix. She'd just get right back up again, look me in the eye and continue to defy me.

No. If we wanted the Vegas gone then we had to do it differently. And I wanted her gone. I was sick of looking at her in my House and around campus.

Sick of watching them with their Royalist club holding court in The Orb. Sick of seeing them learn more and more about their powers each day. Sick of watching her play Caleb like a fucking fool. And most of all I was sick of wanting her and hating her all at once.

My stomach was a knot of constantly warring instincts. I wanted to crush her and hold her at the same time. Every strike I made at her almost seemed to cut me more than her.

When I'd pushed her in that fucking mud, I had to lock my muscles into place to stop myself from diving down after her and lifting her back into my arms. And then I looked into her eyes and saw a moment of hurt there that had nothing to do with physical pain or humiliation but had everything to do with me and what I knew she had felt for me too. I felt like I'd just taken a knife to my own heart and carved a fissure right through it.

Because I knew with every move I made against her I was damaging it more. And I knew that there was nothing I could do to stop myself. I was in full self destruct mode but I refused to go down alone.

It was time we broke the Vegas and got them the hell out of this school. And if I had to break myself to do it then that was just the price I'd have to pay.

I looked down at Terra House as the sun crested the horizon. She still hadn't fucking left.

I roared my anger into the uncaring clouds and turned toward The Wailing Wood, setting a course for King's Hollow right at the heart of it.

I banked hard, tucking my wings close and diving out of the sky as I spotted the wooden roof of the huge treehouse we called our sanctuary.

My weight collided with it and the whole structure trembled beneath me, a groan of protest echoing from it. I wasn't concerned though, this place was born of magic and was more than strong enough to take the weight of a five ton Dragon landing on its roof.

I withdrew into my Fae form with some difficulty. This anger in me had me craving my Dragon form at all times. It was eating me up, consuming me entirely. And I needed it gone.

I stalked across the roof and ripped open the hatch which led inside before dropping down into the wide living area.

I threw a handful of fire into the grate with so much force that it roared to life, flaming half way up the huge chimney before shrinking down to a normal size.

I kicked open the chest in the corner of the room where we kept spare clothes for me and Seth so that we could come here in our Order forms and not have to spend the rest of the night hanging out with our junk on show.

I stuffed my legs into a pair of black sweatpants then crossed to the kitchenette at the back of the room.

I yanked open a drawer and took out the spare Atlas I kept there.

I sent the same message to all three of them at once.

Darius:

King's Hollow. Now. There's something we need to discuss.

I drummed my fingers on the counter impatiently as I waited for them to reply. I didn't care if it was five in the morning, they'd come.

Seth:

On my way. Make coffee.

I scowled at the coffee machine like it had just insulted my mother. He could make his own fucking coffee.

Max:

This had better be good, I'm gonna have to skip out on morning sex for it...

I didn't reply to that either. I just waited to hear from Caleb. Fucking

Caleb who had Vampire hearing and couldn't be that fucking busy with Roxy that he hadn't heard my message come in. I glared at the screen, a red tick appearing to let me know he'd read it.

I waited. And waited.

No reply.

Darius:

This is important, Caleb.

He read that too. Still no reply.

Darius:

Tell me you're on your way.

Darius:

I'll come and drag you out of your bed if you don't come willingly.

Darius:

Answer your fucking messages.

I ground my teeth, smoke pouring between them. I could fly to Terra House and dig him out of it if I had to. I'd carry him here in my claws and remind him that I was king of every beast in the land. Nobody fucking ignored me when I called.

Caleb:

I'm busy.

I almost smashed the fucking Atlas. A roar ripped from my throat and I launched the copper coffee pot across the room with enough force to lodge it into the wooden wall.

A whine caught my attention as a huge, white wolf bounded into the room from the stairwell. Seth shifted in a heartbeat, his eyes wide with concern.

"What's going on?" he asked, striding towards me with his arms held out like he was gonna hug me.

"Seth, I swear to the stars, if you hug me with your fucking dick out I'm gonna rip it off," I snarled and he pulled up short with a whimper.

He quickly hooked a pair of sweatpants from the chest in the corner and pulled them on to cover himself.

I turned my attention back to my Atlas, forcing myself to type slowly when I kept hitting the wrong buttons.

Darius:

I know who you're busy doing. This is about her and you'll want to hear it. Get your ass here now.

"What's going on?" Seth asked again warily, moving towards me with his hands twitching. He wanted to hug me. I could see it written all over his face but I was pretty sure he could tell that I'd tear his arms off if he tried.

"Caleb would rather stay in bed with Roxy Vega than come to his brothers when we call him," I snapped.

Seth sidled closer and looked down at the messages on my Atlas, pushing his long hair back out of his face. Just as he did, Caleb replied.

Caleb:

Give me an hour.

Caleb:

Or two.

Caleb:

;)

Did he just send me a fucking emoji?!

I slammed my fist into the Atlas so hard that the worktop beneath it cracked right down the middle. Bits of broken glass embedded themselves in my fist and blood spurted out of my hand. I actually welcomed the pain. I needed it. I needed something other than rage. I glanced down at it and noticed a jagged piece of glass lodged in my wrist. It must have hit a vein because blood was pissing out of it like a waterfall.

"Fuck, Darius!" Seth caught my arm then flinched back with a whine as my blazing skin burned him.

My shoulders started shaking, my wings demanding to be set loose from my flesh. I was about to lose my shit entirely.

Just as the feeling of the transformation engulfed my chest, a wave of calm washed over me instead and I fell still.

"What the hell have I just walked in on?" Max gasped, his gaze swivelling between the destroyed Atlas, Seth and my bleeding arm.

I bared my teeth at him and his power hit me harder, his brow pinching with concentration as he tried to wrangle the angry beast inside me.

"Cal sent him an emoji," Seth whimpered. He was pacing, moving close to me and backing up again, his gaze moving to the pool of blood which was getting bigger and bigger beside me.

Max frowned then pointed at my wrist. "Let Seth fix that."

I didn't move. Seth approached with a frown, reaching out to take my arm. I didn't fight him off. The rage in me had dimmed a little under Max's influence but it was by no means gone.

Seth winced as my skin burned him again but he didn't pull his hand back, taking the burns as he dragged the sliver of glass out of my wrist then pressed his hand over the wound to heal it. I couldn't even feel it anymore.

As soon as it was done, he wrapped his hand around mine and healed that too, my skin forcing out the rest of the glass as it knitted over.

Seth threaded his fingers through mine as he finished, whining softly as he shifted into my personal space, taking the burns caused by my touch.

I growled at him, a warning low in the back of my throat but he ignored me, pressing forward.

"Seth, I don't think that's a good idea," Max murmured, sweat beading on his brow as he fought with all his might to wrangle my rage under control.

Seth ignored him, wrapping his arms around my waist and nuzzling into my neck as he pressed his bare chest to mine in a tight embrace.

My growl deepened as I warned him to get the hell off of me and I could feel Max fighting as hard as he could to stop me from lashing out.

"Don't be angry," Seth tried. "I'm here, Max is here, Cal will be here soon-"

At the mention of Caleb I lost it. I shoved Seth off of me so hard that he crashed into a cupboard, making the door cave in before he fell inside it.

I snarled at him as more smoke coiled between my teeth and Max darted between us, holding up a hand in offering.

I was half inclined to bite his head off but I managed a curt nod instead.

The moment Max's hand landed on my bicep, the effects of his power multiplied tenfold.

My limbs stopped trembling, the heat withdrew from my skin and I felt the Dragon settle back down beneath my flesh.

I took a deep breath, then another.

Seth scrambled out from the destroyed remains of the cupboard. He didn't even look pissed at me. In fact it looked like he was still more concerned about *me* than him. He made quick work of healing the burns I'd given him but I couldn't quite calm myself enough to offer him an apology.

"I'll call Cal, tell him it's important," Max murmured and the set of his jaw told me he was angry with the Earth Heir too. That was something at least.

413

He eyed me carefully as he withdrew his hand from my arm and though I felt a good measure of anger returning, I still held it under control.

I moved to the counter and placed my palms flat on it as I waited for him to make the call.

Max placed his Atlas down between the three of us, hitting the speaker button as ringing filled the air.

We waited. And waited.

It rang out.

I gritted my teeth as the others glanced at me warily and Max hit redial.

It rang out twice more before he finally answered.

"Yeah?" he asked, sounding so fucking casual I wanted to rip his throat out for it.

I didn't trust myself to speak so I let Max do the talking.

"We're waiting for you at the Hollow. This is serious, Cal, don't dick us around. We'll come and get you if you won't come willingly," Max said in a low voice.

Seth whined a little in agreement.

Caleb let out a long sigh like *we* were the ones being unreasonable.

"*Fine.*"

"That means *now*, not in a few hours," I growled, unable to hold back on commenting any longer.

"Yeah, yeah, let me just see if I've got any clothes left in one piece and I'll be there. Make coffee," he added lazily like he couldn't tell just how much he was pissing me off.

"I'll have it ready," Seth said encouragingly. "Just the way you like it."

I shot him a death glare.

"Thanks," Caleb said. Just before he cut the call I heard the soft murmur of Roxy's voice in the background and my heart twisted angrily in my chest.

He was letting her play him for an idiot and he didn't even realise it. But it was past time he found out.

Seth headed across the room and proceeded to prise the coffee pot out of the wall as if it was a totally normal thing to have to do.

I crossed the room, heading for the couch then turning away from it at the last moment. I couldn't sit. This pent-up energy inside me was writhing too much for that. I moved to stand before the fire instead, drawing comfort from the flames as they blazed at my back. I was at home with fire. It lived in my veins. It was a part of me.

Caleb shot into the room a second later, dropping into the armchair to the left of the room and kicking his feet up onto the coffee table like he'd been there the whole fucking time.

I glared down at him and he looked right back at me mildly like he wasn't the least bit concerned that I might just kill him.

My gaze trailed over his appearance. His blonde curls hadn't been styled at all and they were all messed up, sticking up in random directions. He wore a pair of sweatpants and a wrinkled t-shirt and just above the collar of it, a love bite showed against his skin.

My gaze narrowed on it. Why hadn't he just healed it away? Did he even know it was there? When had she given him that? Was it last night when she went to him? Had they even slept at all? Were they literally in the middle of it when we were trying to call him? Had she had her mouth on his neck just a few moments ago?

Smoke filled my mouth and I fought to swallow it, refusing to let him see just how much those thoughts pissed me off.

Seth appeared with two mugs of coffee, offering the first to me but I only scowled in response so he set it down on the coffee table.

Caleb took the second with a word of thanks, covering his mouth as he yawned widely. Seth returned to fetch more coffee for him and Max before dropping down beside him on the couch.

"Little Vega keep you up all night?" Max teased, putting a good deal of effort into acting normal. Like I hadn't just completely lost my shit and half trashed the place.

"I can hardly keep up with her," Caleb joked, sipping his coffee as he leaned back in his chair.

"No. It seems like she's able to run rings all around you without you even having the faintest fucking idea," I agreed.

Caleb slid his gaze to mine slowly but he didn't even show a flicker of irritation. "What's that supposed to mean?"

"It *means*, that while you've been chasing her all over campus and letting everyone and anyone see how whipped she's got you, Roxy and her sister have been laughing at you the whole time."

Caleb set his coffee down on the table, running a thumb over the hickey on his neck like he wasn't even aware he was doing it. "You wanna explain what you're going on about or just keep on ranting?" he asked. "Because from where I'm sitting, it just sounds like you're jealous."

Seth sucked in a sharp breath and leaned back on the couch, pressing himself against Max like he was expecting a fight to break out at any second.

I bit back the response I wanted to give Caleb as my gut lurched uncomfortably. *That's not the fucking point.*

"Give me your Atlas, Max," I said in a low voice, holding out my hand.

Max instantly tossed it to me and I quickly logged out of his profile and into mine, pulling up my emails. Specifically the folder containing all of Roxy's emails which I'd forwarded to myself when I snatched her Atlas from her last night. When I'd had time to go through them, what I'd found had both surprised me and confirmed what I'd been worried about. I might have been a tiny bit impressed too but I wasn't going to mention that.

I opened up the order confirmation for a life sized, inflatable Pegasus sex doll with the name Tory Vega printed on the invoice clear as day then tossed it into Caleb's lap.

Caleb sat up a little straighter as he looked at it. He fell still. Unnaturally still. And Max shifted uncomfortably in his seat as he read the new emotions flooding out of him.

"Is this true?" Caleb growled, his jaw ticking.

Seth leaned forward to take the Atlas so that he and Max could look too.

"Of course it is," I snapped. "She ordered glitter and horn shaped vibrators too. Even a fucking riding crop with your name stamped on it in rainbow colours. The two of them must have started that whole rumour about you."

"But how did they get an inflatable sex toy into your room?" Max asked. "Didn't you say whoever did it got it in there while you were in the shower? They don't have enough control over their magic to break through a locked door and reseal it that quickly, not to mention quietly enough to-"

"She got into my room last night," Caleb breathed. "She sent me a message to get me to leave and within two minutes she sent me a selfie of her sitting on my bed. She said I'd left the window open, but I knew I hadn't..."

"Shit," Max breathed.

"And instead of questioning her on how she got into your room like that you just fucked her?" I asked scathingly.

"It wasn't exactly the most pressing thing on my mind. I was more interested in the fact that she was in my bed, not on figuring out how she got there," Caleb quipped.

"Seriously?" I snapped like he was an idiot.

Three sets of eyes turned on me like *I* was the one asking a ridiculous question and I rolled my eyes. Yeah, okay if Roxy Vega showed up in my bed mysteriously and wanted to get in my pants then I probably wouldn't have started asking many questions either. *Dammit.*

"Fine. But this proves she did that and Gwendalina was obviously in on it too. We thought they just got over what we did to them after that party but they clearly didn't. They've been fighting back against us in ways we didn't see coming and being pretty fucking clever about it too."

"Well we know they did that to Cal but what else is there to say they've done more than that?" Seth asked.

Caleb had fallen very quiet, his gaze narrowed on a distant point as he seemed to be lost in thought.

"They were responsible for the fire in my room," I said in a low voice.

"But I thought Milton-" Seth began but I cut him off.

"No. It was them. Roxy admitted it to me and Orion."

"Then why isn't she dead already?" Seth asked angrily.

Fire simmered in my veins at that suggestion and for a fleeting moment I wanted to throw myself between him and Roxy to keep her safe from him. I shook the thought off irritably, dismissing it as quickly as it had come.

"We can't just kill them," I snapped. Even though I knew he hadn't really meant it. There was a lot of leeway for us to do what was necessary with the twins, but death and maiming were obviously out of bounds if we wanted to keep our claim. "Besides. She stole something from me while she was there that I can't have anyone finding out about. She promised to stay quiet so long as I do too, so I can't out her for it."

The other Heirs looked at me curiously but didn't question me. They knew I kept secrets from them. They also knew I did it to protect them from the knowledge not because I didn't trust them with it. Hell, they'd probably figured out half the shit I was up to long ago but it was like an unspoken rule that none of us ever mentioned it.

"Darcy was in that detention with us when we cleaned Griffin shit off the roof of Jupiter Hall," Max said in a low voice. "She knew how badly I reacted to that stuff. And I had my cousin ask around Starlight Academy about it. There's not so much as a rumour of one of them having sabotaged my kit. I wanted to get revenge on the asshole who'd done it...but maybe it was never one of them."

"How would the Vegas have gotten access to the kits though?" Seth asked. "Only members of the team can-"

"Members like Geraldine Grus?" I asked in a low growl.

"I'm gonna fucking kill them!" Max bellowed, leaping to his feet as his eyes lit with certainty.

Seth got up and caught hold of his arm with a bark of anger. "You can't hurt Darcy," he said, looking like he was in pain. "She's my Omega - *fuck*. I can't do anything to her unless she challenges me as her Alpha."

Max tore out of his grip, running for the door anyway and Seth took chase.

"Wait!" I called before everyone lost their heads. "There's no point in us just going at them head on like we have before anyway, all it ever does is make them rise up stronger and more defiant."

"He's right," Caleb said quietly from his chair. "They won't be beaten like that."

Max fell still, anger coiling through the room like a tangible force as his Siren gifts spread it through the air.

"You need to break that bond with her, Seth," Max snarled at him.

"I will," Seth growled. "They haven't even struck a blow against me yet, but they'll be coming for me next. I haven't had anything happen to me lately except..." He scratched the back of his head curiously, like some dark thought had just occurred to him. "Except for me catching fleas..."

"They aren't the goddamn pied pipers for Werewolf fleas," Caleb grunted. "There's no way they could give you fleas. At least... not without summoning them with an Aquarius Moonstone..."

"That's Sophomore year magic," Max said. "How would they even know about it?"

"There's a whole library full of spells just sitting there if they wanted to find one," I said, not believing for one moment that anything was beyond those girls.

Seth stared at me for a long moment as horror filled his gaze before tipping his head back and howling at the ceiling. The sound was full of rage and bloodlust, a thirst for vengeance that needed to be sated.

"My whole pack have abandoned me because of those fleas and that fucking *girl*! We can't let this stand. I'll make her challenge me tonight!"

Seth turned and started charging for the door but I stepped into his way, grabbing his arm to halt him.

He looked up at me with a frown and a dark smile pulled at my lips.

"No," I agreed. "We can't let this stand. But we can do so much better than last time."

"What are you suggesting?" Max asked, drawing closer to me as he fed on the dark thread of my emotions.

"I think we let the Vegas try and get through The Reckoning. If they don't, problem solved, they're gone anyway. But if they *do*, we make sure they wish they never had."

Seth's eyes glimmered with darkness as he took that in and he stopped straining against my hold on him.

"We'll take them down?" he breathed, his ache for vengeance dancing on the air between us.

"Oh we'll do more than that," I assured him. "The Vegas won't know what hit them."

"I'm dying for a *little* revenge at least." Max cracked his neck. "We're owed some pay-back."

"Hell Week," Caleb spoke for the first time in a while, his eyes a cold abyss. "We can terrorise them under the guise of Hell Week for now. Then if they make it through The Reckoning, we'll go after them for real."

A dark smile pulled at my lips as I looked around at my brothers. We'd let the Vegas think they had one up on us for now, because by the time we came for them again, they wouldn't even know what hit them.

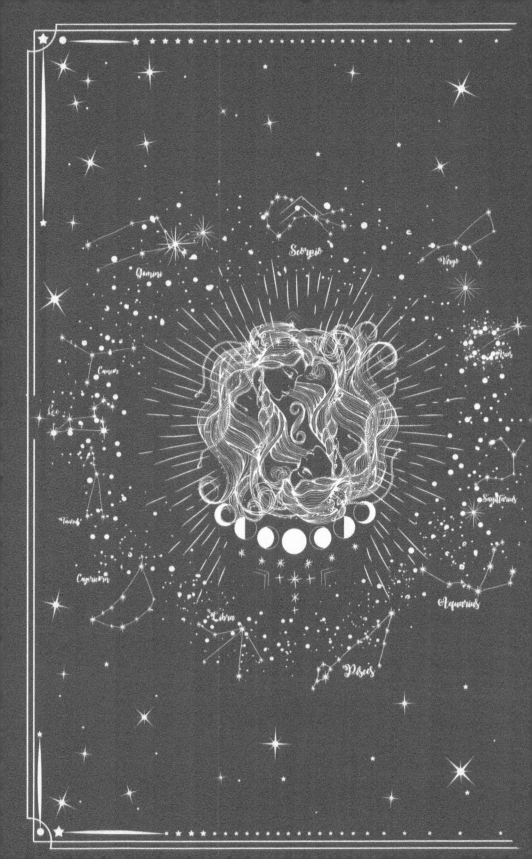

DARCY

CHAPTER TWENTY FIVE

Tory had come to my room just after five am, murmuring sleepily about how Darius had seemed pissy at Caleb and she didn't want to go back to Ignis House before curling up in my bed and falling asleep.

Although I was concerned about how much time she was spending with one of the Heirs, I hadn't voiced it. I simply double checked the door was locked and slid in beside her without comment. Tory could run circles around that douche and I knew he'd never get into her heart enough to hurt her. She was used to keeping her emotions separate from sex. Unlike me, who apparently slept with a guy one time and let him claim a piece of my heart already.

Since sharing a sofa bed in Chicago, sleeping next to my sister had become something of a comfort to me. And I had the feeling she felt the same way. Maybe that was why we ended up in each other's rooms so regularly. When we were together, we were safe. Tory had been my only constant in life and no matter where we were or whatever happened to us, I knew I always had her.

I remembered dressing up as warrior princesses as kids, building a fort out of blankets and pillows then using sticks as swords to fight off our imagined enemies. Nowadays that game was a little too real. We were Solarian princesses with actual enemies who possessed sharp claws and teeth. But they were worse than just beasts, their tongues spun words that were either as sharp as knives or as sweet as honey.

I'd come to feel sorry for Seth in the past few days and Tory was drawn to Caleb whether she liked to admit it or not. Maybe Darius too. And as much as I wanted to despise them to my core, the Heirs weren't just black and white. But I couldn't imagine a time when we could ever make amends. They'd wronged us too deeply, left wounds which we were still struggling to heal. But every day felt like I was rising from that pain, growing beyond it into something powerful, something strong enough to face them.

I shifted closer to my sister as warmth built around us in our cocoon of safety. After she'd told me about the shadows which had tried to claim her, I couldn't stop thinking about it. I wanted to confront Orion about dark magic, to demand he tell me more just so I could try and understand why he wielded it. But the reaction he'd had after we caught them in the cave made me think he wasn't going to open up about it anytime soon. Not that that was going to stop me from trying.

I willed myself to drift off, wanting to get a decent rest before my Fire Trial later today but my mind wasn't cooperating.

I swear the temperature is dropping. It's freaking freezing in here.

I started shivering, drawing the cover tighter around us as the chill inched in.

BOOM. Thunder cracked so loudly I was certain it came from inside my actual room. Lightning flashed and I screamed as a single dark cloud illuminated on my ceiling before rain poured from it in torrents.

"Shit!" I sprang out of bed, immediately stubbing my toe on my nightstand and pain made more curses pour from my lips.

"Ohmagod." Tory leapt out of bed as I held my foot, hissing between my teeth. "What's happening?"

"Hell Week," I groaned. "I'd bet my life on it."

Screams sounded through the tower and I hopped toward the door, unlocking it and wrenching it open. Freshmen were stumbling into the hallway, soaking wet and furious.

Tory and I hurried out to join them in our pyjamas and the pain finally eased from my toe.

Two dark figures appeared at the end of the corridor, cast in shadow in the dimly lit hall and wearing the black cloaks of Hell Week but no masks.

"You have two minutes to get to the stairway," Max's booming voice filled the air. "If you don't bring shoes, you'll regret it. The rainstorms won't stop until you're all out so if anyone's hiding, I suggest they get the fuck out now."

Diego crept out of his room in a raincoat done up to his chin. Tory nudged me and I found she'd grabbed shoes and coats for us and we quickly put them on.

"Everyone out!" Seth barked. "Move move move!"

I shared a *do we really have to do this?* look with Tory before heading after the rest of the freshmen, a yawn pulling at my mouth. Diego moved to my side, swearing loudly in Spanish as we headed toward Seth and Max.

As we passed between them, they moved in close, trapping Tory and I as Diego slipped away ahead of us.

Max's hand curled around my wrist and squeezed so tight I winced.

"Hey!" I gasped, trying to tug free of him. "Be afraid, little Vegas," he purred. "Be very afraid."

"Run," Seth hissed and the two of them released us.

We darted away and they chased after us, corralling us to the top of the staircase. My brows lifted as I found the stairs entirely encased in ice, shimmering like glass as it created a perfectly smooth slide down the huge spiralling steps.

All of the air freshmen were gathered at the top, looking around nervously and Seth didn't give them a second's warning as he blasted air at their backs. Ten fell down at once, screaming as they skidded over the ice at a furious pace. Then another ten, then another.

I spotted Kylie in the next line up, looking to Seth pleadingly before he threw out a palm and mercilessly sent her tumbling down the slide with another group.

When only eight freshmen remained as well as us, Seth pushed Diego over the edge followed by the other seven. He caught my arm, tugging me into his chest while Max took hold of Tory. I opened my mouth to speak, but Seth darted forward, dragging me back against his body and launching himself down the slide.

A scream tore from my throat as we skated down it at high speed, round and round all the way to the bottom. Seth clutched me tighter as we reached the end and I yelled in alarm as we were plunged into a huge pool of ice-cold water which filled the atrium.

My heart nearly stopped as I sank into the freezing depths, kicking hard to escape Seth's iron hold. We breached the surface where freshmen were coughing and spluttering as they tread water. I turned to look for Tory just as Seth cast air at the door, sending it flying open so we spilled out of the tower onto the grass beyond. He never let go of me as we skidded across the ground, then hauled me to my feet. His eyes locked with mine and my heart thudded harder at the sight of his impenetrable expression.

"Where are you t-taking us?" I asked through chattering teeth.

His lips were tight and I hoped this was part of the Hell Week act as he prodded me in the ribs to get me to start walking.

"That way," he murmured in my ear but I turned, searching for Tory, relieved when I saw her darting away from Max to join Diego.

I ducked away from Seth to meet them, shivering as the cold air beat around us.

Seth and Max stayed at the back of the group, herding us across the plains of Air Territory like cattle. I noticed Seth casting air around him and Max to dry out their clothes and frowned as I tried to ignite enough heat in my body to do the same, but the air that twisted between my fingers was cold and useless.

My teeth chattered louder as we reached The Wailing Wood and I tried to draw fire into my blood as Tory had taught me. I managed to chase off the deepest bite of the cold, but it wasn't nearly enough.

As we headed under the orange glow of the lamps, a large group became visible up ahead. The freshmen were gathered on the path, all of them from fire, earth and water, their clothes as soaked as ours.

"That's the last of them!" Seth called out and Caleb appeared, shoving freshmen aside as he walked toward us. I instinctively searched for the final Heir but he was nowhere to be seen.

"Keep walking!" Caleb hollered, moving toward us as the rest of the freshmen hurried on.

We stepped forward to follow but Caleb barred our way, his jaw locked tight and his black cloak fluttering around him in the breeze.

"I'm not sure I'm into the Count Dracula look," Tory joked and I raised a brow hopefully, waiting to see if Caleb's furious mask might crack. But it seemed they were all playing up to the Hell Week bullshit tonight.

"Move," Caleb growled, jerking his head toward the rest of the freshmen.

Tory rolled her eyes, stepping past him and I glanced over my shoulder as Seth and Max moved up behind us. Caleb waited then fell into step with them like three horsemen of the apocalypse – *but where's the fourth?!*

Seth started howling and the noise sent a shiver racing up my spine. We quickened our pace to join the end of the queue of freshmen and I hunted for our friends amongst the masses.

We soon arrived in The Howling Meadow, moving into the long grass and huddling close for warmth.

"This is bullshit," I whispered, shifting even closer to Tory to share body heat.

Seth, Caleb and Max remained on the verge of the trees and everyone turned to them expectantly, the sound of my chattering teeth drilling into my skull.

"Welcome to the nine circles of hell," Max announced, raising his hands into the air. Lights swirled into existence in huge rings, spreading away from him, floating out across campus and expanding into enormous circles of colour. The smallest ring encased our group in a glimmering green and the next one ringed the edge of the meadow in blue, then more and more colours reached out into the darkness.

"If you're going to survive the next hour, you need to make it beyond the ninth circle," Caleb said with a glimmer in his gaze. "You are all soaking wet, but the pools you were dunked in wasn't water. It was Faesine."

A collective gasp of horror sounded around us and Tory and I looked to each other in confusion.

Seth smiled darkly as he gazed between the two of us, picking up from Caleb. "For those of you who don't know, Faesine is a highly flammable substance. It's entirely odourless except to one creature who can smell it a mile away."

The three Heirs parted and a deep growl sounded from the trees which sounded like it belonged to a damn dinosaur. Two reptilian eyes appeared between the boughs then Darius's enormous golden form stepped form the darkness, towering over the Heirs. He raised his huge head of shining scales, roaring to the sky and fear drove a blade into my heart.

"This is a joke right?" Diego called, his tone panicked.

"The only joke here is pathetic Orderless *un*Fae like you. You're an insult to our school." Max spat on the floor, but his eyes were on us like those words hadn't been for Diego at all.

I reached for Tory's hand without hesitation and our magic rushed to meet each other's. I relaxed a little as the flow of our power expanded between us. *This is just a Hell Week stunt. Just a game.*

"In case you don't believe us about the Faesine…" Seth took his shirt off, tossing it to the ground and stepping back. Darius release a spurt of fire at it and a huge hole exploded into the ground as the substance reacted, causing a green blaze to burn where it had been.

Seth unbuckled his pants. "You *will* run. We'll ensure that you do." The second he finished stripping, he leapt forward, bursting into his enormous wolf form and baring his teeth at us. The crowd flinched back as he snapped his powerful jaws and Darius stepped out of the trees.

Seth moved toward Max, dropping down to let him climb onto his back and the Water Heir held on with one hand while raising the other. Air danced around him and leaves spun in the breeze as the vortex grew, warning us that this game was about to begin.

Caleb set his feet like he was preparing to run at us, his fangs snapping out and a low snarl emanating from him.

"Holy shit," Tory breathed and I clutched her hand tighter.

"There's no rules about not fighting back," I whispered and Caleb's eyes flipped to me, a warning blazing in them. *Oh crap.*

"Three!" Max cried. "Two!"

Darius lunged forward, taking off into the sky with several powerful wingbeats. His huge form shadowed the moon as he soared high above us, turning sharply and releasing an explosion of fire from his mouth.

"One!" Max roared and we ran like hell.

Every freshman in the meadow split apart, pouring into the trees through the coloured rings of light, racing for the opposite side of the field, casting domes of air and water around themselves for protection.

Tory and I darted for the nearest trees, a blaze of fire tearing overhead as Darius unleashed his power. The earth was torn up behind us as Dragon Fire split it apart and the heat washed over my back, spreading adrenaline into my limbs.

We'd passed through the first two rings already and I could see the next one way off through the trees, the purple light calling us on as we ran as hard as we possibly could.

A baying howl rang out behind us and heavy paws crashed through the undergrowth following the path we'd just trodden.

Water magic crashed to the ground in front of us, freezing instantly into a sheet of ice. We were running too fast to stop and we both threw out our free hands to cast fire.

"Wait – no fire!" I screamed at the last second, remembering the Faesine. My feet hit the slippery surface and I skidded into Tory, taking her to the ground. I groaned as we untangled ourselves as quickly as we could, trying to ignore the bruising in my limbs. Tory turned to melt the ice with water and I threw out my hands, casting a wall of earth as Seth leapt into the air, his teeth bared and Max yelling a battle cry from his back.

A crash and a yelp sounded as they collided with it and a laugh bubbled from my throat as Tory caught my hand, yanking me upright. We sprinted on, the sound of screaming freshmen carrying all across the woodland. The darkness was thick, but if we kept our eye on the purple ring, we wouldn't lose our way.

We finally darted through it and I panted as we increased our pace, racing through the trees and tearing toward the yellow ring further off at the edge of the forest.

Two freshmen screamed close to our right, then another to our left, the sound of falling bodies making fear slice into my flesh. A huge shadow sailed overhead but I refused to look up, keeping my gaze firmly on that ring.

Three down, six to go.

A rush of air warned us a second before Caleb appeared, shooting vines from his hands and tangling us up in them. We crashed to the ground and he leered over us with a satisfied smirk, raising his hands and making the vines tighten and tighten.

I cried out in pain as thorns grew along the edges and drew blood.

"What the hell, Caleb?" Tory spat then yelped as more thorns dug in to her.

"Just a little prank. Can't you handle the heat, sweetheart?"

The roar of a Dragon echoed in the distance and panic crawled under my flesh. Caleb looked up, his eyes horribly dark as he seemed to be waiting for something. Then he sprang over us and darted off into the trees.

I hunted for Tory's hand, clawing through the mud as I fought against the vines and she did the same. Our fingers met and earth magic burst from our bodies at the same moment, withering the vines so they became brittle and we hurriedly broke free of them, rising to our feet.

"Why'd he run off?" I asked, wiping my muddy hands off on my thighs. Despite the cold, I was so full of adrenaline I could hardly feel it now. But that might have been because I was frozen into numbness.

"No idea," she said and her breath fogged before her. "Let's move. Get this bullshit over with before he decides to come back."

Screams rang out up ahead and we darted away from them, speeding on toward the edge of the wood. We broke free of the trees the same moment we passed through the yellow ring and found ourselves in Earth Territory. Hills spread out ahead of us and the next ring was half way across the exposed plain of land.

A rush of paws sounded behind us and a flash of white fur made my pulse elevate. Seth tore away from us and screams called out in the direction he took.

"Let's run for it," I breathed and Tory nodded, wordlessly casting a shield of air around as we sprinted out across the grass.

Other freshmen burst from the trees, evidently having been waiting for someone to break away first. Nearly thirty others sprinted across the grass and terror shredded my heart as Darius soared overhead. He swooped low, releasing hellfire down on the freshmen. I blinked against the burning light, tossing a desperate glance over my shoulder in fear of him actually setting someone ablaze. He circled a group of five, setting the grass alight around them so they were penned in within it. He turned, banking hard and capturing another group within a fiery circle.

It's just a game. Nothing to worry about. And I sure as hell want to win it!

Tory's hand slipped from mine as we ran so fast it became impossible to hold on to each other. We practically dove through the next ring, setting our eye on the second to last one in the distance. We were tearing toward the Pitball Stadium now and the orange ring blazed before it, encouraging us onward. Darius's roars fell away behind us and I gasped for breath, slowing just a little because of the searing stitch in my side.

Tory pulled me along, more used to running than I was and I made a mental promise to myself that I'd start joining her on those daily runs.

We charged through the orange ring and spotted the final one just beyond the stadium, the shimmering silver colour calling us on. No other students were behind us and the world seemed to fall eerily quiet as we raced past the stadium to where a thick cluster of trees grouped around the back of it.

We were so close, just a hundred feet. A laugh escaped my throat as we charged through it, running into a circular clearing at the heart of the trees and resting our hands on our knees as we dragged in air.

"Holy…hell," I panted, my lungs burning and my muscles aching.

"We won," Tory said breathlessly, laughing and standing up straight.

I sighed happily as I looked around at the copse we'd run into, lunging forward to hug her with an excited squeal.

"Winner winner chicken dinner," Caleb's voice made me freeze as he appeared out of the trees to our right and I released Tory with a lump in my throat. Seth appeared in sweatpants on the opposite side of the clearing and Max moved out of the trees across from him. The cracking of a twig made me lurch around and Darius appeared in sweatpants, his expression darker than I'd ever seen it. We were penned in and I had the awful feeling it was intentional.

"No one else made it to the final ring," Darius announced to the others. "Anyone who made it beyond the trees got cordoned in by my fire."

"Not many got out of the wood," Caleb said with a dark smile.

"Well we won your game," I tried with a shrug. "Guess we'll be going..."

Tory shifted closer and we turned to face Caleb – the safest bet – walking in his direction.

He cocked his head as we approached and fire blazed to life in his hands. "Careful, Vegas. You wouldn't want to go up in flames."

"Yeah, I'm sure the press would love to hear about how the four of you barbecued us in the woods." Tory rolled her eyes. "Fun's over, Caleb. I'm dog tired and I wanna go back to bed."

Caleb didn't smile, his eyes sliding over my sister in a way that unsettled me. He extinguished the fire in his palms, flicking his hand and the earth trembled beneath our feet. Slabs of dirt shot up underneath us, making us stumble back to the centre of the circle. The four heirs closed in as one and real fear inched into my gut.

Seth raised a hand, knocking Tory and I into Darius with a gust of air.

Darius wrapped his arms around us, igniting flames in his palms so we had to shrink back into his body to keep away from them. "Accidents happen at Zodiac all the time..."

"Come on man, they know we didn't actually coat them in Faesine. I only put it on my shirt to freak them out," Seth said, his eyes locked on me.

"Seth!" Max threw a punch into his arm and he lurched away with a whine.

Relief filled me over the Faesine but it was short-lived as Darius shoved us at Max with a blast of water and I spluttered, clutching onto Max's arm and preparing to fight back. Max snared us in shackles of ice which encased our whole hands. Panic seized me as I tried to burn my way through them but Max's power was fierce, halting my magic where it pressed against my palms.

I waited for his Siren gifts to push into us too with dread writhing in my gut, but it never came. Tory locked eyes with him, a threat in her gaze. She'd reveal his darkest secret if he broke his side of the bargain and used his Siren powers against us, and it looked like he wasn't going to risk it.

"You can go back to bed, little Vegas. You just have to beg," Max said with a sneer. "I want you on your knees telling us how we're all your kings and how you're so sorry for ever showing your faces in Solaria. And once we're satisfied, you can go."

"We'll never beg you," Tory spat.

My heart lurched as Max shoved us forward with a gust of air, forcing us down to our knees in the mud. Darius took out his Atlas, aiming it at us with a wicked cruelty in his eyes. "Give us a good show for FaeBook. Let's remind the school who you are; a couple of rats who crawled out of the cesspit of the mortal world and tried to rise above their station."

A deep determination filled me and I clenched my jaw, silently vowing that those words would *not* pass my lips. I glanced at Tory, finding the same resolve in her eyes and she lifted her chin in defiance.

"*Beg*," Max growled, his voice thick with Coercion which rammed against my mental shield. I flinched under the force of it, refusing to let it in.

Seth growled, pacing back and forth on the verge of the circle.

"She's not hurt," Max spat at him and Seth nodded, but his expression remained taut.

Caleb stepped forward, tilting Tory's chin up to face the camera. "*Say it, sweetheart*," he tried to Coerce her and she blinked hard, pressing her lips together as she fought against his power.

Max gripped my hair, tugging to make me to look up at him and I battled a wince as pain flared through my scalp. "*Beg me.*"

His magic pushed at my will, making the words rise to my lips. A weight of pressure mounted against my mind and drove needles into my skull. Part of me wanted to beg and beg until he ended this suffering but I managed to hold out through sheer willpower.

Darius stepped closer, angling the camera down at us, a furious snarl leaving his lips. "What the fuck?" he snapped at Caleb and Max.

Max huffed, leaning down so he was right in our faces. "*BEG US!*" he commanded, the fullness of his power nearly forcing me down the easier road. Seth barked, stepping toward me and Caleb shoved him back, wrapping his arms around him.

I just have to say the words and this pain will stop.

But if I do, I'll never forgive myself.

My skin tingled from the glassy ice encasing my hands and I drew heat to my palms once more, willing it to burn away Max's magic with all my heart. Relief filled me as it turned to water and Tory's fingers snared mine as she managed it too. I immediately interlocked them, a fiery blaze seeming to pass under our skin. It rushed through me, coating my veins like a barrier and I gasped as the pressure of Max's Coercion started to fade.

"You can't stand there, you're in the shot." Darius kicked mud at Max and he backed up with a huff. The wall of fire passing between Tory and I grew hotter, forcing his will from our bodies entirely.

"Earth," Tory whispered and I nodded to her, understanding that the word was for me.

"What?" Darius snarled, his eyes suddenly dropping to our hands as he realised we were free.

Anticipation clutched my heart as I slammed my free hand to the mud at the same time as Tory, throwing my power into the soil and asking it to do what I bid.

A powerful tremor gripped the ground and the Heirs stumbled backwards in surprise. With our combined magic wielding the earth beneath us, it was easier than ever before. A surge of tremendous power sped from our skin and a shockwave exploded out from us, knocking the four of them from their feet.

We were up in a heartbeat, leaping over Max and sprinting out of the copse. Adrenaline coursed through my blood and made my pulse rocket. Shouts of pure rage sounded behind us and we cast a fierce air shield just as vines swung at us from above, wielded by someone's earth magic.

They crashed against our shield and I ducked instinctively, but they didn't make it through. We pressed our advantage, speeding across Earth Territory as fast as we could. The freshmen had escaped from the rings of fire Darius had cast, the grass smoldering and charred where they'd been.

We raced to The Orb, blood pounding in my ears and making me lightheaded as we finally stumbled inside, muddy and exhausted. The rest of the freshmen were gathered there as well as most of the A.S.S.

"There they are!" cried a freshman girl with pigtails. "I saw them get through the final ring – they did it!"

The Heirs burst through the doors behind us with furious expressions, halting as the entire A.S.S stood up, their hands raised as they started clapping.

"To the only freshmen to make it through the ninth ring of hell!" Geraldine cried and a grin spread across my face as I looked to the Heirs, daring them to deny it.

Their eyes burned into our backs as we walked over to join our friends, showered in compliments as we went. Rage burned so hot from Darius, I felt the heat of it rolling up my spine. But I didn't care how angry they were that they'd failed their sad plans of soiling what little reputation we had. We'd fought the Heirs and won. And that felt incredible.

A yawn tore its way out of my throat as I arrived in Fire Territory for our trial, exhausted after the morning we'd had. I'd studied hard last night, practising all the fire magic I knew and refusing to let any other distractions in, but my mind was currently full of the Hell Week prank we'd endured. But that was the idea. To make the trials even harder to complete. The only thing that mattered was getting through my exam, so I had to focus.

I'd managed to avoid Orion since our argument and was on a solid streak which I didn't plan on breaking until after we'd passed The Reckoning. The problem was, the time apart from Orion was telling me something that scared me; I cared for him. A lot. And knowing things between us were in stormy, shark-infested water, was akin to slowly pushing a blunt object into my heart.

I'd tried and failed to talk to Diego about his uncle a bunch of times since Orion had asked, but I had a plan. On Sunday, everyone would be heading to the Fairy Fair in Tucana and I was going to ask Diego to go with me. He couldn't avoid me if we spent the whole evening together alone.

"Hey," I said, smiling as I met Tory and Sofia outside their House, their clothes changed from the muddy, wet attire we'd been left in earlier this morning. Other freshmen were peeling away from the door, heading in the direction of the Fire Arena. "You guys ready?"

Sofia nodded a little nervously but Tory smiled.

"Yep. Let's do this." My sister had a spark in her eyes that ignited a fire in my chest. After fighting off the Heirs, I was on a high which I hoped would carry me through the day and it looked like Tory was still riding it too. We were half way through the trials already and I was ready to cross another one off the list.

We soon arrived at the towering Arena, joining the line of fire freshmen who were on their way in. A strange noise reached my ears, playing on repeat up ahead. A girlish giggle then a splash. Giggle, splash, giggle, splash. What the hell?

Some of the freshmen started laughing as they emerged in the Arena and Tory and I pushed forward to see what the source of the noise was.

On the far side of the Arena, filling the crescent stone seats that rose up to the roof were the Heirs and their fan club. Geraldine and the A.S.S had the remaining seats, seeming oddly quiet as we arrived. Their eyes were all on something above our heads and I turned to look back at the wall which towered above the archway we'd arrived through.

Projected there was a two second clip which alternated between the moment Tory dove into that swimming pool and Seth cut off my hair. The giggle evidently belonged to Kylie who'd been filming me from the bushes. Shock gripped my heart as the two most painful moments we'd experienced in this place bounced back and forth like some sick action replay.

I was hot all over as I turned away from it, moving closer to Tory as we marched on through the sand.

"I wanna destroy them," Tory said under her breath and I nodded.

"This is because we beat them this morning," I breathed, trying not to let them see me shaken as jeers called out from the Heirs' nasty friendship group of mindless sheep.

Professor Pyro ushered us toward the changing rooms to follow the other freshmen, but we stood firm. We'd made a decision last night and we weren't going to back out on it. Sofia cast a worried glance back at us, but I gave her a comforting smile and she headed away.

"We're not going to wear the protective suits, Professor," Tory said, giving her a stare that dared her to try and force us.

She looked between us in surprise. "Well I suppose that's up to you, but the school won't be liable if you burn yourselves."

"We won't," we said in unison then shared a grin over our twin moment.

"Off you go then, line up over there." She pointed to a shimmering golden line of magic that extended right through the centre of the Arena.

We headed that way, standing side by side and facing the opposite wall. Nova was sitting at a table with a female professor with silver hair, the chair beside her empty and waiting for Pyro.

The stands were buzzing with noise, drawing my attention to the Heirs once more. Seth was giving me a glare that spoke of absolute rage and I frowned at him, confused by the sheer hatred I saw pulsing in his gaze. I mean, sure he disliked me. But he hadn't exactly been acting his usual callous self lately. Not since he'd made me his Omega.

I turned to Tory as more freshmen appeared, lining up beside us in their skin-tight silver suits. "Do you get the feeling Seth is extra pissy today?"

She glanced over her shoulder, giving him a sweeping look then turning back to me. "He looks like someone took a shit on his grandma."

"Like *we* did you mean," I muttered and she shrugged.

"Maybe he's just playing up to his pathetic friends."

"True," I said, but I still had a niggling feeling that that wasn't quite it.

Pyro moved to stand in front of us, giving us a tense look as she waved a hand to draw silence from the crowd. All that remained in the quiet was the giggle, splash, giggle, splash of that godforsaken video. *FML. Are the teachers really going to leave that playing?*

Pyro didn't seem to notice it, smiling at us all. "Your Fire Trial will shortly begin. You will be required to walk across a narrow bridge from one side of the arena to the other while casting a shape out of fire approximately ten inches in diameter."

"You can just cast my dick then, Tory!" Caleb cried out and she scowled at him.

Darius shot him a glare that could have murdered a small village and all of their farm animals.

"Yes well, I'd prefer if the object were more sanitary, but you may cast whatever you please," Pyro said, looking a little flustered. She ran a hand over her hair then smiled again. "You will be graded on the complexity, clarity and the length of time you keep the magic in form. If you lose focus, simply recast the object and continue. You will have just twenty minutes for this trial. Good luck." She raised a hand and a timer appeared above us made of fire then she turned and headed off to take her seat at the table.

"Where's the bridge?" Tory murmured and the second she said it, the ground parted right down the golden line, splitting into two crescents and drawing us backwards. Below it was a fiery pit of hell that made me want to hurl. Lava spewed up ten feet below us and twenty narrow metal bridges stretched between the continually extending gap.

"Oh my god," I breathed as the ground slid to a halt and we were left on one side of the blazing inferno. It was fifty feet across, the heat of the lava already raising the temperature in my blood and sparking a flare of power under my skin.

"Begin!" Pyro cried and the clock started counting down.

Tory and I moved to the nearest bridge and I tried to avoid looking at the terrifying sight below as I decided what to cast. I spotted Sofia moving to a bridge a few over from ours, her face fixed in concentration as she cast a diamond above her hand. Tory flexed her fingers and a fireball burst to life in her palm, shifting and moulding until a small motorbike hovered above it. She grew it to the required size, her brows pinching together.

"Be careful," I said, my heart stammering as she stepped onto the bridge. It was barely wider than her shoe.

I swallowed hard, moving forward and raising my hand. I cast an intricate flower above my palm, painting on as many details as I could as I focused. Without the protective suit, the fire seemed to move to my will so much easier, like it was an extension of my flesh.

I steeled myself as I stepped out onto the bridge, carefully placing one foot in front of the other. The blazing heat around me did nothing but fill me with energy and a tingling sensation in my shoulder blades made me wonder if my Order form was simmering under my skin, drawn to the inferno. *Maybe I really am a Dragon.*

Tory was just a foot ahead of me and students moved in my periphery. I caught sight of Sofia's magic flittering away in her hand before she quickly recast it and my heart panged for her. I drew more energy to the flower hovering above my palm, making the petals fall away like embers and Geraldine cheered.

A smile pulled at my lips, but it was short lived as a huge spray of fire exploded up from the lava to my right. Then on my left too. Pockets of pure magma burst into the air and flames roared so keenly they nearly licked my skin.

A scream caught my ear, but I couldn't look to see what had happened as a collective gasp sounded from the audience.

I set my eye on Tory's back and didn't stop moving.

The Heirs were suspiciously quiet but Marguerite led a cheer, seeming to grow more and more agitated every time she belted it out, like us not being burned alive at that current moment was irritating her. "Let the Vegas burn! Let the Vegas burn! Let the Vegas burn!"

The bridge beneath me trembled violently and I released a gasp at the same time Tory did. Either side of me, the other platforms were beginning to shake too. With every passing second, the tremors grew stronger and fear took root in my chest.

"Look forward!" Tory called to me anxiously. I was unsure on my feet at the best of times, let alone on a tiny bridge above a pit of goddamn lava.

Heat seared my eyes as I clenched my teeth, trying to keep my balance, but as I took another step I lost it. A swooping sensation accompanied my scream. My flower fizzled away to nothing as I fell, reaching out desperately to catch myself.

I caught the bridge at the last second, dangling off it, fire spewing below me and flaring against the soles of my shoes.

Panic dug into me. If I used any magic other than fire to get up, I'd fail this exam. But if I didn't, I might fall. The violent tremor finally stopped and I released a slow breath as I tried to haul myself up.

Tory dropped down to help me, her motorbike evaporating. My heart jolted as she caught my hand and pulled me to my feet. We steadied ourselves by resting our hands on each other's shoulders and her gaze burrowed into mine as she checked I was okay. Marguerite's chant had died away and one glance that way showed me the Heirs were on their feet. Darius's hands were raised, but he dropped them the second I met his eyes.

"I'm sorry," I said to my sister, furious with myself.

"Don't be. I'd never leave you."

"I wouldn't leave you either." I squeezed her arm then braced her as she turned around. We recast our fire shapes and continued on. We'd fallen behind a lot of the students, but a quick look told me plenty were going even slower than us, their magic stuttering out over and over again. One girl had resorted to shimmying along on her butt, not even casting magic as she focused on just getting the hell across.

Pitchy screams made my heart lurch and I glanced to my right as a fierce blue light bloomed in my periphery. A raging hot fireball hurtled through the air on a magical rope like a wrecking ball, swinging across the centre of the Arena. I caught hold of Tory's shirt in a moment of sheer panic, tugging her back a step as the blazing ball swept past us. The second it hit its highest point it started rushing back again.

"Go go go," I urged and we ran forward as fast as we could.

Heat scorched the back of my neck as it swung by once more and I took a breath to try and steady my heart. Miraculously, we'd both managed to keep our fire casts in place, but nearly half the other students had lost focus and dropped theirs. I caught sight of Sofia recasting hers and a couple in the audience who must have been her parents cried out in encouragement.

We were over half way and one look at the timer told me we were still making good time. Pockets of fire lit up ahead on the bridge itself and yelps sounded around us as people were burned by the flash fires. They sizzled out as quickly as they came, reigniting in completely random spots so we had no chance of predicting them.

Students were slowing to a halt as they tried to figure out how to cross this next obstacle. Those who'd gotten halfway even had to retreat as they were burned.

"Shit," Tory cursed. "Let's just go for it."

"Do it," I agreed, my heart jack-hammering in my chest.

She started moving forward as fast as was sensible and I hurried to follow.

Fire flashed between us and I waited for it to vanish before darting past the blackened spot. We managed to avoid the fires by luck alone for several seconds, but our luck ran out.

At the same moment, fire blazed beneath our feet. I flinched but no pain came; the flames singed the bottoms of my leggings but I was somehow completely fine. I looked up in confusion, finding Tory glancing back at me with the exact same expression on her face.

Muttering broke out amongst the crowd and I felt the judges eyes on us like a row of hawks.

"Keep going," I said, flustered and confused as we moved on.

When fire flared at my feet again and the same thing happened, we both quickened our pace, throwing caution to the wind. I didn't know what it meant, but I sure as hell was gonna take advantage of it.

We soon took the lead, hurrying toward the end of the bridge and I couldn't believe we'd almost made it through the trial.

A huge door made entirely of fire bloomed at the very end of the bridge. Our final challenge. One other student reached the end a few platforms across. She reached out to touch the door, then yanked her hand back as it burned her.

"Can we get rid of it?" I suggested to Tory.

"Maybe, but..." She reached out and I felt everyone in the Arena staring as she pushed her fingers into the fire. She turned her hand side to side and my lips parted.

"Leap of faith?" she asked.

"Okay but be safe." I bit into my lower lip.

Tory raised her hand as the motorbike remained firmly above it then leapt forward, landing on the other side of the door. I didn't wait for my rational side to kick in, I darted forward and jumped after her.

Heat washed over me. My clothes singed, but nothing else. I landed beside Tory and we dropped the fire casts in our hands, falling into each other's arms as we cheered.

Geraldine's side of the crowd went crazy, but as I looked to the Heirs, I saw something in their eyes I never thought I'd seen in them before. Fear. Darius's gaze shifted between us and laughter built in my throat. If we really were impervious to fire, he couldn't use it against us. And as a Dragon Shifter, that had to suck.

I started laughing and Tory joined me as she flipped them the finger.

The four of them stood, marching out of the crowd and leaving the Arena so fast, I was certain they were going to discuss this turn of events. But I didn't care. We'd completed our third trial and discovered how strong we really were in the process.

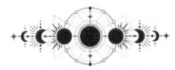

We headed to The Orb for an evening of celebrating with the A.S.S and to top off one of the best days ever, Geraldine taught us a spell to boobytrap a huge tower of cupcakes on our table. When Max predictably came over to steal one, the entire pile exploded in his face, coating him head to toe in frosting. By the time I headed back to Aer Tower with Diego at my side, a permanent smile was etched onto my face.

Principal Nova had sent Tory and I an email stating that she expected us to emerge as a rare kind of Dragon any day now. Though she'd not heard of any kind that were impervious to fire so she was hopeful that we would be a very rare breed.

I wasn't sure I was ready to shift into a creature that size, but I imagined it was something I'd get used to in time. Especially if it meant the Heirs no longer screwed with us.

As I rounded into eleventh floor with Diego, I caught his arm before he headed to his room. "Diego, the Fairy Fair is on Sunday."

"I know," he said sullenly. "Sofia is going…"

"Yeah." I frowned. "So I thought maybe you might wanna go with me? Could be fun?"

His eyes brightened. "Oh, yeah. That sounds great, chica."

"Good." I grinned and he pulled me into a hug where we clashed heads and I awkwardly patted his back then stepped away. "Night then." I slipped away to my room and pushed the key into the lock. Except it was already unlocked.

My heart stammered as I pushed the door open, finding Seth Capella lying on my bed.

"What the hell?" I demanded, stepping into the room. "Get out."

He sat up, his eyes frighteningly dark as he rose to his feet. What was with him today?

My blood chilled as he stalked toward me and I almost backed up into the corridor to escape. But this was *my* room and he was the one trespassing.

"Fire doesn't burn you," he stated, cocking his head with a wolfish look that said he was on the hunt for his next kill. "But I bet vines can choke you. And air can suffocate you." He toyed with both Elements, one in each hand.

"What's up with you?" I breathed, conjuring an air shield to protect myself.

He licked his lips, stepping closer then suddenly slapped on a smile which was somehow more terrifying. "Nothing little Omega. Are you going to challenge me soon?"

"Challenge you?"

"Yeah that's the only way you can get out of my pack. So challenge me, babe. I'm hungry for the fight. Don't keep me waiting too long." He walked out of the door and I leaned back against the wall, waiting for my heart to settle before quickly shutting and locking it.

Why is he so damn angry?

A thought entered my mind which held me hostage with terror for one long moment.

My eyes whipped to the desk and I hurried forward, pulling the top drawer open with a pang of absolute dread. *He hasn't found it, please tell me he hasn't found it.*

Horror filled me. It was gone.

I almost went into complete panic mode when I spotted it peeking out from behind my desk lamp. My heart lurched as I grabbed it, clenching my fist around it.

I didn't leave it there. Did I?

I tried to recall the last time I'd moved it, but between my Elemental Trials and daily Hell Week pranks, my mind drew a blank. I must have moved it. Seth would have killed me if he'd found it.

I breathed a sigh, stuffing it into my top drawer and letting my worries ebb away. Seth was just being his usual unpredictable self. One minute he was all over me and the next he was trying to destroy my life and make me renounce my claim like a jackass. His moods changed like the wind and hell if I was gonna let him rattle me.

MAX

CHAPTER TWENTY SIX

I strode along the glass tube which created the corridor in Aqua house, glancing above my head as a shoal of glimmering silver fish swam overhead. The sun was setting and the light which made it this deep into the lake was quickly diminishing. Soon it would be too dark to see the view through the glass structure and the calming sight of the creatures beneath the lake would be lost to me.

For a moment I considered shifting into my Order form and heading out for a swim to see if that might relax me. But I shrugged the idea off. What I really needed was an outlet for this anger, not a way to try and calm it.

After watching the damn Vegas ace their Fire Trial, I'd ended up with a face full of fucking frosting courtesy of Geraldine goddamn Grus. But because of the sneaky way she'd gone about setting that trap for me I hadn't even been able to challenge her over it. It would have seemed weak to start throwing about accusations, especially while I was covered in cake.

My Atlas started ringing in my pocket and I hooked it out, raising an eyebrow as my Dad's name appeared on the caller ID.

"Hey, Dad. What's going-"

"I don't have time for pleasantries, Max," Dad said quickly and I didn't miss the excited tone to his voice. "The FIB have just apprehended a Nymph - a *live* Nymph!"

"Shit," I breathed, falling still in the middle of the corridor as I gave him my full attention. I waved a hand quickly, forming a silencing bubble against any nosey fuckers who might be lurking nearby before I went on. "Are they interrogating it?"

"That's why I'm calling you," he said briskly. "They're bringing it to the Court of Solaria now so that we can perform the interrogation ourselves. We've never had an opportunity like this before and the other Councillors agreed that we should handle the situation personally."

"Is it safe?" I asked, unable to halt the creeping fear which slid through me at the idea of my dad getting close to one of those things. There was a good reason why they were never apprehended. A Nymph's rattle could disable even the strongest Fae if they were close enough and one wrong move could lead to them getting their probes straight into your heart. It wasn't worth the risk.

"That's the genius part of it," Dad said, barking a laugh as his excitement bled through the phone. He was just as powerful as me and even the tone of his voice could transfer emotions when he was hyped up. "Agent Sky came up with the idea to cut its fingers off before healing the stumps. No probes! It's completely disarmed and primed for a safe interrogation."

"That's...wow. So you think you'll be able to get some answers out of it then? Locations, numbers, plots?"

"Oh I'm confident of it. They'll be transferring the captive here within the hour. And I convinced the other Councillors that it would be educational for you and the other Heirs to observe the interrogation."

"No shit!" I cried, a grin biting into my cheeks.

"Yes shit," Dad laughed. "So gather the other boys and get here as quick as you can. I take it Darius has stardust to hand?"

"Of course he does," I joked. "When do you ever see a Dragon without a pocket full of it?"

Dad chuckled again. "I imagine Lionel would bathe in the stuff if it wouldn't get lodged in his butt crack, just because he could."

I snorted a laugh too. Dad always liked ribbing on the other Orders, laughing at their shows of power. We both knew that the only real power that counted was ours - if you could make people feel the same way as you then you never lost an argument. Of course, the Councillors and other Heirs were strong enough to combat our power so it didn't make a difference to our relationships with them, but almost everyone else we met fell under our sway easily enough.

"I'll call the guys now," I said. "We'll be there within the hour."

"Good." Dad hung up and I sent a quick message to the other Heirs telling them to get their asses here ASAP.

I dropped the silencing bubble and started jogging as I headed up to my room.

I opened the metal door and stepped into the huge glass dome which was my home here at Zodiac. The lake rose to the centre of the glass bubble, lapping around the middle so that my room was half submerged. I looked up at the darkening sky as the last rays of the sun painted it in streaks of russet. The moon hung low in the sky already, almost full and lighting a hunger in my flesh. The closer we drew to the Lunar Eclipse, the more the moon called to me. I was really looking forward to the party that would take place that night. Inhibitions went to hell during an Eclipse and Fae followed their most primal emotions. It was refreshing for me to see people acting on the emotions I could feel pouring from them rather than just trying to repress them all the time.

I touched my fingers to the glass wall of my room and created a layer of ice to grow over the orb, blocking the view of the lake and the sky to make sure we had privacy.

I stripped out of my clothes and found a grey suit in the back of my closet, changing into it swiftly. If we were seen at the Court of Solaria, no doubt our photographs would be taken to go with a fluff piece about us helping with the war effort in tomorrow's papers. It was important we looked the part if we were spotted.

I moved to the mirror, pushing some product into my mohawk to flatten it a little then strapped on one of the watches from my top drawer, opting for a platinum piece to compliment the suit.

A knock came at the door and I opened it as Darius strolled in wearing a black suit with a grey shirt beneath it. He nodded to me, but his attention was on his Atlas as he listened to someone on the other end of it.

I spotted Caleb striding up the corridor outside and left the door open for him.

"Just trust me, Mother," Darius said firmly. "I have it on good authority. And if I'm wrong and you spend a night in the mortal world for no reason then what difference does it make? It's worth it to make sure Xavier isn't at risk."

I glanced at him, wondering why he might think his brother was in danger, but he'd taken a seat on the couch with his back to me.

I drew closer to him and a wave of concern swept over me followed by relief at whatever his mother was saying in response.

"Thank you," Darius said, his shoulders sagging. "I'll see you next week once it's all over."

He cut the call and I moved to perch on the arm of the couch as Caleb entered. He'd opted for a black suit too but the white shirt he wore with it was full of creases. He seemed distracted and he dropped onto my bed with a sigh; irritation flowed from him muddled with disappointment, frustration, a touch of rage... all in all I'd say that Tory Vega had done a number on him.

"Is everything alright with Xavier?" I asked Darius, opting to avoid the subject of Tory while the two of them were here. That girl was causing cracks in our group and I wasn't sure that they'd heal until we got rid of her and her sister for good.

Darius let out a long breath and for a moment a flicker of fear came from him but he held it in check, clearly not wanting me to read into it.

"He's just going through a few things at the moment. It'll all resolve itself in time," Darius said, obviously not wanting to go in to whatever it was.

I nodded, accepting his decision to keep whatever was bothering him to himself. Sometimes I worried that his secrets would catch up on him one day though. His father had done too good a job of teaching him to bottle things up but sometimes emotions needed an outlet beyond rage.

I shifted my gaze to Caleb and he noticed, leaning back on my pillows with his lips pursed.

"I don't think I can keep seeing Tory," he said darkly, more than a little anger pouring from him.

Darius sat up straighter in his chair, relief and excitement slipping from him. I caught his eye and he shrugged innocently, but not before I felt a touch of his lust too.

Yeah, we need this girl gone before the two of them come to blows over her.

"I thought you were going to keep things the same with her so that she didn't catch on to the fact that we were coming for her?" I asked, though I'd known when Cal said that he'd have trouble doing it. The moment he realised he'd been screwing the girl responsible for making him a laughing stock, his anger had tainted the air all around him so strongly that I could taste it even when he left the room. It was more than that though, he was embarrassed too, knowing she was laughing at him and leading him on. Hell, it pissed me off enough and she hadn't even done it to me.

"I know," he muttered. "I just... I'm not going to be able to keep my temper in check if I'm hunting her. It's hard enough not to be too rough with her when I'm not pissed at her. I don't think I can control myself while I'm this angry and I could end up going too far."

"So rough her up a bit," I said with a shrug. "Maybe she'll like it."

Darius growled at me and I looked around at him in surprise as a wave of anger slammed right into me. Emotions always tasted more potent when they were aimed at me like that and for a second I felt exactly what it was like to have a Dragon point his rage at me.

"What if he ends up killing her?" he snapped like I was an idiot. "The law won't protect him from murdering a royal."

I scoffed and looked back at Caleb but I was surprised to find him nodding.

"I could," he said darkly. "There's a reason why the Vampire Code discourages us from indulging in the hunt. The bloodlust blinds me while I'm hunting and it's...hard to rein it in sometimes."

Darius growled again and I huffed at all the anger in the room.

The door opened and I looked up as Seth came in. He was wearing a black suit too and I groaned irritably.

"Should I get changed?" I asked. "You all look like you're matching on purpose now."

Darius rolled his eyes and shrugged out of his jacket. "Better? Now I look like I didn't even bother dressing properly. The stories will be about that instead of focusing on your inability to match or the possibility that we're conspiring to make you look like the odd one out in a grey suit."

I smirked at him because it *was* better. I hated it when the press made comments about me like that, but Darius just let it all roll off of his back. And with my ability to read his emotions I knew he genuinely didn't care about it, so I didn't even have to feel bad about him taking the fall for me.

Seth moved to take a seat beside Darius, nuzzling into him despite the way Darius shifted back an inch to avoid him. It always amused me to watch Seth pushing his wolfy ways onto Darius and Caleb despite their Orders preferring their space. They tried to accommodate him as much as possible but their natures would always collide to some degree.

"So what were you talking about before I arrived?" Seth asked, his hand moving to Darius's thigh.

I raised an eyebrow at him as I felt a touch of lust coming from him and Seth whimpered guiltily, taking his hand back before Darius could push it off.

"The moon is making me horny as fuck," he complained. "And my pack still won't come anywhere near me. I've got *needs*."

"Tell me about it," Darius complained. "All fucking week it's been getting worse and the Eclipse isn't until Monday."

"Which makes it even harder for me to break things off with Tory," Caleb moaned, falling back onto my pillows dramatically.

"What are you, a teenage girl?" I asked him, taking a pillow from the couch to toss at him. "Just find some other girl to screw."

"It won't be the same," Caleb growled, pulling the pillow over his face. "She's so fucking hot. She keeps surprising me and it makes me so hard I can't-"

"Shut the fuck up about it," Darius snapped, pushing himself out of his seat. "Keep screwing her or don't. I don't wanna fucking listen to any more talk about her or her goddamn sister."

His anger pulsed through the room and I sighed heavily. I was gonna need a rage detox after spending a night in their company. Maybe I could find a Pegasus to screw when we got back from the interrogation; they always had happiness to spare. I wasn't even sure why Caleb hated that rumour so much. Who didn't like screwing a girl who smiled the whole time like you were doing her a favour with every thrust?

Seth got up too and moved closer to Darius with a whimper, reaching out to comfort him. Darius batted him away but Seth persisted, brushing his hands along his arms and whimpering like a kicked puppy every time he was rejected.

I swiped a hand over my eyes.

"Is your guard dog going to keep us waiting much longer?" I demanded, checking my watch.

"You know Lance." Darius shrugged. "He'll be late for his own funeral. But if I show up without him Father will be... disappointed."

I pushed my tongue into my cheek. Yeah, disappointed enough to beat the shit out of his son no doubt. Darius had never told us what Lionel did to him, but we all knew. I'd felt the emotions coming from him after one too many run ins with his father and Cal had overheard Lionel screaming at Darius while kicking him until his ribs broke when we'd been at their house for a barbecue once. He'd tried to intervene but his mom had stopped him. When Darius had returned, he'd been healed like it had never happened and we'd tried to confront him about it. He hadn't confirmed it or denied it. He'd just thanked us for giving a shit and told us not to worry about it. As if that was possible.

Seth wrapped his arms around Darius who growled in response. He didn't appreciate us feeling sorry for him and I was pretty sure it would only be another moment before-

Darius shoved Seth off of him and he fell back onto the couch with a whine.

"I'm not a hugger, Seth," Darius snapped. "How many goddamn times do I have to tell you?"

Seth whimpered again. "I know, I know. But you look like you need one and I'm sleeping on my own. My pack should be huddled all around me but I'm in that bed with no one to snuggle and I need to snuggle!"

Darius rolled his eyes and I snorted a laugh, slipping down beside Seth and pulling him under my arm. He released a groan that was damn near sexual as he folded his arms around me, nuzzling into my chest. The relief that poured from him coated the back of my tongue and my gut twisted as I felt a sharp twist of pain coming from him. He was hurting. This separation from his pack wasn't healthy for him.

"Come and sleep here tonight," I offered, needing to make him feel better. His pain hurt me too and I couldn't just leave it alone. "You can be the big spoon."

"Really?" Seth asked excitedly, peering up at me like I'd just promised him the moon. "You promise?"

"Fuck knows why, but yeah." A smile tugged at my lips as I felt just how happy that made him and he swiped his tongue straight up my cheek.

Caleb laughed at us and my smile widened as I felt him pushing some of his anger aside in favour of amusement.

"If you're starting on an orgy I might just wait outside until you're done," Orion's voice came from the door and I twisted in my seat to look at him.

A torrent of relief and happiness spilled from Darius as his special buddy arrived and he strode straight across the room to meet him, pulling him into a tight embrace. They stayed locked together for several long seconds and Orion ran his hand up and down Darius's back. The emotions coming from them were so strong that I could hardly feel the twist of jealousy I usually got when I saw them together.

The four of us were as close as four brothers but Darius had this special relationship with Orion that didn't include us. It was kinda sad how it made me feel like a jealous little bitch but there it was. The one thing a Siren had to do was own their own emotions and I couldn't really deny it. When Orion was around, Darius dropped us like sacks of shit. Okay, maybe that was a bit of an exaggeration but it felt that way sometimes. And I knew neither of them had chosen to undergo the Guardian bond so I didn't even have the right to feel the way I did. But I couldn't help it. And neither could Cal and Seth.

Seth started howling loudly as Orion and Darius kept hold of each other.

"I thought you didn't like hugging," he growled when he couldn't take it anymore.

Caleb laughed and I joined in as Darius finally stepped back.

"Well maybe I just don't like hugging *you,*" he teased, pulling a pouch of stardust from his pocket.

A stab of hurt came from Seth and I frowned.

"Don't be a dick, Darius," I snapped, squeezing Seth tighter.

"Oh for fuck's sake," Darius muttered. "Come here then, puppy."

Seth bounded out of the chair and leapt on Darius like he'd just declared his undying love for him instead of offering a consolation hug. He jumped into Darius's arms and knocked him back onto the bed where they fell on top of Cal who got dragged into the hug too.

I laughed as the mood in the room switched dramatically and amusement, happiness and friendship filled the air. I got up and dove on top of them as well, earning myself more licks from Seth as he alternated between all of us.

"Come on, Orion," Seth called excitedly. "You can join my honorary pack for the night."

"Not a fucking chance," Orion replied, folding his arms as he stayed well away from us where we were all tangled on the bed.

Darius laughed as he got up, offering me a hand to help me up too. Seth pinned Caleb down and licked him straight up the centre of his face and he spluttered as he shoved him off.

"We're going to be late at this rate," Orion said casually and we all looked at him in disbelief as we moved closer together.

Darius tossed the stardust over us and the next second we were floating through the stars, the room melting away from us as we shifted through the world in little less than the space between heartbeats.

My feet hit the ground and I looked around at the others as they appeared too.

Cameras started flashing instantly as the paparazzi spotted us and I heard my name mixed with the others' as the reporters tried to snag our attention for a comment.

Orion darted away from us straight into the building as we turned and posed for a few photos to keep them happy.

"We don't have any comments to make at this time," Darius called and we headed into the Court of Solaria before they had much chance to protest.

The moment we walked through the huge rotating doors, my father's P.A., Cressida, descended on us. Her platinum blonde braids were pulled back into a high ponytail and her full lips pressed into a thin line which was the only indication she gave of being irritated that we were late.

"Here you are!" she gushed. "They just brought the Nymph in. Your parents are already waiting in the interrogation room."

We followed her further into the building, passing several security doors and more FIB agents in their black uniforms than usually filled the halls around here. I guessed it was a precaution with the war taking place but all the tension surrounding us made me uneasy.

We headed up a dark staircase and Cressida led us into an observation room beside a pane of one-way glass so that we'd be hidden from the Nymph. The interrogation room beyond the window was still empty, its white walls gleaming expectantly as it awaited the prisoner.

The Councillors looked up as we entered the room and we all moved forward to greet our parents.

Dad smiled widely as he saw me, his excitement infectious as he drew me into an embrace.

"Have you gotten taller?" he teased, straightening his spine as we stood eye to eye.

"You saw me a few days ago," I replied, shaking my head at the tired joke.

Seth and Cal were both grinning at their moms as they greeted them too but Darius and Orion only exchanged a curt greeting with Lionel.

I extended my senses towards the Fire Councillor, wondering if I should be concerned for Darius tonight but I only detected the faintest hint of disappointment from his father. He was one of the strangest people I'd ever read. Whenever I got near him it was like he was void of emotion. A blank canvas. Either he kept himself in complete control or he was some kind of path. Sociopath, psychopath... *both.* I certainly didn't envy Darius his life with him whatever he was.

My dad noticed my attention swivelling to my friend and his father and led me over to join them, picking up on my concern. I'd spoken to him about Lionel once but there was nothing he or the other Councillors could do about him. To challenge him would be to challenge the Celestial Council itself. And Solaria couldn't afford the unrest that would cause, especially with the Nymphs circling ever closer and the Vega Heirs reappearing.

"Nice to see you, Professor Orion," Dad said, offering his hand.

Orion shook it briefly, his emotions in control too, though his discomfort spilled out a little. He didn't like being read by Sirens. But we were fairly used to that reaction.

"You too, Lord Rigel," Orion agreed.

"I suppose you'll have your hands full with the Lunar Eclipse on Monday," Dad joked. "I wouldn't fancy the challenge of trying to wrangle a school full of randy teenagers with the moon working against me!"

"Gah! *Dad!"* I complained, scrunching my face up in disgust.

"Oh come on," Caleb's mom, Melinda, piped up. "You boys are practically adults now. We all feel the urges of the moon when the Eclipse comes."

Lionel laughed darkly, his gaze sweeping over Melinda in her tight fitting dress as a hint of lust leaked from him.

Christ, I'm going to be sick.

"That we do," Lionel agreed.

Caleb visibly shuddered. "No you don't, Mom," he snapped. "I don't want to even hear a suggestion that you do!"

Melinda laughed. "Well you should. You're Eclipse-conceived after all."

"Fuck! Don't tell me that!" Caleb covered his ears and the Councillors all laughed like it was hilarious.

"Actually, Cally, I've been meaning to talk to you about this," Melinda added. "Your father and I have decided it's best you come home for the night on Monday. Vampires feel the bloodlust too keenly during the Eclipse and it's not worth risking any...*incidents.*"

Seth snorted loudly and his Mom, Antonia, nudged him in a way that wasn't really reprimanding but was obviously meant to be seen that way.

"I can control myself," Caleb complained. "I don't need to go home like a-"

"I'm sure Professor Orion can attest to the difficulty of controlling his nature during an Eclipse?" Melinda asked, casting her gaze on Orion so he was forced to respond.

"It can be...a challenge," he agreed slowly.

"I bet it can," Antonia murmured, running her eyes over him.

"*Mom!*" Seth barked. "The Eclipse isn't for two days for the stars' sake!"

"See, Cally? A *challenge.* Your own professor admits it. So you're coming home to make sure you don't kill anyone and cause a scandal."

"But *Mom-*" Caleb began just as the door opened in the interrogation room.

We all looked around and silence descended like a cloud over all of us as the Nymph was dragged into the room.

My eyes widened as I took it in. I'd seen a few Nymphs in their true form before, but that had been in the midst of battle or after they were already dead. The nightmare before me sent ice sliding through my veins.

It was over a foot taller than the four FIB agents who dragged it into the room. Its skin was rough like the bark of a tree and thorny horns extended from its skull. Its eyes were black like the Shadow Realm it was born from and its face was a picture of horror.

The creature's arms were bound behind its back with chains of fire but as it was thrown to the ground, it turned and my stomach clenched as I spotted the stumps where its fingers should have been. The wounds had been healed to stop any bleeding but the thought of what had been done to them made me clench my own hands into fists defensively.

Excitement built around me and the four Councillors filed from the room, leaving us to watch as they headed in to start the interrogation. Dad clapped me on the shoulder as he went, obviously noticing my concern and I gave him a tight smile as he headed off to join our enemy in that room.

The FIB agents left as our parents entered and the Nymph moved up onto its knees as it was surrounded.

Seth whimpered softly as his mom drew close to the creature, brushing his shoulder against mine for reassurance.

Dad had shed his suit jacket on the way into the room and he slowly rolled his sleeves back as Antonia stalked towards the Nymph first.

Lionel and Melinda stood back, watching as the Nymph raised its head to survey them with its black eyes.

"We need information which you have," Seth's mom said, stopping in front of it. "And we *will* get it from you before you die. It's up to you how difficult that is."

"The shadows will welcome me back for dying a warrior's death," the Nymph growled, its voice guttural and low. "I do not fear pain or death."

Antonia flexed her hand and the Nymph was thrown back against the wall with a blast of air. Its head collided with the white tiles and blood splattered across them at the impact.

My father moved to her side and water shot from his palm, slamming into the creature before creating an orb around its head. The Nymph started thrashing as it fought for air and Dad's jaw clenched as he held the magic in place until it started convulsing.

The water cascaded to the floor before the creature could lose consciousness and Antonia started weaving air through her fingers again.

"Tell us where your forces are massing," she demanded.

The Nymph glared up at her and took in a deep breath, a loud rattle filling the air.

I sucked in a sharp breath as Antonia and my dad dropped to their knees under the influence of the creature's power.

Seth caught my arm, a howl leaving his lips as he cried out to his mother.

Melinda and Lionel staggered as its power hit them too but Lionel snarled as he stepped forward.

Cries went up from the corridor as FIB agents called out for backup and the five of us moved so close to the glass that we were practically pressed against it.

"Tell us!" Lionel yelled, a roar escaping him as he managed to run at the Nymph despite the heavy rattle of its power filling the room.

My own knees were growing weak as it wielded its dark magic and my dad clutched his chest like he could hardly breathe.

Smoke slid between Lionel's lips as he called on the Dragon beneath his flesh for power and threw his fist into the Nymph's face.

Blood flew and he yelled out as he hit it again, his powerful frame brimming with rage as he threw his fists like hammers into the Nymph's face.

On the fourth blow, the rattle was cut off and the Nymph was knocked to the ground.

Lionel didn't stop. He was screaming at it, demanding the information he wanted while kicking and punching, more and more blood spilling over the white tiles as he lost control.

Dad got to his feet, drawing Antonia back instead of moving towards Darius's father.

"Lionel, stop!" Melinda demanded but he just kept kicking and kicking until the Nymph wasn't moving at all.

Silence fell heavily among everyone and I dragged in a long breath.

"He just...killed it," Caleb breathed, a frown gripping his features. "Now we won't get any information from it."

"It was too powerful," I growled. "Even without its probes it just disabled some of the most powerful Fae in Solaria." I knew we needed the information that creature had held, but I couldn't get the image of my dad on his knees out of my mind. I was glad it was dead.

"That monster never would have talked," Seth said in a low voice. "The only thing they deserve is death."

"Well, it makes a change to see him turning that rage on someone who deserves it for once," Orion muttered.

"Kinda looked like he went easy on it to me," Darius replied darkly.

I turned to look at him with a frown, wondering if he'd really had to endure that level of anger at his father's hands. One look at his face gave me my answer and I shifted uncomfortably as I gazed back into the room where blood was steadily spreading across the ground.

I reached out with my power, pushing through the glass and focusing on Lionel Acrux. His face was fixed in a mask of anger and disappointment but as I pressed a little harder with my power, I found the truth of what he was feeling beneath the mask.

Joy. Exhilaration. Relief.

And that might have been the most terrifying thing I'd experienced all night.

TORY

CHAPTER TWENTY SEVEN

We stood in the caves where we had our Earth Elemental lessons with the rest of the freshmen while we waited for the final trial to begin.

This one was different than the others. The stands were outside the caves and we were alone down here while Professor Rockford and the other assessors stood waiting to start the trial.

I stepped from foot to foot as nervous energy ticked through me. This was it, the final trial.

"When we make it through The Reckoning we need a night out," I said to Darcy as we waited for the last of the students to arrive.

"Hell yes. Dancing and drinking and no Heirs. We should go to Tucana again, or maybe somewhere even further away."

"We could get out of the Academy for a whole weekend?" I suggested with a grin. "Hit up our stipend for a five star stay in some fancy hotel and a night drinking champagne."

"Yes please," Darcy said enthusiastically.

We were both going to the Fairy Fair tonight but it wouldn't really be the same kind of celebration as we could have after The Reckoning. Besides, Darcy was going with Diego and Caleb had sent me message after message until I'd finally agreed to let him take me. It wasn't a date though. I was seventy eight percent certain of that. More like a chance to hook up somewhere new. I guessed I'd find out tonight either way.

"The aim of this task is simple," Rockford called in her small voice and I turned my attention her way. "Escape the caves before the time runs out. There are various routes through them and you need to find one that leads above ground...and make sure you don't get eaten."

"Eaten?" I asked, in confusion. "What do you-"

A klaxon sounded and the students all raced forward as one. I caught Darcy's eye and we started running too, caught up in the flood of bodies.

The tunnel curved downhill ahead of us before forking in two directions. The freshmen parted like a tide crashing against a rock, half going each way. We ran left, not really making the choice beyond the fact that we were already to that side of the crowd.

The tunnel curved before splitting again and again, the students around us spilling in different directions while we made snap decisions and hoped for the best.

The further we went, the darker it got. Faeworms and precious metals glimmered on the black walls but it was hard to make out much else.

"How are we supposed to find a way out of here when every tunnel leads down?" Darcy hissed and I chewed my lip, unsure how to answer her. She was right, but how long could that go on for? Surely they'd head up again eventually? What the hell kind of challenge would this be if it was impossible?

"Hold on," I said, catching her arm and pulling her to a halt. "Maybe we should try to be smarter about this. Surely we have to use earth magic to escape this place, it can't just be about running blind."

"Yeah, you're right." Darcy looked around as the rest of the students left us behind and reached out for the cave wall.

She closed her eyes as she concentrated and I looked around, seeing if I could spot anything that might help.

A faint tremor ran through the ground at my feet and I shifted to keep my balance.

"I think we should go right," Darcy murmured, her voice heavy as she concentrated on the feeling of her earth magic.

I opened my mouth to respond just as a guttural roar sounded somewhere in the caves behind us, sending a shiver of fear racing up my spine.

Darcy's eyes snapped open and she looked at me, her gaze filled with the same terror that sound had woken in me.

"What was that?" I breathed.

Darcy shook her head, no words coming out.

The roar came again and I stumbled towards her. "Right?" I confirmed, looking at the narrow passage which led that way. It was darker than the others, narrower too. On looks I wouldn't have picked it but maybe that was a good thing. We should be trusting our magic, nothing else.

"Yeah," Darcy agreed.

We ran for it together and the darkness pressed close as the cavern swallowed us. Up ahead an orange glow seemed to flicker just out of sight, giving just enough light to let me see the walls which pressed in on either side of us.

After a few feet, the passage narrowed too much for us to jog side by side and Darcy slipped ahead of me. We kept going, our panting breaths echoing against the cold rocks as the passage slowly started to curve up hill.

"You were right!" I said encouragingly as we upped our pace a little more.

I reached out to brush my hands over the walls either side of me as I ran and that deep roar sounded behind us again.

"Shit, you don't think she meant that part about us getting eaten, do you?" Darcy begged, looking behind her as she kept running.

"No," I breathed, though it sounded a hell of a lot like a *yes* somehow.

We tumbled around a corner into a wide chamber with a low fire burning at the centre of it, causing the orange glow.

We staggered towards the flames and my heart pounded as I looked around at the chamber we'd emerged in. Seven other passages led out of here, but it was impossible to say which we should follow to get back to the surface.

The growl came again, so close that the earth beneath our feet shuddered with the force of it.

"What the fuck is that?" I gasped.

Darcy was shaking her head, backing up closer to the fire.

I looked between the passages at a total loss.

"We need to feel the way on again," she said, dropping to her knees.

"Okay," I agreed, though I wasn't entirely sure what she meant.

I dropped down too, closing my eyes as I pressed my palms to the dirt beneath us.

I pushed my awareness away from myself, searching with my earth magic for a connection to the rock and soil surrounding us. For a moment it was overwhelming, so much of it pressed in on us from every direction, above, below, to each side but suddenly my attention caught on the space we were in instead.

I felt the fissure in the soil, the divide which ran through it like veins in a body.

The other tunnels branched away from this space and I could push my awareness towards them too, feeling them out as I tried to figure out where they went.

"I'll start on the right, you start on the left," Darcy directed and I quickly agreed.

I dug my fingers into the soil, pushing my consciousness towards the tunnel to my left and trying to figure out where it led. Up and down didn't seem to mean anything to what I was feeling but as the tunnel spread away from us I could feel the rock around it growing thicker, colder, wetter.

That had to mean it went down. I shook my head and drew back to where we were, exploring the next tunnel with my magic instead.

I pushed my awareness into the dark space, but felt it end abruptly in a sharp blockade. There was no opening beyond that, it was a dead end.

"Not the two on the far right," Darcy breathed as she continued her search.

"Must be one of the middle ones," I agreed.

I began to spread my magic out again but just as I did, a huge tremor rattled through the ground beneath me.

I cried out as I pitched forward, the soil and rocks splitting behind me like they were nothing more than soft butter being carved by a knife.

My eyes snapped open and I spun around, the ground bucking beneath me and throwing me back into Darcy just as an enormous roar filled the cavern, rattling off the rock walls and drawing a scream of terror from my lips.

My eyes widened as a huge creature burst from the soil beyond my feet.

It was like a cross between a giant worm and goddamn dragon. Its huge mouth was lined with rows of razor sharp teeth and blind eyes cast about hungrily as it swung its pale head left and right.

"Holy shit," I gasped and its head whipped towards me instantly.

I screamed as it lunged for me, throwing my hands up in panic and casting a huge wave of earth power from my palms on instinct. A wall of rock shot up out of the ground between us and the creature seconds before it could reach us. The sound of crumbling stone rang out as it collided with the wall I'd made and my eyes widened in horror as a crack tore right through the centre of it.

Darcy's hands locked around my arm as she heaved me up. I snapped out of my momentary panic and scrambled after her as she raced across the cave towards the three central tunnels. We hadn't had time to figure out which one we should take and as the sound of breaking stone followed us, we had to take a leap of faith.

Darcy shot into the left tunnel and I was right on her heels as we sprinted into the dark.

The roar came again and the ground at our feet shuddered and trembled as the creature gave chase through the labyrinth of stone.

I had no idea if it was using the tunnel to pursue us or if it might burst from the dirt at our feet at any moment.

We ran and ran, adrenaline coursing through my veins as I pushed my body to its limit and we slowly seemed to put a little distance between us and the hell creature which was hunting us.

The ground was rising slightly beneath us as we went and my heart soared with the idea of us making it to the surface.

"A little further," I panted, refusing to back off the relentless pace while pressing my hand to Darcy's shoulder, making sure I didn't lose her in the darkness.

"We must be close," she panted back as the incline increased sharply and hope strummed a beat in my chest.

The ground still shook, roars chasing us as we climbed up and up, the promise of fresh air and freedom calling my name as our footsteps pounded through the echoing tunnel.

We were nearly there, just another few steps. I was sure that I could hear the sound of the crowd cheering somewhere close by.

My face collided with Darcy's back and I cried out as I slammed down onto my ass in the dirt.

"There's no more tunnel!" Darcy shrieked in panic and my heart skipped a beat as another roar sounded behind us in the dark.

"There has to be!" I protested, crawling forward on my hands and knees as I swept my hands over a wall of soil which blocked the way on.

The creature growled behind us and the walls trembled again.

I pressed my magic out from me, hunting for some way forward, refusing to believe we'd taken the wrong turning. My heart sank as I found nothing but packed dirt all around us, boxing us in, burying us alive, the perfect prey for the creature which drew closer at every moment.

"It's not deep!" Darcy yelled suddenly. "We have to dig our way out. We're only a few meters below the surface!"

I gasped as I realised she was right, the weight of the soil before us was so much less than it had been, we were almost there, nearly free.

"Then let's dig!" I agreed forcefully, throwing myself forward and clawing lumps of soil aside.

Darcy was right beside me and with the help of our magic we burrowed into the wall blocking our way out. I lost her in the dark as I scrambled into a tunnel where the soil fell down all around me, covering me, choking me, suffocating me...

I kept going, digging and digging towards that promise of freedom which was so damn close I could taste it.

The weight of the soil pressed down, the roar of the creature drew close and with a final surge of my earth magic, my hands finally broke the surface.

I grunted with effort as I dug myself out of the ground and suddenly a hand closed around mine. Darcy was dragging me out.

Fresh air surrounded me and I couldn't help the sob that tore from my throat as I gulped it down hungrily.

I shook on my knees, looking up as the cheers of the crowd flooded in on me.

A large group of students were already assembled beside Professor Rockford and the giant timer was ticking down the final minute.

But it didn't matter that we'd come last. We'd made it.

I was covered from head to toe in dirt. Every inch of my body shook with fear and fatigue. But we'd done it. We'd passed the final trial. And no one could say we hadn't earned our placed in this damn school now.

We'd made it through every trial.

And we were here to stay.

DARCY

CHAPTER TWENTY EIGHT

"**F**airrrry faiiiiir!" someone crowed outside my room and I laughed. It seemed everyone in the Academy was going to the Fairy Fair today and I was brimming with excitement after acing my final trial. Curfew had been pushed back until eleven pm tonight to allow students to enjoy the fair, but from the gossip in the halls it sounded like that was because most of the faculty wanted to attend it too.

My hair was half pulled up with a silver clip and I wore a knit black dress with pantyhose, long boots and a leather jacket. I didn't bring anything but my Atlas, keys and some cash for the rides.

Although this was technically a mission to talk to Diego about his dodgy uncle, that didn't mean we weren't going to have a great night. And who knew? Maybe it would cheer him up. He'd been in a mood all week knowing Sofia was going to the fair with Tyler, but I was determined to take his mind off of it. And maybe give him a straight talk about asking her out instead of dancing around the matter.

Tory was going with Caleb and though I was a little worried about her spending so much time with one of the Heirs, it did sound like he was treating her okay when they were alone. I couldn't believe he'd actually stood up for her against Darius the other day. It wasn't exactly an apology, but he was making some effort at least. And besides, Tory knew how to handle men. I'd once seen her kick a six and a half foot biker to the curb because she was (and I quote) 'done with screwing a guy who had smaller balls than her'. That was Tor. And I damn well loved her for it.

The one thing casting shade on my evening was the fact things were still broken between Orion and I. I'd been avoiding him to focus on my trials but that had gone a little *too* smoothly. He hadn't messaged me, hadn't come up to me in the halls, hadn't even shot a glance in my direction whenever I'd come close to bumping into him. I was owed an apology, but if I wasn't going to get one then had to try and move on from him - no matter how much that process would suck. I sure as hell wasn't going to let myself dwell on that tonight, though. I was owed a bit of fun.

A knock came at the door and I pulled it open with a bright smile. Diego had a smart white shirt on with a grey jacket and jeans. He'd cut his hair so it was shaved at the sides and swept back stylishly over the top. My mouth parted as he gave me a crooked smile. He looked good. Better than good. Diego looked *hot*. *What the crap?*

"What do you think, chica?" He brushed his hand over his new hair and my smile widened.

"Sofia's gonna eat her heart out," I teased and he released a laugh.

"Maybe. Come on then, my carriage awaits." He held out his arm and I laughed as I took it, pulling my door closed and locking it as we left.

I felt his eyes lingering on me and gave him a curious frown. "What?"

"You look like la luz de las estrellas."

"What does that mean?" I asked, heat rising up the back of my neck.

"Like the light of the stars," he said and I glanced away, waving a hand to brush off the comment. It was awkwardly nice coming from a friend, though I did sometimes sense Diego liked me more than that. But I hoped I was wrong.

We headed out of Aer Tower where students were moving across campus towards the parking lot and shuttle buses. The night's sky was clear and the air crisp, my breath rising before me from the winter chill.

We walked to Earth Territory and I felt eyes on the back of my head as we headed along the path. I glanced over my shoulder and my heart clenched as I saw Orion taking the path toward Asteroid Place. He stared at me for a long second, his eyes flaring as he took in Diego's arm linked with mine. I pressed my lips together, turning away. I didn't know why he looked so damn angry, he was the one who'd asked me to dig up the dirt on Diego's uncle.

We fetched Diego's rusted red car and it chugged along the road that led out of campus, my excitement growing as we left Zodiac behind.

"One day I'm gonna make something of myself, you know? I won't drive a tin can or ever have to answer to anyone again," Diego said, a fire in his eyes.

"Oh really?" I asked with a grin, glancing over at him as his hands tightened on the wheel. His arms flexed and I noticed actual muscle there. Had he been working out?

"Yeah. My mamá called me last night," he revealed and I wondered if this was my in to ask about his uncle. "She said she was proud of me, Darcy. She's never said that, you know? If I pass The Reckoning tomorrow, she said she'll come and visit me."

"That's great, Diego. So I guess your uncle told her how well you did in the Air Trial?"

He glanced at me. "Come on, we both know I hitched a ride in that trial. And I'm so grateful for it. But my grades are good and I'm getting better at casting air so I guess he told her that." He shrugged one shoulder and I had the feeling he wasn't telling the whole truth.

"He seemed a little...uptight," I said carefully, not wanting to overstep the mark.

Diego's features twitched into a dark expression for a moment, one that spoke of fear. But it was gone as quickly as it came. "He's um…"

I waited for him to find the words, sure if I pressed him too hard he'd shut down this conversation.

"Well he's a bastardo is what he is," he snarled and the ferocity of his tone made my heart beat a little harder.

"Oh?" I breathed.

"He puts pressure on my family, makes them do things…"

"What things?" I gasped and his shoulders tensed as he glanced over at me.

Some horrible memory flashed in his eyes and he swallowed hard. "I shouldn't really talk about it."

"I'm your friend," I said gently. "You can tell me anything." A knot in my stomach reminded me that I was supposed to pass this information on to Orion. But would I really betray my friend like that? I didn't know if I could. And it wasn't like Orion deserved my help right now. But then if Alejandro was up to something dangerous, it could be disastrous if I didn't pass on what I learned...

"Alejandro is el diablo," Diego hissed. "He uses my mother, his own *sister*, and my father for his work. When I was younger, they'd go off for days together and leave me at home with mi abuela."

"What's his work?" I asked.

Diego rubbed his chin, firmly looking out the window. "I don't know," he muttered and I was certain he was lying. The setting of his jaw said this conversation was done and I hoped I'd be able to bring it up again later.

I sat back in my seat and Diego soon put the radio on, our conversation shifting to the fair. It wasn't long before we pulled up on the outskirts of Tucana in a sprawling field set up for parking. Beyond it, the fair was lit up in neon lights and a smile dragged up my lips as excitement flitted through me.

I hopped out of the car, bobbing on my heels as I waited for Diego and we joined the crowd which was heading toward the entrance. A large Ferris wheel and rollercoasters sparkled with lights beyond rows of stands and anticipation built in my chest. I'd never been to an amusement park in my life and I'd always loved the idea of the rides. Tonight, I'd be going on all of them.

I cast an eye around for Tory, wondering if she was here already. There were plenty of students and teachers amongst the crowd and I even spotted Washer up ahead, creaking along in his leather pants with a turtleneck red sweater on. His arm was around a woman with dark hair and my heart nearly stopped when I realised it was Principal Nova. She laughed at something he said, swatting his chest playfully and he grinned at her.

"You've got to be kidding me?" I muttered to Diego, pointing them out. "They're together?"

"No wonder he gets away with murder at Zodiac," he replied.

We headed to the lit up archway with the words *Tucana's Fairy Fair* in curling letters over the top of it. Diego took the lead, paying the entrance fee for us both before I could utter a word of refusal, then caught my hand and tugged me through onto the grass between the first row of stands.

"Thank you," I said. "Drinks are on me."

"I like treating you," he said and the intensity in his gaze made me look anywhere else.

We headed past the stands which were selling an array of strange food and crazy-looking drinks which sparked and bubbled. There were sweets of every kind, from huge cotton candy which changed colour every few seconds, to popcorn which steamed and was coated in melted chocolate, to huge tubs of every flavour ice cream including Faeberry Ripple and Rum and Faeson.

We passed a drinks stand which was selling steaming mugs of hot honey cider and I bought two for us, passing one to Diego. It tasted like a dream, so spicy and sweet with the kick of alcohol burning all the way down into my gut and warming me through.

The next row of stands we came to was a long line of games and I hurried over to one where the prize was a four foot Pegasus stuffed toy. Its horn glittered and every part of its coat shone like stars.

"Ooo," I cooed.

"I'll win you it," Diego said, puffing out his chest as he planted his cup down on the counter. A long-barrelled red gun sat at the centre of it, chained down to stop people stealing it. There was a single large target at the back of the stand conjured by magic, suspended in the air and slowly rotating.

The shady-looking guy behind the counter sidled closer. "Are you going to have a go, missy?" he asked.

"Sure," I said brightly.

"I'll do it," Diego insisted, passing over the money before I could.

I sighed, folding my arms and settling in for the show as Diego picked up the gun. "I just have to hit that target?" he asked the man.

"You have to hit it three times. You get thirty seconds and unlimited shots," the guy confirmed with a mischievous glint in his eyes. "Ready?"

Diego nodded and the guy grinned, stepping aside. Diego lifted the gun and shot at the huge target. An explosion of red light burst from it with a powerful kickback that made him stumble away from the counter. The target shot sideways and the blast exploded into a shower of sparks as it missed. Diego cursed, raising the gun and firing again. This time the target shrank to the size of a pea and Diego missed once more.

"That's impossible," I said with a laugh, but Diego looked deadly serious as he lined up the gun. He took shot after shot, the target darting left, right, up, down, becoming huge, then tiny, elongated, then round like a ball, pinging all over the place.

Diego didn't get a single shot and slammed the gun down in annoyance.

"Move over," the deep voice made my heart churn up and turn to mulch.

Orion pushed Diego aside, dressed in a black shirt and jeans with a leather jacket that looked way too good on him. Behind him, was Francesca.

She looked like the Bonnie to his Clyde, wearing a fitted red dress which hugged her curves and a long black jacket which screamed class. She tilted her head, resting her hand on Orion's arm. "For me?" she asked and I wanted to scream.

Orion paid me zero attention, curling an arm around her waist and tugging her against his hip. "Do you want the blue Pegasus or the silver?"

Diego caught my sleeve to draw me away but something kept me there, my jaw set as I watched the two of them. So close to each other, her fingers caressing him like they'd done it a thousand times.

I thought you were single, jerkface?

"Blue," Francesca decided.

"My favourite colour." He kissed her nose. *Kissed her goddamn nose* while saying how much he loved the colour blue. Why did that hurt so much?

Orion pressed the end of the gun to his shoulder, aiming down the sight. The weaselly man behind the counter restarted the game and the target shot sideways.

Bang. It exploded into a shower of multi-coloured sparks as Orion hit it dead on.

The target reappeared in a tiny form, whizzing about like a bee. Orion shifted the gun so fast I barely saw the movement. Another bang and a display of sparks followed as he hit it again. The third time, I blinked and he'd done it. Won the damn game.

The guy unhooked one of the huge blue Pegasus toys from where it hung on a rack, handing it over to Orion who passed it straight to Francesca. My heart crushed to dust as he slung his arm over her shoulders and walked away, the two of them looking like some movie star couple as they headed toward the drinks stand.

I turned to Diego, slapping a painfully bright smile on my face. "Let's go on all the rides until we puke."

"Er...okay," he said and I snatched his hand, a small and bitter part of me knowing I was doing it to get back at Orion. I despised playing games, but I wasn't going to have him dangle Francesca in front of me and not bite back. It was humiliating.

I towed Diego onto the first rollercoaster we found – which happened to be the biggest – and guided him into the front row. Diego turned sheet white as the bar locked over our waists, his hand gripping mine for dear life.

We shot off so fast, a scream tumbled from my throat and adrenaline surged through me like a forest fire.

Before I knew it, the ride was over and I was laughing my head off, feeling a thousand times better already.

Screw Orion. He's made himself clear. He's done. And I'm not going to let it ruin my night – even if I do go home later and cry into a pillow until I choke. That's later's problem. Now, I'm gonna have a damn good time.

We queued for another rollercoaster even though Diego still looked a little pale from the last one. I spotted Tyler and Sofia getting off the ride and waved to catch their attention. They didn't notice us, but I'd drawn Diego's eyes to them, immediately hating myself for it as Tyler grabbed her by the waist and pulled her into a fierce kiss.

I turned to Diego, feeling shitty that I'd helped set those two up. Especially now I was getting a taste of my own medicine. His eyes were dark, but his response was curling an arm around my waist and drawing me closer. And I let him. Partly because it was freezing and I couldn't refuse a hug and partly because I was hurting hard. Besides, we were using each other. He wanted Sofia and I wanted Orion. Might as well slap on a smile and pretend neither of us gave a shit.

I looked up at Diego and a flame in his eyes roared, like he *did* want this. And I was so unprepared that when he dipped his head and pressed his lips to mine I just froze. Totally, utterly froze.

I spluttered, stepping back, unsure what to say. Did he like me? Or was this to get back at Sofia? Even if it was, he should have *asked.*

We were ushered forward to get on the rollercoaster but suddenly I didn't feel like it.

"Let's get some food," I said quickly, turning and nearly having an aneurism when I spotted Orion near a stand beyond the queue, his eyes drilling into me. His face was an unreadable mask but his gaze told me everything I needed to know. He'd seen Diego kiss me.

I pushed through the queue, my blood too hot as I forced my way out. I needed to talk to Orion. Just for a second. Just to explain. We might have been on bad terms right now but I hadn't meant for that to happen.

"Darcy!" Diego called after me.

There were so many bodies in my way, I just needed everyone to goddamn *move*. Air burst from my palms, forcing a path into existence and people stumbled aside in annoyance. The path cut directly to Orion and pain branded a permanent mark on my heart. He held Francesca against the side of the stand, one hand tangled in her hair, the other locked around her waist as he kissed her. She clung to his jacket, her fingers scraping across his beard as her tongue pushed into his mouth.

Diego caught my arm and led me away, not even noticing Orion there. Because to him it meant nothing. It wasn't the sky falling down, but to me it felt like every star in the heavens were descending and crashing into the earth around me.

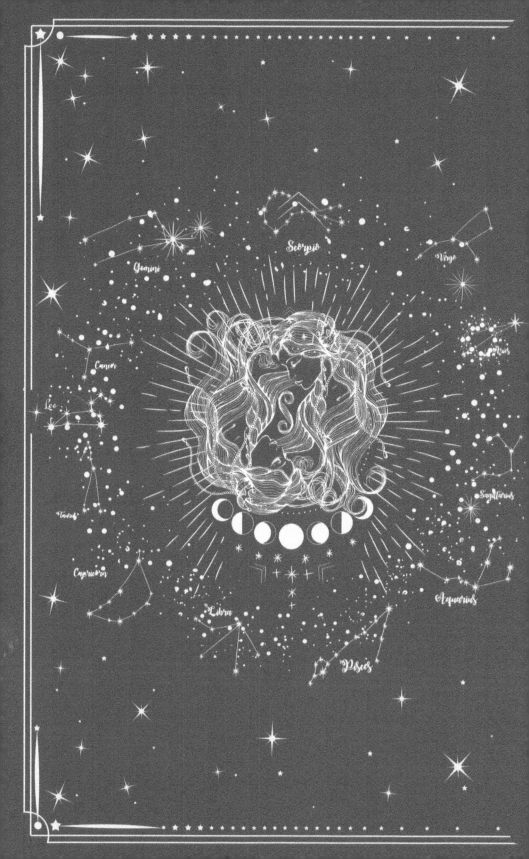

TORY

CHAPTER TWENTY NINE

Caleb was late.

I blew out a breath of frustration as I sipped on my milkshake in The Orb. We'd already agreed to meet late because he had to meet the other Heirs for something before we left, but now I was wondering what the point of going at all was.

I eyed my Atlas as the clock ticked from twelve minutes past to thirteen. He hadn't even messaged me.

And I'm done.

There were shuttle buses heading to the fair and I didn't need a ride in Caleb Altair's no doubt obnoxiously flashy car. I hated cars anyway. Hardly ever rode in them if I could avoid it. They always made me remember sinking to the bottom of that goddamn lake and being trapped. Waiting to die. And even though that fear didn't have its claws in me in the way it used to, I'd still always prefer a bike.

I twisted my long ponytail around my finger as I grabbed my leather jacket from the back of my chair and stood up.

The red crop top and fitted jeans I'd chosen to wear weren't really warm enough for the time of year but I was using my fire magic to keep me warm anyway.

I headed for the exit and sent a quick message to Geraldine, checking where her and the Ass Club were. She'd been begging me to go with them earlier and I'd almost ditched Caleb in favour of a night with her anyway. I'd only decided against it when Justin Master had suggested he be my *escort* for the night. I'd tried to make a joke about him being a male prostitute which had gotten him so flustered that I'd dropped the idea just to save him the torture of my company for the evening. He really loved the idea of the Vega Princesses but I knew I didn't live up to his prim and proper fantasies one bit. And though being a disappointment in that regard was highly amusing, it got a bit draining too. I just wanted a night of freedom.

My Atlas buzzed in my pocket and I pulled it out to find Geraldine's reply.

Geraldine:

Oh hula beluga! Everyone's just jumping in their jackets to hear you'll be joining us! Let me know when you're here and I'll get you some cotton candfae!

I smirked to myself at her exuberant response and upped my speed a little as I headed to the north of campus where the shuttle busses would be ferrying people to the Fairy Fair in Tucana.

I made it to the gates at the edge of campus, passing by the parking lot and heading to the bus shelter where a crowd of students were already waiting for the shuttle bus.

I skirted the crowd, not recognising anyone and not really wanting to find out if they were amongst the Heirs' fan club, then took a seat on a low wall beside the shelter to wait.

My Atlas buzzed again and I pulled it from my pocket.

Caleb:

Where are you?

I raised an eyebrow at the tone of the message, it was half seven now. Half an hour since we'd arranged to meet and this was the first I'd heard from him.

Tory:

Heading to the fair.

Caleb:

Why didn't you wait for me in The Orb?

I snorted. Who did he think he was? As if I was going to sit about waiting for half an hour to see if he decided to grace me with his presence. In fact, aside from messaging me about going to this damn fair, he'd been suspiciously absent ever since I'd spent the night in his room. Maybe he'd been annoyed that I didn't wait there for him to come back from his mystery meeting with the other Heirs, but I wasn't gonna hang around in his room without him there. It was weird. I hadn't even intended to stay the whole night in the first place. So when he'd gone I'd got my shit together and left too.

Tory:

I was under the impression you weren't coming.

Caleb:

Tell me where you are now, I'll come get you.

No apology then.

No thanks.

I looked up just as someone came to sit beside me and smiled as I recognised Milton. He'd become a bit of a permanent feature at our tables in The Orb, though I was glad to see he hadn't bowed to peer pressure and started wearing an Ass badge.

"Don't often see you alone," he commented. "Aren't you spending the night with Darcy?"

"She's on a date," I replied with a shrug. *Fake date, but still...*

"And you're not?"

"I got stood up," I said, a smile tugging at the corner of my mouth. I wasn't sure why I found it so amusing but I did. It seemed kinda fitting; everything in this place was always working against me, why would my love life be any different? Besides, I hadn't been looking for Caleb to ask me out in the first place so I was hardly going to start sobbing about it when it never even got off the ground.

"Shit. And I thought *my* life was pathetic," he teased and I couldn't help but laugh.

The growl of an engine made me look up as a flashy black sports car came skidding to a halt at the curb right in front of us.

My lips parted as the door opened, swinging up into the air like it was the goddamn Batmobile before Caleb got out.

"What are you doing here?" he asked me, a frown tugging at his brow as he drew closer.

Milton swiftly got up and moved away as Caleb shot him a dark look and I pursed my lips defiantly.

"Catching the bus. What does it look like?"

"I...you said you were coming with me," Caleb said, looking at me like he couldn't figure out what the hell was going on.

"Yeah. And then you left me waiting around for you without bothering to let me know you were running late. So I ditched plan A in favour of meeting my friends." I shrugged at him. It wasn't that hard to understand. I wasn't going to be jerked around by some guy who wasn't even my boyfriend.

Caleb just stared at me like I was speaking some other language and I got to my feet as the shuttle bus arrived.

I took a step towards it and he caught my hand to stop me.

"Are you getting on the bus?" he asked with a frown.

"Yeah. If you let go of me."

"But..." Caleb pushed a hand into his hair and let out a long sigh. "I'm sorry alright?"

I raised an eyebrow in surprise and waited to hear the rest of it.

"I recently found out some shit that kinda made me think about some things differently." Caleb narrowed his navy eyes on me like he was trying to figure something out. "And I don't know what to think anymore."

"About what?"

"I can't tell you," he replied, his jaw tightening.

I shrugged and turned back for the bus but he caught my hand again, halting me.

"Come with me to the fair, Tory...please."

"Christ, you look like you're gonna cry if I say no," I teased.

"Shut the fuck up and get in the car," he replied with a smirk.

"That's more like it." I let him walk me to the car and got in beneath the ridiculous door before Caleb shut it for me.

I instantly hit the button for the window, the knot in my chest loosening as it descended. *Fucking cars.*

He went around to the other side and slid in behind the wheel, starting up the engine which gave a deep growl that vibrated right through my bones.

I turned to find him smirking at the look on my face. "You said you liked big engines," he reminded me.

"I was probably referring to bike engines but points for effort. Minus points for making me look like a stuck-up prick arriving at a fun fair in the Batmobile though so you're back to minus ten."

"How does that work out?" he asked.

We shot away from the curb and down the road and I was pressed back into the leather seat as he accelerated quickly.

"You stood me up."

"*You* stood *me* up," he countered. "I was just running late."

"Well next time send a message, asshole, or you won't get another shot," I said with a smirk but I meant it. I wasn't anyone's fool and I wouldn't let him mess me around.

"Point taken."

I eyed Caleb as he drove. He was leaning back in his chair, one hand on the wheel, his muscular figure on show beneath a tight fitting white t-shirt. His hair was too neat, styled back with product to tame his curls. I preferred the way it looked when I'd been clawing my hands through it.

"What are you looking at?" he asked without turning his gaze from the road.

"You," I replied with a shrug. He was nice to look at, it shouldn't have been that surprising.

His gaze slid to me for a moment and suddenly the air in the car felt a lot warmer.

"You should put your seatbelt on," he commented.

"I know," I replied but I didn't do it. *Never again.*

Lights of every colour lit up the horizon ahead of us and I leaned forward as we drew closer to the field where the fair had been erected, a grin on my face like a little kid. But I didn't care. I'd never had money to do this kind of thing before and I was looking forward to it more than was probably normal for someone my age.

We suddenly veered left and I looked at Caleb in surprise as we turned away from the highway and he guided the car up a steep hill into the darkness. I couldn't see anything beyond the light of the headlights and the cool air coming in through my open window sent a shiver down my spine.

"I think you took a wrong turn," I teased, twisting in my seat to look back down the hill at the twinkling lights of the fair.

Caleb didn't respond but he put his foot down a little more, the engine roaring as we climbed higher and higher into the hills.

"Caleb?" I asked, looking at him as he continued to ignore me.

His mouth was set in a thin line and I shifted uncomfortably in my seat, looking around again. Everything beyond the windows was pitch black, endless darkness filling the space around us. I had no idea where we were and as he took a sharp turn, the lights of Tucana and the Fairy Fair behind us were stolen away.

"Where are you taking me?" I asked, a frown pulling at my brow.

Caleb didn't respond but his hand shifted to the controls on his door. My window slid closed and a heavy thunk sounded as the doors locked.

I spun around in my chair as a spike of adrenaline kick-started my heart.

My hand made it to the door handle and I yanked on it automatically, rattling it as it refused to respond to my attempts to open it.

"Let me out of the car," I breathed, a shiver running down my spine.

Caleb ignored me again, guiding the car back and forth around hairpin turns which had my pulse hammering with panic.

I snatched my Atlas from my pocket, meaning to message someone or call someone or-

Caleb snatched it out of my hands, flicking it off before throwing it over his shoulder where it fell into the small space behind his seat and out of sight.

I lifted my hand, magic tingling in my fingertips as I tried to figure out what spell I could use against him safely while we were travelling at this speed.

"Don't," Caleb snapped, snatching my wrist and shoving it down into my lap.

"If this is some new game of yours, I'm not enjoying it," I breathed and he released a hollow laugh.

"I'm not playing, sweetheart," he promised me.

The car suddenly shifted off of the road onto a gravel track and I was almost thrown into the window. Maybe he'd been right about the seatbelt.

Caleb slammed his foot on the brake, his hand landing in the centre of my chest as he did, clamping me back against the seat so that I wasn't thrown through the windscreen.

He cut the engine and the lights in the car fell away, leaving us in darkness.

"What's going on?" I breathed, my fingertips tingling with power but I knew I was outmatched by his skill. I needed to bide my time, find out what was going on and hit him with a strong blast of power when he wasn't expecting it if it came to that.

The silence stretched for so long that I almost wanted to scream just to break it.

"I've been thinking, Tory," Caleb said in a low voice, turning to look at me in the darkness. "That maybe you'd like to try something with me."

"What?" I asked, my hand sliding to the door handle again and tugging on it lightly, just in case. It didn't budge.

"There have been a lot of stories circulating about me and the kinds of things I like to take pleasure from."

I pressed my lips together but I didn't offer a comment. I was aware of the Pegasex rumours...*obviously.*

"So if you and me are gonna work then I guess you'll have to accept the fact that I'm also hopelessly addicted to Pegasus ass according to the latest stories."

Silence stretched. I couldn't see Caleb very well in the dark but I knew he could see me just fine. He would have heard that spike in my heartbeat too. This whole thing was designed to rattle me. But I wasn't going to let myself get rattled.

I bit my lip and leaned towards him slowly, dropping my voice like we were sharing a secret. "Well...maybe when my Order emerges I'll be a Pegasus and I can make all of your fantasies come true."

Caleb locked me in his gaze and his jaw tightened a fraction as he looked at me in the dark. "Would you like that?" he asked in a dangerous voice.

"What?" I breathed, my heart beating a little faster as he continued to look at me like that.

"You wanna be my Pegasus?" he asked, shifting closer to me and catching me by my waist.

He yanked me out of my chair with a surge of his Vampire strength and pulled me over to straddle him. I gasped in surprise as he held me tightly, my heart thundering in fright which I knew he could hear.

"Well?" he prompted, gripping me harder.

My lips parted, unsure what he wanted me to say. I knew he hated that rumour, why was he trying to get me to say I wanted to play a part in it? Why had he brought me all the way up here just to ask me this? Trepidation spilled through my body but I refused to balk.

"You like the idea of me all covered in glitter?" I teased, reaching up to touch his face.

Caleb caught my hand and pinned it to my side. "Maybe the rumours are true," he breathed, his voice dipping from seductive to dangerous. "Maybe I want to whip you with a riding crop with my name printed on it and ride you around like my own personal pony. Maybe I want you to wear a bridal and neigh while I'm screwing you."

My lips parted as I looked at him, searching his navy eyes for some hint of where this was coming from. And suddenly I knew. He'd figured it out. Somehow, he knew it had been me who spread those rumours.

I swallowed as I continued to look at him, wondering if I should just call him out on it, try and get him to see the funny side... But everything about his posture and the way he was holding me said he didn't find this the least bit funny.

I licked my lips slowly and he watched the motion with hunger in his gaze. He might have been pissed as all hell with me but I didn't want to believe he'd hurt me.

"Or *maybe,* I want to play a real round of our usual game," he growled.

My brows pulled together in confusion as he unlocked the doors, the sold thunk echoing in the silence.

"I don't under-"

"It's dark up here, Tory," Caleb snarled, leaning close to my ear. "And there are monsters in the woods. You should probably *run."*

The door swung open beside us and he shoved me out of his lap so that I fell out of the car, catching the doorframe at the last second to stop myself from sprawling in the dead leaves.

"Caleb," I began but he shot out of the car so quickly that my heart leapt in fright.

"Run," he barked, his fangs snapping out and the look in his eyes making me stumble back a step.

I hesitated, looking around at the clearing he'd parked up in. We were in the middle of nowhere, half way up a mountain by the looks of it and there were thick trees all around us. Even if I managed to escape him, I'd be hopelessly lost out here and he'd taken my Atlas from me.

"I don't want to," I said, fighting to hide the tremor of fear in my voice.

Caleb lunged at me and I screamed, throwing my hands up as I cast a huge gust of air at him. He was knocked back and I turned and fled, racing into the trees as fast as I could with terror coursing through my limbs.

Caleb's dark laughter followed me as I ran and I knew in my heart that this was hopeless. He was a fucking Vampire. He could outrun me in a heartbeat and the sound of my feet pounding through the dead leaves was so loud I might as well have been building a fire with my name written in flames and an arrow pointing right at me.

I skidded into a clearing and my sneakers caught on a log hidden beneath the leaves. I hooked it into my grasp without thinking about it and continued to run.

Caleb whooped excitedly as he gave chase and ice splintered through my veins.

I kept running, taking a route downhill in some desperate bid to outpace him.

A force like a battering ram collided with me and I cried out as I was thrown back into a huge tree.

Fire flared to life as I flung it from my palms and Caleb released his grip on me as he lurched aside to avoid getting burned. I swung the branch at him with a scream of defiance and it crashed against the side of his head with enough force to knock him off of his feet.

Caleb snarled as he threw his own magic back at me and vines twisted their way up out of the ground, coiling around my arms and twisting them behind my back.

"Fuck!" Caleb cursed, stalking towards me so that the light of the flames still burning beside us illuminated the blood pissing down his face from the head wound I'd given him. He pressed a hand to the injury, healing it with a grimace before closing in on me again.

I fought to regain the use of my arms but his vines only tightened and with my hands immobilised, I couldn't cast any more magic.

"You hit me with a fucking branch!" Caleb growled, looking down into my eyes.

"You were hunting me like a goddamn psychopath," I spat back.

Caleb stared at me for several long seconds, his chest rising and falling deeply as a frown gripped his features.

He shook his head like he was dismissing some idea then snatched me into his arms before I could say anything else.

We shot back up the hill to his car and he pushed me down roughly to perch on the hood.

Caleb's lips twisted as he looked at me and I fought to calm my panicked breathing as I sat before him, my arms still tied at my back.

"Is this what turns you on then?" I snapped when I couldn't take it anymore. "Terrifying people? It's a long way from glitter and riding crops."

"What's to say I don't like both?" he growled darkly, his eyes narrowing. "Everyone thinks I spend my time chasing after glittering horse assholes. That rumour must have come from somewhere. *Right?*"

I lifted my chin as he moved closer to me, refusing to drop my gaze. Yes we'd started that rumour about him. And no, I wasn't sorry. It was nothing compared to what he and his friends had done to us. I shrugged slowly, like his question was as interesting to me as talking about the weather.

"Didn't you just win the game?" I asked, dropping my voice as I shifted against my restraints, leaning a little closer to him instead of recoiling. "Doesn't that mean you get to bite me now?"

"No, the rumours say I wanna fuck a Pegasus," he reminded me in a growl as he stepped closer too, his knees pressing against mine until I parted them so he could stand between my thighs. "So, *maybe* I need you to play the part of the horsey for me now."

A long beat of silence passed between us and I looked deep into his eyes. He was angry as all hell but there was something else in his gaze too. A kind of plea, like he wanted me to prove something to him. I just didn't know what. But I was willing to push my luck to see if I could find out. Because we'd been playing this game for long enough now. And he should have known that I wasn't going to bow out.

"Well I heard you have a thing for their horns," I breathed, shifting my hips forward so that I was pressed against him. I smiled just a little as I felt his body reacting to mine. "So surely that means you'd want me to shove one up your-"

"No," he snarled, taking hold of my waist between his hands. His grip was tight but not bruising, I was beginning to think he might be backing down a little. "I think what I wanted was a big, plastic Pegasus doll with a hole in its ass to-"

"Don't you already have one though?" I asked, leaning forward so that my lips were almost touching his.

Caleb tightened his grip on my wrist, stopping me. "You wanna come back to my room and watch me screw it then?" he offered in a tone that was all threat.

"Only if you let me film it," I countered, trying to push him towards laughter. If I could just break through this anger then maybe...

"If you wanna make a dirty movie with me then you're gonna have to star in it too," he said, his breath washing over my lips.

"The last time you and your friends filmed me you were trying to kill me," I reminded him.

"That wasn't me."

"You were still there."

Silence hung between us for a long moment and heat built in the space dividing us but neither of us moved to close the distance parting our lips.

"You promised to punish me for that," Caleb murmured eventually.

"And maybe I did," I whispered.

Caleb's hand moved to my face in the dark and I flinched a little at the unexpected touch. He trailed his fingers down my jaw, tipping my chin to the side slowly, exposing my neck to him. My heart was still pounding but the fear was slipping into a thrill, excitement buzzing through my veins. I was toying with a monster and I might have actually wanted him to bite me for once. I needed it. A release to this tension coiling between us.

He leaned in close, running his nose up the arch of my throat and inhaling deeply. "Do you still hate being my Source, Tory?" he asked softly.

"Most of the time," I replied.

"What about now?" His hand slid to grip my ponytail and he tugged it hard enough to make me gasp. The vines fell from my arms and I used my hands to steady myself on the hood of his car.

"I think that right now...I might just like it," I whispered.

Caleb groaned and his fangs snapped out, driving straight into my neck as he continued to hold me tightly. He wasn't gentle with me like he usually was, his anger showing in the depth of his bite and the growl which clawed up the back of his throat.

I moaned as he drank deeply, taking more and more until I began to feel light headed. My hands landed on his shoulders, my fingers biting into his flesh in return for the rough treatment. But I was pulling him closer not pushing him away. My head spun dizzily and for a fleeting moment I wondered what it would be like to die like this. Held in the arms of a beautiful monster...

He finally released me and I sagged back against the hood, blinking at him as a wave of dizziness washed over me.

My body was thrumming with the remains of fear and more than a little desire and I could feel how hard he was between my thighs too.

"You still wanna go to the fair?" Caleb asked, smiling darkly, riding the high of my power.

"Yeah," I replied with a small smile of my own. "I wanna go to the fucking fair."

Caleb leaned forward and kissed me hard. It was punishing, bruising, the taste of my blood coating his tongue and the feel of his skin making heat rise everywhere he touched me. I bowed to his desire as he pinned me in place, feeling the anger burning lower in him with each passing moment. He knew it had been me. But he wanted me more than he wanted revenge. At least for now.

He stepped back, looking down at me with heat in his gaze, healing the bite on my neck with a brush of his fingers.

"Then let's go have some fun."

I offered him a smirk and he left me to slide off of the hood and return to my seat. As soon as the ridiculous door had closed beside me, he started the engine and the headlights blazed to life.

The car shot away down the gravel path and I leaned back into my seat in a bit of a daze. Caleb had taken so much blood and power from me that I felt dizzy with it, but all in all I felt I'd escaped that fairly unscathed. Especially if I'd been right in thinking he knew the truth. Clearly neither of us were going to address it directly. But it seemed like we'd come to an understanding at least. I just had to hope it stayed that way.

DARCY

CHAPTER THIRTY

I sat with an untouched veggie burger on my plate while Diego made his way through his own hamburger.

"You okay?" he asked around a mouthful of meat.

We were under a gazebo which looked over an ice rink and I'd been staring at the couples circling it for a solid ten minutes. Maybe longer.

"Yeah," I said, turning to him. "Sorry I just…" I wasn't sure how to finish that sentence. *I just saw the teacher I screwed kissing another woman and now my heart hurts.*

"We can just go home, if you want?" he asked.

My eyes trailed to the ice rink again and I spotted Tyler twirling Sofia around by the hand. Diego followed my gaze and I checked to see his reaction but his expression didn't give anything away.

"Diego, I did something bad," I said, guilt eating me up.

"What?" he asked, looking to me with a frown.

"I…" I glanced down at my burger. "I helped set Tyler up with Sofia,"

I couldn't bring myself to look at him as silence spanned between us.

Diego rested a hand on mine and I glanced up in surprise, his intensely blue eyes making my heart squeeze. "Because you feel this connection between us?"

"What?" I gasped. "No...I'm sorry. I mean, you're a great friend, Diego."

"Oh."

"I'm sorry about Sofia," I reiterated.

"Well she looks happy," he sighed. "And you're right, we weren't exclusive. I'm not sure she wanted to be anyway. Maybe we're better as friends."

"Like us?" I asked hopefully and he broke a smile.

"Yes, chica." He stood. "How about we take a turn on the Faerris Wheel with some hot fudge?"

"That sounds like heaven." I stood and followed him out of the gazebo.

We were soon queuing for the Faerris Wheel and I gazed up at the large white carriages which slowly revolved above us, finishing the hot fudge we'd bought on the way to it. As we reached the front of the queue, we walked onto the metal platform and I climbed into the carriage as a couple vacated it.

Diego moved to follow but a shadow bashed into him and I gasped in horror as Orion knocked him onto his ass and climbed into his place beside me.

"I need my Source," he barked at Diego as he scrambled upright.

"Hey – no!" I shouted, fury tearing through me. I jumped up to get out but Orion caught the back of my dress, tugging me down into my seat. He locked me in place with one arm and sank his fangs into my throat.

A short scream ripped from my chest, the sound piercing and travelling right across the fair. It wasn't any harder than he normally did it, but it felt like an utter betrayal to do this to me now.

The guy attending the wheel whistled to himself as he casually locked the gate and we moved upwards at an ever-climbing pace.

"Get off of me!" I shoved Orion, trying to force my magic to work, but he had it firmly in his grasp.

He grunted, tugging his fangs free, but not removing his arm where it was locked around my waist. He moved his face into mine, his teeth bared, making real fear push into my veins. In that moment, he was a wild animal and running from him was impossible. We were stuck together for the next twenty minutes and I knew for a fact he'd done this on purpose. He waved his hand to cast a bubble of silence around us and anger pierced my chest.

"This has gone far enough," he snarled, the ferocity in his tone making my heart beat out of rhythm. "You brought him here to piss me off."

My mouth opened as disbelief coursed through me. "You *asked* me to talk to him. And you're not exactly here on your own, Professor," I snapped.

"Lance," he demanded forcefully.

"No," I hissed, trying to unknot his fingers from my dress. "I'm not calling you that because we're not a thing anymore. I do not screw taken guys. If *Fran* doesn't give you what you need in the bedroom, then I'm certainly not going to."

His eyes glittered and a dark smile pulled at his mouth. "She isn't my girlfriend."

"Right. Is that why you rammed your tongue down her throat earlier? Because she's *not* your girlfriend?"

"You're a hypocrite," he pointed out and his smile fell away dramatically. He dragged his thumb across my mouth, wiping it hard and I wriggled to try and stop him, but I was completely cornered.

"What the hell are you doing?" I shoved his arms, but he ignored me, keeping me in place as he pushed his knee into my thigh.

"I'm trying to get Diego Polaris's saliva off of my girl," he growled.

That sentence did so many things to me it was unreal. Anger, rage, delight at the last bit. Then confusion at the last bit too because in what world was I *his* girl? We'd gone from flirting, to screwing like we loved each other, to tearing each other's throats out in the space of a few days. The relationship had expired before it had even started and I was left in the aftermath of a tornado, unsure how to put my life back together.

I pressed a hand to his chest, needing room to breathe but he wouldn't give it to me. The scent of him was blended with Fran's rose perfume and fury reared in me even sharper.

"Diego kissed *me*. I was caught off guard. But you kissed her because you wanted to."

Do not cry, Darcy Vega. Do not fucking cry.

His lips pressed into a tight line and a dangerous energy hummed between us. "You know why I did it."

"Don't do that. You always turn it back on me, expecting me to read your damn mind," I snarled, trying to push him back but if anything he shifted closer. His hand landed on my thigh and I snatched it away. "And don't do *that*."

"Why?"

"Because we're done," I said breathlessly. "It was a one night thing, let's move on with our lives."

"Do we *feel* done to you?" he asked in a baritone voice that made my insides curl like burning paper. He lifted a hand to heal the bite mark which was throbbing on my neck and his gentle touch sent a delicious shiver along my spine. I despised myself for how good that felt and quickly swallowed the emotion away.

The honest answer? No way in hell did this feel done. I was still so angry, but there was a part of me which couldn't cut free from Orion. He was in my blood like poison. Or maybe more like sugar. It was hard to know which. Either way it was probably bad for my health.

He waited for my answer and my heart thumped erratically, practically suffocating me.

"I can't believe you kissed her," I hissed, those treacherous tears threatening to break free.

We were nearly at the top of the Faerris Wheel now and I could see right across the fair. It was beautiful, a sea of lights which constantly flickered and danced. The laughter that carried from below spoke of how much fun everyone was having here and I so wanted to be one of them, instead of feeling like this.

"You brought Diego here on a date to hurt me," Orion said and the tone of his voice said he really was hurt. I mulled over whether that was true. Maybe it was.

"You asked me to talk to him."

"You know I didn't mean take him on a fucking date," he snarled, two chasms of magma opening up in his eyes.

I looked away and he caught my chin, drawing me back to look him in the eye. "When I saw you leaving campus with him, I called Francesca."

My heart thumped painfully hard, full of an ache, a desperate need to believe this was just some stupid game we'd both ravelled ourselves up in. "To get even?" I confirmed.

He nodded. "Biggest fucking mistake of my life. I'd rather bleed than feel what I did when I saw his mouth on yours."

"So you kissed her to get back at me?" I bit at him, trying to mentally erase the image of his hands all over her like that.

"Yes," he said, drawing away a little, his brow furrowed.

Silence passed between us.

"I'll ask you again. Are we done, Blue?" He clutched my arm so tight it almost hurt. We were walking the line of pain and I didn't know if being with him or not being with him would hurt more.

Slowly, I shook my head and his posture relaxed as if I'd told him the world wasn't gonna end. "But maybe we should be. Part of me doesn't want this to be done, but you hurt me."

"You hurt me first." His jaw locked tight and I shook my head at him.

"What I did was *not* on the same level." I glanced away. Since when were we some exclusive couple anyway? Did I really have the right to tell him not to see other women when we'd spent one night together? Maybe I didn't. But hell, maybe I wanted to.

He sighed, reaching out to cup my cheek but I pushed his hand away. Desperation flashed through his eyes. "I'm sorry, okay? I shouldn't have kissed her."

The earnestness of his words made me almost give in. Maybe I *could* get over the Fran stuff but not what had happened to Tory. This whole argument had gotten out of hand. And at the root of it was what he'd done in that cave on the beach.

I nodded stiffly.

"If you want to hurt me in future, use your hands," he said with a dark look. "I think physical pain would be preferable."

"Well I won't stop wanting to hurt you until you apologise for what happened with Darius and Tory," I said. "You never said sorry and that's what breaks me the most. You don't care about what you did." Tears burned my eyes but I blinked them back, cursing myself when I was sure he'd seen them.

"You need an apology, Blue? Fine. I'll give you the best one I can think up." He kissed the corner of my mouth and it burned with promises before he stood, climbed over the gate and jumped.

"Oh shit," I gasped, lurching forward and spotting him landing on the ground below with the aid of his air magic. He headed off into the crowd like he hadn't just action-manned his way off a fifty foot metal wheel and I gazed after him, feeling like I was standing in the wake of a natural disaster.

When the wheel finally descended, I found Diego waiting for me with a scowl on his face. "That vampiro is a rude piece of shit," he muttered. "Are you alright?"

"I'm fine. And he's not a piece of shit," I said on instinct.

He arched a brow at me. "Oh please tell me you don't have some pathetic crush on him, Darcy. That would be tragic."

Heat raced under my skin. My pulse was spiking and a blaze of fire was building in my chest. I bit down on my tongue nearly hard enough to draw blood.

Just say no. Tell him you don't.

Why was it so hard to force the words out? It was just a simple lie. But the way Diego spoke about him made a tigress sit up inside me and lick her lips. I wanted to destroy him for talking about Orion that way. I might have been mad at him, but Diego didn't have the right to talk about him like that. It was as if I had no control over myself for a second. Like a beast really did live in me.

I managed to rein in my anger enough to speak rationally. "I know you don't like him, Diego, but-"

"No buts," he cut me off, his eyes flashing. "I don't just dislike him. I *despise* him. I wish a plague of fucking death on him. In fact, I wish he hadn't survived the battle at the Pitball stadium."

I slapped him so hard I was as stunned as he was as I withdrew my hand. My palm print remained flaring on his cheek and he stared at me with a murderous glint in his eyes. He stepped forward and I stumbled back a step before remembering I was ten times as strong as him. But for half a second, it didn't feel like that, power seeming to radiate from him.

"I thought you were different," he said slowly. "But you're just like your whore of a sister, pining after bastardos who treat you like dirt and who only give you a second look because you'd drop onto your knees for them any time they liked. Es patético." He turned his back on me and walked away into the crowd, seeming to trample on my heart as he left.

My lower lip quivered with rage and it took a long moment for me to pull myself back together. *How dare he say that to me?*

I took out my Atlas, desperate to message Tory so I could find her, but I hesitated. She was probably having a good time with Caleb and I didn't want to ruin that for her. At least one of us should enjoy the fair.

My throat was tight as I walked mindlessly through the crowd, figuring I should probably just catch the shuttle back to Zodiac.

"Pretty laddddy," a woman sang and I spotted her outside a House of Mirrors, the orange walls tall with oddly shaped windows. "Come inside and find out who you truly are," she said enticingly. She wore nothing but a sparkly pink crop top and tiny shorts, a veil covering her mouth and her eyes painted with elaborate make-up. An ethereal tune called from inside the house and she shook her hips in time with it, beckoning me in.

"How much?" I asked, figuring, why not? Might as well try and get my mind off of the shitstorm that was this night.

"For you? Two auras," she said, holding out her hand.

I fished a couple of coins out of my purse, handing them over and she waved a finger at the silver curtain covering the door, drawing it back with a gust of air.

I stepped inside and as the curtain fell behind me, the sound of the fair was completely blocked out. That strange music hung around me as I moved down a dark corridor lit by red lights. At the far end of it was a large mirror with a glowing blue frame. Above it, a word sparkled in silver. *Past.*

As I drew closer, my heart beat harder. I was me before I'd come to Zodiac, standing in my foster father's kitchen. Pete was sitting at the table doing a scratchcard, ferociously rubbing off the silver coating. I stood before the coffee machine, anxiously waiting for it to finish pouring so I could leave. I remembered this day and I almost wanted to walk away before Pete's next words. I couldn't remember them exactly, only the lasting sting they'd caused.

"Fucking lost. Again. Guess I'm stuck with you and your sister a while longer."

Stuck with us. I frowned bitterly. We'd never been wanted anywhere, but this was the hurt of my past. I didn't live there anymore. And that seemed clearer than ever now as I stared at the girl in that memory, clutching the counter with a hopeless expression. I wasn't her anymore. I had hope. I had people who wanted me and I wanted them back.

I turned into the next corridor and the image faded away. I travelled up a ramp, the walls seeming to turn around me in a tunnel, blue lights flashing as I headed toward the next doorway.

I stepped into another corridor, passing a long line of mirrors on the wall. Above them were the words, *who do you want to be?*

Each mirror showed me as something different. I was still me, but my clothes, hair and makeup changed as I passed each one. A laugh fell from my throat as I paused in front of one showing me as a clown. In the next, I twisted through the air and morphed into a beautiful white Griffin. In others I had red hair, black, silver. I was a stripper swinging on a pole, then a warrior with a sword. Finally, I stepped in front of the last mirror and the word *present* glowed above it. I was just me. And I was good with that.

I headed through another curtain and found myself in a room made from mirrored glass. The walls, the floor, the ceiling, all of it was perfectly polished and reflected me endlessly in every direction. I hurried across it, slipping into the next room and finding one final mirror waiting for me. The corridor was lit by low blue lighting and the mirror at the end seemed to be entirely blank.

I walked toward it, eyeing the word *future* above it.

I frowned as flames erupted at the bottom of it, a tangle of blue and red fire. Above, I realised the mirror wasn't blank at all. It pictured the night sky and at the heart of it was a shadowy moon which seemed to burn like embers. The words from the Devil card Astrum had sent to us came to mind.

The answer to your question will be revealed on the Lunar Eclipse.

I had a thousand questions, but I hoped one of the most important ones would come to light tomorrow.

The mirror suddenly shifted into a door and the light brightened. I turned the handle and found myself back outside, the fresh air blowing against my cheeks.

I smiled at the woman attending the attraction and she waved a little creepily as I walked away. *Weird.*

I shivered as I headed along, feeling better after the distraction and deciding to stay a while longer. *Who says I can't have fun on my own?*

I grabbed a hot cocoa from a bar and soaked in the atmosphere, perusing the stands full of trinkets and crystals. *That sonuvabitch Diego. How could he say that about me and my sister?*

My Atlas pinged and I took it out, half hoping Tory fancied meeting up but the message was from Orion.

Lance:

I'm ready to make my apology.
Come to the circus tent in five minutes.

I stuffed my Atlas away with a frown and located a sign pointing toward the tent. I wondered if I should go, but I was too curious not to.

I followed the signs, twisting through the labyrinth of paths toward the circus tent. It loomed on the edge of the fair, a huge dome of purple and red with flashing lights ringing the roof. Fire breathers were gathered outside, shooting colourful displays of flames up toward the sky.

I followed a queue inside and found a ring of stages circling the interior. On each of them was a strange act, from contortionists who wrapped themselves into actual knots, to illusion acts and beautiful dancers who leapt through rings of fire of their own creation.

At the back of the tent, a crowd was gathering and I frowned as I headed that way, searching for Orion. I moved through the throng of bodies, finding a stage with two huge metal chairs beside one another with manacles on the arms and legs.

Above the stage hung a sign reading *The Numb Man* and beneath it was a sparkling crown suspended in a glass box.

A man in a long black coat and nothing but shiny blue shorts underneath it leapt onto the stage, twirling a cane. "Welcome to the Cirque de Sol-Fae! I am your host, Rusty Star. Gather around, we have a daring contestant backstage who wishes to take on The Numb Man!" he cried and a cheer went up from the crowd. At his words, a huge man the size of a small elephant stepped onto the stage, bare chested with his enormous belly hanging over his waistband. His eyes were hollow and his face blank as he took a seat in the metal chair on the left.

A beautiful woman in a gemstone encrusted bikini with a huge pink feather pluming up from the back of her bottoms leapt onto the stage. She tethered the man into the chair with the manacles, locking his wrists and ankles in place with flourishing movements.

"Please give a warm welcome to our fearless contestant, Lance Orion!" Rusty gestured with his cane to the other side of the stage and my mouth fell open as Orion walked onto the platform shirtless with a smirk on his face.

He took a seat in the remaining chair and the girl locked him in place with a wicked smile. He searched the crowd, his gaze latching onto mine and he seemed to relax despite his current situation. I gave him a questioning look but he just smiled wider as the girl stepped away and moved between them to where a huge red lever jutted out of the stage.

"If our contestant can outlast The Numb Man in this dangerous game, he will win our incredible prize. The crown of glory!" Rusty pointed to the glass box above and it lit up in a shower of golden sparks. "The Numb Man has a pain threshold higher than anyone who has ever stepped on this stage. No one has *ever* won the crown, so will our latest contestant be any different?"

Pain threshold?? I looked to Orion, shaking my head, asking, *what the hell are you doing?* with my eyes.

"Are you ready, Diamond?" Rusty asked his assistant and she nodded, taking hold of the lever. He turned back to us with a manic gleam in his gaze.

"Each chair is hooked up to an increasing flow of electricity. Whoever taps out first will lose the game."

Wait - what???

"All you need to do is raise your hand and the electrocution will stop," Rusty said and laughter filled the air as Orion flexed his muscles against the restraints holding him down.

Rusty tittered. "Alright, you can just say the words, Mr Orion."

"You're assuming I'll tap out first," Orion said with a dark grin.

An *oooh* went up from the crowd.

"*Don't,*" I mouthed to him, shaking my head but he ignored me, settling back in his chair like he was about to get a spa treatment.

"We have a very confident competitor, ladies and gentlemen. Let's see how long his confidence lasts," Rusty said with a vicious smile, gesturing to Diamond. "Pull the lever!"

She yanked it back and my heart lurched. Orion winced, his hands curling into fists as the sound of zapping and crackling energy filled the air alongside thundering music.

The Numb Man smiled broadly, having no reaction to the electricity at all.

"Higher!" Rusty commanded and Diamond drew the lever back further.

Orion's jaw tightened and his eyes spoke of pain, but he didn't shout out.

This is crazy!

"Higher!" Rusty called again and Orion finally released a gasp of pain, but still he didn't break. He looked straight at me as his muscles hardened and his shoulders began to shudder.

"You've proved your point!" I yelled, but he didn't call it off.

The Numb Man remained sitting there without even a flicker of pain on his face. Orion was going to damn well die out of sheer stubbornness.

"They don't even hook up the numb guy. It's all a scam," someone said behind me and my heart tumbled in my chest.

"Higher!" Rusty commanded.

Orion roared in pain and panic seized me as I wheeled around to look at the person who'd spoken behind me. A couple of the bikini-clad girls had gathered there to watch. Which meant they worked here, which also meant they goddamn knew that numb guy wasn't hooked up.

"Higher!"

"No!" I shouted, turning back to the stage. Veins were shining in Orion's arms and his chest gleamed with sweat. The Numb Man glanced over at him with a frown like he'd never seen anyone take the game this far. I knew in my heart Orion wasn't going to stop. So I had to do something.

I pushed my way through the crowd, slipping around the back of the stage into the shadows and heading through a curtain. There was no one there so I quickly hunted for a plug to pull so I could stop this madness.

I found what I was looking for and sucked in air as I spotted the plug for the chair which wasn't hooked up.

Numb Man, my ass.

In a moment of madness, I plugged it in. A bellow of pain sounded from the stage and I sprinted back out from behind the curtain, hurrying into the crowd.

"STOP STOP!" The 'Numb' Man cried and Rusty looked around at him in alarm.

"Diamond!" he snapped and she pushed the lever to turn off the electricity. Orion took in a lungful of air, slumping forward, his hands balled up into tight fists.

Diamond hurried to untether The Numb Man and he barged past her off the stage, trembling as he went. She moved to help Orion and I looked around, desperate to go to him, but knowing I couldn't with a whole crowd of people watching.

"Our first ever winner, ladies and gentlemen!" Rusty recovered from his obvious shock and applause rippled through the air.

Orion staggered to his feet, lifting a hand to heal himself and I relaxed as the pain in his posture ebbed away.

Rusty cast magic at the glass box to bring it down, opening it with a reluctant expression and holding it out to Orion. "Congratulations," he said through a smile that was so obviously false it made me hiccough a laugh.

Orion grinned, taking it. "And here I was thinking this thing was rigged."

"Never," Rusty said, clearing his throat.

Orion headed off the stage and I moved through the crowd to try and find him. A line of teachers walked into the tent and I paused, turning the opposite way, my heart fluttering anxiously.

My Atlas pinged and I took it out.

Lance:

Do you want a ride home?

My heart beat frantically as Washer stepped past me, making a beeline for a bunch of the performers in bikinis.

I tapped out a quick reply, frowning as Washer's hand landed on one of their bare backs.

Run for your life girls.

Darcy:

Are you freaking crazy???

Lance:

Yes. For you ;)
Come with me.

I tapped my foot anxiously, angry but desperate to see him too.

Darcy:

Okay, where should I go?

Lance:

Behind the tent is a fence that borders the road.
Wait on the other side of it.

I headed out of the tent, chewing on my lower lip as I circled around to the back of it, finding a high wooden fence at the edge of the field. No lights shone this way and I was pretty sure I was safe from being seen.

I gazed up at the top and pushed air out of my palms, propelling myself over it. I landed on the street on the other side, stumbling only a little and smiling at how well I'd managed it.

The street was quiet, the opposite side of the road leading into a thick woodland. No streetlights were in sight and my breath clouded before me like a ghost in the moonlight.

It was a few minutes before headlights flared and a fancy red Faerarri pulled up beside me. The windows were blacked out but it was pretty obvious who owned this car. The passenger window slid down and Orion leaned across to look at me.

I slapped the side of the door, my anger pouring out. "How could you do that? You nearly gave me a heart attack."

"To be fair, I nearly gave myself a heart attack, Blue, so can we call it even?"

I shook my head, blinking back those damned tears which kept coming for me tonight. I kicked the front wheel and his brows pulled together. "Can you stop attacking my car? She doesn't like it."

I sniffed, turning my back on him and staring up at the moon. Tears blurred it into a fuzzy white ball of cotton wool and I tugged down my sleeve to dab them away. A shadow filled my vision as Orion sped in front of me, his expression taut.

"I didn't mean to upset you," he said, sounding lost. "I don't apologise very often. It's not a very Fae thing to do. Did I not do it right?"

I smacked his chest as another tear spilled over. He caught it at the edge of my chin, wiping it away with his thumb.

"You could have just said the words," I whispered with another sniff and he gave me a hopeful grin, inching closer into my personal space.

"I'm sorry." He pressed his hands either side of me on the car and my breathing hitched.

"You smell like her," I murmured.

"Then make me smell like you," he commanded and I caught his lapels, dragging him down to meet my mouth. Our kiss tasted of tears and desperation. The hurt between us blurred in the middle then faded to nothing like the rain had come to wash it away. Forgiveness was never easy, but the knot inside me finally came loose and I could breathe again.

"Come on," he said, stepping back. "This evening is still salvageable."

"I wish we could stay at the funfair together." I frowned.

"Well...I hear another funfair has popped up in my bedroom for the night," he teased.

A laugh broke free of my throat and Orion grinned, pushing a lock of hair behind my ear.

"If you want to go back and find your friends, I get it." He squeezed my hand and I interlaced my fingers with his.

"Hm, well I quite like the sound of this other funfair. Is there a rollercoaster?"

"No but there's a slip and slide?" he offered.

I laughed as Orion tugged the door open and I dropped into the seat. I put the window up as he shut the door and he shot into the driver's seat at speed.

Quiet fell between us.

The heavy thump of my heart was almost loud enough for me to hear let alone him with his super-sonic ears. I wet my mouth as he drove off down the road, wrangling my emotions.

"Where's Fran?" I asked lightly.

He chuckled. "You know, she'd really kill you if she heard you calling her that."

I shrugged. *She can try.*

"She got called into work. Apparently there was a Nymph sighting in east Tucana. The anonymous caller was very insistent," he said, tilting his head innocently and my mouth fell open.

"You didn't?"

"I did." He barked a laugh. "Where's Polaris?" he asked, his voice dropping as he barely concealed the bitterness in his tone.

"We had an argument," I said tersely, a knife twisting in my gut at the memory.

"About?" he inquired, reaching over and placing his hand on my knee. Even through my pantyhose I felt the blazing heat of his skin and my body responded with a surge of adrenaline.

"You," I admitted.

He shot me a concerned look. "He doesn't know anything, does he?"

"Of course not, he just thinks I have a crush on you and that I'm pathetic for doing so. And a whore apparently."

His grip tightened on my knee and sparks skittered beneath my skin.

"Fuck that kid, I'll tear him a new one the next time I see him," he snarled.

"I might join you in that." I rested my hand on his and he wrapped his palm around mine.

"You're freezing." He released a wave of warm air that rushed over me and reminded me of the other night when I'd shown up soaking wet at his house.

Orion turned down a dark road where the trees leaned overhead, creating a long tunnel for what seemed like miles.

"So have you forgiven me now?" he asked with amusement in his voice.

"Technically you owed the apology to my sister," I pointed out and he gave me an incredulous look.

"By the stars, am I going to have to electrocute myself again for Tory Vega?"

I laughed. "You know that numb guy wasn't hooked up to the mains right? Well, he wasn't until I hooked him up myself."

"What?" he gasped.

"Yep." I squeezed his fingers.

Orion pulled over to the side of the road and my brows shot up as he dragged me forward and slammed his lips against mine. I was half choked by the seatbelt and he quickly released it, my heart rate climbing as his tongue pushed into my mouth. I clambered into his lap with a surge of excitement, straddling him and clawing my hands into his hair as I devoured his kiss. His hands slid under my dress and I urged him on by lifting my hips, lost to how much I wanted him.

A deep growl emanated from his throat as he found his way barred by my pantyhose. He ripped a hole in them between my thighs and I sucked in a breath of surprise.

"Orion!" I laughed but my laughter turned into a moan as he found his way into my panties and pushed his fingers inside me. "You owe me a new pair," I said breathlessly.

"I'll get you a whole new wardrobe if you make that noise again."

"What noise?" I panted and he pumped his fingers harder, drawing a needy moan from my lips.

"That one," he grunted, shifting his free hand between us to undo his jeans.

I arched upwards to give him room and my head banged against the roof. We both laughed and he removed his hand from my pantyhose, tugging my dress over my head.

"Let's get rid of these." He tore my pantyhose in half and I gasped as he peeled them off my legs.

"Hey, how about we tear some of *your* clothes?" I tugged at his shirt and he caught my wrists with a mischievous grin.

His eyes travelled down my near naked body and the lacy red underwear I wore while sucking on his lower lip. "I've missed this." He kissed my collar bone and tingles rushed beneath his lips. "And this." He curled a lock of my hair around his finger and brought that to his lips too. "And these." He squeezed my breasts and I giggled. "Hm...you're missing something though."

"What?" I frowned.

He reached behind his seat and produced the crown he'd won at the fair, placing it on my head. I smiled so wide my cheeks hurt.

"Better," he said, his eyes becoming hooded as he rested his hands on my thighs and drew me closer.

"If you go around placing crowns on my head, you're going to be in trouble," I teased and his mouth skewed.

"Well let's not tell anyone then," he said, leaning in to kiss my neck.

I started unbuttoning his shirt, aching for the feel of his flesh against mine. Our movements grew more frantic, his kisses turning to bites, his fingers pinching, while I clawed at his chest to get the buttons open and finally pushed his shirt over his athletic shoulders.

He tugged my bra down to free my right breast, his mouth encasing my hardened nipple and sending pleasure shuddering through me. A tight ball of need grew in the pit of my stomach and I rolled my hips over his crotch, his arousal bulging against my panties. He groaned appreciatively, sucking harder against my sensitised flesh.

I lifted up on my knees to free him from his pants and my ass bashed into the steering wheel, setting the horn off.

I snorted a laugh and Orion tugged me forward by the hips again to stop the noise.

"This is way more difficult than I expected," I joked and he grinned devilishly at me.

"Definitely worth it though." He freed himself from his boxers, pushing my panties aside and all amusement fell away as he guided my hips forward.

I rested my forehead to his, inhaling as he pushed into me. He hissed between his teeth as I lowered onto him, moaning as he filled me up inch by inch.

I started riding him and he chased my mouth for kisses as I writhed on his lap, delighting in the incredible feelings his body delivered me. His fingers dug into my hips, pushing me down on him in a glorious rhythm. I rolled my neck, bracing my hands on his shoulders as I took what I so desperately needed from his flesh.

"Don't fight with me again," he demanded, his teeth raking against my ear.

"Don't give me a reason to." I sank my nails into his shoulders, making him groan and thrust harder between my legs. One of my knees banged against the parking brake and the other slammed into the door, but I didn't care about the bruises. I'd take all of them in payment for this bliss.

My hips quickened to meet his and we fell into a sweaty, breathless tangle of limbs and wanton kisses. He wrapped one hand in my hair and tugged hard enough to hurt. "That's for Polaris," he growled as I yelped.

I scraped my nails down his chest so hard I drew blood. "That's for Fran."

He looked down in surprise, then released a breathless laugh. "I like you angry."

"Let's not make a habit of it though," I panted.

"Deal," he groaned as he pushed into me again.

I pressed one hand to the window, my spine straightening as an urgent pressure built between my thighs. Orion's hand rode the curve of my spine before forcing me onto him, finishing me. Pleasure cascaded through me like an exploding rainbow and I clung to him as he drove harder and faster into me, finding his own release, grunting my name in the back of his throat.

My legs trembled as I came down from my high, slumping against him as I lost all the energy in my body. I rested my head against his shoulder, our breaths burning hot, leaving a fog on the windows around us.

He trailed his fingers up and down my bare thighs, my skin overly sensitive to him. He tilted my chin up, kissing me so sweetly it seemed to coat my lips in sugar. My hand rested against his chest where his heart beat like the wings of a powerful bird and I smiled at the feel of this formidable man struggling for breath because of me.

I climbed off him into my seat, finding the crown in the footwell where it had fallen off at some point. We both dressed in silence but we kept catching each other's eye and sharing grins.

When I was decent – apart from my lack of pantyhose– Orion restarted the engine and headed on down the road.

"So did you get any information from Polaris during your *date*?" he asked.

"You're never going to let that go are you?" I mocked.

"It just fucks me off that you can go out in public with *him* and not me."

"Well that's how it is," I sighed, turning to gaze out of the steamy window beside me. I painted a grumpy face on it and wrote Orion above it.

He glanced over, breaking a smile. "Is that what I look like to you?"

"Not quite." I added angry eyebrows and fangs, turning to grin cheekily at him.

He laughed and I smiled satisfactorily.

"Diego didn't say much about his uncle, just that he's an asshole. And that his mother and father go off with him sometimes to help him with his 'work'." I shrugged. "Is that useful?"

Orion remained quiet for a moment. "Yes it gives me a couple more Fae to look into. Much as it pains me to say it, I'd appreciate if you keep spending time with him. See what else he'll say about them. But no dates."

"Well that's gonna be pretty difficult as I'm majorly pissed at him and I'm guessing he is at me too."

"What's he pissed at you for?"

"I slapped him," I revealed.

"Good," he growled. "But he deserves more than that for calling you a whore."

"Actually...I slapped him *before* he said that." I twisted my fingers into my skirt as rage burned inside me at the memory.

"Why?" Orion asked.

"He said he wished you'd died when the Nymphs attacked," I forced out, my throat closing up.

Orion's grip tightened on the wheel. "I'm going to kill him."

"You can't. He'll know I told you. And I didn't exactly deny that I have a thing for you, if you go after him he might figure out there's something between us."

"What kind of thing do you have for me?" He shot me a mischievous glance.

"It will sound crazy," I said slowly.

"I like crazy. Did you not get the memo when I tried to cook myself earlier?"

"Promise you won't laugh?" I asked, heat invading my cheeks.

"On the stars."

I nodded, looking out of the window so I didn't have to see his reaction when I told him. "When we were in the battle and you were about to die, I felt compelled to save you. Like...if I didn't a part of me would die too. And ever since then, that part of me is getting stronger like it's become this tangible thing that lives in me. I've never been a jealous person before but when I see you with Francesca it's like I turn into an animal with nothing but basic instincts." My cheeks burned hotter and I didn't dare look at Orion's face, unsure why I was baring my soul to him right then. I rarely trusted anyone enough to spill my heart out to them, but I always wanted to with him. "I told you it was crazy."

He took my hand, winding his fingers between mine and pressing his mouth to the back of my knuckles. I chanced a look his way and my heart pounded as I found nothing but happiness in his eyes. Then he said six words that made my heart shine like the moon. "Good, because I feel it too."

CALEB

CHAPTER THIRTY ONE

I guided my car down the road with half an eye on Tory in the seat beside me as she fixed her damn lipstick like we hadn't just had the craziest fucking argument of my life on the side of a mountain. Did anything ever faze that girl? Or had she really just been through so much shit in her life that what had just happened between us wasn't even a big deal to her?

I didn't know. And I couldn't figure it out. She was a closed book and it drove me mad. Girls usually chased *me* but with her I honestly felt like she wasn't even interested half the time. Which didn't make sense because I was goddamn hilarious and the sex was fucking mind blowing so what else did she even want?

Her window was open and she still hadn't put her seatbelt on. What did she have against seatbelts? I swear the girl had more mysteries in her travel preferences than I had in my whole life.

We turned towards the fair and the sidewalks slowly filled with people. I flicked the button beside me to close her window and she cast a glance my way out of the corner of her eyes, her fingers flexing like she wanted to hit the button to drop it again instantly. But if she didn't want her face plastered all over tomorrow's Celestial Times then she was better off hidden behind the blacked out windows.

I drove right past a no vehicles sign and kept going beyond the crowds of people walking into the fair on foot until I turned right alongside the gates where the other Heirs' cars were already parked. A security guard eyed my car with disapproval, his lips set in a thin line but he didn't make any attempt to come and tell me to move it. If he wanted me to, he'd have to make me and he knew he wasn't strong enough to do that.

"Full disclosure, the press will have recognised my car. Do you wanna pose for photos or let me carry you the hell away from them?" I asked, turning to look at Tory as I cut the engine.

She looked out through the tinted glass and I followed her gaze. Sure enough I spotted several paparazzi with cameras eyeing the car hopefully already.

"Well as the press seem to think I'm a sex addict it might not look good for you to be seen with me," she commented. "They'll think you're my latest conquest."

"I am," I said with a grin which drew a laugh from her. "Does that mean you're accepting my offer of a ride?"

"I guess so." Tory looked at me, her gaze trailing down to my chest as she pursed her lips.

I looked down too and cursed as I spotted the bloodstains all over my white t-shirt. The girl had hit me really damn hard with that branch. It was pretty hot.

"Kinda looks like you're a messy eater," she teased. Her fingers brushed her neck absentmindedly where I'd bitten her, sending a zip of energy straight through my body to my dick.

I cleared my throat, looking in the back of the car like I might find something in the tiny space between the seats to change into. I spotted my Pitball jacket and hooked it into my grasp, shrugging it on and zipping it up to cover the bloodstains. I found her Atlas down there too and handed it back to her without mentioning the whole *I snatched it like a psycho* thing from earlier.

The navy jacket was lined with silver stripes and my name was stamped across the back of it in shining silver letters. It was hardly subtle but I was always recognised wherever I went anyway so it didn't make much difference.

"You look like an extra from Grease," Tory said, smirking at me.

"You got something against being my Sandy?" I asked, unclipping my belt as I leaned over her to open her door.

She snorted a laugh as I hooked my arms around her waist, not giving that a response. But I was fairly sure that snort meant she didn't see me as much of a Danny. *Fair point.* He never kidnapped Sandy and drained her of her blood up a mountain like a serial killer. Of course Sandy never would have been able to handle the kind of man who did that so I guessed Tory wasn't much of a Sandy either. Aside from that leather jacket and tight jeans, pity they weren't leather too...

The door opened and I leapt out of the car with Tory's arms around my neck and her warm body against my chest.

I used my Vampire speed to shoot straight through the gates, tossing a wedge of auras at the kiosk to cover our entrance fee before the paparazzi could get any shots of us. I dove into the crowd, speeding between vendors and rides until I spotted Seth, Darius and Max moving towards the log ride.

I came to a halt a few meters away, calling out to them to let them know I was here.

Tory slid out of my arms, cast a single look at the guys and turned her back on them before walking away.

All three of them tensed, glaring at me with questions in their eyes which were gonna need answering before I could spend the evening with Tory.

I held a finger up at the guys and darted after Tory, catching her hand and tugging her to a halt. My gaze hooked on her lips which she'd painted blood red and I had to resist the urge to kiss her.

"I need to talk to the other Heirs for a sec, wait for me, yeah?"

"Sure," she replied sweetly. Too damn sweetly. "I'll just have a look at some of the stands."

I narrowed my gaze on her for a moment but I couldn't figure out her angle so I pressed a kiss to her cheek before heading back over to the other Heirs.

"Nice job there, Cal, looks like you really scared the shit out of her in the mountains," Max said sarcastically as I stopped in front of them.

I'd known this was coming when I backed out of the plan to scare a confession out of her and leave her up that mountain on her own. It hadn't been a part of the plans we'd been making for after The Reckoning, but I'd been so angry about the Pegasex bullshit that I'd insisted on breaking things off with her and I'd wanted her to know exactly why too. The other Heirs hadn't put up much of an argument against it and Darius had been all for it. Which wasn't a surprise because he'd made it clear that me hooking up with Tory pissed him off something chronic and he'd obviously been pleased I was going to call time on it. Except now I wasn't. And one look at his face let me know he wasn't fucking happy about it.

That had absolutely been my plan right up until I'd gotten her up there and looked her in the eyes. I thought she'd crumble when I pushed her. I thought she'd cry or beg or...something. But she just stared me in the face and lied. She didn't even bother to lie well. She knew I'd caught her out and she just owned it. Pushing back at me and daring me to do something about it or let it go. And it was so fucking hot that I'd chosen option B. I didn't know what it was about Tory Vega, but I was fast becoming addicted to it.

"Yeah well..." I glanced over at Tory as she started talking to some girl selling sparkling balloons shaped like various different Order forms. "I took her up there and did what I said but-"

"But then she started sucking your dick, right?" Seth asked with a smirk.

Darius growled at him and I laughed.

"No. She wouldn't admit it," I said. "And I thought about leaving her up there in the dark and I just didn't want to do it. We need to make sure they don't claim their throne, but we don't have to be total assholes in the process. And if I forget the fact that she's a Vega then I don't have any reason not to keep seeing her," I said, knowing the words would damn me but fuck it, it was the truth.

"But she *is* a Vega," Darius snapped like it was the only thing that even mattered. And maybe it was. Or maybe it should have been.

"Yeah. Well I'm an Altair. And I don't do what I'm told by anyone, so you can save your lecture," I snarled back.

"Are you sure you know what you're getting into with her?" Max asked, shifting closer to me. "That's not just lust you're feeling anymore."

Darius growled again and Max shifted his attention to him, his eyebrows drawing together sharply.

"That girl is trouble," Max said darkly, his eyes whipping between me and Darius as he fed on the emotions bubbling around us.

"Pfft, maybe I like trouble. It doesn't mean I'm going to forget what's important to us. Or Solaria," I said firmly and Max nodded, relaxing as he read my emotions on that too.

"So keep screwing her if that's what you want," Seth said with a shrug, pushing a hand through his long hair. "Just so long as it doesn't change anything else."

Darius looked like he was fighting hard not to add anything on the subject and I decided against baiting him on it. If he'd wanted a shot at Tory then I wasn't what was standing in his way; he was the one who had made her hate him like she did. And if he had some other reason to object to what I chose to do then it was up to him to say it to me or not.

"It won't," I replied firmly. "The Reckoning's tomorrow anyway, chances are she won't make it through. Even if she does we've got better plans to put the Vegas in their place than me breaking her heart."

Seth snorted with amusement. "I don't think there was ever much danger of you managing that," he said, nodding towards something over my shoulder.

Tory had just stepped forward to take her turn at the Siren kissing booth. The guy who pulled her into his arms wasn't wearing a shirt and he was built like a tank. He started saying something to her which made her laugh loudly enough for us to hear it. She hadn't kissed him yet and I had no intention of letting it happen either.

"Can't she fight off a Siren lure yet?" I snapped as I stalked towards her with the other Heirs in tow. Irritation slid beneath my skin that she hadn't even learned to keep up a basic mental shield like that.

"He's not using a lure on her," Max said casually and I snapped around to him with a frown.

"What do you mean?" I demanded.

"I *mean*, your little Vega chose to go up there without him needing to use any power on her at all," Max said with a smirk. "Maybe she's more likely to break *your* heart than the other way around."

I swore at him as I shot forward to stop that Siren asshole from touching her but Darius had made it there first.

"Back off," he snarled at the kissing booth douchebag and the Siren instantly did as he was told, shifting away from Tory like she was contagious.

Darius caught Tory's arm and tugged her away from the stand while she tried to claw his fingers off of her. He moved her to stand before him and she shoved his hand off of her aggressively.

"What the hell do you think you're doing?" she spat, glaring at him with so much venom in her gaze that I halted my advance on them.

"Stopping you from embarrassing yourself and ending up all over the press tomorrow in a story about how you have to pay for kisses as well as having a sex addiction," he replied scathingly. "You're welcome."

"I was asking him about which charity the kissing booth is raising money for," she bit back instantly. "Not paying for a fucking kiss. Unlike *you*, I don't just pay my way through life, living off of Daddy's credit card. But I do have a stipend that's stupidly generous and a fucking conscience and I was trying to do something decent. Which I guess you wouldn't know jack shit about."

Darius cast a look over his shoulder at the sign announcing the fact that the kissing booth was raising funds for a charity and I shifted uncomfortably as I read it too. *Missing Moon Orphanage.*

Tory and her sister were orphans twice over and even though I'd never gotten any details from her about their childhood, I knew it wasn't all sunshine and roses.

When we turned back to Tory she was already gone.

"Nice work, man," I snapped at Darius as I pushed past him to chase her down.

"You were gonna punch that asshole too," he called after me, but I ignored him. Partly because he was pissing me off lately. Mostly because he was right and I was just lucky Darius had gotten there first.

I pulled my Atlas from my pocket as I followed her and sent a quick email to the family lawyer, getting her to set up a donation to the Missing Moon Orphanage from my trust fund and asking her to send me a confirmation ASAP.

I caught Tory as she drew close to the hook-a-duck stand and turned her around to face me.

"You have some really annoying friends too, you know," I said before she could say anything.

"Oh yeah?" she asked, rolling her eyes. "I bet you can't even name any of my friends."

"Darcy," I said quickly and her lips twitched with amusement.

"Name five more and I'll let you off the hook for your asshole associations."

"Come on, we both know you don't have five more friends. You're not that likeable," I teased and I got a full smile in response for that.

"Three then and you can name your prize," she offered.

"Grus," I said instantly, smiling widely.

"I'm gonna want a full name for the prize."

"*Geraldine* Grus," I said enthusiastically. I couldn't even really claim to dislike that girl, she was a goddamn machine on the Pitball pitch and at least she was consistent with her beliefs. She was an open book. Sure, it was set to a page I didn't like much but at least I knew she wasn't a conniving asshole like a lot of the Fae I knew. With her you knew exactly where you stood without having to second guess it.

"That's one," Tory conceded.

"And, errr..." I pushed a hand through my hair but found the curls sticky with drying blood as I did. I dropped my hand irritably, hoping it wasn't noticeable. I'd wiped the blood off of my face in the car but it wasn't going to come out of my hair without a shower. "You know...the little one with the nice ass and the pixie cut. I wanna say she's called...Sorange?"

"Not even at all," Tory laughed and I knew I had her again.

I pushed my advantage and caught her hand, wrapping my fingers between hers as I pulled her into a walk. I could feel the guys watching us but I couldn't deal with them now. I had my sights set on Tory Vega tonight and I wasn't letting her slip away.

"Okay, that's two," I said, ignoring the eye roll I got for counting Sorange as a win. "Aaaaand...Hat Boy."

Tory gave me a full laugh for that one and I turned towards her, capturing her lips with mine before she could stop me.

She didn't resist much, her lips moulding to mine as she gave in to the heat between us and I pressed her back against the hook-a-duck stand. Her lips parted for me and I wrapped my hands around her waist beneath her leather jacket, the soft skin of her stomach warm against my palms.

A kid swore at us as I nudged him and accidentally made him lose his duck which quacked angrily as the spell released it and it splashed away.

Tory pressed me back and I sighed dramatically as she moved away from me, but she let me take her hand again as I fell into step beside her.

I glanced over my shoulder and found Darius scowling at us - no surprises there - Max had folded his arms while he watched us and Seth mimed striking a whip at me. I wasn't even sure I could deny it at this particular moment. Tory Vega was getting under my skin and I wasn't sure I could do much to stop it. I shrugged at the other Heirs like I didn't give a shit what they thought which was mostly true anyway, and drew Tory away from them into the crowd.

"So what do I get for my prize?" I asked casually as I eyed the brightly coloured stands and vendors peddling all kinds of strange and wonderful things.

Tory was drinking everything in with wide eyes and a smile played around her lips which actually made her look kind of innocent for once.

"You just had your prize," she said dismissively.

"You would have let me kiss you anyway!" I protested.

"Not likely," she teased.

Her eyes fell on a guy selling brightly coloured sticks of cotton candfae and I tugged her towards him knowingly. I ordered her one and tossed the guy a twenty when he asked for two auras, drawing Tory away again without bothering to wait for the change.

Tory raised an eyebrow at me as she took a bite of her cotton candfae which was changing from pink to blue to lilac as she held it. "Why did you do that?" she asked me, casting a look back at the vendor who was grinning like that tip had just made his day.

I shrugged. "That money doesn't mean anything to me, it makes him happy. Why not?"

"Aaand?" she pushed, her eyes picking me apart like I was just so damn easy for her to read.

I sighed. "*And* it doesn't hurt my reputation for people to think of me as generous. When I'm sitting on the Celestial Council one day and I make some choice that that guy's friends are pissed about he'll be there saying, 'I met Caleb Altair once, he was damn decent - gave me an eighteen dollar tip on some cotton candfae."

"There it is," she said with a satisfied smirk, taking another bite.

"It's still a nice thing to do," I protested. "Ulterior motives aside."

"Sure," she agreed like she didn't agree or maybe she did, I couldn't fucking tell and she was already walking away again.

My Atlas pinged in my pocket and I pulled it out, grinning at the email from the family lawyer.

"I thought I'd make up for the whole kissing booth thing back there," I said, holding out the email for her to look at.

She raised an eyebrow as she read it. "You donated ten thousand auras to the orphanage?" she asked, her lips parting in surprise.

A grin was tugging at my lips in anticipation of what she'd do next but instead of the hug, tears of joy and making out sesh which would undoubtedly lead to me getting her back in my bed again tonight, she frowned at me.

"Why?" she asked warily. "What exactly is it that you want from me?"

"I..." I pushed a hand into my hair, unsure how this seemed to have had the opposite effect to what I'd wanted. "I thought it would make you happy."

Tory looked at me for a long moment, twirling the cotton candfae between her fingers. "You know what I like about you, Caleb?" she asked like she was asking me a math problem.

"Everything?" I suggested.

Tory rolled her eyes. "I like it when you don't try so hard. I don't need you to make grand gestures or buy me sweets. I'm not your girlfriend and I don't want to be."

Ouch.

"So why don't you just save the bullshit for a nice girl who needs hearts and flowers because that's not me. I'm not impressed by shit like that."

"So what are you impressed by?" I asked, needing to know more than I liked to admit.

"I just want someone to make my heart beat faster," she said in a low voice that had me drawing closer to her as I looked into her dark eyes. "To challenge me and make me laugh and push back against my bullshit. I want to be forced out of my comfort zone and I want to feel excited, exhilarated, *afraid.* But not just because you're an asshole. Because I want to feel alive."

"So not much then?" I confirmed teasingly. This girl was going to be the death of me. I couldn't resist that glint in her eye or the challenge in her tone and I was pretty sure she knew it.

"No, not much." She smirked as she finished her cotton candfae and released a blaze of fire magic in her palm to destroy the wooden stick it had been wrapped around.

"Fuck it then, come on." I snatched her hand and this time I didn't try to hold onto it all sweet and innocent, I just tugged her through the crowd behind me.

The Fairy Fair was the same every year and I knew by now where all the best parts of it were found. We wound between countless people and I dragged Tory on when she spotted Geraldine Grus and her Ass idiots. She waved at them but didn't try very hard to get away from me and I smirked to myself, knowing I had her attention again.

A shadow stepped into my path and I scowled as Hat Boy himself set his eyes on my date.

"Are you okay, chica?" he asked, catching Tory's other arm so that she stopped to speak to him.

"Yeah," she said brightly. "Caleb's just showing me around the fair. Where's Darcy?"

Hat Boy's gaze darkened slightly and he shrugged. "She blew me off. Turns out our date didn't mean as much to her as it did to me."

"Speaking of dates," I interrupted loudly. "We were actually-"

"What happened?" Tory asked, cutting me off and my irritation grew a notch as she chose to give this loser her attention instead of me.

"We were having a really good time, we even kissed and then-"

"You what?" Tory gasped.

I growled as he continued to dominate her attention and lifted her wrist to my lips, pressing a kiss against her skin. Her heart beat a little harder and I smirked as I moved closer, kissing her neck instead.

"Yeah she..." Hat Boy paused as I wrapped my arms around Tory's waist and she put a half assed effort into batting me off. "Can we go somewhere to talk in private?"

"Oh, ummm. Me and Caleb were kinda-"

"Please, chica," he begged and I moved behind Tory, dragging her body back to press against mine as I kept my arms around her.

"I think she's made her choice," I growled, scowling at him. "Tory doesn't wanna spend her evening with you any more than her sister did."

"*Caleb,*" she hissed but I ran my fingers down her sides and a laugh escaped her too.

"Forget it. Eres una puta como tu hermana." He turned and started walking away but I flicked my fingers at him, making the earth tremble beneath his feet so that he almost fell.

Tory sucked in a breath in surprise but I ignored her. "I'm pretty sure you just called my date a whore," I growled.

He looked around at us again, his face paling but he didn't deny it.

Tory looked at her so-called friend for a long moment then just shook her head. "I just wanna enjoy the fair," she said, glancing around at me. "Leave it."

Hat Boy looked between the two of us with anger swimming in his gaze but his power was so low he wasn't even worth my time. "You heard her. Fuck off," I snapped.

He scurried away from us and I grinned as I tried to kiss her again but she pushed me off.

"You're such a dick," she said halfheartedly.

"Isn't that why you like me?" I challenged.

"No. I like you because you're half decent in bed."

A shit eating grin bit at my cheeks at that comment. "I'll work on convincing you of the other half tonight." I promised, snatching her hand again so that we could get back to our date.

"Not likely," Tory muttered but she let me drag her on with a smile playing around her lips.

We made it to the big, dark tower in the centre of the fair and Tory tipped her head back, looking up at the sign above the entrance which read *House of Horrors*.

Her eyes lit with interest and I grinned at her as I headed towards the queue. Tory slowed down as we reached the back of it, but I tugged on her hand to keep her moving. I was a Celestial Heir; I didn't queue.

Tory gave me a look that said I was an entitled prick and I smirked, letting her know I agreed.

We reached the front of the queue without anyone daring to voice a complaint and I pulled a few aura notes out of my pocket, pressing them into the hand of the guy running it.

"Make sure we get the full experience," I said to him in an undertone and he smiled knowingly, casting a look Tory's way.

She was paying more attention to the big fake spider hanging over the entrance than she was to us though so I wasn't sure if she'd heard me. Either way, if she wanted to feel alive, I was gonna deliver.

The guy handed over four bracelets and I slipped two over my wrists before turning and doing the same to Tory.

"What's this for?" she asked, eyeing the silver bangles.

"They stop you from casting magic in case you panic," I said. "It can get kinda intense in there and they don't want anyone accidentally burning the place down."

"So we're just leaving ourselves vulnerable?" she asked slowly.

"Hardly," I teased. "The bangles slip right back off again. They aren't FIB manacles, just a backup in case of panic. But if you're afraid..."

Tory straightened her spine at that insinuation and shook her head, making her high ponytail swing back and forth.

"I'm pretty sure you're the one clinging onto my hand like the sky might come crashing down if you let go of me," she countered.

"Let's see if you're still feeling so brave on the other side," I teased.

The door opened for us and we stepped inside, walking over creaking floorboards as I released my grip on Tory's hand and let her go ahead of me.

She didn't hesitate and I followed her silhouette in the darkened space as creepy music came from speakers hidden somewhere. I resisted the urge to sharpen my eyesight with my Vampire gifts, letting the dark press in on me so that I could enjoy the House of Horrors the same way as her.

As we headed down the long corridor, something brushed against my ankle and I almost flinched.

Tory gasped, falling still a few paces in front of me before stumbling back a step and bumping into my chest.

"There's something in here," she breathed, her heart beat spiking a little just as another small body scuttled over my sneaker.

I only offered a dark laugh as I nudged her to get her moving again. The summoning room always gave me the creeps but I wasn't going to let it show. I wanted to see how she coped when she realised we were surrounded by rats.

Tory headed further into the dark space, her pace slower now as she tried to figure out what was going on and I followed a few steps behind.

A high pitched squeak came from our right and she stilled. She was nearing the centre of the room now and any moment-

Tory stepped forward and the panel beneath her feet flipped up, revealing the pale glow of a huge summoning crystal. The second it was revealed, the rats went wild, flooding towards it from everywhere, scampering over our feet, brushing against our legs, dropping down from the pipes and beams which ran along the ceiling.

Tory screamed and started running, darting towards the doorway which fell open ahead of us, allowing red light to pour into the room.

I chased after her, flinching as a rat fell onto my shoulder and dislodging it as we raced through to the red lit room.

"Were those real *rats*?" Tory demanded, swiping at her body like they could still be crawling over her.

I laughed as she shuddered in disgust. "Yeah, they summon them there, I hear they're nice, clean rats though - no plague carriers."

She gaped at me like I was insane but before she could say anything else, the door to the rat room snapped shut and the floor beneath our feet began to tremble.

Flames sprang to life beside us and Tory spun towards them in surprise. More fire licked along the ceiling then to our left, but this room didn't seem to offer any fear for her and she just looked around at the magic curiously. After seeing her performance in her Fire Trial I wasn't that surprised that she wasn't afraid of the flames but as she stepped towards them with her hand held out, I quickly shot forward to stop her.

"What are you doing?" I demanded, holding her back as her fingers danced close to the flames. We'd all seen them walk through fire like it was nothing during that trial but I'd assumed it was more to do with their magic than them actually being fire-proof. People weren't just immune to burning.

"I wanna know if I'll burn with my magic blocked off," she said, looking up at me with flames dancing in her eyes.

"I don't think that's a good-"

Tory yanked out of my grip and pushed her fist straight into the flames. After half a beat, a laugh fell from her lips and she looked up at me excitedly.

"Maybe I'll be an even bigger Dragon than Darius and I can beat the crap out of him with teeth and claws," she joked.

I couldn't help but laugh at the idea of that. Darius already equalled his father's size in Dragon form and they were the biggest of their kind recorded in a century. If her and her sister really were bigger than the Acruxes I didn't think it would sit too well with them. It probably wouldn't really be a good look for them either, especially as Lionel flaunted his Order form like it made him royalty of his own kind. I imagined his reputation might take a hit if the two Vegas turned out to be bigger badder beasts than them. It would strengthen their claim to the throne too. It'd be better for all of us if they emerged as a common Order, preferably something non-threatening. But everything I knew about Tory Vega and her sister made me think that was a pointless hope.

She pulled her hand back from the flames as more and more fires sprang to life all around us. The way on was up a winding staircase at the far end of the room and Tory jogged up it quickly. I could hear her heart pumping with the thrill of this place and I smiled to myself knowing I'd succeeded in giving her one of the things she'd requested at least.

On the next floor the creepy music was louder and as the door closed behind us, the floor started to tip.

Tory caught my arm, her fingers curling around my bicep and making heat wind through my body in response.

The lights stuttered out and a creepy voice started singing a nursery rhyme.

Tory released her grip on me and started forward, holding her arms out to the sides a little to balance herself as the floor continued to shift.

A panel slid open to our left and Tory flinched as a woman dressed like an old maid leaned out, throwing a gust of air magic at us as she shrieked threateningly.

We were knocked back against the opposite wall which instantly spun around, flinging us into a dark space. Tory caught my hand again as she almost fell and I smiled when she didn't release me.

Another panel slid open and the maid appeared again, striking us with air magic as she screamed curses our way.

We were knocked into the path of a guy dressed like a servant who cast more magic at us, knocking us through another hidden door. Then another.

Tory let out a little shriek of surprise each time one of them appeared again, half laughing as we were knocked back and forth and tightening her grip on my hand so that she didn't lose me.

I held her firmly, laughing too as I let myself forget all about her Order and her claim, my inheritance and Solaria as a whole. For a little while I wasn't going to worry about any of it. I'd asked her after the Nymph attack to draw a line between our personal relationship and our political one and I was going to stick to my own word on that. When I was with her like this, I wasn't going to think about any of that other stuff, I was going to just stay in the moment.

We were knocked through a final door so hard that we fell to the ground, hitting soft mats which were there for that very reason.

Tory fell on top of me and she laughed, leaning down and pressing her lips to mine way too briefly. I tried to catch her hand as she pushed away from me but she danced aside, skipping ahead as she started climbing the next set of stairs.

A roar echoed from somewhere above us and Tory paused for half a second before hurrying on.

I chased after her, meaning to claim a proper kiss but she made it to the room above before I could.

A steady drip, drip, drip sounded from somewhere in the dark and I hesitated, wondering if she really wanted to face the water horror or if I should just run her through it with my Vampire speed.

But I got the impression Tory Vega didn't want her hand held to get her through anything. Every day she was proving herself to be Fae through and through and I was pretty sure she'd rise to this challenge just like everything else.

Soft splashes sounded as we walked out into the room over the thin puddle of water which lined the floor.

"Caleb?" Tory breathed in the dark and I shifted closer to her.

"Yeah?"

"These sneakers are new, I don't want them to-"

The floor fell away beneath us before she could finish that thought and a flood of water fell over us. Tory screamed as she plummeted down the slide and I laughed, my voice echoing around us as we shot down so fast that it felt like I'd left my stomach in the room above.

We skidded out into a dark room at the bottom and Tory got to her feet, offering me a hand to pull me up just as three guys in black cloaks with their hoods drawn up stepped from the shadows.

They raised their palms at us, chanting in deep voices as they advanced and Tory shrieked again, backing up and tugging me with her. Her heart was pounding and her eyes were alight with exhilaration as she let herself fall into the fear of the place.

She tugged on my arm, yanking me towards the elevator which stood open on the far side of the room as the guys in the cloaks drew all of the water back out of our clothes and hair with their magic.

As soon as they'd done it, they ran at us and Tory yelled out as she dragged me into the elevator, slamming her thumb on the single button in the dimly lit cube again and again.

The doors slid shut just before they reached it and she sagged back against the wall as the elevator began to ascend, biting her lip in amusement.

I caught her waist and pulled her closer to me just as the lights flickered overhead. Her hands fisted in the material of my jacket as the elevator came to a halt and the lights died all together.

Half a heartbeat passed before the whole thing plummeted towards the ground way too fast and she screamed as she clung to me for dear life.

I tightened my hold on her, adrenaline rocketing through my limbs as we fell. The elevator slowed before it could hit the ground and Tory laughed nervously as the lights flickered back on and it began to climb again.

"Having fun?" I asked her, as she pressed her face against my chest.

"Hell yes, but this place is insane."

The doors opened again behind us as we reached the top floor and she stepped out of my arms as she looked along the corridor which spread away from us.

Tory glanced at me hesitantly for a moment before moving out.

I fell into step beside her as she looked back and forth, trying to figure out what would happen next.

A prickle of anticipation slid down my spine as I heard the hidden door behind us easing open but Tory didn't notice it.

I fought the urge to look back as two large sets of feet padded into the space behind us.

We made it several more steps before a low growl sounded and Tory whirled around to look at the two Manticores at our backs.

"Holy shit," she breathed, her eyes widening at the beasts who looked like lions with giant leathery wings and scorpion stingers for tails.

The Manticores let out huge roars and leapt at us. Tory screamed, snatching my hand as she started running and we raced away from them down the corridor to the opening at the far end which showed the star speckled sky outside.

Two sets of huge paws thundered after us as we ran as fast as she could go and I looked back over my shoulder just as the first Manticore pounced.

His teeth clamped down on a mouthful of Tory's leather jacket and she shrieked as he lifted her clean off of the ground, taking off and shooting out of the opening in front of us. Half a second later, the second Manticore caught me and I whooped excitedly as I was lifted off of my feet and we shot out of the building up towards the sky.

I caught sight of Tory for a moment as the beast flew higher and higher and then all of a sudden, it released me.

I yelled out as I fell and Tory's screams came from somewhere close as she plummeted towards the ground too.

The wind whipped around me, my stomach lurched and the ground rushed ever closer.

At the last second, a cushion of air wrapped around me, folding me into it before I could hit the concrete and go splat.

We hung suspended for a moment, hearts racing as we looked at each other, grinning like a couple of kids.

The magic released us, flipping us around so that our feet hit the ground and Tory leapt on me a second later.

I laughed as I caught her and she wrapped her arms and legs around me, kissing me so hard it was almost punishing. Her hands fisted in my hair and her ankles locked tight behind my back as her tongue brushed against mine in a way that made me hard almost instantly.

"Fuck, Tory, I can't get enough of you," I murmured against her lips and she laughed just as I shoved her back against the wall of the House of Horrors.

My hands moved beneath her jacket, skimming her perfect tits over the material of that tiny crop top as I ached to rip it off of her right there.

"Ah, Mr Altair?" a nervous voice came from beside us and I pulled away from Tory with a growl of irritation.

The guy running the House of Horrors flinched at my expression but he barrelled on all the same.

"It's just that the next participants in the House of Horrors will be falling right on top of your heads any moment if you don't vacate the area," he said anxiously, glancing up at the sky.

Tory laughed as she unhooked her legs from my waist and pulled me away from the wall even though I had half a mind to order him to shut the whole attraction down until we were done here.

She pulled the magic-restricting bangles off of her wrists and tossed them in a bucket by the entrance and I followed her lead as she dragged me out of the attraction and back into the mayhem of the fair.

"What do you want to do now?" I asked her as she looked up at me with bright eyes, her heart pounding and cheeks flushed.

I was half hoping she'd say she just wanted to leave and head back to my room or maybe even just find some quiet corner around here to have her way with me but of course she didn't.

"Everything," she replied with a grin. "I want to do it all."

"I'll do whatever makes you happy," I replied, throwing my arm over her shoulders as I led her towards the next ride. And the strangest thing was, I was pretty sure that was the truth.

Darcy

CHAPTER THIRTY TWO

Lance:

I'll make it worth your while if you pass The Reckoning today.

#motivation #seemeafterclass

Darcy:

I can't believe you just hashtagged me!

Lance:

I can't believe you're not in my bed right now.

#missyourpeach

Darcy:

I also can't believe you just admitted you want me to pass The Reckoning.

Lance:

It's complicated.

You got that right.

I snorted a laugh, tucking my Atlas in my bag as I headed out of the door. The Reckoning was held in The Howling Meadow at dawn and as usual I had no idea what to expect. The one thing I was glad of though, was that after this morning, it would be over. And though I was nervous as hell, we'd done well in the trials and I just had to hope we could succeed at this final challenge.

No matter what happened though, I knew Tory and I had each other. And that was enough. We'd been through so much together during our lives, but since we'd arrived at Zodiac our bond had grown even fiercer. We would ride out the storms of our fate together, hand in hand. And no one could ever take that from us.

I spotted Diego further down the stairwell and a lump bulged in my throat as anger opened up in me again. If I was going to get information about his uncle, I'd have to suck it up, but that didn't seem like a possibility right then. I was just too damn furious and today was too damn important to waste my energy on him.

He threw a glance over his shoulder, scowled when he spotted me then quickened his stride. I shook my head at him, tutting under my breath. *Jerk.*

I followed the other freshmen outside where it was still dark and someone barged past me, nearly knocking me on my ass.

Kylie seemed to be walking on air as she hurried ahead of me with Jillian jogging after her. "*All* night?" Jillian was saying to her.

"Yeah, I haven't even had time to wash the glitter off. He was still all over me this morning. He said he can't get enough of me," Kylie said, flicking her hair over her shoulder as they headed away.

Ew. One guess who she's been screwing.

I fell to the back of the air freshmen, wrapping my coat closer around me as the wind picked up. We passed through The Wailing Wood and Tory caught my eye beside Sofia and Tyler. She waved me over and I quickened my pace, glancing over at Diego who pointedly walked away from us.

"How was the fair?" Tory asked, looking like she had a thousand things to say to me. We fell into a discussion about Caleb and the Heirs and I was horrified by what Caleb had done to her at the top of some mountain. But she seemed to think he'd made up for it. I wasn't entirely satisfied by that, but Tory had clearly decided to keep seeing him. I told her about what had happened between Diego and I – leaving out the rest of my night with Orion - and she cursed his name, glaring over at him across the meadow.

I itched to tell her the truth about Orion and wondered if I should just do it. She wouldn't tell anyone. But even as I considered it, a sharp pinch in my gut reminded me that if she knew about us, she could get in trouble for covering my ass.

No, Orion and I had to figure out what the hell we were actually going to do about this insatiable thing we'd wrapped ourselves up in. It had to remain between us until then. And probably after then too.

Professor Zenith and Principal Nova appeared in long navy robes, moving in front of us with serious expressions. Ringing the edge of the field was a set of bleachers full of spectators. They were packed with the usual crowd of the Heirs and their fan club and Geraldine and the A.S.S., plus a whole host of hopeful looking parents.

Nova lifted her chin, gazing across us from left to right. "Today your fates will be decided. Each of you have been given a score between one and ten based on your performance in the trials you undertook this week. You will receive those scores…now." She waved her hand and numbers appeared above all of our heads in glittering blue sparks.

I looked up, finding a nine above my head and I squealed with joy as I spotted the same above Tory's. Geraldine went absolutely crazy, crying out our names with actual tears rolling down her cheeks. The A.S.S joined in, drowning out the heckles coming from the Heirs' friends. The Heirs themselves were huddled together, their eyes dark as mutters passed between them.

I looked to the other freshmen around me hopefully, finding Sofia with a five and Tyler with a seven. Diego had a glimmering three above his head, his shoulders hunched as if he wanted to shrink away from it. Despite my anger at him, I couldn't help but feel a small pang of disappointment on his behalf. It wasn't like I wanted him to lose his place at the Academy, but an apology was definitely due if we were ever gonna see eye to eye again.

Nova clapped her hands to draw our attention. "No matter how low or high your number, you may still fail or pass the final assessment depending on how well you do in this test. The Reckoning will judge how strong of will and heart you truly are. How much you deserve your place at this elite academy. You will then each be given a final score which will decide whether or not you stay on at Zodiac. If your total is less than twelve, you will lose your place this very day."

Nerves danced through me as Nova directed us to create a circle in the field like we had on the night of The Awakening.

I stood between Sofia and Tory, our fingers interlaced and locked tight.

"Good luck," I said under my breath as Zenith and Nova took to the centre of the field and Sofia and Tory murmured it back.

Zenith raised her hand to the glittering night sky which was on the cusp of dawn, closing her eyes for a long moment. Silence spanned across the meadow; even the crowd were quiet and I wondered if they'd been told to be this time.

"Look to the stars, freshmen! It is time for your Reckoning!" Zenith said dramatically and I lifted my head with a deep inhale, taking in the expansive dots of light above.

"Optio vobis faciam!" Zenith cried and I felt her voice right down to the pit of my soul. The stars seemed to twist, turning and turning until I was trapped in the vortex, unable to move as they snared me in their powerful aura.

A weight fell over me like the pressure of a waterfall and darkness descended, taking everything and everyone with it.

A hovering sensation filled my body and I felt as though I was suspended in a chasm of nothingness for a million miles in every direction.

"Hello?" I called out, panic squeezing my heart and stealing my breath.

"Hello? Hello? Hello?" My voice echoed back to me a hundred times, overlapping and merging until it made my ears ache.

Absolute silence pressed in on me again and I hung there with only the drilling thump of my heartbeat for company. I drew fire to my fingertips and it flared brighter than I'd ever seen it, flickering with power in electric blue and blazing scarlet.

Whispers brushed my ears that sent a sliver of fright into my chest. I wasn't sure if they were coming from inside my head or from the abyss surrounding me. Something told me they came from the stars themselves, somehow neither feminine nor masculine, they just *were*.

"Gemini of air, fire, water, earth, daughter of a king, twin soul and Fae born of ash and fire...it's time to face The Reckoning."

The blackness appeared to peel back like the page of a book and I found myself on a dark, suburban street before a burning house. The flames reached into the air, seeming to lick the sky itself. An anxious crowd were gathered on the road beside two huge fire trucks.

I wanted to move closer, my instincts drawing me toward that house. A mere thought transported me to the front of the crowd and my heart clenched as a firefighter shouted orders to his crew, shaking his head as if he'd already given up hope. Fear lapped in my chest as I realised what I was witnessing.

I blinked and it was dawn. The crowd had dispersed and only one fire truck remained. The blaze had reduced the house to a blackened husk. A shadow shifted in my periphery and I turned to see a tall figure standing at the end of the street, head bowed and body cloaked. A flicker of glittering light shone in their palm and I was certain it was stardust. A wave of their hand and the magic swallowed them up.

A baby's cries caught my ear, then another and my heart stumbled.

"Sir!" a male voice drew my attention back to the house and a fireman came marching out of the wreckage with a bundle of blankets in his arms. "The twins survived! I pulled them out of the ashes."

My heart pounded harder and harder as I finally understood why we hadn't died this night. We were impervious to fire. Impossible as it seemed, it was clear as day now.

But who was that Fae standing on the corner watching? A pit of dread in my gut told me it meant nothing good. No one was supposed to know about us. We were Changelings. So how could anyone have been there to witness this night?

My birth mother? My father? Who else knew? Did they die before or after this night?

"Gemini," the whispers filled my head again. "The wood burns hottest at the heart of the fire. The more hardship you face, the stronger you become."

The vision faded away and I found myself standing in an office. Tory and I sat on the floor together, we were five, the absolute image of each other. But I had a cast on my arm which was covered in scribbles and Tory had a paper chain bracelet on the same arm.

"It's not working out," my foster mother, Mrs Fairchild, spoke to a woman across the desk, her voice hushed. "They're *impossible*."

This memory seemed more vivid now, like I'd locked it away, buried it so deep that I'd almost forgotten it had happened. The young me and my sister looked up, hearing what she was saying.

"Tory breaks every toy or game I give her and Darcy always has scrapes and bruises like she's *trying* to hurt herself. They snuck out of my garden into the neighbour's last week and climbed into her son's treehouse. It's a miracle Darcy didn't kill herself when she fell. I just don't have the nerves for it anymore."

"Perhaps you could try-" the administrator started.

"I'm done trying," she said, standing and moving to place a kiss on each of our heads before walking out the door.

I felt the crack in my heart Mrs Fairchild had caused all those years ago, breaking me apart again for a moment. The confusion, the feeling of Tory's hand curling around mine, the uncertainty of where we'd go next.

The vision shifted once more and I had the awful feeling the stars were about to drag me through every painful moment of my life. But the next thing I witnessed was a blur of Tory and I standing before ten different schools, each day marking the first at each one. We were older in every vision. But as they progressed, I noticed we looked stronger as time went on, our eyes hardening, our posture straightening. The stars weren't trying to hurt me, I realised. They were showing me how we'd been *made*. How after each rejection and hurt, we'd lifted our chins a little higher, built our armour a little thicker.

A clamour of noise filled the air. All of the insults I'd ever received in my life that had stuck with me. Given to me from nameless mean girls at school, teachers, foster parents, friends. The words which had left a scar on my heart.

Clumsy. Unwanted. Weird. Stray. Too quiet. Too broken. Too poor.

The pain of it all built up in my chest like water against a dam. I shied away from it as the darkness swallowed me once more, covering my eyes.

"Stop it," I snarled, forcing the visions to recede and the stars listened.

As I opened my eyes I found myself facing Tory. I smiled my relief, moving forward to touch her but the image of her rippled and changed, morphing into Seth instead.

I shrank back, but his expression was softer than in real life, warmer.

The stars whispered to me again, sending a little tremor through me. "Adversaries surround you, Gemini. But do you know which ones are your true enemies?"

Seth became Max, then Caleb then Darius. Each time the vision changed, their expressions became more frightening, the promise of pain in their eyes.

Darius shifted into Sofia, then Diego, Geraldine, Tyler, Kylie, Nova, Angelica, Washer, Marguerite, a hundred faces I knew from the corridors of Zodiac, each looking angrier than the last, their eyes full of hate. The Councillors appeared next, ending with Lionel who looked like the devil himself, his eyes two chasms of hellfire. His face became Orion's and my throat tightened as a cold wave of hate emanated from him.

"Darkness breeds darkness," the stars whispered as I continued to gaze at him, a thick shadow seeming to cling to his form. "What does a Fae do when their back is against the wall, Gemini?"

My tongue grew heavy as I mulled over the answer to that question. "They fight," I breathed.

"And what does a Fae do with their heart?"

I swallowed as Orion moved forward, reaching toward me almost lovingly, but then a dagger appeared in his hand. The same one he'd had in the cave the other day. He took my arm, holding it above my wrist and I winced, trying to pull free of him.

"They guard it," I answered, dragging my hand away from him and his form disintegrated like grains of sand on the wind, leaving me in total darkness once more.

"And what will a Fae do to claim their rightful place in Solaria?"

The answer slid onto my tongue as easily as breathing. It was instinct. Something I'd known about Fae this whole time, but had failed to truly acknowledge. It was why the Heirs hurt us, why Orion helped them, why Lionel controlled them all.

"Anything."

The darkness drew back like a tide and the night sky shone down on me once again. A glittering number twenty shone above my head and I blinked heavily as I shook off the oppressive feel of the darkness which had claimed me.

I turned to Tory beside me, her eyes wide as she gazed up at the blazing number twenty above her head too. All around us, more and more numbers appeared above the students circling the field, but none as high as ours.

Beside me, Sofia had a glittering fifteen and I quickly looked to Diego, quietly relieved to find he'd just passed with a twelve. Kylie had a bright eighteen and Tyler had the same.

A horrified wail caught my ear and I spotted a girl falling to her knees as she started crying, her number eleven meaning she had lost her place at Zodiac. Nearly thirty hadn't passed and a mixture of tears and anger clamoured around us as everyone broke the circle.

Nova called out, "The Reckoning is over! Those of you who scored less than twelve, you are dismissed." She gestured to The Wailing Wood. "Please pack your things and head home before midday.

Sadness filled me as I watched the dejected students heading over to their families at the edge of the field, falling into the arms of their parents. Sofia squealed at us before running across the field to hug her family and the rest of the crowd did the same.

I turned to Tory and smiled, tears welling in my eyes. "Did you see the fire?"

She nodded, blinking back her own tears. "I saw everything. And I think I get why we had to go through it all now."

I pulled her into a hug as a tear rolled down my cheek. "Me too."

"Did you see the Fae after our house burned down?" she whispered into my ear and I nodded against her shoulder.

"What do you think it means?"

She remained silent a moment. "I don't know. But I get the feeling it's nothing good."

"Congratulations," Max's dark voice made me pull away from Tory and I found the four Heirs lined up in front of us. Fear juddered through me, but I wasn't going to let them ruin this moment for us.

"Thanks," Tory said. "Are you here to give us warm hugs?"

Darius tsked. "We're here to give you a message."

I ground my teeth, staring back at him. "Why do I get the feeling I've heard this message before?"

Max stepped forward, an aura of calm emanating from him that my heartbeat slow a fraction. "We don't intend on letting you graduate, little Vegas."

Seth sneered, brushing his hand over Max's arm. "It's going to hurt."

"You might wanna get out now while you still can," Caleb said and Tory pursed her lips at him.

"You've proved you're Fae. We don't intend on underestimating that fact," Darius snarled. "So enjoy the Lunar Eclipse tonight. It will be the last night of peace between us. But every night after that...when you lay your pretty little heads down on your pillows, I want you to remember we're coming for you. In the dead of night, at the break of dawn or the fall of dusk. You won't know when and you won't know how, but what you will know is that we're coming. For. *You.*"

He turned and walked away and one by one the other Heirs followed, leaving me shaking from head to toe.

Words echoed in my mind, branded on me from the voices of the stars.

What will a Fae do to claim their rightful place in Solaria?

Anything.

TORY

CHAPTER THIRTY THREE

Attention All Students, the following is a safety notice and we advise you take all of the information in this notification seriously.
*Tonight is the **LUNAR ECLIPSE**.*

All Fae will be struck by the urges of the moon and will be guided by their most base instincts and the truest desires of their hearts and flesh.
As such, the faculty have made the following recommendations:

1. Remain alone in your rooms throughout the evening with the door locked.
2. Turn off your Atlases to avoid the temptation to send provocative messages to your fellow students via social media.
3. Take a sleeping draft or two to try and bypass the night without succumbing to the urges.
4. Make sure you have cast your monthly contraceptive spells so that when rules 1-3 fail to work you will not come crying to the faculty about

unexpected pregnancies.

Please try to remain safe and enjoy your evening.

- Principal Nova.

I read the message for the second time and couldn't help but smirk. For all intents and purposes this was a warning to say that in all likelihood a lot of people would be getting laid tonight so don't forget to use contraception. The rest of it was just nonsense and she knew it.

In amongst the Hell Week madness I'd heard more than a few excited whispers about the Lunar Eclipse and the sorts of things that people got up to during it.

Even thinking about tonight was getting me hot under the collar and it wasn't even dinner time yet.

I bit my lip as I dropped my Atlas, wondering what I'd do tonight after our celebration dinner. Caleb had gone back to stay with his family for an Eclipse celebration after The Reckoning but I found I was glad. After the fun we'd had last night I'd been looking forward to spending more time with him. But then he just went straight back to threatening me with the other Heirs after The Reckoning and I realised that I really wasn't cool with his whole Jekyll and Hyde act.

When he came back from his visit with his family I planned on making some new rules for us to play by and if he didn't like it, then maybe I'd just have to cut him loose. Which was a damn shame because he was really hot. But I wasn't going to let him have it both ways. He wanted me or he wanted to get rid of me and he'd have to decide which.

The fact that he wouldn't be around tonight made me wonder if the moon would start driving me towards someone else or if it was all just a load of nonsense and an excuse for Fae to hook up with whoever they liked. The idea that an Eclipse could have that much sway on us almost seemed ridiculous but I guessed if the faculty felt the need to send out a warning there must have been some merit to it.

Thanks to Orion's wildly awkward sex-ed class, I knew how to cast the contraceptive spell and the last one I'd cast was still in effect. So if I did happen to find myself in anyone's bed then at least I wouldn't have to worry about that.

I turned to look at my latest online shopping arrivals, trying to decide on an outfit for our celebration dinner at The Orb just as my Atlas pinged again.

I glanced down at the author of the message and my heart did a kind of awkward somersault, lodging in my throat for a moment before dropping all the way down into the pit of my stomach.

Darius Acrux - 1 new message.

My lips parted and I shook my head slightly, trying to shake off the fluttery feeling in my stomach as I picked it up and opened the message.

Darius:
All members of Ignis House are hereby invited to the Moon Party in Air Cove tonight at sundown. Come ready to party like your house is on fire and someone stole all your clothes. It's gonna get messy and you'll all be showing up to represent the hottest House on campus. Attendance isn't optional. Show up or ship out.
- Your humble House Captain.

I blew out a breath, refusing to admit that a small part of me was disappointed to find that message hadn't been personal. It wasn't like I wanted him to be sending me messages anyway. If he had, I'd just have to delete it. And probably block him too.

I dropped my Atlas back onto my bed and stepped out of my clothes as I prepared to start trying on outfits for tonight.

My skin felt hot and I fanned myself with my hand, crossing the room in my black underwear as I moved to open the window.

The sky was painted orange as the sun began to set and I paused for a moment, admiring the view and enjoying the cool breeze that danced over my flesh.

As I looked out at the sky, my gaze fell on a pale, white orb which hung low on the horizon. The moon was up already.

A shiver ran down my spine as I looked at it for a long moment, every inch of my skin starting to come alive like an electrical current was dancing across my nerve endings.

I bit my lip and turned away from the view, snatching my Atlas back into my grasp and typing out a message.

Tory:

Thanks for the invite but I'm not sure I've got anything appropriate to wear. What's the dress code?

As soon as I hit send my stomach dropped and I tried to un-send it again. I tapped the screen, bashing my hands against it again and again as I tried to figure out a way for that message not to have just been sent.

A notification flashed up at the bottom of the screen and my heart lurched uncomfortably.

Darius Acrux is typing.

No, no, no, no! What have I done??

Darius:

I'm sure you'll look good enough in anything you wear. Just turn up as you are.

I looked down at myself in my underwear and laughed. That would certainly help my reputation as a sex addict, wouldn't it?

Tory:

No, I think that would be wildly inappropriate actually.

Darius:

Why?

How could three little letters make my heart race like that? I read his message four times which was excessive for a one word response but I didn't know how to reply to it. I just kept blinking at it until he sent another message.

Darius:

Send me a photo and I'll give you an honest opinion.

If I thought my heart had been racing before then that was nothing to what it was doing now. Of course I wasn't going to send him a photo. I was standing in my underwear not wearing some awful outfit like he thought I was. Unless he didn't think I was. Maybe he knew exactly what I was wearing. But how could he? And why was I even considering sending him a photo when I obviously wasn't about to do it?

Darius:

I dare you...

Fuck it.

I moved towards the mirror which hung beside my door and paused as I noticed my eyes seemed kinda strange. I leaned a little closer, looking at my pupils which were wide and dilated like an anime character. I frowned at the strange appearance of my eyes for a moment before my original task tugged at my attention. I kicked on a pair of heavy boots which still had mud on them from when I'd worn them out in the rain and a smirk pulled at my lips.

I took a deep breath, held my Atlas up and took the photo.

Heat prickled along my skin as I toyed with the idea of pressing send or delete. I wasn't really going to send Darius Acrux a picture of me in my underwear.

Was I?

I snorted at the idea, moving my thumb to hit delete and swiping send instead.

My gut lurched, my eyes widened and I quickly followed through with the rest of the vague plan I'd had when I'd half considered this outrageous idea. Fuck knew what was getting into me tonight.

Tory:

See? My shoes don't match, I look ridiculous...

My heart beat an unsteady tune in my chest as I tried to figure out why the hell I'd just done that. Not that it mattered. He saw me in that tiny bathing suit in Water Elemental class all the time anyway. And he'd burned all my clothes off that time too, so he'd already seen everything there was to see of my body. It was no big deal.

The words *Darius Acrux is typing* had been sitting at the bottom of my screen for way too long now. Either he was about to send me an essay or he'd half written a response and forgotten about it or he was having trouble deciding exactly what to say back to me.

Why the hell had I messaged him again?

Could I blame the moon? I sure as shit wanted to. My heart was beating too fast. Too damn fast.

A knock sounded at my door and my heart nearly leapt out of my chest.

My lips parted. I glanced at my Atlas which still held no reply and moved towards the door uncertainly.

I wanted to ask who was there, but I couldn't quite get the words to pass my lips.

I slowly turned the door handle and pulled it open a crack.

"What were you doing, taking a shit or something?" Darcy joked as she pushed her way inside and I let out a shaky laugh, quickly closing the door again behind her.

She was already dressed in a grey skirt and cute top, her blue hair loose and curling around her shoulders.

Her gaze slipped to the filthy boots I'd paired with my underwear and her brows pinched.

"What are you wearing, Tor?" she asked on a laugh.

"Umm..." I wasn't even sure how to explain the fact that I'd clearly had a mental break, so I kicked my boots off by the door and moved back to looking at my wardrobe instead.

"Holy mother of crap! Are you sexting Darius Acrux?" Darcy gasped and I spun back around to find her holding up my Atlas which I realised too late I'd left open on the bed with the messages right there for her to see.

"God no!" I snapped. "As if! I just...sent him a single photo which was a joke, not sexual at all!"

"Your underwear is transparent," she pointed out and I looked down, shaking my head but it actually kinda was.

"I...I'm gonna blame the moon," I said because I seriously had no other excuse and I was feeling really damn hot again and I could see the damn moon out of my open window like it was laughing at me. I pointed at it to emphasise my point and Darcy laughed.

"Okay well the *moon* might want you to cover up before we actually head out though, yeah?" she suggested.

I smirked at her teasing tone and pointed at the array of new clothes I had yet to pick between.

"I can't choose, that's how I ended up asking for Darius's help in the first place."

"And he suggested those boots?"

"He did not." I bit my lip. "Shit, you'd better keep me away from him tonight if one glimpse of the moon is all it takes for me to start sending him half naked photos," I joked, but I kinda meant it. And I kinda hoped she didn't and I ran into him anyway. *Shit.*

"Caleb losing his shine so soon?" Darcy teased as she started rifling through my options.

"Yes. Well no...we had so much fun last night at the fair and afterwards in his room too..." I smirked at her as she shook her head in mock disgust. "But then this morning he's all *you'd better watch out, I'm coming for you,* like a total dipshit-"

"Darius was pretty heavy on that idea too," Darcy pointed out.

"Yeah, I know. But he doesn't pretend to be anything else. Like with Caleb he's all, *let's just be us and keep the feud stuff separate.* But that's easier said than done, you know? Because one minute I'm laughing my ass off with him and sleeping in his bed and the next he's like *I'm gonna get you out of the school and make you and your sister bleed.* And I just wanna punch his stupid fucking face."

"I'm feeling that," Darcy agreed. "You should totally punch him." She hooked a dress out of the pile and held it out for me. It was white with pale lilac blossoms all over it, the top was fitted while the skirt flared out. I'd bought it with Darcy in mind and we both knew it.

"The moon wants you to wear this tonight," Darcy said. "If you look innocent, it thinks you might act it too."

I smirked at her as she tossed the dress to me and I pulled it on. It hugged my figure and skimmed my knees.

"Am I seriously wearing this?" I asked in amusement. It was cute and I wasn't sure I could pull off cute.

"You are," she agreed, pushing me down into the chair by my desk as she started fiddling with my hair. "So, we were up to you wanting to punch Caleb's face and somehow explaining why you're sending dirty photos to Darius because I'm still lost as to how he's any different..."

"Right. Yeah. Well he's different because he doesn't pretend to be anything apart from an asshole," I said, biting my lip as I let my mind wander in Darius's direction.

"And assholes are hot." I could hear Darcy rolling her eyes without even having to see it. Yeah, yeah, I was singing an old tune. We both knew it. I was an addict and I may have been heading for a relapse if this moon got its way.

"Hate sex is hot," I said and Darcy groaned.

"I see where this is going," she stated.

"You don't. It's not. I'm just saying..."

Darcy laughed and I joined in.

"It's the moon," I added.

"Sure it is," she agreed. "Well I've done what I can to make you *look* innocent. Let's hope you manage to act it."

She stopped playing with my hair and I stood up to look in the mirror, smiling at the loose curls she'd given me to compliment the pretty dress.

I slipped on a pair of white sneakers with it because we were heading to the beach and heels would have just made me look like a gazelle on crack walking on the sand.

"Does the moon have anyone in mind for you?" I asked, looking around at my sister with a sly smile. She hadn't hooked up with anyone since that whole Seth cutting her hair bullshit and I was worried she was overthinking the whole trust thing with men again.

"Oh...well..." Her cheeks flushed a little and she opened her mouth like she was going to say something.

"Oh my god! You're totally holding out on me, who is it?" I demanded.

She hesitated and in the silence that followed, my Atlas pinged. Darcy leapt on it and I bit my lip, trying not to hope for it to be Darius and failing.

"It's just Geraldine," she said and a little sinking feeling dropped through my chest. "She's checking how long we'll be."

"Tell her fifteen minutes," I said. "*So* who's the lucky guy...?"

Darcy laughed dismissively. "No one in particular, but you know, the moon is making me think maybe I'll just keep my options open."

I frowned as she avoided my gaze but if she wanted to keep her crush a secret I wouldn't push it.

"Fine," I sighed. "But if you get laid I'm expecting all the details tomorrow."

She snorted in amusement and gave a non-committal noise.

"Oh, I know, let's go overkill," Darcy said excitedly, changing the subject. She moved to my side and twisted a lock of my hair between her fingers, frowning in concentration as a little vine grew from the palm of her hand to coil around it. Tiny lilac flowers sprung to life along the length of it and I smiled widely at her display of magic as she tucked the end behind my ear.

"Look at you, Darcy. Anyone would think you're a fully fledged student of the best magic school in Solaria," I complimented.

"Damn straight I am," she agreed.

A knock came at my door again. Louder than Darcy's had been.

I widened my eyes at her and her mouth fell open.

She mouthed *who is it?* and I shrugged because I didn't have a clue. Then she mouthed *Darius?* and my eyes widened like saucers.

I picked up my Atlas, seeing that he still hadn't responded to my shameless half naked photo before slipping towards the door with Darcy right beside me.

My palms were slick as I reached for the door handle but I slapped a look of *couldn't give a shit* right on my face. I'd sent the damn picture so I'd have to front it out.

I opened the door and my tongue stuck to the roof of my mouth as I found Darius leaning on the doorframe.

His gaze slid over my dress slowly and heat crawled along my skin everywhere he looked.

"You sorted out your problem then?" he asked casually.

"Umm... I decided on different shoes..."

Please floor, swallow me now. Or him. Or my sister who is standing right behind this door.

"I think I preferred the other option," he said, moving a little closer to me.

"Well *I* think Tory looks really nice in this dress," Darcy said, yanking the door all the way open so that she was revealed beside me.

Darius moved back an almost imperceptible amount but everything about his posture seemed to change.

"Doesn't she look *nice?*" Darcy pressed.

"Holy shit, Darcy. No one wants to look *nice,*" I muttered.

"Nice girls do," she hissed back pointedly.

Darius laughed and the sound rolled right down my spine and into my soul.

"Roxy's not a nice girl," he said, his gaze fixed on mine, his pupils larger than normal in his endlessly dark eyes. "No matter how pretty she looks in that dress."

He turned and walked away from us before I could utter a response.

I sagged against the doorframe and turned to Darcy with my eyebrows raised. "How did he make 'pretty' sound dirty?" I asked, my voice rough.

"He didn't, Tor," Darcy said with a sigh as I moved back inside to grab my things. "That was all in your head."

"Was it, though?" I asked, smirking at her.

"Sadly... no, it wasn't."

I bit my lip against another smile. I had no real intention of going anywhere near Darius Acrux tonight.

Probably.

Maybe.

Sixty three percent.

Dammit.

DARIUS

CHAPTER THIRTY FOUR

I made it to the common room before I stopped walking. My Atlas was burning a hole in my pocket, but at this point if I looked at that picture she'd sent me one more time I was actually going to self combust.

I moved towards the biggest fireplace in the room and leaned my back against the wall beside it, tugging at the neck of my t-shirt which was suddenly feeling tighter than it had earlier.

I kept my gaze fixed on the foot of the stairs which led up to the dorms. Waiting. Not that I'd admit it to anyone but myself. But I had no other reason to be standing here. I was already late to meet Lance, I was definitely waiting.

Someone came down the stairs and my muscles tightened in anticipation for a moment but I sagged back against the wall as I recognised Marguerite.

I should leave.

My fingers flexed with the desire to pull my Atlas out again. I could settle on some kind of reply to send her at least. One which didn't involve me showing up at her door like I expected...what exactly? For her to have suddenly forgotten she hates me? Or maybe to ask her who the moon was pushing her towards tonight. Because I'd known before the sun rose this morning exactly where it would be pushing me. I just couldn't tell if she'd fall under its spell for me too.

I crossed my arms as the urge to take my Atlas from my pocket seized me again.

"You're looking so lonely over here, Dari," Marguerite purred as she walked straight towards me.

I hated her calling me that. And her hair needed dying again. Nothing about what she was presenting me with was working for her.

I skimmed my eyes her way once then looked back towards the stairs.

"I'm all ready to party with you, Captain," she tried, reaching out to run a finger down the centre of my stomach until she reached my waistband.

I caught her hand in my grip and pushed it away. "What part of *done* don't you grasp?" I asked, still not looking at her.

"Remember the last Eclipse?" she breathed, leaning closer to me despite the aura of *fuck off* I was definitely exuding.

"Not particularly," I replied.

"C'mon, that was the first time we kissed," she pushed. "It was so hot."

"Fuck knows how many girls I kissed that night," I replied dismissively. "Don't count yourself too lucky." It was probably a dick thing to say but it was true. An Eclipse always brought people's desires to the forefront of their minds and I tended to have more than a few girls circling around me at all times. They always took a shot at me once the moon rose. And I'd said yes to more than a few of them in the past. Not tonight though. I only had my eyes set on one girl tonight and the joke of it all was that I knew she wouldn't be looking back. Or at least I had known that until she'd sent me that photo.

"I'll let you do anything you want to me," Marguerite offered, dipping her voice in a way I guessed she thought was seductive but came off desperate which was not attractive in any way.

She leaned forward like she was going to kiss me and I raised a hand, placing it over her face and pressing down so that she fell back into an armchair beside the fire.

"Stop embarrassing yourself," I muttered as I pushed off of the wall.

Roxy Vega had just walked into the room.

She looked...I didn't even know what to make of her dressed up like a freaking prom queen but I liked it. I wanted to pull the flowers out of her hair and get her white dress filthy in the mud.

Her gaze found mine and she bit her bottom lip in a way that made me hard just looking at her.

She was holding her sister's hand, Gwendalina tugging her along like a puppy on a leash. The two of them cut through the room quickly, clearly not planning on stopping for any reason.

I watched as they passed, caught between approaching her and not. The moon wasn't fully up yet so I still had some control. Not a whole hell of a lot, but some. Not that I ever seemed to have much around her in the first place.

I clenched my fist tightly and waited for them to leave.

I needed to see Lance. I couldn't get distracted by a girl. Even *the* girl.

They made it to the door and Roxy looked back over her shoulder at me. I almost went to her and asked why she'd sent me that photo. I almost called her name. I almost-

Her sister tugged her hand and they were gone.

I released the breath I'd been holding and swiped a palm over my face.

If I got near that girl when the moon was up then there would be no stopping me. I'd be begging on my knees for a moment of her time and she'd probably be laughing in my fucking face.

I should have asked her why she sent it.

Fuck.

I half considered following her but I was late. Lance was always late but still...he'd probably be at his own house on time.

I turned sharply and headed out of Ignis House, half considering shifting just to get there quicker. But it was pretty hard to disguise a big ass golden Dragon descending upon Asteroid Place. Much easier to sneak in there in my Fae form.

I headed off down the path as quickly as I could without running and soon gave in to the temptation to look at my Atlas again.

I flicked open my messages and looked over the photo she'd sent me. If she hadn't followed it up with the message about her shoes not matching I doubted I'd have ever even seen the filthy black walking boots she'd put on.

Her head was tilted to the side, half a smile lifting her full lips like she knew she was toying with me.

It was hardly the first photo a girl had ever sent me of her in her underwear, but there was something about it that I couldn't work out.

It should have been pretty simple. Girl sends half naked photos - not so subtle hint she wanted in my pants. But Roxy wasn't an open book. She hadn't offered me that photo; I'd dared her to show me what she was wearing. And she wouldn't blink. Because she never fucking did. The filthy shoes were her way of flipping me off and saying this isn't sexy. Even though she'd failed pretty abysmally if that had been her intention. I'd never stared at a photo that hard in my fucking life before. What was that smile about? Why did she send this? What would she taste like? *Fuck.* If she wanted me hooked she had me. I just didn't know if she wanted *me.*

I made it to the gates before Asteroid Place where the faculty lived and punched in the key code Lance had sent me. I ducked inside, taking an indirect route through the chalets ringing the complex so that I could avoid passing the swimming pool where I could hear a clamour of voices and splashing. I guessed that meant the faculty had already started their Eclipse celebrations.

I made it to the back of Lance's house and pushed open the patio door as I let myself in. I felt the moment I stepped through his silencing bubble, his magic sliding over my skin like a caress.

"Lance?" I called, looking around the open space but there was no sign of him.

I strained my ears and heard the shower running so I headed to claim one of his beers while I waited. I checked the clock. I was twenty minutes late which meant he was even later than that. *Asshole.*

I should have gone after Roxy.

I strummed my fingers against my leg and drained my beer, Atlas firmly in pocket. The sun was setting fast and I could feel the moon tugging at me to move. It wanted me to find her.

I closed my eyes, staying still through pure force of will.

When I couldn't take it anymore, I headed for another beer.

Lance was taking his sweet time in the shower.

The sound of splashing and high pitched laughter caught my ear outside and I crossed the room, twitching the curtain aside at the front of the house so that I could look out at the swimming pool.

I frowned as I instantly saw way too much pasty skin and a whole host of teacher tits. It looked like the faculty were gearing up for a fucking orgy. Half of them were naked already or wearing thongs and speedos which should have been illegal. There was a reason most of them stayed covered up in tweed blazers and I sure as hell wished I'd remained in my little bubble of headspace where none of them ever took them off.

"Who wants to make my helicopter take off?" Professor Washer called loudly as he balanced at the end of the diving board thrusting his hips so that his dick swung round and round in circles.

I dropped the curtain with a grimace, wishing I could burn the images from my mind.

"Enjoying the view?" Lance asked, laughing as he stepped into the room in a pair of jeans, his bare chest still damp from the shower.

"I'm scarred for life here," I groaned in disgust.

"Well I got a fucking invitation to that little slice of hell so how do you think I feel?" Lance joked as he moved forward to embrace me.

We hadn't had much time alone together this week and it always made the bond a little stronger when we were reunited. The sign for Libra on my skin had been itching all day, begging me to find him.

I wrapped my arms around him tightly, releasing a breath as I leaned my head on his shoulder and just stood there holding him for a few moments. We were beyond the point where we questioned the way this fucking thing made us feel about each other after all these years and I was just glad it had never progressed any further than occasional spooning.

I tried to pull back but Lance didn't release me, his fangs grazing against my neck as a soft growl escaped him.

"For fuck's sake, Lance," I muttered, straining against him. "If you bite me on the Eclipse you'll probably start trying to suck my dick right after it." This bond between us did all sorts of crazy shit and the way we were drawn together when he bit me was so intense on a normal day that we'd sworn off doing it for fear of how it might escalate. He only drank my blood if we had no other option now and him falling prey to the bloodlust because of the moon didn't count as a good enough reason for me.

He sighed dramatically, loosening his hold as he fought against his Order instincts.

"You're probably right," he agreed. "And I'd be so fucking good at it that you'd fall in love with me before the morning."

I laughed as he finally managed to pull his fangs away from my flesh.

Lance's beard tickled my neck and I drew back, shoving him off of me playfully like I hadn't just been nuzzled right into his goddamn skin. He smelled of cinnamon. And dammit but I loved that smell.

"They're safely away?" he asked seriously, moving to pour himself a bourbon as I sank back onto the couch and finished my beer.

"Xavier just texted me," I confirmed. "Him and Mother were about to use stardust to travel to the mortal world. They won't be back until tomorrow when the moon is gone and he can be sure he's safe from Father again."

"Good," Lance said, a grin tugging at his lips as he tossed me a new beer. "It feels pretty fucking great to beat that asshole at his own game. And it's too late for him to find a replacement before the moon comes up."

"Yeah," I agreed. "Looks like he's in for a night of disappointment and solitude."

"To beating him at his own game," Lance said, holding his drink out to me so that I could tap my bottle to it.

"To beating him altogether," I growled.

"Soon," Lance agreed darkly and I nodded.

I drank deeply and leaned back against the soft cushions, feeling like I was king of the goddamn world for once. Outsmarting my father felt so good I just wanted to bask in the feeling of it forever.

"So where's the secret Eclipse party being held tonight?" Lance asked.

I smirked at him, offering an innocent shrug. "What party?"

"You expect me to believe a bunch of teenagers are going to ignore the opportunity to celebrate the end of Hell Week and stay in on the one night they get a free pass to screw whoever the hell they like? Pfft."

I smirked at the idea of screwing whoever the hell I liked and Lance leaned closer to me as he noticed.

"Are you going to tell me who you've got your eye on then?" he asked.

"It's a terrible idea on so many levels," I said, not sure if I should tell him or not. He knew how important it was that we take down the Vegas so that when I took my Father's place on the Celestial Council it would still be strong enough to face the Nymph issue without faltering. We couldn't risk the unbalance their return could bring. But the Vegas as *the Vegas* were a problem simple enough to discuss solutions to. The girls themselves were a whole different situation.

"Tell me. I'm a poor old man destined to lock myself up in this place or get molested by Washer in the pool party from hell. I need to know that people still have fun somewhere in this world," he begged.

I smirked at him then pulled my Atlas from my pocket, eyeing the picture Roxy had sent me for the thousandth time.

"If a girl sends you a photo of her in her underwear, she wants to screw you, right?" I asked, frowning at myself for even asking this question but it just didn't seem that simple somehow.

"Generally I'd say that's a pretty clear indicator," he joked.

"Even when that girl hates you about as much as is humanly possible?"

Lance hesitated, his gaze dropping to the Atlas in my hand even though I held it so he couldn't see the photo. I wasn't sure why but I didn't really want to start showing it around to anyone else. She'd sent it to me. It was mine.

"Would this girl happen to be seeing one of your friends?" he asked slowly.

I clicked my tongue dismissively. "Caleb has a different girl every other week. She's not his girlfriend and he's shared a girl with Seth before so..."

"So you don't think he'd care?"

Caleb had already sent me several messages warning me not to go near Roxy tonight and I'd happily baited him by responding with a message that simply said it wasn't up to me, it was up to the moon. He'd threatened to sneak out of his parents' manor and come back to school but I knew that was a load of shit. There was no way he'd be coming back which meant he wouldn't get in my way, but that still didn't mean she'd want me instead.

"Oh he'd care. He just couldn't say much about it. Besides, like I said, she's made it clear she's not his. It's her choice to make." *And I want her to be mine.*

"And you think she might choose you?" Lance asked slowly, raising a brow.

"You're sounding sceptical as fuck right now, Lance," I snapped. "I'm not trying to pretend she doesn't hate me. I'm just wondering if hate is the only thing she feels about me."

"Well...there's only one way to find out, isn't there?" He smiled knowingly and drained his drink.

"And if she tells me to fuck off?" I demanded.

"Then you get to taste the bitter sting of rejection for the first time in your life," he teased. "It'll be good for you."

I groaned, placing my bottle down on the table as I stood.

I rolled my shoulders as the Dragon stirred beneath my flesh. It was dark out now, the moon was all the way up and I needed to expel some of the energy the moon was pushing into me before it drove me insane.

"Where's Lance?" Principal Nova's voice came from outside. "He should be here for this, I *need* him..."

"I'll find him, my popkin," Professor Washer replied instantly. "He's probably just a little shy. We'll have to be gentle with him!"

"Oh hell, you have to rescue me," Lance begged, looking towards the front of the house where he was no doubt using his Vampire hearing to listen as Washer approached the front door.

I snorted a laugh. "You have to promise not to go all dickhead teacher on us and break up the party," I warned.

"I swear on my life, just get me out of here," he said and I smirked as I led the way to the back of the house.

Lance shot away from me, returning before I'd even made it to the rear door with a t-shirt and sneakers on and I headed outside just as Washer rang the doorbell.

Lance locked the back door and we slipped away through the chalets until the sounds of the pool party were left behind and we made it out of Asteroid Place.

I led the way into Air Territory, intermittently complaining about Roxy Vega while trying to psyche myself up to track her down.

Every step I took was getting me closer to her, I could feel it. But I couldn't move too soon either. I knew my chances with her were slim at best so I had to play it just right if I wanted her to give me the time of day.

We headed to the top of the cliffs above the cove and I took a seat in the long grass beside my friend as we looked down over the bonfires burning all along the beach.

It didn't take me long to spot Roxy. Her white dress stood out on the sand and her laughter carried to me on the wind like that particular sound had been picked out just for me.

I leaned forward, shifting back and forth as I looked down at her, wondering if there was any point to this. Was I even going to go down there? I could feel every nerve in my body crying out to follow the call of the moon and go to her but what if she just turned me away? All the time I lingered between doing it and not doing it, there was still a chance and I knew I was hesitating in the what if.

"Just go," Lance snapped eventually. "Tell her how you feel. Lay it the fuck out and find out if she feels it too. You won't get rid of that need by sitting beside me dry humping the grass."

I laughed at that and turned to look at him. "You think she'll even listen?" I asked.

"I think you have to find out. We've been together for an hour now and you've spent fifty nine of those minutes talking about her. I can't bear it anymore. Leave this old man to sit on the cliff and go get your girl."

I got to my feet, shrugging like I didn't much care either way but the way he'd just called her *my girl* made the Dragon purr beneath my skin.

"Fine, but if it blows up in my face then it'll be your fault if we end up spooning tonight," I warned him.

"Suck it up buttercup, she's just a girl." Lance grinned at me and I turned my back on him.

She wasn't just a girl though. Not to me. She was the one girl I shouldn't want, the one I couldn't have, the one I didn't need. And yet I did. And everything in my life could be damaged so badly by that need that I'd fought it tooth and claw up until this point.

But apparently I was about to let the moon call me out on my bullshit. Because deep down I knew that every time I pushed her, every time I hurt her, each time she snapped at me and got back up, she'd been chipping away at my resolve a little more, breaking down my walls a little more. And even though I knew that all the things I'd done to her had only pushed her away from me, they'd each drawn me in a little closer every time.

I'd pushed her for her hatred because a moment of her scorn meant more to me than what it cost. I took her attention whatever way I could get it because all the time it was on me it lit me up and made me burn. And I wanted to burn with her more than I think I'd ever wanted anything in my life.

I headed down the trail to the beach with one thing on my mind and the determination to get it if there was even the slightest chance I could.

Roxy Vega, I'm gonna make you mine.

DARCY

CHAPTER THIRTY FIVE

I sat on the sand beside Tory with a beer in my grip, surrounded by the Ass Club before a blazing bonfire. Sofia and Tyler were making out like there was no tomorrow, barely coming up for breath. As far as I knew, Diego hadn't come down here tonight and I felt kind of sad that he was missing out on the fun. I hoped we could patch things up between us soon, but it was still pretty hard for me to move past what he'd said. Especially as he hadn't even apologised.

I spotted Max perched on a rock like a muscular male version of The Little Mermaid further along the beach, surrounded by girls. His navy blue scales were on show, defining every firm plane of his body and shining with the sea spray. Every time he said something, the girls around him all giggled and he brushed his hands over them to feed on their happiness. A strange hum was emitting from him and when he set his eye on a girl across the beach, they got up and joined his growing harem.

"Is he luring them over?" I asked Tory, nudging her and she looked to him with a frown.

"Looks like it. Let's not catch his eye. I do *not* wanna be his prey tonight."

We turned away and I took another sip of my beer, smiling up at the bulbous full moon above. The glow of it seemed to find its way under my skin and right into my veins. Any time I looked at it too long, the wild beast that lived inside me flexed her limbs like she was on the hunt. And who she wanted, was unquestionably Orion.

"Damn moon," I muttered, sipping my beer.

"Huh? Did you say Dragon?" Tory turned to me, her brows reaching for hairline as hope glittered in her eyes.

"No, Tor." I patted her arm, knowing she was going through a similar hell to me right now. Even if the guy she lusted after did want us destroyed, the moon wanted what it wanted, so what could she really do but wait it out?

I sighed internally. There was no way Orion could join us tonight and I couldn't exactly go wandering into the teacher's quarters moondrunk - though a part of me really freaking considered it. *Oh hi Principal Nova I'm just looking for Professor Orion because if I don't screw him six ways till Sunday the moon is gonna cry.*

Yah, maybe not.

Darius appeared on the beach, his eyes falling on us and his lips twitching. I frowned over my shoulder at him as he eyed up Tory. She hadn't noticed him yet and I wondered if I should point him out before he fulfilled that promise in his eyes and came over.

He stood there for so long it was kind of awkward. His grand speech from this morning rang in my head and an angry heat flared up my back, seeming to spread through my skin. I blinked and he was gone, strolling off down the beach and swiping a beer from a crate at the base of Max's rock.

My mind drifted back to Orion and I shook my head at the huge silver being above us in the sky. *Give me a break, Mr Moon. I can't have him tonight.*

Someone played reggae music from a speaker and the slow, rolling rhythm of it bled over me. We'd been told the entire party was encased in a silencing bubble created by the Heirs themselves so the teachers wouldn't easily find us. Though I imagined if they wanted to, they wouldn't have to look that hard.

Geraldine got to her feet, pulling her top off and revealing her large cleavage. "Who's up for a skinny dip, friends?" She shed the rest of her clothes and I laughed as more of the A.S.S jumped up. Angelica tore off her dress excitedly before sprinting into the water hand in hand with Justin, their bare asses making me laugh harder.

Geraldine planted her hands on her hips as she stared down at us with a gleam in her eyes. I had to admire her confidence and in all fairness, her body was so in shape I couldn't blame her.

"To the wild and wet waters I go!" she bounded away but a deep hum filled the air and she turned her head sharply toward Max. I glanced his way, finding his eyes dripping all over Geraldine, his Siren power urging her to go to his harem.

She started moving that way and I jumped up to catch her hand but she moved the sand beneath my feet to make me stumble back onto my ass.

"Geraldine!" Tory called after her in alarm.

She moved to the edge of his rock and he waved his hand to make the girls around him part, luring her in. "Hey Grus," he purred.

"Oh my salty sea cucumbers, you are quite the merman, aren't you?" she tittered and I got up again, moving forward with Tory, ready to drag her away from him.

"Yeah baby. Do you wanna see *my* sea cucumber in private?" Max offered.

Before we reached her, Geraldine turned toward the sea. "Actually, you can keep your oily dolphin flippers to yourself, Max Rigel." She ran into the sea and he stared after her in shock.

"She broke his spell," I said with a laugh and Tory and I retreated into our group.

"She's so badass." Tory dropped back onto the sand and I moved to her side.

My Atlas buzzed in my bag and I took it out while Tory fell into a conversation with Tyler and Sofia as they finally broke apart. I chewed on my lower lip as I realised who it was from, quickly peeking at the message.

Lance:

Need to see you. Aer Tower. Ten minutes.

Yes yes yes!

Shit, how am I gonna excuse myself? I hate lying to Tor, dammit.

"I think I'll go put my bag back in my room. My stuff's getting all sandy," I said to Tory, knowing it was a crappy excuse but she was a little tipsy so maybe it would fly. Plus all my dreams had just come true so screw it.

"Sure. Go and knock for Diego while you're at it," she said. "He needs to sort his shit out and apologise. No point in him missing out on tonight just because he's a grouch."

"Yeah, I'll try." I got to my feet with a surge of excitement, heading up the beach and brushing the sand off my skirt as I went. As I exited the warm bubble that the A.S.S had cast to keep in the heat of the fire, I shivered in the wintry air.

I hurried toward the path that led up from the cove, my pace quickening as the moonlight soaked into my skin. I felt almost high, unstoppable. And I knew exactly what I wanted. It was tall, bearded and had a bad temper when provoked. If I didn't see him, the moon would definitely make me go mad. I was a slave to it and hell if I cared.

Air Territory was dead quiet as I headed across the flat plain toward Aer Tower. Heat flooded my veins as I moved to the entrance, glancing around for Orion with adrenaline in my blood. When he didn't show, I shot him a message.

Darcy:

Where are you???

He replied quickly.

Lance:

Polaris is staring out of his window like an axe murderer.
Plan B: Come to The Wailing Wood.

Darcy:

Now who sounds like an axe murderer?

Lance:

I'd never murder you with an axe.
I'd use my teeth.

I giggled, quickening my pace to a jog as I headed towards the forest, the moonlight glowing off of the path and sending a shivery kind of energy into my blood.

I raced along the track, slipping between the boughs, for once not afraid of coming here in the dark. I was invincible tonight.

I slowed my pace as the shadows fell over me, moving from the orange glow of one lamppost to the next.

As I moved into a long stretch of darkness, my heart pumped faster and I stilled, a prickling sensation on the back of my neck telling me I wasn't alone.

Hot hands caught my arms and pinned me against the nearest tree face forward, sending my pulse skyrocketing. My cheek pressed to the bark as

Orion's scent surrounded me. I didn't even mind the nag of pain in my arms, a smile pulling at my mouth.

"You're in trouble, Miss Vega," he said into my ear. "You're out after curfew."

"My teacher told me to," I said breathily, relishing the game.

"Do you always do what you're told?" He brushed his fangs down my neck and my whole body convulsed.

"No...are you going to punish me?" I dragged in the dangerous air emanating from him, turning my head to try and capture his mouth with mine, but he evaded me.

His hand pressed firmly against my lower thigh and the heat of his skin chased away the cold, burning into my flesh.

"Do you want to be punished?"

Hell yeah I do.

I nodded keenly, my heart beating like the wings of a hummingbird as I waited, daring him to do it.

He lifted his hand and slapped it against the back of my thigh, making me gasp. *He actually did it!*

I barely had time to recover before he did it again, higher this time as he pushed up my skirt. Heat burned between my thighs and a whimper of pleasure escaped me. He'd either cast a silencing bubble around us or we were taking one hell of a risk because between the smack of his hand and my yelps, it was pretty obvious what was going on if anyone was close enough to hear. I was so intoxicated by the urges of the dawning Eclipse that I didn't even care, I just wanted him. And his hands. And his-

His palm clapped against my ass and I moaned as I caught the back of his neck, drawing him down and turning my head to find his lips. Before I managed it, he flipped me around, pulling me tightly into his arms and sinking his tongue into my mouth. Every inch of my body came alive with that kiss. I could almost taste the moonlight which was driving my instincts tonight, burning inside me like a silver flame that could never go out.

He broke the desperate kiss long before I was ready for him to, pushing my head to one side and digging his fangs into my throat instead. The sharp pain gave way to pleasure and the animal in me took over entirely. He pinned me in place against the tree and I clawed at his back, a sizzling sensation rolling up my spine and across my shoulder blades.

I needed something specific. But I couldn't tell what.

Orion was frantic as he bit me and I knew he was trying to hold himself back, the power of the Eclipse hanging over him, drawing the hunger of his Order form to the forefront of his mind. He needed this just like I needed to... *to what?*

I flexed my neck, frustrated as I rolled my shoulders and ached for some sort of release I didn't understand.

"You're very fidgety," Orion said as he pulled away, smirking at me.

"I know," I gasped, running a hand into my hair. "I just feel like I need something. Like...like..." I shook my head, struggling to finish that sentence.

"Sex?" he asked hopefully and I laughed. "Do you think we can sneak into your room? I think I want to punish you some more."

"*Lance*," I giggled. "It's not that. I mean, okay it's a bit that. But it's something else too. My shoulders itch and...I dunno."

He frowned, taking me seriously at last. "Turn around."

I raised a brow at him. "Are you going to spank me again?"

He chuckled darkly. "Not right now." He took hold of my shoulders and turned me to face the other way. Then he pulled up my shirt, gently running his thumbs over my shoulder blades, causing a divine shiver to run through me.

"*Ohhh* that feels so good."

He did it again with a laugh and I arched into his hands, desperate for more.

"Wings," he announced. "You're gonna have wings. Darius reacts the same way when-" He didn't finish that sentence.

"You caress his shoulder blades?" I finished for him, bursting out laughing.

He groaned, releasing my shirt. "This bond I have with him makes us do weird shit sometimes, alright?"

"Tell me more about that." I turned to face him and I could see he wanted to, but then his guard went up and he changed lanes.

"I told you you'll be a Dragon. The Eclipse make the needs of our Order forms more urgent. Like right now I want to bite you and...hunt you. Though I'd never actually do the second thing." He frowned darkly. "My parents were kind of fond of hunting their prey, but it's no joke. Fae have been killed playing up to that particular part of a Vampire's nature."

Shit. Note to self: tell Tory to stop doing that with Caleb.

"Let's stick to biting...maybe you wanna bite me somewhere else tonight?" I placed my hand on his chest, knotting my fingers in his shirt and he nodded excitedly. "I'll distract Diego upstairs while you sneak into my room."

His eyes glittered hungrily and he leaned into my ear with a playful grin. "I'm gonna run my tongue over your shoulder blades till you can't stand it."

I giggled, dancing away from him onto the path. "I hope you didn't do that to Darius."

He barked a laugh. "Can you hurry up? I'm losing my mind over you already."

I turned away, my heart rising in my chest as I started jogging back to Aer Tower with excitement bursting inside me like fireworks.

One day soon I'm gonna have goddamn wings!

SETH

CHAPTER THIRTY SIX

Kylie ground herself against me as I lay back in the sand. My pack were going at it twenty yards away and Kylie seemed keen to start the party too. But she wouldn't do it here. Not with an audience. Maybe that was why I hadn't offered yet.

Her mouth ran down my bare chest and she tugged at my belt to unbuckle it. With the power of the full moon pulsing through my veins and the Lunar Eclipse looming ever closer, I was reduced to my most basic instincts. The problem was, they weren't urging me after Kylie. Last night I'd hooked up with her, trying to screw a certain someone out of my head. But I'd failed. And it was eating me up from the inside out.

"Come on, Sethy," Kylie urged. "Let's go somewhere private." Her hand rubbed over my crotch and Seth Junior made a real good effort for her.

Her pupils were full blown just like everyone else's on the beach. The moon was urging me on and though she wasn't my first choice tonight, she'd make a decent enough second. I let her pull me to my feet and guide me away from the cove, stepping behind a high boulder when we were far enough from the party for her to feel comfortable.

She tugged her top off with a giggle and unhooked her bra just as fast. I gave her a hungry look, tugging her closer by the waist and squeezing her tit. It was freezing out so I cast a bubble of heated air around us and the goosebumps settled down on her flesh.

She took out a packet of Pegasus glitter from her pocket and I smirked as she poured it into her palm and slid her hand down her skirt. Yeah, that shit did not work. But I kinda liked the tingly feeling it gave me and the way it made my dick look like I'd fucked a rainbow afterwards. The only problem was, tonight I didn't really fancy a rainbow. There was only one colour on my mind, in fact. Blue.

Kylie dropped her panties, leaving her skirt in place and starting to dance for me. Shit was amusing so I leaned back against the boulder and took a swig of my beer, focusing on getting hard.

Come on, do it for the moon, Seth Junior. Forget about the Vega chick. She is so far off the menu, she's not even on the specials board.

Kylie gazed up at the sky, raising her hands as she swung her hips to a tune located solely in her head. I caught her arm, dragging her against me and shutting my eyes. Her lips met mine and I kissed her savagely.

"Let's pretend you're my Omega," I purred. Definitely not because I wanted to pretend she was my *actual* Omega.

"Okay," she said excitedly.

"Turn around," I commanded and she did so.

I kept my eyes shut as I dragged my mouth across her shoulder, shifting her hair aside and imagining it belonged to Darcy.

"Stay quiet," I said and Kylie nodded as I nuzzled into her neck.

I started to get hard and I sighed. *Finally.*

I pushed her onto her knees, dropping down and taking her roughly from behind, my eyes clamped shut as I concentrated. She started crying out as I slammed into her and I lifted one shoulder to ram it against my right ear.

"Oh Se-*thy*, Sethy baby, I love you."

Shut up shut up shut up.

I dug my fingers into her hips. "Quiet, Omega," I barked, but she didn't and I felt my hard-on sinking like a flag down a pole.

"I love you," she gasped again.

Yep, my boner is officially dead. RIP buddy.

"Er...Sethy?" she squeaked as I stopped, a horribly long moment passing between us where she realised what had happened. "Are you okay?"

"I'm fine," I snapped, getting up from my knees and yanking my pants up. Fucking Vega Twins. What was with them? It was like they were sent from the stars themselves to screw with me and my friends. Ever since they'd shown up, we'd faced more problems than we had in our entire lives. Now my dick couldn't even perform. *My freaking dick!*

Where even was Darcy right now, huh? I hadn't seen her with her friends for most of the night.

I bet she's off screwing the guy she's secretly seeing. Well. Fuck. That.

If Caleb could chase Tory's tail as much as he pleased, I was going after Darcy tonight. Our plans still stood. I would rain down hell on her for the flea stunt. But the moon was firmly controlling my libido tonight and every emotion I'd felt toward that girl since she'd arrived at Zodiac was welling up inside me, fit to burst.

Just for tonight, I'd make her see how good we could make each other feel. I'd win her round and she'd be pinned beneath me before the Lunar Eclipse even started. I groaned, thinking about it, adrenaline ricocheting through my body. All of that blue hair wound around my fist while I made her body bow to mine. *Yes.*

"We're done, Kylie," I said. "It's been fun. Really." I tossed her her shirt and she stared at me as it hit her chest and fell to the sand at her feet.

"What?" she gasped.

"Sorry, babe. This has run its course. You're a sweet chick, but I've been screwing my pack for months. I'm sorry you thought we were exclusive. We never were."

She hooked up her shirt from the ground, pulling it on then stormed toward me. Her hair burst into coils of angry snakes, her skin turning green and her teeth sharpening to points. Man, I'd really found that hot once. But not anymore.

"You don't mean it!" she shrieked.

"I do," I sighed, running a hand over my face. "And babe?"

"What?" she snarled.

"Pegasus glitter doesn't kill Werewolf sperm." I shrugged innocently. "Feels kinda good though. For guys. I mean, I dunno what that's like for you but..." I shrugged again and her hand crashed into my cheek with the force of air magic behind it. I let her do it because, well, she was owed it. I'd cheated on her for a really fucking long time. I reckoned she knew that though. I didn't exactly keep it a secret. The burn in my cheek sizzled away and I gave her an apologetic expression.

"Seth Capella you are an *asshole*," she growled, her eyes swimming with tears. Every snake on her head bared its fangs at me and I wondered if she'd attack me again.

"I know," I grunted.

She shoved me in the chest then clawed her fingers around my neck, her lower lip quivering. "You loved me once though, didn't you? You can do it again."

I really considered lying to her. I did. But I didn't want to mindfuck Kylie Major anymore - or actually fuck her. She deserved better. I shook my head, leaning in to nuzzle her cheek in apology but she shoved me away.

Her lips tightened for a second as she surveyed me. "Darcy Vega doesn't want you, you know that right?" She stormed off and I waited until she was gone, downing the last of my beer before throwing the bottle against the cliff wall so it smashed into a thousand pieces.

Bitch.

I locked my jaw, heading back along the beach on a hunt for the girl who was driving me to insanity tonight. I was gonna prove Kylie wrong and myself right. Darcy wanted me, she just had trouble admitting it because it was hard for her to look past what I'd done to her. But she'd liked me once. When she'd first come to Zodiac, I'd had her. Why did I have to go and fuck that up? The hair stunt hadn't worked anyway. She could have been mine by now and I wouldn't feel like my heart was constantly trying to bash itself to death on my ribcage every time I saw her.

Why is being bad so fucking hard when it comes to her?

I asked every member of my pack - who were way too moon-high to be pissy at me tonight -if they'd seen her until finally Frank pointed to the path that led back up to campus.

"Think I saw her head that way." He caught my arm before I could leave, his fingers brushing down my chest. "Forget the Vega girl, come have some fun. We can put aside our issues for tonight...Alpha." His voice was full of lust and I could practically see the moon in his eyes as he stared at me. I imagined I was at the top of a lot of people's moon lists tonight, but I wasn't interested. Even if it did feel euphoric to be called Alpha again. I glanced past him to the orgy my pack were shamelessly having in front of the entire party.

I'll probably win them back if I stay. But...Darcy.

I pulled free of Frank's grip and picked up a bottle of rum, heading away without a word.

"We'll be here when she rejects you, Alpha!" Frank called, howling to me as I went but I refused to look back.

Maybe she won't this time.

I headed up the path, jogging all the way to Air Territory and searching the horizon. I looked to Aer Tower, my eyes travelling up to her room on the eleventh floor where the light was on. I bit down on the inside of my cheek, knowing she was up there fucking some douchebag.

I huffed, pacing back and forth at the top of the hill. She had to come back this way eventually if she was gonna re-join the party, so I dropped down onto the path and leaned back against the sandy bank on one side of it. *Then I'll see who said douchebag is.*

I opened the rum, taking a long swig as I waited.

When she heads back to the beach I'll make her see that whoever this waste of space fling is, he's not gonna satisfy her like I can.

I took another long drink.

I bet his name's Brody or something just as lame. Fucking Brody.

I spotted Darius at the bottom of the path, alternating between sipping on a bottle of beer and pacing. He kept looking across the beach then returned to drinking and pacing. He was too far away for me to shout out to him and frankly he looked like he was having his own personal pity party. If we teamed up, it would be the most pathetic Moon Party we'd ever thrown.

Go get laid, man.

He eventually headed off down the beach again and I frowned, wondering if I should go after him. But the moon was encouraging me to sit my ass there until the girl I craved came to me. So that was just what I was gonna do.

I'd made it through three quarters of the bottle by the time Darcy arrived. I heard her laugh and wasn't sure if I'd imagined it or not. I tried to get up but shitballs I was drunk. I crawled forward, poking my head out of the pathway. She was in some muscular guy's arms, his mouth was against her neck and her eyes were swimming with delight as she clawed at his shoulders. They thought they were alone. But they weren't fucking alone.

"Brody," I growled, dragging myself to my feet ready to knock him out. The guy lurched back a step and my vision doubled for a second.

What? My head spun as I stared at the guy standing there. *I must be seriously fucking drunk.*

"Orion?" I slurred.

He glanced at Darcy then me. "Thanks for the drink," he shot at her and I frowned.

Oh yeah... Vampire.

"You're not Brody." I waved Orion aside. "Go back to your cave."

"You're drunk, Capella," he said in warning. "Go back to your House."

I stumbled toward them and found Darcy looking at me with something that might have been concern. Or maybe I was just being hopeful.

"You're not the boss of me, asshole." I shoved Orion aside except I didn't. Because his hand crashed into my chest and I stumbled towards the cliff edge.

"Did you see that?" I balked at Darcy. "He tried to throw me off the fucking cliff."

"Seth," Darcy said carefully. "Maybe you should go to bed." She reached for me and I caught her hand, bringing it to my cheek and smiling at her.

"You'll come with me though, right babe?"

Orion knocked me on my ass so hard the sky spun. He leaned over me, teeth bared. "Get out of here or I'll start taking House Points."

I threw air at him but he blocked it, throwing it back at me. I grunted in fury, pushing myself to my knees as he evaporated the spell. "I need to talk to her. You've had your blood, now fuck off."

Orion's eyes sharpened like knives. "I'm not going anywhere."

I snorted. "Oh you're not, are you? Well I'll take Darcy with me. She's my Omega. I need to have some wolf words with her, *sir.*"

Orion put himself between us and Darcy caught his arm, leaning around him. I looked between the two of them with a frown, feeling like I was missing something here.

Orion pushed her aside and she stumbled back. "Go to the beach, Miss Vega."

"No – wait," I begged. Shit, what was that pleading tone I'd just used? That didn't sound like me. It kept pouring out though. "Talk to me for five minutes, Darcy. That's it. I won't touch you."

Orion went to object but Darcy stepped in. "Go ahead, but you can say it in front of Professor Orion, too."

I sighed heavily. "Fine. But back up." I pointed at him and his hands curled into fists. He did not move.

Darcy gave him a look of encouragement and he growled as he marched away several feet to give us some space. I knew he'd hear us with his fucking bat ears, but whatever. He was just some dried-up-dreams teacher who would bow at my feet one day.

I drew my shoulders back, the moonlight throbbing against my back. "I broke up with Kylie," I told her, lifting my chin with a hopeful smile.

"Oh right," she said, folding her arms, having barely any reaction to that.

The fuck was with her?

"The moon drives you toward the people you want most. I know it's fucking crazy because I'm gonna be your enemy again tomorrow, babe, but you must feel this too. The moon is making you hot for me, right?"

Orion shifted in my periphery, but I ignored him. I wasn't doing shit wrong. He could stand there like a perverted tree listening in on his students if he wanted to, didn't matter to me. He could stay there while I screwed Darcy into next week too if he fancied. Not my issue.

Darcy's eyes widened and I took in her dilated pupils with a deep, burning lust in my core. *Yeah, she was so into me right now.*

"I don't know how to make myself clearer to you, Seth. I'm not interested. The moon is *not* driving me anywhere near you."

Orion released a breath of laughter and a snarl left my throat. Rejection cascaded through me as I took in the hard wall in her eyes. The one that firmly said no to me.

"Liar," I spat and she raised her hands to defend herself. Not that I was gonna do shit. Not tonight. But fuck her. Fuck her so fucking hard. I was Seth

Capella. How dare she make a fool of me?

"I know what you did," I said in a deadly tone.

Her eyes flickered for a moment. "I don't know what you mean."

I stepped forward, sensing Orion moving in my periphery. I looked to him with a sneer. "Why don't you go back to your fucking job, sir?"

He squared his shoulders at me and I wondered how much trouble I'd be in if I started pounding on him.

I moved closer to Darcy and felt her shield press against my skin. I lay my palms flat on it and ran my tongue up the dome of air.

"That's the last time you reject me, Omega." I turned and marched away, heading back to the beach to find someone to get drunk with. Caleb came to mind and I howled to the sky, wishing his mom hadn't made him go home for the Eclipse.

I jogged down the track, trying to drag my mind away from Orion and Darcy up on the hill. But it was damn impossible. Something kept circling in my mind and I wasn't sure if it was induced by the rum or not.

If he bit her...where was the blood?

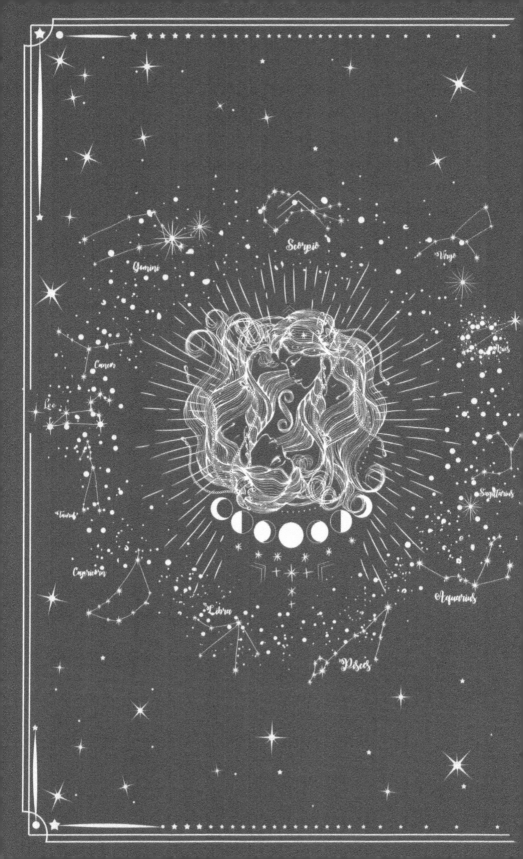

TORY

CHAPTER THIRTY SEVEN

I lay back on the sand and pushed my hands through it, carving little fissures all over its surface and trying to cool the ache in my flesh. I was hot. Too damn hot. And my back was burning more than everywhere else.

I wriggled against the sand, trying to ease the feeling of need in my flesh because I didn't know *what* I needed.

Someone changed the music and a heady beat pulsed across the sand just as a shadow fell over me. I blinked up, trying to see who was blocking the light of the fire.

"Galloping gorillas that sea is as chilly as a chestnut tonight," Geraldine gasped, shaking her head back and forth like a dog and soaking me in icy droplets of salt water.

I squealed, rolling away from her and getting to my feet to escape the deluge. She shimmied back into her underwear and started swaying her hips to the rhythm of the music.

"Come and dance, Princess!" she called excitedly, raising her hands to the stars as the beat pulsed louder.

Angelica and several more members of the Ass Club were returning from their dip in the sea too and Geraldine drew them all to her like moths to a flame, creating a dance floor out of sand and moonlight.

Bodies swayed and writhed before the light of the fire and I watched it with an ache in my soul like I wanted to stride straight into the flames.

I took a step forward, tilting my head as the fire seemed to whisper to me, promising me something I'd been waiting for, begging me to come a little closer...

A hand caught mine and before I really knew what was happening, I was twirled in a circle, my skirt flaring out around me for a moment before I was pulled into the group of dancing bodies.

Geraldine tugged me close, her front pressing to my back as she encouraged me to start moving to the rhythm of the beat.

A laugh escaped me as I gave in to her demands, pushing my fingers through my hair as I let the moon draw me into its power.

The more I gave myself to the dance, the sharper the ache in me grew. It needed something...I needed *something*.

More bodies shifted closer to me and hands brushed against my arms, my neck, my thighs. The touch was gentle, innocent but desperate too. Like we were all building towards some great crescendo but no one knew what.

My breaths started to come heavier, my hands trailing over my own body and painting lines of fire on my skin everywhere I touched. But it wasn't enough.

Geraldine started laughing and the sound was thick and heady with lust. I turned to look up at her, finding Max Rigel's arms around her waist. My lips parted in surprise but he didn't seem to be using his gifts on her, if anything it looked more like he was under *her* spell.

They started grinding against each other and I half wondered if this was somehow a part of his plans. But tonight didn't feel like the kind of night that could be messed with. The moon made the rules, not the Heirs, and I decided to trust in its judgement as I shifted away to give them space.

I bit my lip as I slipped between the crowd of bodies, my eyes flicking across familiar faces and strangers alike. Some guys reached out to me as I passed them, some girls too, an offer in their gaze which I could have taken up as easily as breathing. But they weren't what I needed. I needed something else, something darker, fiercer, hotter...

I was searching and I didn't know what I was looking for. Only that when I found it this fire in me might be satisfied.

I closed my eyes, pushing between the bodies and letting the moon guide my feet as the music pounded through my flesh like a war drum. It was setting me free, sending me home, guiding me towards...

My eyes fell open and I took a deep breath of smoky air, the tang of salt dancing across my lips. I'd left the dancers behind and the fire was to my back as I looked towards the dark cliffs.

The strangest sense of urgency filled me and I started to move away from my friends. I kicked my shoes off, feeling the sand shift between my toes as I walked towards the water, following the curve of the shore as I walked along the edge of the sea. Waves lapped over my feet, cooling the heat which simmered inside me a little but not nearly enough.

The sound of the music faded away behind me until I was alone with the crash of the sea and the song of the moon which tainted the air with an almost tangible feeling of expectation.

The cliffs drew closer to the shore the further I walked, until eventually a rocky outcrop jutted out into the water, blocking my way on as the waves splashed against it.

A prickle ran up my spine and I was struck with the certainty that I wasn't alone anymore. The moon had brought someone to me or maybe it had brought me to them.

I turned slowly, looking back towards the cliff as my skin shivered with anticipation.

Darius stepped out of the shadows and I stood looking at him as he approached me.

The wind picked up, my hair billowing around me on a breeze filled with starlight which caressed every exposed inch of my flesh. My dress fluttered against my thighs, heat spiralling along the sensitive skin there as if it was him touching me.

He stopped about a meter from me, the silver glow of the moon highlighting every sharp angle of his features. His chest was bare and his tattoos almost seemed to pulse for a moment, like the creatures painted on his flesh were coming to life tonight too.

"I've been watching you," he said slowly.

My heart beat a little faster at that confession and I tilted my head at him, my hair spilling over my shoulder and drawing goosebumps along my skin in the process. Darius observed the movement like he was starving for it, like anything and everything I did now was fascinating to him.

"Why?" I asked slowly, needing his answer like I needed to draw breath.

"Because that's what I do," he said slowly. "I watch you and hunger for you and ache for you. It torments me like I torment you."

The fire in my veins burned hotter at that confession and I shifted in the sand, biting down on my lip as I looked up at him. His gaze lingered on my mouth and the ache in my shoulders heightened to the point of pain for a moment before fading beneath my flesh again.

"Then why do it?" I asked. "Why not just look away?"

"I'd find it easier to carve my eyes out than I would to stop them landing on you."

My stomach knotted up and I took half a step closer to him.

"So don't stop," I breathed, my heart pounding recklessly in my chest.

"You don't want me to?" he questioned, his gaze burning into mine.

I wasn't sure what to say to that. I knew I should have wanted him to look away, I should have wanted him as far away from me as possible but no matter what he did to me I felt like I kept ending up back here. Something about him just drew me in all over again like I was a glutton for the punishment he inflicted on me, like every blow he dealt me was a caress. I must have been insane to want to pull him closer instead of pushing him away but I couldn't keep denying what I wanted. Even if it did damn me.

"I want..." I said, unsure how to begin to put words to all the things I wanted from him.

Darius was watching me like my answer to this question was the only thing that mattered to him in all the world.

I dropped his eye, turning to look out over the water at the moon which hung low and fat in the sky. It was whispering secrets on the wind, nudging my heart to accept what it needed even though the thought of it sent fear skittering through me too.

I backed up a step and Darius followed, his gaze capturing mine as I moved again.

"Tell me," he begged, his steps mirroring mine until I found my back against the black cliff wall. Nowhere left to run. And I was glad.

I swallowed a lump in my throat but I had no words left. I could only look up at him in the moonlight as he drew ever closer, the gap between us narrowing down until I could feel the emptiness of the space dividing us like a great chasm which needed to be crossed.

Darius shifted closer still, his breath dancing across my jaw, the heat of his body rolling over me and causing my fingers to ache with longing as I held them still at my sides.

Darius reached out for me and gently brushed a lock of my hair behind my ear. Only his fingertips touched me but the path they carved into my skin was pure sin.

A breath echoed down into my lungs, the taste of smoke and cedar caressing my tongue as the essence of him enveloped me.

He towered over me, his fingers flexing to brush the back of my hand in the tiniest touch which sent fireworks bursting through my flesh.

I looked up at him, my cheek grazing against his rough jaw. My gaze fixed with his. Less than nothing separated us from each other and for a moment endless possibilities opened up before us.

"Do you think you could ever forgive me for the things I've done to you?" Darius breathed, his fingertips trailing up my side and lighting fire in their wake.

We were barely touching at all and yet my body was alive with need and longing. I arched my back slightly, my breaths coming quicker as his hand slowly moved to cup my cheek.

I looked into his dark eyes, the sound of the waves crashing heavily behind him and the cold air enveloping us both.

Perhaps I was wrong, but in that moment every piece of me was aching for him, needing him to be all the things I wished he would be.

My lips parted but I didn't speak. I nodded slowly, holding his eye.

His other hand found my waist, his grip tightening as he drew me so close that there was nothing at all dividing our bodies aside from our clothes. I could feel every hard line of his muscular frame pressing to the curves of my body.

I lifted my hands slowly, wanting to touch him, needing to feel the heat of his flesh like the sweetest form of torture.

My heart was pounding a desperate tune, driving me on towards him. The moon had pushed us here and I was beginning to think it knew what it was doing.

My hand slid along the hard line of his bicep, over his broad shoulder and onto the back of his neck where my fingertips pushed into his dark hair.

I angled my mouth towards his, his stubble brushing across my lips and making my back arch with a shiver of energy.

A deep growl resounded through him as he pinned me in his gaze, the cage of his arms tightening around me like he was afraid I might run. But I was done running from him. There was something between us that couldn't be denied any longer and it was time we faced it.

He drew closer, my lips parting in anticipation of his touch.

"There are countless people who would say I'm not allowed to want you," Darius breathed. "But you make me want to burn the whole world down so that I can claim you for my own."

"Then we should burn it down," I agreed.

Darius moved nearer, his lips brushing against mine in a feather light caress which was already enough to light a fire in my veins. My grip tightened in his hair, my other hand shifting on his chest, my chin tilted and Darius inched down-

"Congratulations Darius, you actually managed to do something useful for once," Lionel Acrux's voice smashed through our bubble of peace like a bucket of cold water.

A wave of magic slammed into me and I cried out as I was thrown back, pinned to the cliff by a power so immense that I could hardly draw breath, let alone cast any magic in return.

My heart pounded panic through my limbs as Darius was thrown down onto the sand by his father's magic too.

"Let me go!" I yelled, straining against the force that held me, my eyes locking on Lionel as I fought to figure out what the hell was going on.

"What the fuck are you doing?" Darius demanded, scrambling to his knees before jerking still as his father's magic wrapped around him.

"Just when I'm starting to believe my son is entirely hopeless, he cuts Roxanya Vega off from the pack and allows me to descend," Lionel said darkly, his gaze roaming over me hungrily.

"Let us go!" Darius demanded. "You can't just-"

Lionel snapped his fingers and Darius doubled over, clutching his chest as his father took hold of the air in his lungs, immobilising it to shut him up.

I opened my mouth to scream at him again but he froze the air in my lungs with a flick of his fingers too and a new wave of terror flooded through me as I fought to draw breath.

I thrashed against the bonds that held me but it was no use.

Lionel smiled at me lazily before turning and walking back down the beach, his magic tugging the two of us after him as he went.

Chains of fire locked around me and I stumbled forward as he yanked me into motion. I could hear Darius following but I couldn't turn my head to look back at him.

We rounded the cliff and Lionel gave me half a second to draw in another breath before locking my lungs again.

I stumbled around the rocks and my heart fell still as panic consumed me whole. Darcy was locked in the grip of a huge man whose face was shrouded in the folds of a dark blue cloak. I couldn't hear a single sound she was making through the bubble of silencing magic that had clearly been cast around her, but I could see that she was screaming as she thrashed against her captor.

Orion was kneeling on the sand between three more of the hooded men, blood pouring down the side of his face and chains of fire blazing around his chest as they held him down.

Darcy's panicked gaze locked on me as I was led towards her, tears slipping down her cheeks as she shook her head in fierce denial of whatever the hell was happening.

Lionel yanked me into the silencing bubble and his grip on the air in my lungs disappeared as Darcy's yells filled the air.

"What the hell do you want from us?" she screamed, her furious gaze pinning on Lionel as he drew a silk pouch from his pocket.

"You'll find out soon enough."

My gaze locked with Darcy's as I fought against my bonds and all of a sudden the world disappeared around me.

I was floating, spinning, wheeling through the stars as we were transported to somewhere far away from the Academy and our friends, stardust coiling around me like the grip of fate.

I didn't know where the hell he was taking us. But the fear in my heart made me wonder if we'd ever come back.

DARCY

CHAPTER THIRTY EIGHT

I was sucked through a vortex, blinded, choked. Some other magic had a hold of me alongside the stardust and for a moment I couldn't breathe at all.

My knees hit soft earth and my arms were immediately yanked behind my back and my legs immobilised beneath me. I took in the unfamiliar cliff top I knelt on and the jagged black rocks which burst up from the dark sea to my left. An old crater fell away beneath me with grass clinging to its banks. At the heart of it was a blackened patch of stone which shone like ink.

Fear thundered through me as Orion crashed into the grass beside me, writhing against his fiery binds.

"No no no," he ground out through his teeth. He twisted his arms so violently that he managed to hook something out of his pocket half a second before more people materialised around us.

"What's happening?" I begged as Orion stilled on his knees, his gaze full of recognition as he stared across the field before us. He said nothing and panic gripped my heart as the wailing wind blew between us. "*Lance!*"

Tory and Darius slammed into the grass beside me and I sucked in a breath, turning to my sister with wide eyes.

"Are you okay?" I asked and she nodded quickly, though rage and fear were written into her features.

"Fuck!" Darius spat, staring past me to look at Orion. "Hurry, Lance," he hissed.

"On it," Orion growled, his brow fixed in concentration and hope flourished in my chest.

Lionel Acrux materialised before us with dead eyes that roamed across us.

Fae appeared around the crater from the glittering depths of stardust in navy blue robes. They wore gnarled wooden masks etched with grotesque faces and hollow eyes that made panic spill into my blood.

Lionel turned to greet them and Orion and Darius shared a look that said, *now*.

Orion twisted something into his palm and blood leaked between his fingers. He shut his eyes and murmured under his breath so fast I couldn't catch the words. Black veins spread out from his wrists and a spark of light snapped the magical binds holding him in place. He sprang to his feet, throwing an arm out to release Darius from them too, casting a storm of magic at Lionel in the same instant.

Hope burned brighter in me as Lionel tumbled into the crater, catching himself with air before he hit the centre and twisting around to face them with a snarl. I gasped as every single one of his followers raised their hands, but Darius and Orion's moves almost looked rehearsed.

Darius ran for the cliff while Orion cast a shield around us so powerful that it glowed with pure energy. My heart stuttered as a tumult of hellfire rained down on it from the surrounding Fae and I winced instinctively, tugging forcefully at my binds.

Come on, come on.

My heart tumbled in time with Darius as he leapt off of the cliff, disappearing over the treacherous edge.

Oh my god. He's abandoning us!

Orion dropped one hand and cupped my cheek. His magic pushed against my skin and I knew what he wanted without any words passing between us. I let my walls down instantly, giving him what he needed so my power swept into him and the shield glowed hotter. Tory shifted to try and help, moving up onto her knees and pressing her arm to mine. Her magic gushed into me and I passed it to Orion, our chain of power so fierce it burned through me like lava.

Lionel took charge of the fight and fire surrounded the globe, lighting the entire surface of it in blazing flames

"Holy shit!" Tory shouted over the clamour of noise.

"Just hold on," Orion said through his teeth. "We won't keep them back much longer."

"What?" I cried in alarm, but he didn't answer.

More Fae arrived beyond the crater and every time a new one appeared, they joined the fight against our shield. Orion couldn't spare a single second to free us from the magical binds in case the shield faltered, but I could see him looking our way, his brow taut as he tried to think up a way to manage it.

"Darius will give us a chance to run. We'll have five seconds. I'll break your binds then you *must* follow me over the cliff."

"The cliff?!" I echoed in horror.

"Darius will catch us," Orion swore and Tory and I nodded, having no other choice but to lay our trust in the Fire Heir.

Darius's beautiful and terrifying Dragon form swept up from beyond the cliff, soaring over the heads of the robed Fae and unleashing a blaze of fury on them. Half had to stop and shield while he tore up the ground between them, his fire so intense it burned a mark on my retinas. The other half doubled their efforts in battering our shield and I gave everything I had to Orion, refusing to let our defenses fail.

Two more Fae appeared beside Lionel and my gut jolted as I recognised them. They were unmasked. Orion's mother, Stella, had her hand firmly clamped onto Darius's brother, Xavier, who was as pale as a sheet, his eyes full of horror as he gazed up at Darius overhead.

"ENOUGH!" Lionel bellowed. "Or Xavier will die!" He kicked out his son's knees, drawing a silver knife from his robes and holding it to Xavier's throat. A pit of sickness filled my gut as Darius let out a roar of pain above.

Orion shook his head in horror, looking to Tory and I on the ground. Darius released another bellow and Orion clasped the mark on his arm, his magic falling away and the shield dying with it.

"No!" I begged.

"I'm sorry," he choked at us. "I have to. For him." He buckled forward, holding his arm and Darius came to land beside him with an almighty thud that sent a quake right through to my bones. He shifted back into his Fae form and Stella held out robes for him with a triumphant smile. Darius shrugged them on before storming toward his father. "Let him go or I'll kill you."

Lionel was pressing the blade to his son's throat so hard it was almost breaking the skin.

"An idle threat," Lionel purred. "Now do as I say or Xavier will die. Do not think I will hesitate even for a moment."

"I already put your mother in her place tonight for betraying your father, Darius, let's not cause anymore unnecessary bloodshed," Stella said overly sweetly.

My breathing grew ragged as Darius retreated, his shoulders shaking with fury.

Stella smiled at him, leaning in to caress Lionel's arm. "It's almost time," she whispered excitedly, gesturing to the moon which was on the cusp of the Eclipse then her eyes flashed to Orion. "Will you join us willingly this time, baby boy? Or will you treat your own mother like dirt once again, pretending you're so noble when your own hands weave dark magic on a daily basis?"

Orion's hands balled into fists like he was refusing that fact, but I knew it was true, I'd seen it for myself.

"I'll do as Lionel asks," he growled and I tried to meet his eyes to work out if he meant that.

Please don't abandon us.

I knew we were here for a reason, but I couldn't figure out what it was.

Lionel lifted the blade from his son's throat, shoving Xavier toward one of the masked men behind him. "If Darius makes one wrong move, kill Xavier without hesitation."

"Yes, Commander," came a gravelly voice from behind the mask.

My throat thickened with disgust. How could Lionel be so callous to his own flesh and blood?

Darius moved beside Orion and they shared a look that terrified me. It said they'd given up. That they were bowing to Lionel's whims and I simply couldn't bear it.

"Four years ago, we stood on this very spot," Lionel spoke to his strange followers and I fought against my binds once more, sensing Tory doing the same in my periphery. "We failed to enter the Shadow Realm, but this time will be different. Stella, bring me the scriptures." He waved her closer and she took a long scroll from inside her robes before passing it to him.

My mind churned with what he'd said. *The Shadow Realm? Didn't Orion say that's where the Nymphs come from?*

Lionel continued, "We believe we made an error before in translating The Tenebris Scripturas – the dark scriptures. The word pure is interchangeable with many meanings in the tongues of old. One of which...is royal." He turned to face us and ice inched into my very soul.

"*No*," Orion snarled. "You can't lay a finger on them, Solaria wouldn't allow it!"

"I rule Solaria, Lance," Lionel spat at him. "So bite your tongue or I'll rip it out of your mouth."

My heart jolted at his tone. We needed to get out of here. But I couldn't see any way to do that. I couldn't move and my magic was locked down. Tory gave me a desperate look and I shook my head to tell her I had no ideas.

The silver moonlight bathing us suddenly fell away and everyone looked up. The moon was cast in a dark red shadow as it hung ominously above; the Lunar Eclipse was upon us.

Lionel tore his robe from his back, bellowing, "Begin!" and every one of the Fae raised their arms toward the night's sky, beginning to chant in some dark language I didn't know. It scratched at my ears and twisted my insides as they spoke some powerful spell which I knew for sure had to be dark magic.

Lionel turned sharply and an enormous Dragon ripped from his flesh, his scales like molten jade and his eyes as red as blood. He took off into the sky, the size of him terrifying to behold as he climbed higher and higher, beginning to circle above like a giant bird of prey.

The Faes' chanting grew louder and Orion and Darius drew closer to us, their eyes dark with fear.

A roaring, ripping noise seemed to tear the sky apart and a blazing light grew brighter and brighter on the horizon, appearing to create a fissure in the fabric of the heavens.

My lips parted in terror as a meteor crashed through the atmosphere, a fiery blue tail painting a line across the star-spangled canvas above. It was coming right for us and I began to shake, moving against Tory as we shrank away from the oncoming comet.

It collided with the earth right at the heart of the crater before us, carving deeper into the ground and making the cliff tremor violently beneath us. Lionel soared toward it as the heat of the impact swept over us, making me wince as dirt and debris flew into the air.

Lionel released a line of Dragon Fire which scored against the meteor and the rock burned with dark purple flames. It turned to liquid before my eyes, melting down into a molten onyx sludge which bubbled and sparked. As the intensity of Lionel's fire increased, the liquid started to glitter and the stars above seemed to shine brighter for a moment, making me squint against the glow. I gasped as the liquid fell apart and turned into a huge mound of stardust under the brunt of his tremendous power.

Lionel ceased the fire and roared his triumph to the sky. I finally caught my breath as he came to land beside us, shifting back into his Fae form. Stella promptly cloaked him then turned to us with a frenzied gleam in her eyes which were so like Orion's it made my insides twist. "Stardust made on the night of a Lunar Eclipse takes the traveller to the Shadow Realm. Those of pure blood can survive the transition...so you're our lucky little vessels."

"How can you do this, after what happened to your own daughter?" Orion spat at her and my heart lurched.

"Clara?" I whispered and Stella's eyes snapped to mine.

"Don't you speak her name." Her eyes filled with pain and she clutched at her heart with one hand while pointing at Orion with the other. "And don't you dare blame me, my boy. She made her own choice, she wanted to go. She wanted to be a part of it. Unlike *you* who scorns me at every opportunity. Who turned his back on his own mother."

Orion said nothing, his jaw ticking but I could see a grief in his eyes that weighed a thousand tons.

"What do you want?" Tory demanded of Stella.

Stella looked to Lionel and he waved a hand in agreement, seeming anxious to move on.

"The Fifth Element," Stella said with a keen desperation in her eyes. "The Element of shadows."

TORY

CHAPTER THIRTY NINE

Lionel stalked towards us with a manic glint in his gaze and his long robes billowing out behind him.

"The two of you are going to cooperate with our plans," he growled.

"Go fuck yourself," I spat at him, straining against the magic which still held my arms firmly behind my back.

His fist collided with the side of my face so hard that I was knocked straight down into the grass. A gut churning crack sounded and I was pretty sure he'd shattered my cheekbone. Blood coated my tongue and agony unlike anything I'd ever felt echoed through my skull. I was aware of Darcy screaming beyond the ringing in my ears and Darius started shouting too.

"Don't you lay a fucking hand on her again!" he bellowed and I blinked up at him as he pounded his fists against a shield Lionel had created to hold him back.

Lionel moved forward, gripping a fistful of my hair and wrenching me back up onto my knees so that I had to look at him.

The agony in my cheek throbbed with the movement and I winced as he shook me like a dog with a chew toy.

"Let that be a warning to you," he hissed in my face. "Because the next time you disrespect me like that, I'll take my rage out on your sister."

I wanted to spit in his mother fucking face but he'd threatened me with the only thing I cared about in this world.

My brows pinched as I held my tongue, the fight going out of me in an instant.

"Good girl," he mocked, slapping a hand against my shattered cheek in a patronising gesture which drew a scream of agony from my lips.

Lionel's eyes lit with excitement at the sound and I was filled with the certainty that he was getting off on this. He was a total fucking sadist. This was what drove him; power, dominance.

Darius was snarling at him like a wild beast as he threw magic at the shield which parted us.

"Let her go!" Darcy demanded through a sob as she tried to scramble closer, Lionel's magic halting her advance just as it had Darius's.

"I'll only say this once so the two of you had better be listening well," Lionel purred, releasing his grip on my hair and standing to his full height again before us. "You will both do everything that's asked of you tonight without complaint and as quickly as you can manage. You won't try to run or fight back in any way. We only need one of you for this magic to work so if either of you breaks these terms I won't hesitate to kill the other. Do you understand?"

I looked at Darcy desperately as tears continued to run down her cheeks. I couldn't do anything that would risk her life and I knew she felt the exact same way.

"I understand," Darcy breathed and I nodded, unsure if I could even talk through the searing torture taking place in my face.

"Good. Darius, Lance, make sure they're prepared in their robes. And don't forget that Xavier's life depends on your full cooperation too. I have an Heir, I'm more than willing to trade the spare for the shadows if that's what it takes." Lionel swept away from us, the barriers of his magic falling away so that our arms were released from the restraints and the shields disappeared.

Xavier whimpered in the arms of the asshole restraining him and fear clawed through me as I looked at him. If Lionel was willing to kill his own child for this then I knew there was no chance of pity for us.

Darius caught my hand and tugged me to my feet, his eyes wild with panic as he reached out to cup my shattered cheek in his hand. I winced away from the pain of that small contact and his jaw locked tight with fury and shame as his healing magic washed into my body.

"Roxy?" Darius whispered, trying to catch my eye but I didn't look at him. That wasn't even my fucking name. "I don't know what to do," he breathed, looking from me to Orion and back again.

Orion's features were a blank mask as he held a blue robe out to Darcy, his brow furrowed like he was desperately trying to think up some way out of this but had nothing.

"Are you alright?" Darius asked me, clasping my hand, the robe intended for me gripped in his fist. I reached out and took it from him, looking away as I shrugged it on.

"What difference would that make to you?" I asked coldly. I couldn't believe I'd actually let myself fall for his shit again. Every time I got an inch closer to him it blew up in my face. Why had I let the moon pull me towards him when all I ever got for being close to him was pain?

Darius shook his head, looking back at Orion but our teacher still had nothing to say. We clearly weren't going to be getting any help from either of them now. It seemed like they were against whatever was happening here but they were in no better position to stop it than we were.

"Lance?" Darcy breathed shakily, catching his fingers between her own. "What are they going to make us do?"

"They want you to claim the shadows," he breathed, his tone pained.

I exchanged a look with Darcy but she clearly had no idea what that meant either.

"It's how my sister died," Orion added and my lips parted as fear swept through me, sharp and fierce.

"It's time!" Lionel shouted, beckoning for us to join him by the crater.

Orion and Darius looked like they were trying to come up with reasons to stop us from going to him, but I'd heard Lionel's warning loud and clear. I wasn't going to keep him waiting while he held Darcy's life in the balance.

I took my sister's hand and walked purposefully towards the Dragon Lord as he watched us with a predator's gaze.

The rest of the robed people surrounding us were chanting and stamping their feet, crying out in a language I'd never heard but which set every hair on my body on end.

Fear trickled down my spine as we reached the edge of the crater and Lionel moved to stand between us over our joined hands.

The stardust within the pit seemed to twist and writhe with some hellish magic I could almost taste. Bile rose in my throat in response, terror leaking through my veins. He was going to make us go in there with that foul creation, I could tell. And I didn't think we'd be coming back out again.

"You said you only need one of us," I breathed shakily, unable to tear my gaze from the pit which awaited us. "So just use me. I'll do anything you want. Everything. Just don't make Darcy do it too," I begged.

"No, I'll do it," Darcy interrupted forcefully. "Let my sister go and-"

"I said we *can* do it with one of you," Lionel interrupted in a hiss which warned us to stop speaking. "But the magic will be more potent with two. The only reason I would have for selecting one of you to do the spell would be because the other is dead."

I fell silent, my bottom lip trembling as I looked into my sister's eyes.

"Hold out your hands," he commanded.

The chanting surrounding us was growing louder and louder, the magic building towards whatever terrible conclusion was coming.

I raised my hand palm up and Darcy mirrored me.

Lionel pulled a glittering silver dagger from the folds of his cloak and wielded it above our outstretched hands. He murmured several words I didn't recognise and a rattling cold raced over my skin.

With a slash of his blade, he sliced Darcy's palm open, quickly followed by my own.

I gasped at the pain for a moment as he snatched our wrists and pressed our palms together.

"Now," he commanded. "Go forth and feed the shadows."

Lionel's hand landed on my spine and I fell forwards with a cry of surprise, gripping Darcy's fingers tightly.

I hit the bottom of the crater on my knees, the glittering stardust surrounding us in a sea of black.

"Tory?" Darcy breathed in panic and I looked into her eyes as the earth trembled beneath us.

"Don't let go of me, okay?" I said, not knowing why, only that we were always strongest together. If we were going to survive this then it would be as one. She nodded, the fear in her eyes a reflection of my own as she clung to me tightly.

A hand landed on my shoulder and I looked up to find Stella standing behind me, her eyes dancing with excitement.

Lionel gripped me next, placing a hand on Darcy too.

I wanted to ask them what they were doing but the stardust was shifting like a tide before us. Almost as if something within it was hunting for its prey and I was afraid of what would happen when it found us.

"Make sure my sons take their places too. We must be ready to capture it this time," Lionel growled and a moment later Darius took hold of my free hand.

I turned to look at him and for a brief second all I wanted was to throw myself into his arms and beg him to take me away from here. But I didn't find anything in his eyes but a wall of cold, hard acceptance. His jaw was locked tightly and his eyes were filled with regrets which he didn't voice before he turned away from me.

Pain spiked through my chest, my lips parted and I suddenly felt like something had been stolen from me. Like he should have been fighting for me instead of accepting my fate.

I didn't know why I even thought he might but the fact that he wasn't tore through me like a chasm and a single tear spilled down my cheek.

"Darius?" I whispered, begging for something even though I wasn't sure what.

He looked back at me, a well of pain in his eyes but he didn't have anything to offer me.

"Don't cry," he breathed, wiping my tear away like he thought it would comfort me but I recoiled from his touch, pain flaring in me as he abandoned me to this fate, whatever it would be.

Someone started cursing behind me and I turned my head as Orion was dragged down into the crater too. Chains of fire magic were wrapped tightly around his chest, pinning his arms in place and immobilising him. The robed men forced him to his feet and Lionel tethered his hand to Darcy's with a whip of magic.

Orion's gaze fell on my sister and it was like something was breaking in him.

"Blue..." he breathed, a thousand words seeming to go unsaid as she held his eye, shaking her head at him.

"It's okay," she murmured over and over beneath her breath, even as he continued to struggle, seeming desperate to save her.

"You're strong, Roxy," Darius said in a low voice, drawing my focus back to him. "You can survive this, I know it..."

My lips parted but before I could respond, our combined blood spilled between our fingers and dropped into the stardust before us.

A wave of ecstasy ran up my spine and I gasped as my vision clouded and I lost sight of the world around me.

Shadows clambered through the wound on my palm creeping, sliding, weaving into my veins and forging a path through the fabric of my flesh. They kept going, reaching higher and higher as they spilled across my soul, digging their way into my heart and filling every void within me.

My lips parted and I could taste the shadows on the wind, I could feel them caressing every inch of my body, owning me, flooding me, completing me.

Horror like I'd never known gripped me as all the darkest parts of me were brought to light. Every fear, every hate, each cruel and twisted thing I'd ever done, thrust into the light like there was nothing else to me at all. Panic reared its head in me and I almost lost myself to terror.

But I wasn't alone in the dark. Darcy's presence was strong and constant beside me, the combined grip of our fingers unwavering as the shadows tried to prise us apart.

Voices began to echo to me in the void. A girl, calling out for us to join her. A flicker of brown hair, ebony eyes, blood.

"Come to me."

I looked for her but she wasn't there anymore.

"Find me."

My heart started beating slower as the ecstasy in my veins began to turn to pain. I was trembling but I was burning too, the shadows reaching deeper and deeper within my soul as they tried to lay claim to all I was.

The girl was suddenly standing before us again.

"Release yourselves to me. Join the shadows..."

The flames were hotter now, scorching a path through my soul and I was aware that somewhere I was screaming as the agony of them consumed me.

I'd thought we couldn't burn but I was wrong. I'd never felt pain like this. Chasms of fire carved through my flesh, scoring two great lines across my back, desperate for release.

"I can free you from this pain."

She was reaching for us in the dark, her eyes full of shadows and promises.

But I couldn't reach for her. Darcy still held my hand. And I wouldn't let her go any more than she would release me.

The flames were scalding, searing away my flesh and blazing through me in a never ending torrent of agony. I needed a release. I had to go to the shadows but to do so meant letting Darcy go and I'd sooner burn forever more than do that.

With a cry of pure agony, I fell back instead of forward. Darcy was pulling me with her or maybe I was pulling her. Away from the shadows, falling into the fire.

The pain in my back exploded out of me like a tsunami of pure relief.

The world was burning and falling away and for a moment I didn't realise what had even happened.

But I wasn't dead.

I was flying.

I blinked away the flames and stared at Darcy in complete and utter shock as I took in the fire which engulfed her body. Wings of flaming red feathers burst from her back, beating in time with the slow pace of my heart as she held herself aloft.

Her hair was a twisting mass of living flames burning in darkest red and orange which whipped around her as she beat her huge wings to stay hovering at my side. Flames licked over her skin, casting her flesh in flame and her eyes in darkness. She looked like an angel fallen to the flames, endlessly beautiful and eternally powerful.

"Tory?" she asked, her eyes wide with wonder that told me she was seeing the same miracle as me.

We'd survived. And more than that, our Orders had emerged. And we weren't Dragons at all. For a moment I was at a loss as to what we were, but the knowledge came to me like it had been there all along. We'd been reborn from the flames, rising from the shadows like...

"Phoenixes," I said, staring at Darcy in complete and utter fascination.

Before I could take in any more than that, a heaviness fell over me and I felt the shadows coiling close again.

A cry escaped me as I fell from the sky, clutching onto my sister as the flames tumbled away from us and our wings retreated.

We were caught in a net of air magic before we could hit the ground and thick material wrapped around me as someone dragged me away from my sister.

I fought against the heaviness in my limbs as shadows crawled beneath my flesh, aching for me to wield them.

"Roxy?" Darius begged, shaking me as he held me against his chest.

I clung to the robe he'd wrapped around me as I tried to make my head stop spinning.

Lionel was talking to Stella excitedly and I looked towards him as shadows wrapped around his arms.

"We did it!" he exclaimed, his eyes alight with this new, dark magic. "It worked!"

All around us the robed figures were experimenting with the power the shadows had granted them and for a moment I saw shadows coiling behind Darius's eyes too.

"Get off of me," I hissed, pushing out of his grip as I scooted towards my sister.

Orion was holding her hand against his cheek, his head bowed hopelessly as he murmured to himself. Darcy wasn't looking at him, her eyes were on me.

Darius followed me, staying close despite my warning and I felt the flames which lived in my soul rising in challenge beneath my skin. But that wasn't all that was there. Deep within the confines of my heart, I could feel the shadows lurking, taking root and growing into something unknown.

Lionel strode towards us, his eyes alight with power and success.

"You were both a part of this," he said, his words for Darius and Orion. "You hold the Fifth Element now too. So there's no one you can tell and no more chances for you to defy us. You are bound to us by the shadows and they will never let you go."

"What about them?" Darius asked, pointing at me and Darcy.

Lionel's gaze swept over us. "They've done what we needed them to do. They were just the vessels to channel the shadows to us and they even saved us the trouble of having to cover up their deaths. Take them back to the Academy, we don't need them here anymore."

Orion and Darius exchanged a dark look but neither of them responded, seeming too defeated to even have words.

Lionel snapped his fingers at Darcy and me and I raised my eyes to him slowly.

"You will forget you were ever here," he commanded, his voice thick with Coercion which tied me up in manacles forged of steel. *"You will have no memory of this night other than knowing your Orders emerged. You will forget the shadows. And you will forget that you ever saw me."*

Darcy gasped beside me as the magic tried to drive into her and I looked at her desperately as his commands tightened on me too.

But before my memories could be altered by his Coercion, flames danced before my eyes like an impenetrable barrier. They burned against the power of his magic until his Coercion slipped away on the breeze. I exchanged a look with Darcy which told me the same thing had just happened to her but kept my mouth shut.

Lionel tossed a pouch of stardust into Darius's lap and he lifted it in silence.

"Take them back to the Academy," Lionel commanded. "Inform me if there's any sign of them remembering."

He strode away and Darius pulled a handful of stardust into his fist.

He looked into my eyes right before he tossed it into the air.

"I'm sorry," he breathed. And the world slid away as we fell into the grip of the stars.

Darius Acrux was sorry? He didn't know the meaning of the word. But after what he'd done, risking our lives by tangling us up in his family's psychotic ritual, I planned on making him learn the definition

He was sorry?

Not yet he wasn't.

ALSO BY
CAROLINE PECKHAM
&
SUSANNE VALENTI

Brutal Boys of Everlake Prep

(Complete Reverse Harem Bully Romance Contemporary Series)

Kings of Quarantine

Kings of Lockdown

Kings of Anarchy

Queen of Quarantine

**

Dead Men Walking

(Reverse Harem Dark Romance Contemporary Series)

The Death Club

Society of Psychos

**

The Harlequin Crew

(Reverse Harem Mafia Romance Contemporary Series)

Sinners Playground

Dead Man's Isle

Carnival Hill

Paradise Lagoon

Harlequinn Crew Novellas

Devil's Pass

**

Dark Empire

(Dark Mafia Contemporary Standalones)

Beautiful Carnage

Beautiful Savage

**

The Ruthless Boys of the Zodiac

(Reverse Harem Paranormal Romance Series - Set in the world of Solaria)

Dark Fae

Savage Fae

Vicious Fae

Broken Fae

Warrior Fae

Zodiac Academy

(M/F Bully Romance Series- Set in the world of Solaria, five years after Dark Fae)

The Awakening

Ruthless Fae

The Reckoning

Shadow Princess

Cursed Fates

Fated Thrones

Heartless Sky

The Awakening - As told by the Boys

Zodiac Academy Novellas

Origins of an Academy Bully

The Big A.S.S. Party

Darkmore Penitentiary

(Reverse Harem Paranormal Romance Series - Set in the world of Solaria,
ten years after Dark Fae)

Caged Wolf

Alpha Wolf

Feral Wolf

**

The Age of Vampires

(Complete M/F Paranormal Romance/Dystopian Series)

Eternal Reign

Eternal Shade

Eternal Curse

Eternal Vow

Eternal Night

Eternal Love

**

Cage of Lies

(M/F Dystopian Series)

Rebel Rising

**

Tainted Earth

(M/F Dystopian Series)

Afflicted

Altered

Adapted

Advanced

**

The Vampire Games

(Complete M/F Paranormal Romance Trilogy)

V Games

V Games: Fresh From The Grave

V Games: Dead Before Dawn

*

The Vampire Games: Season Two

(Complete M/F Paranormal Romance Trilogy)

Wolf Games

Wolf Games: Island of Shade

Wolf Games: Severed Fates

*

The Vampire Games: Season Three

Hunter Trials

*

The Vampire Games Novellas

A Game of Vampires

**

The Rise of Issac

(Complete YA Fantasy Series)

Creeping Shadow

Bleeding Snow

Turning Tide

Weeping Sky

Failing Light